Books by Hunter Morgan

Published by Kensington Publishing Corporation

ARE YOU
SCARED YET?

Hunter Morgan

ZEBRA BOOKS
Kensington Publishing Corp.
www.kensingtonbooks.com

ZEBRA BOOKS are published by

Kensington Publishing Corp.
850 Third Avenue
New York, NY 10022

All Kensington titles, imprints, and distributed lines are available at special quantity discounts for bulk purchases for sales promotion, premiums, fund-raising, educational, or institutional use.

Special book excerpts or customized printings can also be created to fit specific needs. For details, write or phone the office of the Kensington Special Sales Manager: Attn. Special Sales Department. Kensington Publishing Corp., 850 Third Avenue, New York, NY 10022. Phone: 1-800-221-2647.

Zebra and the Z logo Reg. U.S. Pat. & TM Off.

ISBN-13: 978-0-8217-7945-3
ISBN-10: 0-8217-7945-1

First Printing: June 2007
10 9 8 7 6 5 4 3 2 1

Printed in the United States of America

My Beloved,

I have been watching you for months. Adoring you. I have saved every photograph of you published in every newspaper and magazine. I have hung on every word you've spoken, on camera and off. You have given me hope that there is still goodness in the world. Honesty. Devotion. I would give my life for you. I wonder if you would give me yours . . .

The Daughter

Chapter 1

The phone rang as Delilah flung open the front door and dashed back into the house. Her keys weren't on the table in the foyer where they belonged. She hurried into the kitchen. Not on the counter where they didn't belong, either.

She was tempted to ignore the ringing phone. She was going to be late to the press conference at Maria's Place. Snowden had just been telling her last night what an honor it was for her, as well as for the Stephen Kill police department, to have one of their own invited to cut the ribbon for the opening of the new wing. He said that kind of good press couldn't be measured; promotions and more money in the department budget, to say nothing of the good will instilled with the community. If she didn't hurry, there'd be no good will for her or the department.

She swept the cordless phone off its base on the counter as she breezed by, glancing at the caller ID screen. Rosemary.

Now she was *really* tempted not to pick up. The phone continued to ring. She went down the hall to her bedroom.

Keys weren't on the dresser. They weren't on the bedside table. "Come on, come on," she muttered.

On the fourth ring, the answering machine clicked on. She heard the canned recording, then an urgent voice from the kitchen. "Delilah? Delilah, are you there? If you're there, could you pick up?" A pause. "Please?"

Her sister was crying. And this wasn't the first call from Rosemary in tears in the last couple of months. Her forty-seven-year-old husband had left her for their thirty-something dental hygienist. Boob job included. Rosemary had had to put her kindergartener in daycare half days so she could go back to work full time. And Callie . . . Their Callie was giving her a run for her money.

"Delilah?"

She spotted her ring of keys on the carpet, half concealed by the bed's dust ruffle. She dropped to her knees, hitting the "on" button on the phone as she grabbed the keys. "Rosemary?"

"Oh, you're there. Thank goodness." Rosemary sniffed. "Delilah, I have to talk to you. I—"

"Look, I'm really running late and I've got a bad battery on my cell, so I can't even call you from the car." She caught a glimpse of herself in the full-length mirror on the bathroom door.

She looked like an honest-to-God policewoman in the dress uniform, right down to the shiny badge and new commendation ribbons over her breast pocket. So why, after eight years of service, did she still feel like a fake?

"I can't talk right now." She pushed her blond bangs out her eyes, the keys jangling as she hurried back down the hall. She left her hat in the cruiser. At least, she hoped to God that's where she'd put it. "See, darlin', I'm late to this thing—"

"Delilah, she's been arrested."

Delilah didn't have to ask who. She was afraid to ask for what.

"She's been released into my custody, but I can't do this. I *can't* keep doing this."

"Oh, Rosemary. I'm so sorry." Delilah halted at the kitchen counter. "I really do have to go, but how about if I call you back tonight? As soon as I get home."

"You . . . you'll call me back?" Another sniffle. "We'll talk about this? Because, Delilah, I've been thinking a lot about this the past few days and I just don't think I can—" Her sister's voice on the other end of the line cracked and Delilah felt a chink open in her carefully constructed armor. She'd separated herself from Callie emotionally a long time ago. It was what was best for Callie. For both of them.

"I swear, on Granny's grave," Delilah said, noticing that her Sticks-of-Georgia accent came back full force the moment she spoke to anyone from home. "I'll call you back." She disconnected before Rosemary could say anything more and laid the phone on the counter.

"Tell me this isn't happening," she murmured, hurrying for the door. "Tell me, Granny, this isn't my worst nightmare coming true."

"Sister Julie!"

"Sister Julie . . ."

Julie was surrounded by a sea of voices, swarmed by the citizens of Stephen Kill, all wanting to offer her congratulations. Have a moment of her time. And they deserved it, every one of the two hundred people milling around. It was these simple, kind, good and generous-hearted people who had made today possible.

"Señora Santori." Julie opened her arms to greet the

closest person to her, a middle-aged Mexican woman in a bright red dress. "Thank you so much for coming." She smiled as she turned away to greet Dr. Cary, a local dentist and heavy financial contributor. "Thanks so much for coming, Jeremy." She shook his hand as she squeezed past him into the dining room that was as congested as the front foyer.

There, the house's administrative assistant, Monica, had cleverly pushed together two old-fashioned farmhouse kitchen tables to serve as a square buffet. The tables, covered in elegant white linen, were laden with finger sandwiches, potato and pasta salads, and fresh fruits. It was a simple but impressive display, from the old silver teapot holding fresh flowers, to the mismatched stacks of china luncheon plates, obtained by Monica from every flea market, yard sale, and antique store within a sixty mile radius of their small town. The dishes, like the shiny, dented teapot, had cost them next to nothing, yet they gave off the radiance of being worth far more than most people would probably first give them credit for. Much like her flock of pregnant teenagers, she thought to herself as she greeted another one of her volunteers.

"Have you seen Detective Sergeant Swift yet?" Monica called over the hubbub from the doorway as she swept a pile of dirty plates off an antique oak sideboard.

"Not yet." Julie smiled, lifting her arms in feigned exasperation. "But how would I know? We're packed to the gills."

"An impressive turnout. You did a super job." Monica smiled back shyly.

"No, *you* did a super job," Julie called after her as Monica disappeared into the kitchen. She raised her voice in a manner that could have been considered inappropriate for an almost-forty-year-old woman wearing a nun's habit. "I couldn't have done it without you!"

"She's right. This is a remarkable turnout."

Julie turned to the soft-spoken black man with the incredible blue eyes. He was so tall that she had to raise her hand to shake his. "Chief Calloway. Thank you so much for being here, and thank you for loaning us your officer."

"We're very proud of Detective Swift, as we are of all our fine officers."

Movie-star handsome in his dress blue uniform, he seemed to exude a confidence in himself that splashed off onto others. With Chief Snowden Calloway protecting the town, everyone felt a little safer. He'd certainly proven his mettle the summer before with those hideous murders. "What a very politic way of responding." She shook her finger at him. "I could use a few lessons. Is Detective Swift here yet?" She took a step back, making way for one of her girls.

"I haven't seen her." He raised his glass as the teenager ducked under his arm to pass from the kitchen into the dining room, carrying an oval china platter of cheese and crackers.

"Need help?" Julie was already moving to greet another volunteer.

"I've got it." Blue-eyed, blond-haired Tiffany set the dish on one of the tables, shifting another plate to make room. Wearing a denim jumper and white T-shirt, she didn't look old enough to be seven months pregnant. She didn't look old enough to be allowed to cross the street alone. "Thanks, Sister."

Tiffany had come to Maria's Place after being put out of her home in Dayton, Ohio, by her stepfather for getting "knocked-up" at fourteen years old. Put out by her stepfather, who Catholic Social Services suspected was the father of her baby . . . After the baby was born and placed for adoption, Tiffany would be returning home, like most of her girls. Home to finish high school, go to college, find a nice man, marry, settle down, and have children she could keep. That was Julie's wish for all eleven of the girls currently staying with her and Sister Agatha.

Maria's Place had been Julie's dream for many years before she saw it begin to come to fruition eight years ago. In a time when pregnancy in teenagers was no longer a shameful secret hidden in families, in a time when young girls showed off their rounded bellies almost as a badge of pride, there was little need for a safe place for pregnant teenagers who couldn't go home. But that didn't mean there was *no* need. It had taken Julie more than ten years to convince enough nuns and priests in the Benedictine Order of the necessity of a haven like Maria's, and then another two for her to find this old farmhouse in southern Delaware and enough church funding to open the doors to her first two girls.

Now, they worked and lived almost entirely off donations, and their program had become so successful that in the last six months they had been able to build a much needed addition to the house. Today was the ribbon cutting, its official "opening," and every volunteer who had worked at Maria's Place or given a contribution since the day it opened had been invited. From the look of the old farmhouse bursting at the seams with guests, it looked to Julie as if they all took as much pride in their accomplishment as she did.

"Sister Julie?" An attractive woman in her early thirties in a pink linen suit slipped between two guests, trying to reach her.

"Yes, I'm Sister Julie." She extended her hand.

"Well, I guess you must be." The woman chuckled. "Only person I've run into in a nun's habit since I arrived. Who else would you be?"

"Actually, there's also Sister Agatha, though I would guess she's in the kitchen. She finds so many people a bit overwhelming." Julie lifted her hand to her wimple to be sure no hair peeked out from beneath the white band. She rarely wore her habit and wasn't entirely comfortable in it. It wasn't required by the Benedictines in the capacity in which she served in the town, and her uniform of the day was usually jeans and a T-shirt; however, for an event like this, it was good for the Catholic Church for her to don her habit, at least for a few hours. "I'm sorry, I didn't get your name?" She shook the woman's hand warmly.

"Goodness, I'm sorry. I'm not new at this. Really, I'm not. I . . . you just surprised me. You're not what I expected."

"Ah, a product of a Catholic education."

"Our Lady of Perpetual Grace, Danbury, New Hampshire. The nuns I grew up with were all well past their one hundredth birthday and sporting hairy moles and wicked rulers." The woman's handshake was quick, but firm. "Marty Kyle, WKKB, Rehoboth Beach. I have the six o'-clock news." She said it as if Julie should have recognized her.

Julie didn't, but then she rarely had time for TV. She did, however, recognize the name. It had been on one of the many press releases Monica had sent out to newspapers and TV and radio stations. PR too good to turn down, Monica had insisted as she made Julie sign each letter personally.

"You have quite a turnout here. There must be close to two hundred people. All volunteers?"

"Yes, I suppose they are, Mrs. Kyle, although we're certainly not checking at the door." Julie laughed. "Financial contributors as well, of course. And then some media representatives such as yourself." She graciously indicated the reporter.

"Actually, it's Miss Kyle. Always a bridesmaid." She chuckled, holding up a ringless left hand. "But please, call me Marty. Now, I know you haven't the time today, Sister. We'll just get your usual sound bites and get you on the local evening news, but I was hoping you might be willing to meet with me for an at-length interview. A Baltimore affiliate is looking for some news segments for a new prime-time Sunday evening newsmagazine and I think Maria's Place might be the perfect subject."

"Have you seen Amanda, Sister Julie?" Tiffany asked, squeezing by with her big belly. "She's supposed to be helping me but I haven't seen her and Sister Agatha is starting to hum. You know how she gets when she starts humming."

Julie kept her smile to herself. Sister Agatha had been with them only a few months and everyone was still trying to adjust. She had very different ideas than Julie on how the house ought to be run, but she was a hard worker and Julie had no doubt that her heart was always in the right place. "I'd be happy to be interviewed," she told Marty, already following Tiffany through the living room, into the hall. "If you'll excuse me."

"Certainly. Thank you. I'll call this week," the attractive blonde called after her.

"Have you seen Amanda?" Julie asked another teen passing them, going in the opposite direction.

Yolanda wrinkled her freckled nose, one hand on her belly, the other wrapped around a pitcher of water. "Bathroom, last I saw her." She pointed toward the back of the house. "But that was like half an hour ago."

"I'll find her." Julie laid her hand on Yolanda's shoulder. "See what Sister Agatha needs."

"But she's humming," Yolanda groaned as she slipped away.

Squeezing past two ladies in large hats, Sister Julie hung a quick right and went down another hall, this one shorter than the main hall that ran through the house. She opened the paneled cross and Bible door into a storage room that had been converted to a two-stall bathroom when they first moved into the house.

She didn't even have to lean over to look under the stall doors. Two feet with purple sneakers were visible beneath the door of the last stall, soles pointing out. Amanda was sitting on the floor.

"Amanda?"

Julie heard a sniffle.

"Amanda, honey. Everything okay? You feeling all right?" She stood in front of the closed metal stall door that looked completely out of place surrounded by hardwood pine floors, plaster walls, and a drop-tin ceiling.

"I'm fine." Another sniffle.

Julie hesitated. "You don't sound fine." She waited and when Amanda didn't respond, she rested her hand on the door. "Can I come in?"

"There's no room," the teenager said, clearly in misery.

"Sure there is. Come on . . ." Julie waited another moment and was rewarded with the metal on metal sound of the stall door unlocking.

Julie slipped in and closed the door behind her. Amanda was still sitting on the floor, but had drawn up her legs, Indian-style, to make room. Julie pressed her back to the cool stall wall and slid down until she, too, was seated on the wood floor. She sat directly across from

Amanda, her ugly, sensible black nun shoes touching purple canvas sneakers. "What's up?" she asked softly.

Amanda shook her head, pressing her lips together, but Julie could tell the fifteen-year-old wanted to say something. She just needed a minute to gather her thoughts. To get her emotions under control. That was all these girls usually needed. A minute to catch their breath.

Amanda tucked a lock of brown hair behind her ear. She was small, fine-boned, and though only six months pregnant, her belly appeared enormous on her five-foot-nothing, normally ninety-pound frame. "Did you read it?"

"Read what, sweetie?"

The girl stared at the small space between their feet. "The article in the news magazine. That boring one we get every week." She sniffed and dragged her sleeve under her nose.

Julie reached up and tugged on a strip of toilet paper hanging next to her left ear.

"You're always saying in civics class that we need to read that stupid magazine. See what's going on in the world. People blowing people up in the desert, suicide bombers, and shit."

Julie ignored the curse word. Cursing was a definite infraction of the rules and if Agatha heard it, there would be instant castigation and punishment—one of the many subjects on which Julie and Agatha didn't quite see eye to eye. But it was Julie's prerogative to let it slide. "This was an article about the Middle East?" She tore off a long strip of the toilet paper and passed it to the teen.

"No." Amanda scowled, snatching the paper from her. She blew her nose on the paper, folded it, and blew again. She tossed it into the open toilet bowl. "About the little boy." She said it so softly that Julie had to lean closer to hear.

"I didn't get a chance to read the magazine this week. I'm sorry. I've been super busy with the ribbon-cutting ceremony and all these people descending on us." Julie rolled her eyes, raising both hands, trying to make a joke about the craziness of their lives the last few weeks.

Amanda drew up her knees, hugging herself as best she could, considering her belly. "You should read it."

"I will. What article in particular did you want me to read? About a boy?"

She nodded, bright, shiny pink lips pressed tightly together. The girls were encouraged not to wear make-up, but it wasn't forbidden. The pink was subtle for Amanda, who usually went for fuchsia or siren red.

"Okay . . ." Julie prodded gently. Outside the bathroom door she could hear voices, laughter, footsteps. She could hear Monica asking people to begin moving down the hall into the new wing for the ceremony in her clear, efficient voice. Julie knew Monica would be looking for her, but she'd just have to wait. A big part of her job here at Maria's Place was listening to these girls. Someone had to.

"They . . . the police or somebody . . . they found him . . ." Amanda squeezed her eyes shut and rested her chin on her knees. "In . . . a closet. L . . . locked in a closet. He was six years old."

Julie waited, knowing there had to be more to the story.

"His . . . his parents had . . ." Her lower lip trembled. "They'd locked him in there for years. Since . . . since he was a baby, they think. I guess they gave him water and food sometimes, but he had to"—she inhaled a shuddering breath—"you know, poop and pee on the floor and sleep in it."

Julie closed her eyes for a split second and then opened them, looking directly at the young girl. "There's no explanation for the sins some people commit, you know that, Amanda."

"It was his . . . his adopted parents," she managed, stifling a sob.

It was as if the proverbial light bulb went off in Julie's head. An *adopted* child had been abused by his *adopted* parents. "Oh, sweetheart." She reached out and took Amanda's hand, her elbow pressing against the cool, porcelain bowl. "That's not the norm. You know that. You've met prospective adoptive parents. You know how well we screen our parents."

"Is . . . is that what I'm doing? Giving my baby away to be locked in a closet?" she demanded, half crying, half shouting.

"No, no of course not." Julie rose on her knees and wrapped her arms clumsily around the teenager, around bony knees and her big belly. She kissed the top of her head. Amanda smelled of shampoo . . . baby shampoo . . . and Julie had to fight the tears that burned the backs of her eyelids. "That's not going to happen. Your baby is going to go to parents who will love and protect and cherish him or her."

"You don't know that," she sobbed. "I don't want to give my baby away! I don't want to give my baby to someone who's going to lock him in a closet."

Julie wasn't sure what to say next. Kids were smart these days, especially fifteen-year-old pregnant kids. They knew what kind of evil was in the world; they'd witnessed it first hand in many cases. And they knew the statistics, and they knew that every once in a while something bad happened to someone good.

"Shhh," Julie hushed, stroking her back. "Don't think

about it. Not right now. You've still got months. *Months* to decide. If giving this baby up for adoption isn't the right thing for you, you know we'll help you. You know we'll do all we can to help you finish school, help you learn how to take care of your baby."

Amanda sniffed and Julie released her to grab more toilet paper. "No. I don't have to do it, do I? No matter what Aunt Jean says."

Julie shook her head.

"I've got months to decide?"

"Months," Julie agreed, passing her the strip of paper. "Now blow your nose, wash your face, and go help Tiffany in the dining room, before Sister Agatha loses her cool and you end up with extra chores."

Julie rested her palm on Amanda's cheek for a moment. Just long enough to say a quick prayer and then she released her, coming to her feet. "Come on. Out." She pushed open the stall door. She didn't mean to be unkind, but sometimes the best thing for a person whose heart was aching was to do something good for someone else. "Out before we're both in trouble."

As Julie exited the stall, the door from the hall swung open and Monica stuck her head in. "I've been looking everywhere for you. The Lieutenant Governor is waiting to have his picture taken with you."

"I'm coming." Julie smoothed the skirt of her habit. "Amanda needs a little cold water on her face, a minute to get it together, and then could you walk back to the kitchen with her? I imagine Sister Agatha needs help to get the desserts on the table so they'll be there after the ribbon cutting."

Monica clipped her pen on her leather note book, tucking it under her arms as every bit of tension seemed to slip from her face. "I'd be happy to find Amanda a

job." She went to the sink, reaching for a paper towel.
"Come on, Amanda. The cold water will feel good. I
could use some myself." She dipped the towel beneath
the running water and patted her own face.

"Thank you," Julie mouthed as she went the door.

"The Lieutenant Governor," Monica called after her.

Julie raised her hand as she went out the door. "I'm
on it!"

Delilah took every short cut she knew through town,
resisting the urge to speed. At least once a week Snowden got a citizen complaint that one officer or another
was speeding, not on the way to a call, but to get to the
diner to pick up lunch or make it home in time for the
basketball game. Their chief believed no one was above
the law, and it wasn't an issue worth crossing him over.

As she approached one of only three traffic lights inside
the city limits, it changed to yellow. Delilah hit the gas.
"Pink," she murmured under her breath as she cruised
beneath the red light.

She checked the time on the dashboard. It was 3:05.
She was officially late for the ribbon cutting. She signaled and cut into an alley that ran behind a street of
houses all built in the forties, a time when the town had
seen its biggest boom. As she passed a chain-link fence
overgrown with poison ivy, she automatically scanned
the backyard visible from the alley, then the rear of the
dwelling. The house was one of several on Stephen Kill's
patrol list flagged for regular "cruise bys." It was the
home of the town's now deceased serial killer, Alice
Crupp. Because her will was still in probate, her son's
caretakers couldn't yet put it up for sale. Forty-year-old
Mattie was an idiot savant, a man who could barely tie his

own shoes, who could not speak, but had a talent for any kind of keyboard and played each Sunday at the local Episcopal church. Even though the local church's ex-priest and his wife cared for Mattie, everyone in the town felt a certain responsibility for the man, especially considering the circumstances that had revealed themselves the summer before.

The police department kept an eye on the house for Mattie's sake. Once it was legally his, it could be sold and the money invested for the man's future, but vacant as it was now, it was a temptation to teenagers and the occasional vagrant. With all the press last summer surrounding the "sin murders," everyone in town, and entirely too many out-of-towners, knew the house stood empty.

Fortunately for Delilah, the place looked undisturbed; she didn't have time to stop and investigate. The lawn needed mowing and a few bits of trash littered the back yard, but there was no sign of activity. At the end of the alley, she stopped and waited for an elderly man walking his Chihuahua to cross in front of her and continue on the sidewalk. He waved. She waved back, tapping the steering wheel, trying to wait patiently as he hobbled past the nose of the big black-and-white cruiser . . .

"Come on, come on, Mr. Tuttle," she muttered from behind her pasted-on smile. "Could you pick up the pace, Sugar?"

He finally stepped onto the opposite curb and she shot out of the alley, onto the street. In five minutes she'd be there. Seven, tops.

Her thoughts wandered back to the phone call before she left the house. She'd told herself she wasn't going to think about. Not right now. But the harder a person tried not to think about something, the harder it was.

"White elephant in the living room," she chastised herself.

Truth was, Delilah wasn't surprised by her sister's call. She'd known for months it was only a matter of time. At Easter, she had flown home for a week and spent several excruciating days in her parents' kitchen, having her brothers file through and give advice on who ought to be doing what to control their niece's behavior before it got irrevocably out of control. There had been truancy issues at school, failed classes, missed curfews, hanging with a bad crowd. Callie wasn't a bad kid; she was just headstrong and had made some bad choices. That, and she and Rosemary mixed like Pennzoil and spring rain on blacktop. That week, Callie had actually asked Delilah if she could go home to Delaware with her, try a new school, upgrade her friends. Delilah had put the brakes on that before Callie even attempted to suggest the idea to her mother.

Her mother.

It stuck in Delilah's craw. Rosemary didn't deserve this. Not all those years of marriage down the drain for a dental hygienist with double D cups and a double A brain. And she didn't deserve to be trying to deal with Callie's antics while still scrambling to make her way in the business world again and be sure her younger children got their share of attention.

At the edge of town, Delilah hit her brakes at a stop sign, looked both ways and pulled left onto the county road. Ten minutes late.

She was tempted to hit the bubble light and siren. She could scoot right along then . . .

She increased her speed to the posted fifty miles an hour as she left the town limits.

What was she going to say to Rosemary when she called her back tonight? Her "sorries" were more than exhausted. She didn't have any sound advice to offer her sister concerning Callie. What the heck did she know about raising a teenager? Even if she did have any suggestions, she knew her sister would bristle the minute she spoke up. Her relationship with Rosemary, who was twelve years older than Delilah, had always been rocky. Delilah had always gotten along better with her brothers.

Hardwood and pine trees sprung up on both sides of the blacktop road as Delilah followed it out of town. DEL DOT had just repaved the previous fall so the roadway was smooth. She eased the cruiser to fifty-five, then sixty.

She would just have to call Rosemary, keep her mouth shut, and let her sister talk. It was really all she wanted. Rosemary just needed someone to listen to her, to know that Delilah cared, even if she couldn't fathom what Rosemary was feeling right now.

Delilah started into an S curve and tapped the brake. That was a good plan. She'd call Rosemary, she'd let her talk and—

Delilah spotted something in the middle of the opposite lane and immediately pushed down on the brake pedal. At first, she thought it was a brown coat, or blanket, or something, but as she drew closer, she saw it move.

She hit the brakes hard as she pulled off onto the side of the road. "Ah, no," she groaned.

Chapter 2

Julie stood in the kitchen doorway holding open one of the swinging doors. It was 3:20 and there was still no sign of or word from Detective Swift. Julie had almost two hundred guests and media representatives crowded into the new wing for the ribbon cutting and no ribbon cutter. "So what do you think?"

Sister Agatha glanced at one of the many institutional black plastic clocks with white faces that hung in the farmhouse. She had acquired an entire case of them from some government agency and hung them throughout the house that Julie was trying to make homey for their girls.

"I know, she's twenty minutes late," Julie said, feeling Sister Agatha's self-esteem–diminishing disapproval.

Sister Agatha picked up a white terrycloth towel and dried her hands that didn't appear to be wet. She wore a habit identical to Julie's except that she wore hers every day; to Julie's knowledge, the woman had no *civilian* clothes.

"You should have started on time. The Lieutenant Governor shouldn't be kept waiting. He's an important man."

Julie knew she was right. At least half right. Twenty minutes was long enough to keep anyone waiting; they did need to start without their decorated female police detective. She just wished Agatha could say it in a kinder voice. Or she wished she could take what Agatha said at face value without always reading something into her tone. Without feeling she was dealing with her mother and would never meet her approval no matter what she did.

"You're right. Come on. Join us." Julie stepped back to let Agatha pass.

"That's your job, to speak to the reporters, to all those *men*, clamoring with questions." Agatha drew the hand towel along the spotless gold-speckled Formica countertop. Julie knew Sister Agatha didn't endorse the way she had used the press to promote Maria's Place, especially not when Stephen Kill had first drawn the nation's attention last year with the murders. Julie might not have ever convinced anyone to listen long enough to hear the story of Maria's Place if the journalists hadn't already been parked in their vans on the town's streets. But Julie looked at it as if she'd used something bad to do some good.

"I really wish you would join us," she told Agatha, meeting her gaze. The nun had pretty, pale blue eyes, high cheekbones, and lovely skin. It was her frown, the way she pulled back the corners of her mouth and wrinkled her forehead that made her look years older than thirty-two and seven years Julie's junior. "You're as much a part of this place as I am," she insisted. "You should be there beside me."

"The girls may stay long enough for the ribbon cutting, but then send them back into the kitchen." She turned away, snapping the dishtowel over her shoulder. "And no more hiding in restrooms."

Julie opened her mouth to speak, then clamped it shut. *Patience. Patience and humility.* That was what Father

Carter had suggested she pray for last time she had spoken to him expressing her concerns that Maria's Place might not be the best place to be utilizing Sister Agatha's *gifts*.

"Thank you, Sister." Julie backed out of the kitchen, letting the door swing behind her. The "you're welcome, Sister," barely registered in her mind as she hurried down the hall, wondering who the heck she was going to ask to cut the ribbon now.

Delilah carefully rolled the dog over on the pavement and he whined, looking up at her with big, liquidy brown eyes. It was obvious the poor thing was in pain. "What's the matter, boy?" she crooned, looking him over, trying to keep her hands as far from his mouth as possible, just in case he decided to take a bite out of her.

She had no idea how to accurately assess the dog's injuries. She had had the usual emergency rescue training with annual recertification for CPR and HHR required by the department, but no veterinary emergency training.

She ran her hand over his back, the curly hair sticky with blood. It wasn't until her hand reached his rear end that he flinched. "Poor boy," she soothed. "It's okay. I'm just having a look. I'm not going to hurt you."

She knelt on both knees, ignoring the dampness that seeped through her new gray uniform dress slacks. Blood. As best she could tell, it looked as if the Benji-type mutt had a broken or dislocated hip. There were no protruding bones, but the right hip seemed crooked, asymmetrical. And one rear leg didn't look right, although it was too bloody to tell exactly what was wrong.

He'd obviously been hit by a car and from where he was lying in the road, it was pretty clear whoever had hit him must have known they'd done it. There was no way someone wouldn't have seen or felt the collision with this dog. He had to weigh close to forty pounds.

She groaned, patting the dog's head, speaking soothingly to him again. Delilah couldn't imagine what sick jerk would run over a dog and leave it to die in the road, but the driver wasn't her immediate concern. Right now, she needed to get the dog to medical care.

She glanced over her shoulder at her car as she got to her feet. "Be right back, boy."

The dog strained as if he might try to get to his feet, but when Delilah leaned over and ran her hand over his head, he relaxed and lay still. "Atta boy," she called, taking note he wore no dog collar. She hurried back to her car. She didn't need another fool to come around the corner at fifty miles an hour and finish the poor guy off.

Leaving the engine running, Delilah popped her trunk and grabbed a blanket, part of a police unit's standard emergency equipment. Closing the trunk, she unfolded the blanket as she walked back to the center of the road. She squatted over the dog, thinking for a moment. He was pretty big and she was pretty small, barely five foot one. She liked to keep her weight around that of a hundred pound feed sack.

The dog whined and lifted his head off the pavement, looking at her with those big brown eyes.

"Okay, boy, now you're going to have to behave yourself, you hear me?" She covered him with the blanket. "I'm already late. Ya see, I was goin' to this big shindig when you flagged me down," she told him, falling into her rural Georgian accent. "And I don't mind that, I truly don't. But I will mind if I get bit in the deal." She began to gingerly roll him toward her, onto the blanket, off the injured hip and leg. "You see what I'm saying, here, buddy?"

The dog whined and tensed, but didn't raise his head. Once he was in the blanket, she squatted as if she was about to do a dead lift at the gym and then heaved him into her arms.

Delilah groaned with effort as she tried to redistribute his weight in her arms without jostling him. "Been hittin' the Dog Chow a little heavy, there, boy?" Holding him against her body, ignoring the blood that oozed through her freshly dry-cleaned jacket, she slowly rose to her feet and walked toward the car. "Good boy. Good dog," she murmured, keeping her face well away from his. He didn't appear aggressive, but she knew the "better safe than sorry" rule from experience. She and one of her brothers had once tried to rescue a dog from a muskrat trap when she was a kid. They'd both ended up with stitches and a tongue lashing from the pediatrician and their mama.

At the car, Delilah debated whether to put him in the front seat or back seat. In the front, she could pet the dog, keep him calm. In the front, he could also bite her ear off if he got agitated once they were on the road.

"Sorry, pooch." She maneuvered him in her arms, resting one knee against the car so she could get the rear door open without having to set him down. "No canine passengers in the front seat. Strict station policy."

She gently lowered him to the seat. "Good boy," she encouraged, releasing him and easing back. Seeing the seat belt, on impulse, she loosened one strap and buckled it around him, tucking the now bloody blanket around him papoose style. "There you go. Now stay put and we'll have you fixed up in no time."

Delilah closed the door and looked down at her uniform, opening her arms. She was covered in blood and dog hair. "Perfect," she muttered as she climbed behind the wheel and secured her seatbelt. Putting the car in gear, she hit the bubble light and siren buttons and made a U-turn in the road. She reached for her radio. "Looks like we're going to be *seriously* late to the shindig, old boy," she told the dog.

She clicked the transmit button on the old-fashioned style police radio. As the only detective on the force, she had been issued a car, but it was the oldest one in the fleet. It hadn't even been equipped with a cell phone and a computer, although they had been promised to her months ago. "Unit 7 to SCom."

"Ten–Three." The dispatcher's voice crackled over the radio.

"I've got a hit-and-run dog," she said having no idea what the code was for it, not even sure there was one. "Please notify Dr. Eagle of incoming." She glanced at the red numerals on the dash. "She may have already headed home for the day, but if not, see if she can hang around a few more minutes."

"Ten–four."

"And hey, Jer," Delilah said, completely ignoring radio protocol, "could you get a message to Chief Calloway at Maria's Place, let him know I'm going to be a little late?"

By the time Delilah had met the local veterinarian at her office and gotten the dog settled on the examining table and waited with her until a technician arrived, it was five o'clock. Delilah had fully intended to just go home, but Snowden called in and had the dispatcher patch the call to her car. There were still plenty of people at Maria's Place, some media still there, and he wanted her to come anyway. Before she could explain to him that she needed to go home and change, he disconnected.

Delilah was tired, she was annoyed with Snowden, and worried about Callie, Rosemary, and the mutt. The last thing she wanted to do was to show up at a public event in a uniform smeared with blood she'd tried unsuccessfully to clean up in the vet's office bathroom, and the teary eyes she kept wiping at. Dr. Eagle had determined she could probably save the dog's life, repair the hip, but the one rear leg had been crushed and it would need to be amputated.

Delilah knew it was silly to cry over a dog she didn't know, who was going lose his leg but not his life. It was just that . . . it was a day when she felt like she needed a break and no one was going to cut her one.

She pulled up in the cruiser behind a WKKB news van, complete with satellite dish on top. "Perfect," she muttered, grabbing her uniform hat, rubbing the wet, stained spot on her jacket just above her right nipple.

She had barely made it up the front steps onto the old farmhouse porch when applause rippled in front of her, moving from the porch, through the open door into the house.

Delilah felt her cheeks grow warm.

"We're never going to be able to live with you now," one of her fellow officers, standing on the porch, eating a piece of apple pie teased.

She looked at him.

"Jerry called the chief. Told him what was going on with the dog and the vet and all. Chief made a public announcement when he apologized for you not being here." John Lopez winked at her, a forkful of apple pie poised. "Be no livin' with you now, Detective Swift, stalker of serial killers and defender of homeless dogs."

"Eat your pie, Lopez," she muttered, walking in the front door.

"Nice job, Detective," a woman said to her.

"Congratulations," offered another. The hall was filled with people, many she knew from town, some she didn't.

There was more clapping. Someone patted her on the back. She nodded, half smiling, feeling totally out of place. Embarrassed. The dog was lying in the middle of the road. What was she supposed to do? Swerve around it and keep driving? She didn't even particularly like dogs. She was a cat woman all the way.

Halfway down the hall, under the stairwell, surrounded by pretty white and green flowered wallpaper she met Snowden's blue-eyed gaze.

"Detective." He nodded as she approached.

"Chief." She removed her hat. An elderly woman was trying to offer her a piece of coconut cake, but she shook her head. "No, thanks. Maybe in a minute." There were people all around, jostling her, congratulating her, making her really uncomfortable. "Sorry about missing the ceremony," she said quietly, stopping at Snowden's elbow.

He smiled with one corner of his mouth, taking in her shabby appearance before meeting her gaze again. "Sometimes these things can't be helped, Detective. Nice job."

From behind Delilah, a woman in a pink suit thrust a microphone in front of Delilah's face. A man emerged behind her with a camera on his shoulder and a bright light on the camera winked at her. Delilah recognized the woman now—she hosted the local evening news. Young, pretty, and single, she was a bit of a celebrity in the area.

"Here she is," Chief Calloway said, "Stephen Kill's very own Detective Sergeant Swift."

"Detective Swift, could you tell us the condition of the

dog you rescued?" the reporter asked into the microphone
and then shoved it at Delilah again.

Delilah looked up at Snowden, but he only flashed
that little half smile of his again and walked away.

"Detective Swift," Marty Kyle, from the evening news
pushed, "can you tell us about your heroic rescue? We
understand that despite heavy blood loss, the dog is expected to come through surgery, thanks to you."

Delilah clenched her hat in both hands, trying to hide
her stained uniform and looked into the camera, silently
cursing Snowden under her breath as she scrambled to
say something intelligent . . . vowing to get even with him
for throwing her to the media wolves again.

Delilah had just hopped out of the shower when she
heard a knock on the door. Glancing at herself in the
mirror, running one hand through her wet blond hair,
she dropped the yellow towel and reached for her blue
silk bathrobe on the back of the bathroom door.

The knock came again, this time more insistently. It
was the back door. "Open up," came a stern male voice.
"Police."

She took one more quick look in the steamy mirror,
wiping a smudge of mascara from under her eyes, and
hurried out of the bathroom, through her dark bedroom, and down the hall.

He was still banging when she turned the deadbolt
and jerked the door open. "Enough already."

Snowden quickly stepped in, closing the door behind
him. Before she could speak, he grabbed her around the
waist and pushed her against the side of the refrigerator.

"This police brutality?" She closed her eyes, lifting her
chin, feeling the heat of his mouth against her throat.

He kissed his way upward to her ear. "You ducked out of there pretty fast. You okay?" he whispered.

"I fared better than my uniform."

"You know what I mean. The reporters. I didn't intend to . . . put you on the spot like that," he said.

She slid her palm across his smoothly shaven face, drawing in his gaze. "Yes, you did. I saw that evil little smile of yours. You know how much I hate those interviews and you were loving it."

He grinned as he slid her hand over her hip to her back and pulled her against him. Snowden had a way about him she liked. He was never too possessive, never too rough, but he was fun in his lovemaking. It was something she would never have guessed about him. At first glance, Chief Snowden Calloway did not give the impression of being a *fun* guy.

"You're our hero," he teased. "What can I do, but play it up while it lasts? A police force can't buy this kind of good publicity and you just drag it around behind you."

She grabbed two handfuls of his white University of Virginia T-shirt. It was one of his favorite jogging shirts, but he hadn't been jogging. He smelled just-out-of the shower clean and she leaned against him, pressing her cheek to one smooth, hard pec, breathing him in. "You should go back to using the front door. You're going to get caught one of these days, hopping Mr. Jenson's fence."

"Just out for a jog," he said, feigning innocence as he lowered his hand to one of her buttocks and gave it a playful squeeze, pulling her against him so she could feel his groin against her hips.

Delilah let her eyes drift shut for a moment, enjoying not just the pressure of his *man stick* as she and her girlfriends used to call it, but the feel of Snowden's arms around her. She didn't know exactly when it had happened, but this wasn't just about hot, sweaty, forbidden sex with her boss anymore. It was developing into something else. He knew it. She knew it. She just couldn't figure out which one of them it frightened more.

"I was going to pour myself a glass of wine." She lifted her chin to look into his pale blue eyes. He brushed his lips against hers before releasing her. "Want one?" She slipped out of his arms, catching his larger hand with hers before letting it go.

"Nah, I can't stay long."

"A beer?"

"No, thanks."

He leaned against a kitchen cabinet crossing long powerful legs that his baggy cotton gym shorts showed off to a T. Delilah thought he had the most beautifully colored skin, like a cup of coffee with just the right amount of cream in it. Here, in the civilized, almost north, she'd heard it referred to as café latte skin. Where she was from, the description was not nearly as poetic and a heck of a lot more derogatory.

She turned away from him, reaching for the bottle of Shiraz on the counter and a wine glass from the cupboard above. Despite her family's continuous prying, she had not told anyone about her relationship with Snowden. No matter how much her mother needled her about it being "high time she found herself a man," she kept her mouth shut. If her daddy, her brothers, found out she was dating a black man, they'd string them both up.

"Pretty amazing turnout at Maria's Place today." She removed the vacuum stopper from the bottle and poured herself half a glass. She hadn't cared much for wine when she'd moved to Delaware a year and a half ago. Maybe a glass of chardonnay once in a while, but Snowden had introduced her to an entire world of rich, dark cabernets, merlots, and grenaches. What was interesting about Snowden's love of wine was that he never opened a bottle for himself or drank a glass alone the way she did. For him, wine was only meant to be shared with others.

"I think a lot of people were there to see you. Shake your hand," he said thoughtfully.

She grimaced. "I suppose that's good for Sister Julie and her girls, but I'm serious about feeling funny about all this attention. It just doesn't seem to want to go away."

"You made CNN and CNBC." He shrugged broad shoulders. "You're our star."

"But I wasn't solely responsible for tracking down Alice Crupp and you know it." She took a sip of wine, turning to lean against the counter beside him. "We all worked hard to put an end to those killings. You just pushed me out front when the media came knocking."

"I've got news for you, Delilah. You were already out front on that investigation. Besides, it's hard to interview an entire police force in a thirty second sound bite. And everyone likes a hero, especially if it's a—"

"Woman?"

He took the glass from her, watching her over the rim as he sipped from it. "I was going to say blue-eyed, blond-haired knockout with an attitude."

She laughed and plucked her glass from his hand. "You want to . . ." She lifted her chin suggestively in the direction of her bedroom.

"I don't know." He grabbed the end of the tie of her silk robe and slowly pulled on it. "You?"

The robe fell open, partially baring her breasts and offering a glimpse of pale thigh. She really did need to get some sun. "Maybe . . ."

She was just turning to him, lifting her chin to meet

his lips when the phone rang. It startled them both, but she was the one who actually jumped.

"Sheesh," she muttered. She guessed all this sneaking around bothered her more than she thought.

The phone rang again.

"You going to answer that?"

It wasn't until then that she remembered the call earlier in the day from her sister. Delilah didn't curse often; it was how her mama had brought her up, but she was sorely tempted. She was not up to this conversation tonight.

The phone rang again.

Unfortunately, if she didn't answer it, the answering machine would come on and there was no telling what Rosemary might say. So far, Delilah had been pretty good about keeping Snowden almost entirely in the dark about her family. This was not the way she wanted him to start getting to know them.

She reached across him, grabbing the cordless phone from its cradle. "'Lo."

He grabbed the tie of her robe again, but she pushed him away with her elbow.

"Delilah? I thought you were going to call me tonight. You promised," her sister said in her ear, a quiver in her voice.

"I know. I . . . I was. I'm sorry." Delilah glanced up at Snowden and then turned her back to him, setting down her wine glass. "What's going on? What did she do?"

"Marijuana in her locker. This is bad, Delilah. She could be sent away to—"

"Look, someone's here," Delilah interrupted. "You think I could—"

"I've decided," Rosemary said. Either she didn't hear Delilah or she didn't care that her sister had company. "You're going to have to come get her."

"Wh . . . what?" Delilah looked at Snowden. *Sorry,* she mouthed.

It's okay, he mouthed back, reaching for her glass.

Delilah wandered out of the kitchen and down the hall. "Rosemary, I know you're upset," she said softly. "But don't you think—"

"Upset!" Rosemary interrupted. "I'm past upset, Delilah. I'm . . . I'm at my wit's end. I need you to come get her. Keep . . . keep her for the summer. At least until I can . . . I can get my head on straight. Get the kids calmed down and in some sort of routine."

"I'm not sure that's wise for Callie right now." Delilah stood in front of her bedroom doorway, trying to keep her voice down. She'd put fresh sheets on the bed in the hopes Snowden would stop by. She needed him tonight. Needed to feel his arms around her. "I know she knows she's made a mistake. I know—"

"You don't know anything, Delilah!" Her voice teetered on the edge of hysteria. "How could you possibly know, sitting up there in your nice, new town house, getting your name in *Newsweek*? Seeing your face on cable TV?"

Delilah rested her hand on the doorframe, closing her eyes for a moment. "Okay," she said softly. "You're right. You're right, of course, I don't know what you're going through. But I can't talk right now. There's someone here . . . someone from the station."

"You're not going to keep putting me off again, Delilah. I talked to Mama tonight and to Jeb and Jason. They all agree—"

"Rosemary," Delilah said forcefully. "I am not going to talk to you about this when you're this upset. It's not the way for either of us to make any smart decisions."

Rosemary was quiet on the other end of the phone.

Delilah thought she heard her sister crying. She opened her eyes. Rosemary had never been a particularly strong woman. Never very independent. Delilah knew this had to be hard for her sister. But did Rosemary think it was easy for her?

"You sound exhausted," Delilah said gently. "Why don't you make yourself a cup of chamomile tea and let me call you tomorrow after church?"

"I *am* tired," Rosemary breathed.

"I know, sweetie. Have some tea, get a good night's sleep and I'll talk to you tomorrow."

"Okay, but—" Rosemary halted and then started again. "I'm serious this time, Delilah. Callie and I need some time apart. Otherwise—" Her voice cracked. "Otherwise one of us is going to kill the other."

Delilah smiled, but it was the kind of smile she put on to hold back the tears. "Talk to you tomorrow, *Suga*. I love you."

After Rosemary hung up, Delilah stood for a moment in the dark hallway before going back to the kitchen. Snowden was refilling the wine glass. She looked at him, trying to figure out how much he had heard.

"My . . . my sister," she said replacing the phone on its cradle.

His broad forehead creased as he passed her the glass of wine. "I thought you had six brothers."

She lowered her gaze, sipping from the glass. "I do. And one sister."

"Something wrong?"

"There's always something wrong with my sister." She rolled her eyes, then realized that even if it was true, it was unfair for her to speak badly of Rosemary after all she had done for Delilah. She had, after all, basically saved her life. "She's just going through a bad time.

Been married several years and her husband left her for some young bimbo." She lifted one shoulder. "Now Rosemary's had to go back to work full-time; she's dealing with day care and a hormonal teenager."

"She's lucky she has someone like you to talk to."

Delilah looked down at the tile in front of her bare feet. Snowden was an only child, born illegitimately to a white woman. No one in the town ever knew who his father was. To this day, his mother wouldn't budge, not even telling him. Delilah gathered he had grown up lonely and the thought, now, brought a lump to her throat. Here she'd grown up in East Jesus, Georgia, running wild over her grandpappy's farmland, chased by six brothers and a sister, and he'd grown up a few blocks from where they stood, in a tiny house, under the shadow of illegitimacy, further stained by the fact that he was brainy and biracial.

She smiled at him and grabbed his hand, tugging him in the direction of the bedroom. "You coming?" she asked softly.

He hesitated.

It was always this way with Snowden. As if each and every time he came to her place, he was battling with his conscience. They both knew it was wrong for them to be carrying on an affair when he was her boss. But they had both been so lonely before and now, now that they'd found each other . . .

He took her hand in his and lifted it to his lips. "Yeah," he said softly. "I'm coming."

My dearest Delilah,

I cannot tell you how proud I was of you today. You gave up your chance to make headline news again, to be fawned over by your many admirers, just to save a home-

less dog. I had hoped that we might speak today. I saw you in the hall. In the dining room. But you were busy.

There are not many people who would have done today what you did. I don't know that I would have.

That, of course, is why I love you.

　　　　　　　　　　　　　　　　The Daughter

Chapter 3

"Tell me what you want," he whispered in her ear, drawing his hand up her thigh.

She giggled. Wiggled beneath him. He pinned her wrists to each side of her head with his hands and ground his groin against hers. She could feel him, hot . . . hard for her.

"Tell me what you want."

"You know what I want," she panted, looking up at him through a fringe of dark lashes, struggling against his hold on her.

"Say it."

She giggled again, but when he leaned over her, she whispered in his ear. She used naughty words. Foul, dirty, nasty words that her mother would have washed out her mouth for speaking.

He groaned, releasing her wrists and dragged his hot, wet mouth over her bare breast, down her belly. She ceased to struggle, grabbing his hair with her hands, forcing his head lower. She drew her knees up, sinking her stiletto heels into the fabric, forcing him off the couch and down on his knees in front of her. In pale light from his pharmacy desk lamp, she could see his eyes, wide, wild with desire for her.

"Do it," she ordered. "Do it now."

"Do it now, or what?" he dared, pushing out his tongue, teasing her swollen pink flesh with it.

"You know," she snapped, smacking him soundly on the back of the head with the palm of her hand.

"Yes, I know, Kitten," he intoned, now properly remorseful. And then he lowered his head and did as he was told.

Paul Trubant entered the "family room" of the new addition, his faux croc skin briefcase swinging from his hand. "Afternoon, ladies. I have an appointment back at my office at three, so if you don't mind we'll go ahead and get started."

The response of the girls already present in the room was a mix, typical of teens their age. A couple groaned. A couple obediently took seats on the comfy couches and chairs that someone had already placed in a circle in anticipation of the meeting. Monica, no doubt, who was always on top of things. The teens Elise and Tiffany, both blonde and so similar in appearance that they were sometimes mistaken for sisters, continued to stand in front of the French doors that led into the backyard and the new garden Sister Julie was laying out.

Paul took a Windsor-back chair that had probably once stood in someone's dining room. A donation, like most of their furniture. He slid his briefcase between his legs and opened it on the floor, searching for his leather portfolio in which he kept notes until they could be properly transcribed into his records.

The new wing, built onto the back of the farmhouse

that housed Maria's Place, was two stories, providing an additional whopping twenty-five hundred square feet of space that included the all-purpose room they called the family room, two small offices—one for staff and one for volunteers—and a bathroom on the first floor. A new large bathroom with three shower stalls was on the second floor along with two additional dorm rooms that housed three to four girls, depending on occupancy.

Paul was truly proud of what he had accomplished here at Maria's Place in the last year. What they had all accomplished: Sister Julie and Sister Agatha, Monica, and all the volunteers it took to keep the place running. Not only had they raised enough money from private and corporate donations to build the addition, but they had increased their budget to the point that he could be added on the payroll as a part-time staff member. Paul enjoyed his private practice, where he now focused almost solely on teenagers and young adults, but Maria's Place, these brave girls, were his pride and joy. He cared for each one of them and was honored, *humbled,* to be able to help them get through this difficult phase in their lives and move toward growing into well-adjusted, happy, productive young women.

Setting his portfolio on his knees and plucking a pen from the pocket of his oxford shirt, he looked up. "Tiffany and Elise, are you going to join us?"

Tiffany, hand propped on her hip, glanced in his direction. Elise said something under her breath that was not likely to be positive, but both girls slowly made their way in the direction of the circle. Monica entered the room, carrying her ever-present clipboard, ushering three more girls. "Ten today, Paul. Belinda's at the dentist." She looked up over her tortoiseshell glasses, her lips moving as she counted. "One short. Who's missing? Who's missing," she repeated louder when no one responded.

"The new one," Yolanda offered when no one else spoke up. She rubbed her hand over her big belly that was covered by a faded yellow T-shirt with Winnie the Pooh dancing across it.

"Lareina?" Monica lifted both brows until they rose above her glasses.

Monica was good with the girls. And although they thought she was a little dull, a little uncool, unlike Sister Julie who kept up with rock bands and male movie stars, they liked her. They just didn't like admitting it.

"I guess," Yolanda answered.

"She was upstairs puking a little while ago," Izzy piped up, tugging her black Led Zeppelin T-shirt down over her belly before taking a seat in a comfy chair, tucking one foot under her. "I told her, you hurl it, you clean it."

Monica frowned, turning to Paul. "Go ahead and get started. I know you have to get out of here today. I'll find Lareina."

Paul nodded, turning his attention to his young charges. "So ladies, what's going on? Busy weekend. A lot of attention with ribbon cutting Saturday. How'd that go?"

"I don't think we should let all those strangers in our house," Katy said, trying to make herself comfortable on the end of a denim couch. "Someone ripped off my headphones."

"No one took your headphones, you ninny." Elise rolled her eyes as she settled on the other end of the sofa. Her sidekick sat down between them. "I told you. They're down in the laundry room in lost and found." An additional eye roll. "Personally, I think we ought to start charging for unclaimed crap. I'm tired of tracking people down to return it."

Paul scribbled down the date and the names of the girls present and noted that Elise was still feeling resentful of her designated duties in the laundry room in the basement. In the home she had come from, there had been a maid to wash her clothes.

"Do you really think one of our volunteers would steal something from you, Katy?" he asked. "Or did it just make you uncomfortable, having so many people here?"

Katy shrugged.

Paul waited an appropriate amount of time and then addressed the entire group. "How about everyone else? Were you uncomfortable Saturday?"

"I don't know," Amanda said quietly, after waiting sufficient time so as to not be labeled a suck up among the other girls. "It was kind of weird." She nibbled on a fingernail. "But kind of nice, too, I guess. For Sister Julie."

"How so?"

Amanda didn't make eye contact with him. "It's just that she works so hard. She does a lot for us, you know? It . . . it was nice that someone else noticed."

"Sister Julie and Sister Agatha do work very hard," Paul agreed.

"That witch," someone muttered under her breath. "She hardly came out of the kitchen."

His guess was it was Izzy, but he couldn't be sure. He shifted his gaze to her. She stared right at him. Izzy and Sister Agatha weren't the best of friends, but she probably didn't dislike the younger nun any more than any of the other girls; she was just bold and brazen enough to articulate it more often.

Paul held her gaze a beat longer and then let her go. He leaned back in his chair. "Back to Saturday. Amanda's right, it probably was gratifying for many people here to see so many supporters show up." He was hoping to keep

Amanda talking. He'd heard about her tears Saturday and had approached her that afternoon, but she'd been unwilling to say why she was upset. She might not even have known why she was crying. Hormones. All the girls were like that some days. Most pregnant women were. He knew his wife had been.

"The TV crew was kind of neat. I wonder if it was on the news in other states, like at home." Tiffany looked to one of the other girls, her face bright with eagerness. "We might be famous."

"The camera guys didn't film us," Elise scoffed. "They weren't allowed to, you ninny. We're hiding in this dumpy town, remember?"

"We don't name-call." Paul kept his tone even. "Do you miss home, Tiffany?"

She looked at him for a moment. "Not really." She looked past him, to the window, her hand straying to her belly. "I guess. Some. I miss my cat."

Elise and Izzy groaned in harmony. Some of the other girls, who had thus far been quiet, giggled. There was a pecking order among the young women at Maria's Place, just as there was in any boarding school. Elise and Izzy were at the top and the girls looked up to them, or were at least envious of them, for no clear-cut reasons beyond the fact that they seemed to be the strongest of the girls presently in the house.

"If you'll recall, I gave you some homework last session, remember?" Paul said, checking his notes. "Involving goals."

More groans.

"So, let's go around the room and share. Short-term and long-term goals, as you see them right now." He tapped his lower lip with his pen. "Yolanda, would you mind going first?"

* * *

Paul ended the session with the girls with plenty of time to get to his office in town to make his three o'clock appointment, but ended up getting hung up with Sister Agatha on his way out the door. She said she was concerned about the effect of so many volunteers coming and going at Maria's Place, especially in the last few weeks, but he very quickly realized it was more about her control than the girls' emotions that she was worried about. He offered to come speak with her further on the subject later in the week, but it still took him ten minutes to get away from her. Sister Agatha could be . . . tenacious.

"I know, I know, I'm late." Paul handed Muriel his briefcase at the door.

"Sister Agatha, again?" she questioned.

"Sister Agatha."

She pressed a cold Diet Coke into his hand. "Mr. and Mrs. Gibson are in the waiting room, should I show them in?"

"Give me three minutes." He ducked into the bathroom, then entered his office from the back hall, through a rear door. He was just grabbing a file off his desk, taking a sip of the soda when the door that led into the waiting room opened.

"Come in, come in. I apologize for keeping you." He looked past the husband and wife to his secretary. "Thanks, Muriel."

"Need anything else?"

"Nope." Paul came around his desk, leaving the Coke can, bringing the file.

"So I can go? Stewart's ortho appointment."

"Go." He waved her away with the manila file." I can

let Mr. and Mrs. Gibson out. Have a good evening. Good luck with the braces."

She waved and closed the door behind her.

"Please, have a seat." Paul indicated an oak dining table with four chairs around it which was perfect for this kind of meeting. He also had the standard couch and two comfortable chairs with a coffee table and end tables on an Oriental rug, but he tended to use that area for single sessions, family meetings, and so forth. Here was where he liked to meet with parents; he felt as if it gave them a sense of actually participating in their child's care. In the Gibson case, Mattie was neither the Gibsons' offspring, nor was he a child, but it was the same principle.

"I enjoyed my time with Mattie, let me tell you first off."

Mr. Gibson glanced askance at his wife. He was an interesting person. They were an interesting couple. Noah had been the town's Episcopal priest until six years ago when he had killed a husband and wife in a drunken-driving accident. He'd spent five years in prison and come home a broken man, only to have been reborn with the help of his wife and the child he had never known existed. He was a strong man, Paul would give him credit for that. And Rachel was a very special woman to have been able to forgive what he did to her and their marriage and help him move on. To add to the complications of their life, they were the joint guardians of a forty-year-old mentally disabled man, who was classified as an idiot savant, something small-town psychologists like himself rarely saw.

"You *enjoyed* your time with Mattie?" Mr. Gibson said. "You're saying he spoke to you? Interacted with you."

"No. No, he did not. Not really," Paul smiled, flipping open the file. "But I observed him playing with your daughter. Coloring with her. He definitely communicates with her, as you suggested. They communicate together."

"What, telepathically?" Mr. Gibson scoffed.

"Noah, please." All Mrs. Gibson had to do was place her hand on his and he relaxed in the chair.

"Sorry, Dr. Trubant." He grinned out of the side of his mouth. "What can I say? I'm a skeptic."

"Of just about everything," Mrs. Gibson injected in a teasing tone. She was very attractive, blond, early forties with clear, determined green eyes. Eyes that reflected a devotion to her husband that Paul rarely witnessed between couples married as long as they had been.

She turned her attention to Paul, folding her hands in front of her on the table. "So, what can you tell us about Mattie? Do you think he could function in a setting like Maria's Place? Do you think he could work there?"

"What I saw, Mrs. Gibson—"

"Please, call me Rachel. This formality seems silly. We've known each other for years."

He nodded, smiling again. "Sure, and please, call me Paul. Not even my clients call me Dr. Trubant. Only my mother, and only when she's trying to impress her friends."

Rachel laughed. Noah smiled.

"Anyway, what I was going to say was that for Mattie's limitations, he seems very well adjusted. Very happy. But also, emotionally very dependent on your daughter."

"It was really hard for him this year, her going to kindergarten. Even though it was just half a day, he missed her tremendously," Rachel said. "We saw a lot of moping around. Some uncooperativeness."

"Which is all pretty much to be expected, considering his attachment to her," Paul assured them. "And, a good reason to try to move him beyond his small world there at your winery. With some additional people in his life, with some responsibilities, with a life of his own, shall we say, I believe he'd show less dependence on her."

"Which would probably be good for Mallory, too." She glanced at Noah. "She recognizes how important she is to him, so much so that she's sometimes hesitant to go to friends' houses for play dates, attend birthday parties. You know, little girl stuff."

"I understand completely. You're good parents to not only take Mattie's needs into consideration, but your daughter's as well. How old is she again?"

"Five and a half," Noah said, making no attempt to hide his pride. "Almost a first grader, she reminds us about a dozen times a day."

Paul grinned, understanding perfectly. He had his own "almost first grader" at home. "From my observations, I see absolutely no reason why, on a trial basis, Mattie can't start working at Maria's. You just need to take it slowly. Stay with him at first, maybe even take Mallory. Make the change in increments."

"We've talked to Sister Julie several times about it," Rachel said.

"She's willing to do whatever it takes to make Mattie comfortable," Noah added.

Paul flipped a couple of pages in the file in front of him. "Now, I know there was some discussion as to whether or not he should be paid, or his work should be considered a donation."

"Mattie receives social security." Noah leaned back in the chair.

He, too, was attractive. Suntanned. Dark eyes. A face that showed he had lived through a lot. Conquered a host of demons.

"And once his mother's estate is settled, we'll be selling

her house and placing the proceeds in a trust," Noah continued. "He has investments and he requires very little in the way of material things, so he doesn't really need the income."

"We just want the money there, you know, so he'll always be taken care of," Rachel finished for her husband.

"I don't have to tell you how noble it is of you to be doing this for Mattie. I know it can't be easy. A man his age, unrelated to you, who doesn't speak."

"It doesn't have anything to do with being noble." Noah glanced down at his hands, the hands of a farmer. "Anyway, so either way, whether he gets paid, or doesn't, your professional opinion is that Mattie can handle this."

"Not only do I think he can handle it." Paul closed the file, looking up at them across the table. "But I think, given some time, he would thrive."

The Gibsons only stayed an additional ten minutes and Paul walked them to the waiting room, letting them out and locking the door behind them. He returned to his desk and worked on some notes for an hour and then picked up the phone and called home.

"Hey, it's me," he said when his wife answered on the third ring.

"Hey, me. No, no cookies. Not before dinner. Cookies after dinner."

"But I want cookies before dinner," he teased, leaning back in chair, smiling.

"Not you," she chastised playfully. "Your daughter."

"My daughter wants cookies before dinner?" He feigned shock. He could hear their "almost first grader" chattering in the background.

"Like father, like daughter," Susan told him.

Paul heard a resounding clatter of metal hitting metal that was so loud he had to draw the phone from his ear.

"Sorry about that," Susan said a second later. "I'm doing that juggling dinner and a toddler thing. Pauly just won't let go today."

"Think the ear infection is back?"

"Maybe. Pauly, honey, please. Please, can you just let Mommy—"

Susan's voice was drowned out by a piercing wail.

"I'm sorry, hon," she said. "Chloe! Could you please come get your brother so I can get dinner on?"

He could tell she had covered the receiver so she could yell to their twelve-year-old daughter. Then she spoke to him again. "What time do you think you'll be home?"

"Actually, that's why I called." He went on quickly. Smoothly. But his heart was already racing in anticipation. "Had to move some appointments around today. I've got a six thirty."

"Not again," she groaned. "Paul, I was trying to make a decent dinner. I thought chicken cacciatore would be nice. Maybe even a glass of merlot?"

"Sounds great." He adjusted their framed family photograph on his desk. It had been taken in the spring for their church directory. "I shouldn't be any later than eight. Why don't you get Chloe to call in pizza and you and I can have a piece and that glass of wine after the kids go to bed?"

She sighed. He could tell she was tired.

"You sure?"

She didn't sound as annoyed now. Maybe a little relieved. Paul knew it was hard for her, coming home from her job as a medical receptionist, picking up Pauly and Annie from daycare. Helping Chloe with her homework, getting her to field hockey practice. It was a lot for her, but she had understood the sacrifices when he went back to school to get his doctorate and then opened his own counseling practice two years ago.

"We ended up having pizza *last night* instead of a real meal. Because I couldn't get dinner on the table."

"Ah, honey, you're being too hard on yourself." Guilt tickled the edges of his mind. Susan was such a good person, a good wife, a good mother. "And if I recall correctly, last week was my fault, too."

She sighed again. "I just wish you could be home earlier sometimes."

"I know, babe. I'm sorry. What can I say? We're doing well. I think my work at Maria's is getting around. We had three people call today asking about new appointments."

"That's great."

He smiled, relaxing back in his leather executive's chair again, the thoughts of guilt slipping away. He worked hard. He deserved a small reward. "Yeah. It is, isn't it?"

The toddler began to wail again.

"I'll let you go," he told Susan. "See you when I get home." He hung up and got out the chair, going to the back door to unlock it. Then he returned to his desk to get some more work done, to wait for her.

Chapter 4

The Daughter sat cross-legged on her bed and unfolded the town's bi-weekly newspaper. She'd picked it up this morning when she stopped for coffee, but hadn't so much as taken a peek. She had savored it all day long, anticipated for hours the pleasure she would have in seeing her Delilah in a photograph on the front page. The joy of reading the lengthy article on her, one so long and detailed that it might take up half the front page and be continued on page three.

The Daughter reached for her beverage cup, took a sip, and at last allowed her gaze to settle on the front page of Stephen Kill's *Leader*. She was disappointed to discover that the headline was about Maria's Place and the ribbon-cutting, which she quickly scanned. Delilah was mentioned, of course, referred to as the town's "star detective," but that wasn't what *The Daughter* was looking for. It wasn't the opening of the new wing at the home for unwed mothers that was the number one news story in the town over the weekend. Everyone knew that.

The Daughter's heart fluttered. Panic tightened in her stomach. She checked the date of the paper, thinking, somehow she'd bought the previous week's paper, although she was certain she hadn't. Sure enough, the paper said Tuesday, June 5. It was today's paper, all right.

But where was the article on Delilah's heroic rescue of the stray dog, named Franklin by the technicians at the vet's office where she had taken him after the accident? Surely the piece was here. Surely *The Daughter* had just missed it. She scanned the front page again, her focus flitting from one article to the next.

A bar ran down the left side of the page outlining the city council's proposal for the expansion of the city septic system to include a proposed development for low-income residents. There was also the table of contents telling a reader where the obituaries were and where you could look up what movies were playing in Rehoboth this weekend. There was also a blurb on DEL DOT's planned changes to Route One to help relieve some of the congestion of summer traffic. A huge article and photograph on some swimmer from Stephen Kill who was home from college.

But there nothing on Delilah and the dog on the front page. Nothing.

The Daughter turned the thin pages in jerky, angry movements, skimming page by page. The article on the college student, Rob Crane, took up nearly half the front page, and a third of page three. There were multiple photographs.

At last, *The Daughter* found mention of Delilah's heroic save. Page twelve, under *Police Beat.* Four lines and no photograph. *Four lousy lines.* Her hands trembled. A four line blurb thrown in between the notice of a sobriety checkpoint being set up on County Road 9 this coming Friday night and the report of the arrest of a forty-year-old man for public urination at a bar outside of town?

Four lines. Four lines and that kid, that punk, who was what, a *swimmer*, got an entire article? *The Daughter* closed the paper on her lap, tearing a page in the process. She stared at the photograph of the smiling Rob Crane wearing a ridiculous yellow Speedo and an equally ridiculous white swim cap on his head. He was grinning. Even his grin was stupid. The same grin he had displayed on the evening news, featured in the weekly "Home Town Hero" spot. Who did Rob Crane think he was? Did he truly believe he was better than Detective Delilah Swift? Did he possibly think he could hold a candle to her?

The Daughter quickly read the article, her anger mounting. Graduated from Stephen Kill High School the previous year, attending St. Elizabeth's College in Eastern Maryland, on a partial swimming scholarship. Won all kinds of medals. An Olympic hopeful, the article said. *Blah, blah, blah, blah, blah.*

She ripped the young man's smiling face from the front page, balled it up, and threw it. Hands still shaking, she turned back to page twelve, took scissors from her nightstand, and carefully, lovingly, cut out the four lines about Delilah rescuing the dog. She then got out her journal and smoothed the tiny cut of newspaper on a page.

"It's not right," she said softly. "It's not fair, Delilah. I know it's not fair." She reached for the Scotch tape and carefully attached the article onto a clean, white page.

"You deserved better," she told Delilah as she closed the pale pink diary and clutched it to her breasts. "He's nothing compared to you. Less than nothing. I know things about Rob Crane. Know secret things. He's not Stephen Kill's rising star." Tears stung the backs of her eyelids.

"He . . . he's a monster."

* * *

"I can't tell you how much I appreciate you stopping by, Bruce, Julie said from the bathroom doorway. "When I called, I told your wife we were in no hurry, it's been leaking for ages. It was just on my list of mountains to conquer."

"Not a problem. I was on my way home. It was on my way," the plumber said. He was lying flat on his back on the tiled bathroom floor beneath one of the two porcelain sinks, both hands above his head, cranking a large wrench.

"Elise, wait, I'm coming!" Tiffany ducked into the bathroom, almost smacking Julie with the door. When she spotted the plumber on the floor, she stopped short. "Oops."

Julie turned to the teen. "Sorry, you'll have use the facilities in the new wing. Mr. Johnson is trying to fix our leaky faucet."

Elise scrunched her freckled nose. "But Sister Agatha just kicked us out of there and I really have to go." She pointed to the two toilet stalls in the old bathroom. "Can't I just—"

"Now wouldn't that be rude?" Julie teased.

"I . . . I can go . . ." Bruce pointed the wrench toward the door, obviously uncomfortable with the situation.

"Out, Elise," Julie ordered.

Elise bounced up and down. "But I really have to p—"

"Out," Julie repeated louder, trying not to laugh, knowing this could be a true emergency for a girl six months pregnant. She just looked so silly, blond ponytail bobbing up and down. "Use the new bathroom, or the one downstairs."

With a groan, Elise walked out the door only to nearly run into Sister Agatha.

"Where do you think you're going, young lady?" The

nun demanded in the hall. "Everyone is supposed to be out of the dormitories this time of day. You should be working on your homework."

"What's with you people? I really have to go," Elise whined, beginning to bounce on the balls of her feet again. "I'll just be a minute," she said trying to dodge Sister Agatha.

Agatha blocked her way. "When there's a perfectly good bathroom here?"

Julie stuck her head out the door. Behind her, the plumber was now beating on one of the old pipes with his wrench. "I'm sorry, Sister Agatha," she said above the racket. "I sent Elise back to the dormitories to use the restroom. We have a male visitor."

"In the women's restroom?" Sister Agatha admonished. She began to hum under her breath.

Julie stepped back to let her bustle past. Sister Agatha never walked anywhere, not when she could bustle. The hem of her black and white wimple fluttered behind her.

Elise took off toward the new wing and relief.

"The leaky pipe," Julie explained, following Sister Agatha into the bathroom. "Mr. Johnson was passing by and was kind enough to stop and have a look at it."

Sister Agatha looked at Bruce still lying on the floor, now digging through a tool box, then back at Julie. "It's not Tuesday," she said sternly. "Tuesday is maintenance day. All maintenance calls are scheduled on Tuesdays."

"I understand that, Sister, but Bruce was kind enough to—"

"There are reasons why we have these rules, Sister Julie." Sister Agatha stepped out into the hallway, lowering her voice. "We simply cannot continue to have men coming and going any time they like."

Embarrassed that Sister Agatha wasn't being more gracious, Julie closed the bathroom door behind her as she entered the hall. "He's donating his services, Sister. Today was when he could come by. Otherwise, it might have been weeks."

"There are reasons I've set up these schedules," Sister Agatha repeated. "We cannot constantly have people coming and going in this house. Men walking freely about our halls at four o'clock in the afternoon when there are girls up here unchaperoned."

"I escorted him upstairs. I've been standing there the whole time." Julie rested one hand on her hip. "Sister, he's doing it for *free.*"

"Nothing is free," she challenged. "There's always a price and I fear the cost of these *free* services could result in a cost that can never be monetarily repaid." She made a fist, lifting it to emphasize her point. "We are responsible not only for these young women physically, but morally as well. Surely you know the dangers of unchaperoned teenage girls with men?"

Julie almost laughed aloud thinking of something her grandmother used to say about the horse already being out of the barn. And Sister Agatha was worried about the girls having sex with a fifty-five-year old, balding, pot-bellied, crack-bearing plumber? Julie would have laughed, except that she knew Sister Agatha was being entirely serious.

"These so-called volunteers coming and going all times of the day and night. No system in place to monitor where they are or what they're doing in the house. Do you realize that at this very moment there is a strange woman in the kitchen counting our saucepans?"

"That's Emily. She's not a stranger. She's just home from college. Her parents own a restaurant in Rehoboth and have offered to give us some new stainless pots and pans. She's taking inventory to see what we need." Julie opened her arms. "You know me. I can't cook. I don't know what we need."

"She's wearing an inappropriate shirt that bares her midriff and two of our girls were seated on the floor with her, conversing."

"Sister Agatha, Emily is completely—" She cut herself off halfway through her sentence. It was senseless to go on. Once again, Sister Agatha was not going to see this the same way Julie saw it. "I'll speak to Emily about her clothing." She lifted her chin in the direction of the closed bathroom door. "As soon as Bruce is done and I've escorted him from the house."

"The girls should be doing their homework." Sister Agatha started down the hallway toward the front staircase, her black Hush Puppy shoes slapping on the hardwood floor. "We may only have a few days left of school, but they will not be excused from their work. We have a responsibility to their education while they're here."

"Sister Julie," Monica called, waving the cordless phone, passing Sister Agatha at the head of the stairs.

Monica was a ray of sunshine in the storm-clouded hallway. "It's Marty Kyle, from the TV station. She wants to set up an interview with you. I tried to tell her I make your appointments, but . . ." Monica shrugged good-naturedly.

Monica had come to Maria's Place almost two years ago, a true Godsend, Julie was sure of it. New in town, Julie had run into her at the Chamber of Commerce. They'd struck up a conversation and Julie had learned that Monica was seeking an administrative assistant position. She'd interviewed, Julie had given her the job, and she had quickly become Julie's right-hand woman.

"Not a problem." Julie reached for the phone.

She had learned a great deal in the last year about dealing with the "outside world" as well as the church, and one of those things was that some people just had to "speak to the top." One of Monica's duties was to deal with as many phone calls as she could, giving Julie time to do other tasks, but sometimes, some people just wouldn't take no for an answer. They didn't want the director's assistant, who usually knew more than the director. They wanted the big cheese.

"Hello," Julie said into the phone. There was no answer and the phone sounded dead. "Hello?"

Monica took the phone from her, hit a button and handed it back to Julie. "She was on hold," she whispered.

Julie smiled, nodding, lifting one finger. "Marty, this is Sister Julie, how can I help you?"

"Sister Julie, thank you for taking my call. I wanted to tell you again how impressed I was by Maria's Place," said the reporter on the other end of the line. "By the whole program."

She spoke smoothly with a tone of self-importance Julie found prickly. But Julie knew very well you didn't have to like a person to accept their gifts, whether it was a compliment or hard cash. "Thank you very much. It truly is amazing that so many people could work together for a cause like this."

"As I was telling you Saturday," she continued, "I was wondering if I could interview you."

"I'd be more than happy to be interviewed."

"Great, how does Monday look for you, Sister?"

"For that, I'll have to hand you back over to my assistant, Monica Dryden. She handles my calendar."

"Oh, well . . . certainly," the reported said, obviously miffed.

"Let me give you back to Monica. I'm looking forward to talking to you." Julie passed the phone.

"Monica Dryden here, Miss Kyle. Just let me have a look at Sister Julie's calendar." Monica started back down the hall, her low-heeled black pumps click-clicking on the hardwood floor.

Julie had told Monica a million times that she was welcome to dress causally at Maria's Place. Julie certainly did, but Monica insisted on what she saw as business-appropriate wear that generally meant at-the-knee-length skirts, polyester blouses, and plain, low heels with pantyhose. Always with hose. The girls liked to poke fun at Monica's sometimes severe, often plain, attire, but Julie admired her. She didn't know Monica's story, exactly, or what life she came from; Monica didn't share much in the way of personal information. But she was a hard worker and she stood up for what she believed. She refused to crumble under "peer pressure," even if it was from a handful of pregnant teenage girls.

Julie stepped back into the bathroom where the plumber was still prone on the floor beneath the ancient sink. "So, Bruce, are we going to have to issue last rites?"

Marty gently set the receiver on its cradle as she worked her jaw, fighting her annoyance. It amazed her what idiots some people could be. Opportunities right under their nose—opportunities only people like Marty could offer—and they wanted to get snotty with her? Pass her off to some little ninny?

She rolled back from her desk in the office chair, pulling open the bottom drawer to remove the heels she'd brought to wear with her suit tonight on the air. She had half a mind to cancel the whole damned Maria's Place interview. Sister Julie could just get her damned free publicity elsewhere. She kicked off her black pumps, replacing them with three-inch heels.

Marty didn't care if the woman was a nun. She'd

known women like Sister Julie her whole life. They talk sickeningly sweet to you, they smile and pretend when they speak to you that there's no one more important in the world to them. But the truth is, no one is more important to them than themselves. They're just good at hiding it. No one, not even a nun works the way Sister Julie had worked for that house for knocked-up girls, without expecting something in return. Without *getting* something in return. Marty wondered what Sister Julie's angle was. Was it the glory of having everyone fawn over her or was it something darker? Whatever it was, she hated to feed into it.

This nun story, this Maria's Place, was too good a piece to pass up. The news magazine she was interviewing with, *News Night,* really went for saccharin stories like this one. It might well be her ticket out of this shit-hole station.

Marty worked her jaw. Just one more irritation to add to her already irritating day. First, a dead battery this morning in her car. Then a problem with her credit card limit when she'd tried to charge a battery at the gas station that towed her. Coffee spilled on her skirt at the morning meeting, one of her stories cut from tonight's line-up. The list seemed endless.

She rubbed the knot on the back of her neck, watching through the glass of her tiny office as people passed back and forth like puny, mindless ants. What she needed was a drink. A little relaxation tonight after work.

She glanced at the telephone. Contemplated her choices.

After a moment, she dialed.

It rang four times before he answered.

"I was getting ready to hang up," she said with annoyance.

"I had a client. He was just leaving."

"You want to get together tonight?" She wrapped the

phone cord around her finger, turning her chair so that her back was to the glass wall of the newsroom. "After?"

"I . . . I don't know," he hemmed.

Marty was tempted to hang up. To tell him to go fuck himself. Trouble was, *she* wanted to fuck him. "I'll wear your favorite heels," she cooed into the phone. She slid one long, tanned leg out for her own scrutiny. "I've got fishnet stockings in my car."

"I . . . I shouldn't," he said.

"Of course you *shouldn't*," she snapped. But then she changed her tone, practically purring. "But that's why you will . . . See you tonight." She hung up before he could answer.

He would be there. She knew he would. He always was.

Friday night, Rob pulled into the parking lot just after nine. He took the time to park on the far side of the building where his truck couldn't be seen from the road. Not that his parents usually went this way, but they had gone over to the beach for dinner. He didn't want to take any chances getting caught. Not that they would *do* anything. It was just a hassle he didn't want to deal with tonight. A long lecture on the hazards of drinking. Drinking and driving. The importance of an athlete staying in shape, even though Rob wasn't swimming competitively right now.

He grabbed his wallet off the dash as he climbed out of the red Isuzu pickup. Shoving it into the front pocket of his cargo shorts, he entered the dumpy bar through a side door where there was a single long cooler of beer and wine. He pushed his wrap-around sunglasses back on his head so he could see.

The Pit was mostly a bar, but this side, an old storeroom,

served as a package store. Standing in front of the glass door, Rob pretended to decide what he wanted as his gaze strayed to the counter. If the cashier tonight was the little brown man, he was in luck. He never asked for ID. If it was his skinny-ass wife, Rob was in trouble. He might as well walk away now and not risk her being on the rag and calling the police on him.

Behind Rob, the outside door opened. Another patron. He scooted down a little in front of the cooler. There wasn't a lot of room because of the cardboard cases of beer stacked in the aisle. He glanced sideways to see an attractive woman in a short skirt, tank top, and very high heels peering into the glass door beside him.

She looked at him.

He looked at her.

She smiled.

He looked back at the Buds in front of him and grinned to himself. She liked him. She was old. Had to be at least thirty. But she was hot. She was *definitely* hot.

He looked at her again.

She smiled. "Long day," she said.

"Yeah." He thrust one hand into his pocket.

"Hot night for June." She opened the cooler and pulled out a six pack of Coronas.

Rob liked bottled Corona a hell of a lot more than Bud in a can, but most of his pay check from his summer job went into his college account. Even with the partial scholarship, it wasn't cheap, going to St. E's, living in the dorm. And his parents had his brother and sister to put through college, too. They provided plenty to pay for college, but he was expected to contribute.

He opened the door in front of him, savoring the chill of the metal handle and the feel of the cold air that tumbled out of the cooler. He loved that feel. That first rush of cold air. It was like that blast of cold water when he dove into a pool.

"Headed to a party?" she asked. She'd let the door swing shut. She had her beer, but made no move to go to the counter. She was hanging back because she wanted to talk to him. Obviously, she thought he was hot, too.

"Yeah, maybe." He lowered his wrap-around surfer sunglasses, a smooth move he knew, and stared at her through the dark lenses. *What the hell*, he thought. *You're only nineteen and this well hung once.* "You want to come?"

She smiled, never taking her eyes off him. She wore a lot of make-up, but she had nice lips. Red. Wet.

"I don't know," she said, smiling almost shyly. "Not sure if that's such a good idea, but . . . you want to party?"

"Like . . . alone?" It was all he could do not to stammer.

"Close door," the owner barked from the counter. "Let cold out. Beer get hot."

Rob uncurled his fingers, letting the door close. He wondered if he was dreaming. He could still feel the cold air from the cooler on his face. The door made that sucking sound as the rubber vacuum gasket sealed.

"You like Corona?" the woman asked him.

She'd taken a step closer to him. He could smell her perfume.

"Yeah. Sure," he managed.

She stepped back, opened the door and grabbed another six pack. "My treat." She looked right at him and there was no mistaking that hungry look in her eyes. That horny look.

"Meet you at your car?" she whispered.

Chapter 5

"Sorry to call you in on a Saturday, Swift." The shift commander approached Delilah in the narrow hallway of the stationhouse. He was wearing the same uniform as every other officer on the force, he used the same dry cleaner everyone else used, but Johnson's creases always seemed sharper to Delilah. The gray fabric of his summer trousers a little crisper.

"Kline is on vacation and Thomas called from the ER. Apparently he may have broken his arm trying to surf." The fifty-something-year-old with his buzz cut and no-nonsense demeanor made a face of disdain. "Chief's the one who said to call you in. Said you wouldn't be doing anything, anyway."

She frowned, wondering what Snowden was doing in on a Saturday afternoon. But she knew the answer. Paperwork. He didn't have any more of a personal life than she did. "I'll have you know, Johnson, I had a busy and stimulating afternoon planned. I was going to rearrange my underwear drawer while I watched NASCAR."

He passed her a manila file folder and raised both

hands as he went by her. "I ain't touchin' that with a ten-foot pole. They're in *Interview One*."

Interview One was the only interview room in the tiny station. Stephen Kill police officers interrogated victims, criminals, and witnesses alike in the stark, eight-by-ten room. Fortunately, they had few interviews of any nature to conduct. With the exception of the murders that had taken place the summer before, Stephen Kill had always been a quiet, law-abiding town. The force mostly issued traffic citations, settled the occasional domestic dispute, and visited schools, churches, and volunteer organizations, educating the public on various safety issues.

When Delilah had made detective, she'd been thrilled, but the truth was, these last few months, she'd been missing patrol. With few cases in need of any investigation beyond who took down Mr. Capadona's "No Hunting" signs again, she was forced to run many of the education classes. Delilah was quickly learning that she just wasn't cut out for talking to senior citizen groups about the 911 system in the state or teaching CPR to Girl Scouts. Not her idea of serious cop work.

Delilah opened the manila file. Johnson had told her on the phone that it was a missing person report, but hadn't given any further information. *Rob Crane, age nineteen. Missing twelve to eighteen hours.* She knocked on the door and turned the fancy stainless steel knob that could be locked from the outside with a state-of-the-art passkey that hung in the break room. The thanks for the four-thousand-dollar "door system" could be given to Mattie McConnell, a local resident who had escaped from this very room and stolen a police car the previous summer.

"Good afternoon," Delilah said, putting on her cop face as she entered. She offered her hand to a tall, slender man with a receding hair line. He was fit, somewhere in his late forties. "I'm Detective Swift."

He shook her hand. "Yes, of course. We've seen you on the news, in the papers. We . . . we're contributors to Maria's Place. We were at the ribbon cutting Saturday. I'm Robert Crane, and this is my wife, Sandy." He indicated the woman seated at the small interview table.

Delilah shook Sandy Crane's hand; she didn't really remember either of them, but Mrs. Crane's face looked vaguely familiar. Probably bumped into each other in line at the post office or the drug store. She was small, petite framed, about the same age as her husband. Short brown hair, no make-up. She was wearing Bermuda shorts and a rather unfortunate pink and green plaid blouse.

"We apologize for making you come in on a weekend, Detective. I told the officer, it really wasn't necessary."

"I insisted we come," Mrs. Crane said, nervously tucking a lock of graying hair behind her ear. "Something terrible has happened to Rob, I just know it."

"He's nineteen, Sandy." Mr. Crane used a *Father Knows Best* tone of voice with his wife. "He's out sowing his oats, is all."

The worried mother looked at her husband, then at Delilah. "This isn't like him," she said. "To not come home. To not call."

"Would you like a seat, Mr. Crane?" Delilah indicated the only other vacant chair at the small table.

He shook his head.

Delilah slid into the chair, removing a pen from her jacket pocket. Her position as detective didn't require she wear a uniform, so she generally wore khaki pants, a knit shirt, and a blazer over it to conceal her side arm. It wasn't that she didn't want people to know she carried a gun; it was just that she knew it made people uncomfortable. Especial law-abiding citizens like Mr. and Mrs. Crane.

"When was the last time you saw Robert . . . Rob," Delilah corrected herself.

"Yesterday after work." Mrs. Crane knotted her hands, pressing them onto the table top. "About five-thirty. I would say it was five-thirty, wouldn't you, Robert?" She didn't give him time to respond. "Rob came in from work. He works part-time for Robert's brother Dave. Landscaping. Well"—she lifted narrow shoulders— "mostly mowing lawns, but he makes good money and he enjoys working for his uncle. Rob asked me about our plans for the evening. I was emptying the dishwasher. I told him we were going out to get something to eat, just his father and I." She half smiled. "It was our anniversary last night. Twenty-one years."

"Congratulations." Delilah took notes on a blank sheet that Johnson had attached to the official missing persons form he had already filled out in square, masculine printing. Information he had probably taken over the phone when the call had come in. "And did Rob say where he was going?"

"No." Again, Mrs. Crane looked at her husband. "He . . . he didn't say anything to you about where he was going, did he?"

Delilah heard a catch in her voice. It was subtle, but it was definitely there. She turned to Mr. Crane. "So you spoke with Rob last night after he got home from work, as well. Separately from Mrs. Crane?"

He hesitated. "Yes."

Delilah looked back to Mrs. Crane and then down at her notes. "And did your son mention where he was going?"

"No. He did not."

"What time were you expecting him home?"

"Midnight," Mrs. Crane said emphatically. "I know Rob is practically grown, practically a man, but when he's in our house, he follows our rules. We all agreed to that when he was still in high school. *Midnight*," she repeated.

Delilah flipped the paper over, glancing at the form. "Do you know if your son spoke to his sister or . . . brother?"

"They weren't home. Josie, she's nine, was spending a night with a friend. Peter had Little League practice and then he was going home with the coach's son. So we could have our anniversary dinner."

Delilah nodded. "And which of you actually saw him last?" She looked up when neither answered.

"Robert, I think." Mrs. Crane nodded.

Delilah waited to see if he would say anything. He didn't. "I see you've already written the names and phone numbers of all of Rob's friends in the area." She glanced at Johnson's form again. "We'll check with them of course, but did you call his friends?"

"I called everyone I could think of. Even his roommate at St. Elizabeth's who lives in Virginia. They aren't that close, but I had to try." Delilah scanned the list of handwritten names and numbers. There were a few girls' names, but mostly boys. "Your son have a girlfriend?"

Mrs. Crane shook her head. "Rob is an excellent student and a swimmer. You probably read the newspaper article about him this week. In the *Leader*?" Her pride was plain in her voice. "He didn't really have time for a girlfriend."

"Did he date?"

"In high school? Not much. You know, kids don't really date these days. They *hang out*." She gave a little laugh.

Delilah glanced up at Mr. Crane. "How about you, sir, any knowledge of a girlfriend?"

"Not that Rob doesn't like girls." Mr. Crane gave a macho chuckle. "But nothing serious. As Sandy said, Rob is focused on his schoolwork and his swimming. He's truly a gifted athlete."

"And what about alcohol? Does he drink?"

"He's only nineteen," Mrs. Crane said.

"Not much, you know, sneaks a beer here and there," Mr. Crane offered. "Athletes like Rob are very conscientious about what goes into their bodies."

"And what about drugs?" She tried to sound as non-accusatory as possible, just as she had been trained. "Prescription? Legal? Illegal?"

Mr. Crane frowned, his tone now touchy. "My son doesn't do drugs, Detective."

"I apologize, but I have a list of questions I'm expected to ask. Please don't take offense." Delilah studied Johnson's form for a moment and then looked to Mrs. Crane. "You said you called all of Rob's friends. Did anyone see him last night after he left your house?"

"Yes. Jamey Pratt. They were friends in high school. He went to Jamey's house after he left home, apparently. Around six-thirty. The boys ordered pizza. Watched a movie. Jamey thought he left around eight thirty or nine o'clock." Mrs. Crane reached out. "His name and number are there on the top. His cell number, too."

"And did Jamey say if Rob told him where he was going when he left his house?"

She shook her head. "He said he didn't know."

Delilah made a small mark next to Jamey Pratt's name. Just because a kid wouldn't tell another kid's parent where his friend was going didn't mean he didn't know. He was the best lead she had.

"And Rob was driving the '97 Red Isuzu pick-up, is that correct?"

"Yes."

Delilah was quiet for a minute, checking to be sure she had all the information she needed. Mr. Crane was probably right, the boy was probably just out "sowing his oats." Sleeping off a drunk most likely. "Well, I think I have what I need for now." Delilah rose, closing the folder. "We'll make some phone calls. Alert our officers on duty to keep a look out for Rob and his truck. We'll find him, Mrs. Crane."

"And . . . and what should we do now? Should we wait here? We already drove around town looking for him, but maybe—"

"You should go home, Mrs. Crane." Delilah turned to Mr. Crane. "You should both go home and wait there in case Rob shows up or calls. He has a cell phone, right?" She flipped open the folder again.

"Yes. That number is there, too. We tried calling it, of course. I think I filled his mailbox with messages. Rob will have to use all of his minutes checking his messages." Mrs. Crane tried to make a joke, but it was weak. "Maybe . . . maybe the police can trace any calls he made from it since yesterday?"

"We'll see what we can do. In the meantime,"—Delilah opened the door—"please go home and wait. Someone will call you the minute we know something. And, of course, if you hear from Rob, you need to call us."

Mr. Crane waited for his wife to rise from her chair. "Thank you, Detective."

Delilah offered a half-smile, one she hoped was reassuring, and walked them to the lobby door. She watched them exit the building and then she went back down the hall toward Snowden's office.

She couldn't imagine what it was like for Mr. and Mrs. Crane to have a child missing, even one Rob's age. Even if it was just a matter of a college kid having too much to drink and sacking out at a friend's house. She knew it had to be terrifying. Being parents had to be difficult enough as it was; she didn't honestly know how people got through this kind of stuff.

Delilah knocked on the doorframe and stuck her head through the open doorway. "Call Swift in? She doesn't have a Saturday night date anyway?"

Snowden smiled from behind his desk, but he didn't look up from his computer screen. "That what Johnson said I said?"

"Doesn't matter." She entered the office and stood behind the two leather chairs in front of his desk. "I interviewed the Cranes and sent them home. I'll start making phone calls. Let our patrol know who we're looking for, description of the vehicle he was driving, the usual."

"He's probably sleeping off a drunk." Snowden hit the print key on his keyboard and the printer to his left on a small secretary began to hum. He looked up at her. "He'll be home soon enough."

"That's what I was thinking." She tapped the file folder on the back of the chair. "But the parents say he doesn't drink. Doesn't do drugs. No girlfriend."

"Your parents knew you drank when you were nineteen?"

She lifted an eyebrow. "Heck, no! My daddy'd have killed me."

Snowden smiled. "Tillie Calloway would have tortured me *before* she killed me."

She gave a low whistle. "You really are old, aren't you, Chief?"

He snatched the freshly printed sheets off the printer tray. "You need something *else,* Detective?"

She smiled, but she didn't respond. The door was open, anyone could walk by. They were always careful at work, no matter what shameless thoughts went through their heads. "I'm going to make these phone calls. See what I can find out."

"Keep me up to date."

"Will do." She walked out of the office, hoping she'd find Rob Crane before dark as they both predicted. That would give her time to get home, change the sheets, and take a shower before Snowden arrived.

Rob woke slowly, disoriented. His room was dark. The bed hard. *No . . . not his room. Not his bed.* A sense of panic fluttered in his chest as he threw both hands out to feel the hard ground beneath him. He raised his head and then cringed, fingering the back of it. His hair was damp around the sore spot. Crusty.

He didn't know where he was. How he got here. It was damned dark. Maybe he wasn't awake. Maybe he was still dreaming.

But images flashed in his mind like flipping pages from an old black and white textbook. He wasn't dreaming. They were real. *This* was real.

He remembered the beer cooler at The Pit. The feel of the cold door handle.

The chick.

He sat up and his hands fell to his lap. His shorts were unbuttoned. Fallen halfway down. He pushed forward onto his knees and hastily jerked them up over his boxers.

The beer. He drank a lot of beer.

First he drove his truck and she passed him beers. He'd gotten wasted pretty quickly, though exactly how, he wasn't sure. He hadn't had that many . . . had he?

He remembered turning onto the old mill road. Barely more than a trail now. She'd been laughing. Teasing him. Flirting with him.

He had liked her. She was easy to talk to for a woman her age. She knew all about his swimming. Asked him things.

He parked. Took a leak and then they made out in the front seat of the truck. Then . . .

Rob's head was pounding. It was hard to think. He sank back on his heels, still fighting the panic in his chest. So dark . . .

He remembered the taste of her mouth on his. He had wanted her. She had said there was a place they could go. He had thought she meant her apartment, at first. They'd taken a path through the woods that all the kids in town knew about. It led from the mill road, across Old Man Tuttle's property, right into town. A mile maybe, on foot?

Rob remembered wondering why they hadn't just driven to her place, but they were having such a good time. The air was hot, and sweet with the coming of summer and she had been wearing perfume. A faint scent that made his breath catch in his throat when he leaned closer to her. Made him hard.

They had cut across people's yards, just like back when he was in high school, him and Jamey and others sneaking out after curfew. Dogs barked. He'd heard the rumble of window air conditioners. Cars on the street. The occasional voice caught on the wind.

It had been very dark out, the moon hidden by clouds.

The only light had been from what came through closed blinds on the houses, and the street lights in the distance.

She'd led him through a gate, around a dumpster, past an aboveground pool. Somebody's yard. He hadn't known exactly where he was. Too drunk and too horny to care.

Rob's chest tightened as the memories came back faster. They had stopped beneath a big tree. She had backed up against the trunk, pulled him against her, let him kiss her neck. Squeeze one breast. She had whispered in his ear. Made promises so nasty he thought he'd blow his wad right there.

Rob wasn't a virgin . . . not *technically*, but he wasn't exactly that experienced, either. He had wanted her so bad. She had tasted . . . *felt* . . . so good.

She had led him through the dark, down steps. He remembered hesitating, but she had whispered in his ear again. Dirty words that had urged him forward.

He'd let her lead him down the steps, into a pitch darkness where no street lights penetrated. Into *this* dark.

Rob began to shake, looking around him, trying to see something. Anything in the inky blackness.

She had touched him through his shorts. It had felt so good that he had been afraid it would all be over before he got started. He remembered fumbling with her bra strap.

Then, out of nowhere, his head had felt as if it exploded. He must have fallen. Hit the floor. Her voice. Then nothing . . .

Now this. Overwhelming darkness. Dampness. The hard ground beneath him. "H . . . hello?" Rob called, trying not to be afraid.

He rose slowly to his feet. Felt dizzy and had to close

his eyes for a minute. Thought he might vomit. But the nausea passed, and he opened his eyes again. He thrust out his hands to feel his way like a blind man.

"Anyone there? Annie?" She had said her name was Annie.

"Annie?" he called tentatively. Then again, louder. "Annie?"

His hands found the rough planks of a wall. It rose from the floor upward, higher than he could reach. Keeping his palms on the wall, he shuffled his feet, following it. Four steps and he hit another wall. Rob followed it all the way around. He found what he thought were the seams of a door, but it wouldn't open. There was no handle.

He was in a room of some sort. Small. Eight by six feet, max.

He swallowed hard, pressing his hands against the wall. He was thirsty. His head really hurt.

He didn't understand. He felt tears sting behind his eyelids as he fought to stay calm.

She had done this to him, hadn't she? Annie? Locked him in here. But where was *here?* *What* was here?

It was just a dark room, but right now, it felt like a tomb.

Chapter 6

Delilah leaned against the kitchen counter and waited for the coffee pot to fill. She could hear the shower running and it made her smile. Snowden had spent the night, something he didn't often do.

She watched the dark liquid drip rhythmically into the glass carafe. She'd received no call from the station last night and this morning when she called in, she discovered that there was still no sign of or word from Rob Crane.

Delilah had been so sure he would show up last night that this morning she was a little bewildered. Where the heck was he?

Yesterday she'd talked to his friends on the phone and stopped by to see his buddy who worked at a local sub shop. Jamey had stuck to his story, saying he didn't know where Rob had gone after he left his house. Delilah had checked in some of the obvious places a nineteen year old might go on a Friday night: the minimart, the diner. No one had seen him. With lack of any evidence to the contrary, by bedtime, she'd settled on her original theory that Rob had been up to some minor no-good and was sleeping it off at a friend's. Maybe reluctant to go home, knowing he was busted. But now that he'd been missing more than twenty-four hours, she wasn't so sure. She'd been so laid back about the whole case that this morning she had a serious case of the guilts.

Now, she had to expand the possibilities to include the idea that he might no longer be in the area. Had he taken off to see an ex-girlfriend? Did he have an argument with her parents that they hadn't told her about? Had he just decided to get out of Dodge for a few days to make his parents sweat? Scare them, maybe? Or was he the kind of person who didn't think about others, just acted on impulse? All these scenarios running around in her head were entirely possible. Likely even. What worried her was that this didn't appear to be a run-of-the-mill "kid left town."

Fortunately, Delilah had followed normal procedure for a missing person report and notified the officers on duty, providing a description of Rob and his vehicle. And even though yesterday he hadn't been missing long enough to *officially* be missing, she'd also given the State Police and several small town forces in the surrounding area a heads up.

The phone rang and she grabbed the handset off the counter. It had to be the station. The kid had showed up somewhere.

"Swift," she said into the phone.

"Delilah?"

She wasn't expecting to hear from his sister, not on a Sunday morning. Sundays, Rosemary was at church half the day. She glanced in the direction of the hall. The shower was still running.

"Hey, Rosemary," Delilah said cautiously. She reached

for two matching mugs from the cupboard over the coffee pot. "How are you this morning?"

"She's on her way," Rosemary said.

Delilah set both mugs on the counter. "I'm sorry. What? Who's on her way?"

"Callie," Rosemary exhaled. "I put her on a plane five minutes ago."

"Put her on a plane for *where*?" Delilah asked, dumbfounded. She reached for the coffee carafe.

"There. She's flying into Salisbury. She won't be there until three because she has a connecting flight in Philly. You have to be at the airport to pick her up."

Delilah set the coffee pot back on its base without pouring any. For a moment, she was speechless. Callie was coming *here*? "Rosemary . . ."

"I know. I know. We should have discussed it further. I should have called you sooner. But I just decided last night. I can't do it, Delilah." Her voice broke. "I can't do it anymore. Bruce called yesterday and he wants to have lunch. He . . . he wants to talk, but he just can't deal with her nonsense. Not right now. I need you. I need your help in this. I think he's serious. He left her. The woman. He's staying at a hotel and he wants to come home."

"That's wonderful." Delilah tried to sound supportive, unable to help wondering if it was wonderful that your two-timing husband wanted to come home. But her thoughts strayed for only a second before they bounced back to Callie. "Rosemary, I can't believe you put her on a plane without telling me. Does Joseph know about this?" He was their oldest brother, only eighteen months younger than Rosemary. He'd been there for them both all these years. "Mama and Daddy?"

"I didn't tell anyone." Rosemary sounded like an emotional basket case, but she was dug in. Delilah recognized that determination in her voice all too well. There was no way she was going to change her sister's mind about this. Not right now. Not when she was dug in like this. Besides . . . Callie was already in the air. She was already on her way whether Delilah wanted her here or not.

Delilah bristled at the thought. "She's fourteen. She shouldn't be flying alone."

"That ridiculous. Kids fly all the time, seven, eight years old," Rosemary defended herself. "If she's old enough to buy pot alone, I think she's old enough to fly alone. It's not like she's flying to Pakistan or something."

Delilah closed her eyes for a moment, exhaling. What was she going to do? Callie couldn't stay here.

Suddenly she realized that the shower was no longer running. Snowden would be out of the bathroom in a minute, coming down the hall for his morning coffee.

"Okay. I'll be there to get her." Delilah gripped the phone. "Three o'clock. I'll pick her up. We'll talk. I'll try to see what's going on in her head. But she can't stay, Rosemary. She can't stay too long. Just . . . just a few days. A week or so, maybe. Just long enough for you to get yourself situated." She heard the bathroom door open. "Look, I have to go to work this morning if I'm going to be in Salisbury at three. I've got a missing teenager. We'll call you tonight and let you know Callie arrived safely."

Delilah was reaching for the coffee pot when Snowden appeared in the doorway, naked except for the towel wrapped around his waist.

"Any word on the kid?"

She shook her head, her back to him, not trusting herself to speak yet. She poured the coffee slowly, trying to give herself some recovery time.

Callie here? Mild panic tightened her chest. She couldn't have Callie here. She didn't know anything

about teenagers. She didn't really even know Callie very
well. And what about Snowden? No one could know
about the two of them. How on earth logistically could
they possibly see each other with a fourteen year old
sleeping in the spare bedroom?

"That wasn't the station?"

Delilah completely blanked out. "I'm sorry?"

"The phone call. That wasn't Johnson?"

She had to clench her hand to keep it from shaking as
she slid the coffee carafe back onto the hot plate and
turned away from the counter, headed for the fridge.
She knew she might as well come clean now. It wasn't as
if he wasn't going to notice a teenager in the house the
next time he came over.

"That . . . that was my sister Rosemary, again. She . . .
we decided it might be a good idea if my niece came to
stay for a few days." She looked up at him quickly, then
down again as she walked back to the counter with the
small carton in her hand. "Give them both a break."

"That's nice of you. Might be what they need." He
took the cream carton she slid along the counter toward
him. "When's she coming?"

Delilah dug into the sugar bowl for a second heaping
teaspoon. "Today."

Snowden looked up. "Today?"

She gave him a quick smile, thinking she better just
give him the whole story now. "I guess things have been
a little crazy. Callie was expelled for marijuana posses-
sion so she's already out of school. My sister's husband
wants to talk about reconciliation. He . . . he's Rosemary's second husband."

"Ah, so he's not Callie's father."

Delilah lifted her cup to her mouth, blew, and took a
sip. It was so hot it burned her lips. "No." *Okay, so that*

was at least half the story. She wiped her mouth and reached for the spoon to stir the coffee. It needed more sugar.

Snowden leaned against the counter and Delilah couldn't help but marvel at the way he could keep his towel wrapped around his narrow hips, barely covering "Christmas" as her granny had always said. The towel just hung there, well below his belly button, like a modern miracle of terrycloth, revealing nothing and yet promising . . .

She dumped another spoon of sugar into her coffee.

"She have a serious problem?"

Delilah set down her coffee cup and went to the pantry. No bran cereal and fruit for her this morning. It was definitely going to be a Pop-Tart kind of day.

"A serious drug problem?" he asked.

She pushed aside the Red Rose teabags, a bag of sugar, flour. Sure enough, behind a little bag of cornmeal was her emergency stash of S'more Pop-Tarts.

"When aren't drugs serious with a fourteen year old?" she asked, tearing open the top of the box.

He eyed her choice of breakfast food, but made no comment. He was such a health and exercise nut that she doubted Pop-Tarts had ever crossed his lips.

"You know what I mean," he said. "First time she's been busted? Other drugs? Alcohol?"

She leaned against the counter beside him, exhaled and dug a packet out of the box. "Suspended twice this year, before the expulsion. Smoking cigarettes in the bathroom, then skipping school, I think. Arrested for underage drinking about two months ago. Rosemary caught her smoking weed around the same time." She listed the offenses as if she was reading off a grocery list rather than a rap sheet. "But she's not a bad kid. She's really not." Delilah put the box down so she could use both hands to attack the paper and foil wrapping between her and the chocolate marshmallow pastry.

"So what do you think you can do for her that her parents haven't been able to?"

"I don't know, Snowden." Her tone came out more waspish than she intended and she tugged harder on the "easy open" corner that wouldn't budge. "It's seven o'clock in the morning. I'd thought I'd have my coffee before I started solving the world's problems."

"Okay," he said.

Just like that. No anger. No hurt feelings. Just *okay*. Sometimes it really irked her that he was so in control of himself. Of his emotions.

"Okay," she repeated with a nod, at last gaining entry to the seemingly impenetrable Pop-Tart pack.

"I better go." He left the counter, carrying his coffee cup, still pulling off the magic towel act.

Above the edge of the towel, Delilah could just see the barest hint of cleavage between two muscular brown buttocks as he walked away. She crammed pastry into her mouth. She had to give the man one thing, his no Pop-Tart rule had certainly carved a fine pair of man-cheeks.

Delilah gripped the wheel of the police cruiser, staring at the blacktop that ran beneath her, driving on autopilot, thoroughly absorbed by the thoughts flying around inside her head. She was going to have to step on it to make the airport on time.

Where could this kid be? What was she going to say to Callie? What was she going to do with her? Statistics suggested a missing nineteen-year-old male who had disappeared had either done so voluntarily or met with a tragic accident. Foul play was rarely involved.

Rob Crane's family and friends all swore he wasn't the kind to just take off. That he was too responsible a young man. They insisted he would never voluntarily worry his friends and family this way. If that was true, where was he? Had he driven his car off some back road bridge and drowned? Or had his family and friends merely misjudged Rob? Had he met a girl in Rehoboth and made a road trip to South Carolina in pursuit of tourist tail? What made Rosemary think that if she couldn't do anything with Callie, Delilah could?

The sun was strong, the Sunday afternoon hot, and she kicked up the air inside the car. She picked up the Salisbury bypass, following the signs toward the municipal airport. It was two forty-nine. Minutes to spare. But with every moment that passed, she was dreading this more and more. It wasn't that she didn't love Callie, because she did. With every ounce of her heart. But she didn't know Callie. Shoot, Delilah barely knew herself. She was having a hard enough time figuring out her own life; what to do about Snowden, about the job she loved and despised at the same time, whether moving away from home to take this job in Delaware really had been such a good idea.

Delilah pulled into the small parking lot, took a ticket from the nice elderly gentleman in the booth, and pulled into the first open spot she saw. She grabbed the leather backpack she used as a purse and approached the quaint, small town airport terminal. Inside, she passed through a thorough but friendly security station and was waiting for Callie at the windows facing the runway when the plane rolled up. As passengers began to disembark on the tarmac and make their way into the building, Delilah took a deep breath and smiled. There was no turning back. The teenager was here and she was going to deal with it. They were going to deal with this situation together.

Delilah almost missed her. Almost let her pass right by. She'd been looking for a blond, hair much the same color as her own, about her height. A tall, willowy redhead with a shoulder-length, hip haircut, and a frown walked into the waiting area and halted, shifting the orange backpack hanging off her shoulder. She wore ear buds in both ears, the white wires hanging down each side of her face, disappearing into the backpack.

"Callie?"

The young woman turned. She'd definitely grown taller since Delilah had seen her back in the spring.

"Oh," Callie said, almost seeming surprised anyone was there for her. "Hey."

Delilah forced her smile even wider. Callie did not smile back.

"Have a good trip?" Delilah put out her arms. Her family was the huggy, kissy type. There were embraces and smooches around every time someone walked in or out of the house. It had driven Delilah crazy as a teen.

Apparently, the tradition had the same impact on Callie. Instead of allowing Delilah to hug her, Callie ducked, managing to shrug away before Delilah caught more than a thin shoulder.

"You know they don't feed you on flights any more?" Callie walked away, heading in the same direction as the other passengers. *Baggage.* "Not unless you're like flying to China or some bullshit like that."

Delilah looked at the teen with one of those exaggerated second takes you saw on TV. She couldn't believe Rosemary would allow such language. Had Delilah or Rosemary or any of their brothers ever used that word in her Mama and Daddy's house, the kids would have had her mouth washed out with Dawn dish detergent.

Delilah was so shocked she didn't know what to say. She hated to have Callie under her charge less than a minute before she started correcting her.

"Can we like stop and get something? I only like Arby's and Chick-fil-A," Callie said. "I don't do Mickey D's. Dog burgers." She spoke with that unmistakable southern drawl that made Delilah homesick at once.

"Okay. Sure. I guess." Delilah shrugged, trying to go with the flow. "I was going to throw burgers on the grill, but we can stop if you're really hungry." Callie bobbed her head and it took Delilah a second to realize she was nodding to the beat of the music in her ears, not responding to the conversation.

They waited for the bags in silence. People milled about. Hugged. Laughed. A young couple stood to the side of the baggage carousel and snuggled, making Delilah envious. It sometimes bothered her that she and Snowden had to be so careful. That she couldn't so much as lay her hand on his arm in public, for fear of being seen.

Delilah glanced at Callie. She felt as if she should be saying something, but she didn't know what to say. Callie seemed to be content to listen to her music and stare off into space with an obviously practiced look of boredom on her face.

They picked up her bag and headed out of the terminal. "Look, Callie," Delilah said, walking beside the teen.

Either Callie couldn't hear her or was ignoring her.

Delilah exhaled with a puff of air and caught her niece's attention, signaling for her to turn down the music.

"Yeah?" Callie said.

Her tone suggested annoyance, but Delilah was determined not to make judgments based on what Rosemary had to say about the teenager. If she was going to try to help Callie, help her family situation at home, she had to use her own instincts. She also felt as if she needed to give Callie a chance.

"I was saying . . . we're right over here." Delilah cut between the cars. "That I'm glad you're here. I wish it was under better circumstances, but—"

"Mom tell you? The asshole basically kicked me out of the house."

Delilah stopped at the rear of the black and white police cruiser with the words *Stephen Kill Police* painted across the rear side panels. "Callie, you can't use language like that in my house." She spoke quietly, but with authority, the voice she'd been taught to use on the job. "Cursing isn't acceptable."

Callie stared at the car as Delilah inserted her key and popped the trunk. "We're riding in this thing? You've got to be kidding me."

It hadn't occurred to Delilah that Callie would be uncomfortable riding in a police car. But she hadn't had a choice. Her pickup was at Buck's getting new brake pads, and even though the shop did a nice job for a reasonable price, expedient service was not one of its finer attributes.

"Sorry. My truck's in the shop. I drive this a lot. It's good for citizens to see cruisers on the road, even if the officer's off duty."

Callie dropped the suitcase at Delilah's feet and walked around to the passenger's side, turning up the invisible music maker buried in her backpack.

Delilah stared at the suitcase for a minute, then picked it up and heaved it into the massive trunk. She waited until she was out of the parking lot and back on the bypass before attempting conversation with her charge again.

"We don't need to get into it right now, but I want you to know how sorry I was to hear about your arrest." She took a quick glimpse at the teen slumped in the seat beside her, staring out the window, music pouring from her ears. It was loud music, *but at least it wasn't bad.*

Delilah reached over and touched Callie's bare arm, then signaled for her to remove the ear buds. There was no misinterpreting Callie's aggravation this time.

"I said, I was really sorry to hear about your arrest. I know you're too smart not to know the dangers of drugs, but—"

"Drugs?" Callie rolled her eyes and glanced out the window.

Delilah didn't know what she was expecting, but this wasn't it. Surely Callie didn't believe drugs were okay? "Callie—"

"I mean, it's not like I was doing crack or something," the teen said, her tone suggesting Delilah was some sort of idiot.

"I'm not getting into a discussion with you right now, comparing the evils of marijuana to the evils of cocaine." Delilah pushed her sunglasses more snuggly on her head. She could feel a headache coming on. She had smoked marijuana a couple of times when she was in high school, but there was no way she was confessing that to Callie or anyone else for that matter. "Marijuana is illegal, Callie. It doesn't matter what you think of it. Now, fortunately, I think you can go through a program and have this expunged from your record, but you have to get it out of your head that you didn't do anything wrong. Because you did."

Callie shook her head, but didn't say anything.

"What?" Delilah asked.

Callie continued to stare out the window. "Nothing."

"Look, your mom sent you here because she thought maybe I could help. I'm hoping she's right, but you're going to have to tell me what you're thinking."

"So you can tell me I'm wrong?"

"So I can have a better understanding of where you're coming from. I don't know right now what's making you do things I know very well you know are wrong. Is it friends making you feel like you have to? Is it to tick off your parents? I don't know the answer, but I know there's got to be a reason."

Callie crossed her arms over her chest, staring straight ahead now, through the windshield. "You don't want to hear what I have to say."

"I do. I also want to keep you safe and alive." Delilah glanced at the clock on the dash. It had now been forty-three hours since anyone had seen Rob Crane. "You know, I see a lot of terrible things on the job. Things that happen to young people your age. Right now, I've got a missing college student. Nineteen years old. His parents are scared to death."

Callie groaned and shifted her gaze to her window. "Are we getting Chick-fil-A?"

Delilah paused a beat before she answered. She had known this wasn't going to be easy, but she could already see that that was an understatement. Callie wasn't going to be an easy nut to crack. "Sure."

"Cool." Callie bobbed her head as she reinserted her ear buds and slid her hand into her back pack.

As the music flooded the teen's ears and the car, Delilah switched lanes, eyeing the sign marking the next exit. In the right-hand lane, her gaze strayed over the elevated highway to a marshy patch below and her thoughts returned to the missing college student. Had Rob's car gone off the road somewhere? There were plenty of marshy places like this in the area. It had been a wet spring and ponds and wetlands were full. So were sink holes.

Delilah knew that statistics said the kid would show up, but she just couldn't shake the feeling she had that, this time, the stats were wrong.

The Daughter checked the time on the digital clock beside her bed for the third time in the last half hour. It was only six-ten. It was too early to go yet. She had to resist the temptation. No matter how badly she wanted to go, she had to wait until dark. After dark, then she could see him . . . well, go talk to him. She wasn't stupid enough to open the door, not yet at least.

The thought of going there, of talking to him, shot adrenalin through her entire body. She couldn't believe she'd had the guts to do it. It was something she'd thought about on and off for years, but hadn't known she could actually do it. Not just plan it, but execute it.

Killing the fat cow didn't count. That had been different. Easy. It had taken almost no preparation. It hadn't even felt that good. It was just like doing something that had to be done. Something like killing a fly or wiping your ass. But *this* . . . this was different.

The Daughter picked up her scrapbook from the bedside table and carefully opened it, smoothing the first page, a glossy color photo of Delilah from the previous year. *The Daughter* had scanned it, cropped it, then printed it on shiny *Kodak* paper so that it looked like a family shot. Like *The Daughter* had taken it herself.

She drew her finger along the edge of the photo, aching to touch Delilah's face, but not wanting to risk smudging the crisp, clear image. She had been thinking about Delilah all day. She smiled to herself. Not that today had been any different than any other day in the last few months.

She wondered what Delilah was doing. How she had spent her Sunday, the day of rest? She was off-duty, *The Daughter* knew that. Had she risen early, curled up in her favorite jammies and read the newspaper, and sipped tea like *The Daughter* had done? She liked the idea of that, them both reading the Sunday paper, the same articles, laughing over the same funnies, doing the same cross-word puzzle. *The Daughter* wanted to think about what it would be like to do those things together, but she didn't dare. It was . . . too much. Too overwhelming. She felt her heart flutter with a mixture of pleasure and something akin to fear.

She closed the scrapbook and reached for the novel she'd left beside her bed. Soon it would be dark and then she would pay *The Swimmer* a visit.

It was after eight o'clock when the phone rang and Delilah was relieved to have something to do other than look at Callie's back as the teen sat hunched over the computer while Delilah tried to concentrate on the training manual she'd been attempting to get through for weeks.

"Delilah."

She smiled at the sound of Snowden's deep masculine voice on the phone. "Hey."

"Get your niece okay?"

"Yeah. Fine. Everything's fine." She uncurled her bare feet from beneath her and climbed out of the chair, keeping her voice down. "It's a little, you know . . .

awkward right now." She walked into the kitchen for a little privacy. "But I think with some time, she'll be willing to open up a bit with me."

"That's good. Listen, I'm at my mom's right now, but I just got a call from the station." His voice changed in a heartbeat. Delilah was now speaking to Chief Calloway and not her lover. "They found his truck. Out on the old sawmill road. Can you leave her? Meet me there?"

"Oh, sure. Of course." Delilah was already headed down the hall to get her shoes on. "Any sign of him?" she asked, hoping against hope.

"No. Keys in the ignition. Wallet in the glove compartment. But there's no sign of a struggle. No blood."

"Good. That's good isn't it?" She didn't really expect him to answer. "Meet you there in twenty minutes." She hung up and reached for her badge on the bedside nightstand.

Chapter 7

"Miss Kyle, good morning. Come in."

Marty allowed the mousy assistant to escort her through the front door. Her camera guy would be here within the hour, but she wanted to take a little time to talk about the interview with the nun before they began filming. The clearer they both were on what they wanted out of this interview, the quicker they could get it done and the less wasted footage would end up on the cutting room floor.

"Sister Julie is out in the garden."

The woman . . . Marsha, Martha . . . *Monica*, that was it, glanced out the door behind Marty.

What was it with people and cameras? "Crew's coming later. I can find the backyard. Why don't you be a dear and make me a cup of coffee? Black." Marty strode down the hall toward the new wing, her heels clicking on the polished hardwood floor.

Feminine voices floated down the staircase. Girls giggling. Marty wondered exactly what they thought they had to laugh about. They were fifteen, knocked up, and their families had kicked them out of their homes. Marty certainly hadn't thought it was funny. She knew. She'd been there.

"Good morning, Marty. Good to see you." Julie approached the reporter across the new stone patio that had been completely built by donations and volunteer labor. She tugged off her canvas gardening gloves, tucking them into the back pocket of her faded blue jeans. She'd actually considered donning her habit this morning for the filming, but decided against it. It was important to her that who she was and what Maria's Place was came across accurately on television.

"Good to see you. I thought we could chat for a little while before my crew arrives and we start taping. As I said, we'll do the initial filming over the next week and then I'll be back to fill in the holes once we see what we have," Marty said without preamble as she dropped her slick leather briefcase on one of the four wrought iron and glass tables scattered across the patio. "I ordered some coffee. I hope you don't mind." She glanced at the seat of a chair before she sat down.

Julie smiled. She knew she was supposed to love all God's children, but she found some harder to like than others. "I'm glad Monica could be of assistance. I don't know what I'd do without her. She's my right arm and sometimes my left." She chuckled as took the chair across from Marty.

"And not Sister Agatha? She's not your *right-hand man?*"

Julie had to pause for a moment and think how to respond. The woman certainly didn't bother with niceties, did she? Marty also obviously had a way of seeing straight through to the heart of matters. An instinct. Julie made a mental note to remember that. To remember to be careful what she said.

Julie smiled, tugging the flowered gloves from her pocket and placing them on the glass table top. "Sister Agatha and Monica serve very different roles here at Maria's Place. Monica is our administrator. Sister Agatha is in charge of education, both secular and nonsecular. We simply couldn't function without either of them."

Marty scribbled on a legal pad using an expensive pen. "So Sister Agatha is relegated to curriculum, teaching, and Hail Marys, while you run the place and make the decisions? And Monica does the scuttle work?"

Julie had to smile to herself. Marty obviously had self-image issues. It wasn't hard to see through the lavender suit, the snake-skin patterned high heels, the expensive hair cut, and manicure. Julie had been in the nun business long enough to know when someone was hurting inside. "I'd hardly call what our administrator does scuttle work. She takes care of all scheduling for the house and our girls such as maintenance, doctor's appointments, even family visits. She also does all the paperwork the diocese requires, as well as serves as our bookkeeper."

Julie reached out and pressed her finger into the soil inside a red clay pot of impatiens in the center of the table. They needed water. She would talk to the new girl Lareina, see if she might be interested in helping out with gardening. With the new patio and flower beds and additional potted plants, it was obviously going to be a bigger job than Julie could handle these days, even with Mattie McConnell helping out.

"And what about your job? Exactly what do you do?"

Julie waited patiently for Marty to make eye contact with her.

"You understand that I'm just trying to get some information so I know what kind of questions to ask," the reporter said. She tucked a lock of blond hair behind her ear.

"I understand." Julie nodded. "I was hoping, however, that we could concentrate on what Maria's provides pregnant teenagers."

"But no interviews with the teenagers?" Marty was terse.

Julie was firm. "No. I will not allow my girls to be filmed or interviewed. It's important to us here that we respect their privacy and the privacy of their families."

"So how am I supposed to give viewers their point of view? How am I supposed to tell how they got here, how they feel about the place?"

Julie opened both hands. "I can't tell you that. I'm sure you'll find a way, though."

Marty looked down, twisting her mouth. That obviously wasn't the response she was hoping for.

Julie's grandmother always said never offer criticism without also offering possible solutions. "Perhaps you should focus your story on what the house provides and what the volunteers who serve here do rather than directly on our girls. I would imagine you could get as many volunteers as you needed to allow you to interview them on camera."

"He one of your volunteers?" She nodded, indicating someone behind Julie.

Julie turned to look over her shoulder. "That's Mattie McConnell. Actually, he's just been hired to help out. He'll be doing some light handywork around the house. Fixing sticky windows. Gardening, whatever we need."

Marty watched the forty-year-old man drag a rake clumsily across the grass in front of the sixteen-passenger van the home owned. "You're paying him to dig up your grass?"

Julie turned back, beginning to feel that her patience was just about at its limit. "Mattie is mentally handicapped, but he's a wonderful man. Kind. Easy going. He doesn't speak, though, so unfortunately, you won't be able to interview him."

The reporter lifted a finely plucked, thin brow. "It's safe having a man like that around these teenage girls?"

"Perfectly."

Marty turned back to her notes, clearing her throat. "So . . ." She looked up at Julie. "What about the rest of your *staff*? I don't suppose they have privacy issues or difficulty forming sentences. I can interview them?"

"Certainly. I've already warned them. Monica is shy. I'd appreciate it if you'd go easy her." Julie chuckled. "But I'm sure Sister Agatha will be happy to answer all your questions. She has very definite opinions, and I'm sure will be willing to offer a little healthy criticism of the program, just to spice up your interview."

Marty looked up from her pad of paper again, actually seeming interested for the first time. "Is that animosity I hear in your voice, Sister Julie?"

"Certainly not. It's Sister Agatha's job to help me make Maria's Place the best it can be. How can that happen if there are no differences of opinion in the way things ought to be done?"

The French doors opened and Monica stepped out onto the patio carrying an antique silver tray covered with a white cloth napkin. Balanced on the tray were two floral china cups and saucers and matching cream pitcher and sugar bowl.

"Another one of your finds?" Julie asked, indicating

the china as her assistant set the tray on the table in front of the reporter.

"There were only five cups, six saucers, and three dessert plates so I got them supercheap." She looked to Marty. "Anything else I can do for you, Miss Kyle?"

Marty didn't look up. "No. Thank you. Just bring my camera crew out when they arrive." She looked up, gazing out over the patio to the newly tilled and only partially planted flower beds. "I'll have to see what the guys think of the lighting, but this is as good a place as any to start. We'll want inside shots, too, of course, but I'll get back to you on that."

Monica nodded. "Sister Julie, you need anything?"

Julie held up her hand. "Not a thing. Thank you, Monica. Go ahead and get back to what you were doing. I'll keep my eye out for the camera crew." She winked and Monica smiled, slipping back into the house and closing the door behind her.

"So, Marty. You want to ask some juicy questions?" Julie slid forward on the edge of the chair and clapped her hands. "Let's talk about who these girls are, and why we're all here."

"Six days, Snowden. It's been six days. Where the heck is he?" Delilah flopped down in one of the arm chairs in front of him and propped her elbows on his desk, cradling her head in her hands.

"You look tired," he said, his voice almost inaudible.

It was after five and the station had quieted considerably, but his office door was open and anyone passing by could overhear anything they said.

"I *am* tired." She dropped her hands to the smooth desk and looked up at him. "I've got these neighborhood awareness workshops to schedule, that grant application to work on, my exam to study for, and I can't stop thinking about him. Wondering if we've missed something."

"You have to learn to turn it off." He continued to speak in the same soothing voice. "You need to sleep to be your best when you're here."

"It wouldn't matter if I could shut off my brain for a few minutes." She threw up one hand and pushed back in the chair. "Callie is up all hours on the computer. It's weird having someone in the house, walking around in the middle of the night. I just can't relax. I can't sleep."

He raised one dark eyebrow. He didn't have to say anything for his disapproval to register. She frowned. He didn't have a teenager. How could he possibly understand?

"She misses her friends back home. Instant messaging." She gestured. "It's what teenagers do."

He didn't say anything, making her feel as if she had to explain herself even further, which she hated. In the last nine months, the ten years age difference between them rarely seemed to matter, but it was times like this that she felt as if he were offering paternal criticism, something she definitely didn't need. Her father was still alive and well; she got plenty of the real thing.

Delilah glanced away, knowing they needed to discuss this issue, but making the decision to let it go for now. She looked back at him. "I did get one possible lead today. I went by to see the friend Jamey again and I'm sure he doesn't know where Rob is; he's too upset. Anyway, this time when I talked to him, he *remembered* there *had* been talk of a party at someone's dad's house over in Rehoboth. Underage drinking, I'm sure, which is why he didn't mention it in the first place. Jamey didn't know the girl so he wasn't going, but he said he'd ask around and try to find out where it had been."

Snowden leaned forward, tenting his hands on the pile of neatly stacked manila folders in front of him. He had nice hands. A nice touch. A touch she was starting to miss. They hadn't seen each other, except at work, since Callie's arrival Sunday.

"That's good," he said. "That's very good."

She stared at the pewter cup of pens and mechanical pencils on his desk, thinking. "I just keep wondering if we missed something in the truck. Around the truck. What would you think about getting a bloodhound in?" She glanced up. "I know we have dogs available to us through the state police, but I'm talking an honest-to-goodness scent tracker. Go back to where we found the vehicle. He had to have walked out of there of his own free will. The search of the woods found nothing, no sign of struggle, and no evidence that could be linked to Rob."

"You said you found a pile of beer cans."

"*Piles* of beer cans," she corrected. "Kids have obviously been partying in the area where the sawmill once stood. You can tell that they've been piling up over time. We need to start keeping a better eye on things out there, send a patrol car by some nights."

"Maybe the party he went to Friday night was there instead of this supposed *girl's house.*"

"I don't think so. The friend was pretty sure Rob was headed to the party in Rehoboth." She looked up at him. "So what do you think about the hired bloodhound?" She grimaced. "That in our budget?"

"No," he said, watching her. "You've been watching too much TV. Our department can't swing that kind of evidence gathering—for a kid maybe—but this is not a kid. He's legally an adult. Besides, it rained Tuesday night. That severely diminishes the scent."

"So that's a *no* on the bloodhound?"

He exhaled, holding her gaze with his clear blue eyes. No matter how many times she looked into those eyes, she couldn't get over their color. She knew African-Americans, especially those who were biracial, had blue eyes occasionally, but Snowden's were so stunning that she was still surprised every time he looked at her.

"I can't authorize bloodhounds every time someone disappears, Detective."

"Snowden! When was the last time someone went missing in Stephen Kill? 1968?"

"Rob Crane is nineteen. Nineteen year olds take off. His parents said he was under a lot of stress." Snowden— always the voice of reason. "Star swimmer, 3.8 GPA. I don't know the father, but I get the feeling he rides his boy hard."

She crossed her arms over her chest. He was right. She knew he was right. She just hated it when he was *always* right.

"So what do we do now?" Her gaze shifted to the clock on the wall. It was five forty-five. She needed to get home to Callie. She had promised they'd go grocery shopping together and have Mexican night. Tacos. Burritos. The whole shebang.

"You try to track down information on this party. See what you can get there, but other than that, there's not much else we can do."

"And I just tell his parents what? We don't know where he is?"

"We *don't* know where he is, Delilah."

She rose from the chair and walked to the door. "I miss you," she said softly.

"You want me to come by tonight?"

She had to turn back to hear him. "I don't think it's a good idea. Callie'll only be here a few days, and—"

"And you don't want her calling home and telling your family you're dating a black man."

The comment startled her to the point that she didn't know what to say. They had never really discussed the racial issue. Sure, she had joked about her daddy coming after them both, but they had never really *talked* about it. It seemed pointless to her, really, because the bigger issue was that he was her boss. Still, they'd be kidding themselves if they didn't admit race would be an issue in the town. When Snowden had first hired Delilah more than a year ago, in response, someone had painted graphic graffiti on the baseball dugouts at the local ballpark. The images left no doubt in the viewer's mind, due to the use of multiple hues of spray paint, as to the race of the male and female depicted. Stephen Kill wasn't a town that flaunted its prejudices, but that didn't make them any less real.

"Please, Snowden," Delilah said softly, rubbing her temples.

"I'm sorry." He rose behind his desk. "I just—"

She held up her hand and he went silent. She turned for the door again. "Call me later."

It was funny, but he wasn't thirsty any more. His head didn't hurt that much, either.

Rob tried to lick his dry lips because they hurt, but he didn't have any spit left. He was half-lying, half-sitting against the wall. Eyes closed. No sense in using the energy to open them. It was too dark to see anything. There was no day or night in the tiny box of a room, just darkness.

How long had it been?

Days, Rob knew. But he wasn't sure how many, but he knew a man, even a healthy, athletic man his age and weight couldn't last more than five or six days without any water.

God, what he wouldn't do for a sip of beer right now.

He sort of laughed, then choked, and the spasm made him light-headed. He pressed the back of his head against the rough wall and slid down until he was lying on the dirt floor.

It had to be close to five days. Six maybe. She'd come six times, so that made sense. Once each day.

Crazy bitch. She would sit on the other side of the wall and talk to him. Most of what she said didn't make sense. Made even less sense to him now that his mind seemed fuzzy. She talked about socks. About a barbeque grill and how hot the coals could get. She kept asking him about his old girlfriend Shawna. Asked him why he swam. Why he thought he was any good.

Rob had tried to talk to her, at least at first. He tried everything he could think of. He had screamed for help until he was hoarse. Until he was too weak to scream. He had tried to reason with the crazy bitch on the other side of the wall. He'd tried threatening her. He'd even offered her money. He'd promised his parents would pay, no matter how much she wanted.

A sob rose in his throat.

His mom had to be so worried. Not knowing where he was . . . what had happened to him. He rested his head in the crook of his arm.

It was all so unbelievable. Who would have thought something like this could happen here? In big cities, yeah . . . maybe. But Stephen Kill? He knew practically everyone in the town. He'd grown up here.

He wondered if Annie was from Stephen Kill. He

didn't remember ever seeing her before. Probably wasn't even her real name.

His lower jaw trembled. "Mom," he croaked. "I'm sorry. I'm so sorry." No tears clouded his eyes. He cried quietly, his whole body jerking with spasms.

He was so tired.

He reached up to scratch his face, thinking maybe it itched, but his hand fell to his chest like it weighed a ton.

Rob could feel his heart beating. It was too fast. He was breathing too fast.

"I'm sorry." He mouthed the words, his head rolling off his arm, hitting the cool dirt. *I'm sorry I disappointed you, again, Dad.*

Julie pushed open the swinging kitchen door and was surprised not only to find the overhead florescent lights on, but Monica sitting at the table the girls used to prep meals. She thought she had heard her leave just after she'd come in around ten. Must have been a volunteer. The hotline was now manned twenty-four hours a day, thanks to Monica's efficiency. The emergency teen pregnancy hotline offered a kind voice in the middle of the night as well as the promise of help the next day, no matter where in the country a girl lived.

Julie glanced at the wall clock. Eleven twenty. "You still here?"

Monica looked up from a balance sheet and propped her chin on the heel of her hand. She looked as tired as Julie felt. "I wanted to get a handle on these numbers. We've had so much money going in and out in the last few weeks . . ."

"I know. I know," Julie commiserated, walking to the eight burner stainless steel stove to retrieve the tea kettle. "And I certainly haven't been much help to you. I can't tell you how thankful I am to have you Monica."

She smiled and glanced back at the neat columns of numbers.

"Tea?" Julie asked.

Monica shook her head. "I think I'll head home. I have that interview with Miss Kyle in the morning. I have no idea what I'm going to wear and . . ." She let her sentence trail off.

Julie leaned her hip against the sink and watched water from the faucet pour into the tea kettle's spout. "Wear whatever you want to wear and you shouldn't be nervous. She's just going to ask you a few questions about your job here. She may try to wheedle information out of you about the particular situations of some of our girls, but you're tough. I've seen you in action. You can handle her."

"I don't know." Monica pursed her lips, running a Chapstick she had dug out of her skirt pocket over them. "She scares me. No one should be able to walk in heels that high with toes that pointy."

Julie burst into laughter as she slapped the faucet off. "Good point." She walked to the stove and set the kettle on a burner, lighting the gas flame under it. "In that case, she scares me a little, too."

They both chuckled.

"Seriously." Julie walked up behind Monica. She placed her hand on her shoulder, thinking to massage it, but the moment she felt her assistant tense, she released her. Julie knew very little about Monica's past, but she guessed she'd been hurt, emotionally for sure, perhaps even physically. She was skittish around people and very sensitive about being touched. She also had a wrinkled scar on one forearm that appeared to have been a bad abrasion, maybe even a burn.

"I don't want you to sweat over this interview thing," Julie continued, crossing her arms over her chest. "If you don't want to do it, you don't have to."

"No. It's important. If Miss Kyle gets that job with that television station, the story could end up being broadcast nationwide."

The hinges of the door squeaked, and Monica and Julie both looked up to see Sister Agatha. "There you are," she said to Julie. "You weren't in your room. I checked several times."

"I'm sorry." She hadn't seen Sister Agatha since dinner, as it was her evening off. "I was out and then I was down in the basement organizing those storage bins. What did you need, Sister?"

"They've been smoking." Sister Agatha's voice was tight. "I told you they've been smoking and now here's proof." She opened her small hand to reveal two crushed cigarette butts. "I left this matter up to you and what have you done to eliminate it? Nothing. I can tell you that. You've done nothing, Sister Julie!"

Head bowed, Monica quickly gathered her paperwork and rose from the chair. "I should be going. I'll see everyone tomorrow. " She smoothly dodged Sister Agatha and made a beeline for the door that lead to a mud room and then outside.

Traitor, Julie thought wryly. *Deserter.* She'd be sure and give Monica a hard time about it in the morning. "Where did you find them?" Julie plucked the nasty butts from Agatha's hand and carried them to the fifty-gallon trashcan near the back door.

"Flower pot in the yard . . ."

Julie glanced in the direction of the door as she

walked to the sink to wash her hands. The tea kettle whistled. "Just now? You were in the backyard in the dark, looking for cigarette butts?"

"I was checking windows to be sure they were all latched. Open windows are how these young ladies got in these circumstances in the first place," Sister Agatha intoned indignantly. Julie shook off her wet hands over the sink and dashed for the stove to shut off the kettle. "Tea, Sister?"

"Oh, no. You're not going to do this. Not tonight. You're not going to change the subject."

Julie turned her back on the nun dressed head to toe in black except for the small patch of wimple-white. She grabbed a mug off the tree of mismatched stoneware and took a teabag out of a canister. "I spoke to the girls, Sister."

"I think we're past speaking. It's time to dole out punishment. Remove privileges."

Julie poured boiling water over the teabag, watching the steam rise. "And who would you have me punish?"

"You know very well who's doing it. Tiffany and Elise. I wouldn't doubt if they didn't have the new girl involved as well."

Julie pressed her lips together. "I'll speak with the girls again."

"They're taking advantage, that's all there is to it." Sister Agatha drew her hand across the table, sweeping away invisible crumbs and readjusted the chair Monica had pushed in on her way out. "We have rules and rules must be followed. We all have to follow rules, Sister Julie."

Julie pulled open a drawer and withdrew a spoon. "I'll take care of it." She dipped into the cup to remove the tea bag. "Have you had time to look over the new applications? There's one girl, Trina, I think we need to seriously consider."

"No, I haven't. I did my personal shopping and went to church."

Carrying her mug, Julie shot the sodden teabag into the trash can as she went by. "I left the applications on your desk." She blew across the surface of the hot tea, edging toward the door and escape.

"Of course." At the back door, Sister Agatha tugged the chintz curtains over the window closed, turned the lock on the knob and then the deadbolt. "And you'll warn those young ladies that we will not stand for tobacco use in this household."

"I will, Sister." Julie forced a bright smile, touching the cross that hung around her neck. "Good night, Sister. God Bless."

"God Bless," Agatha offered. "This is their last chance," she warned, waggling her finger as Julie went through the doorway. "I'll have every personal CD player and iPod in the house if I find butts again."

Julie groaned as she trudged up the stairs in the dark, trying not to spill her tea. She knew everyone had their cross to bear, but she couldn't help thinking that some days, Sister Agatha was an awfully heavy load.

"Paul?" Susan called sleepily, rolling over in bed and patting the empty place beside her.

He dropped the towel over the back of chair and pulled up a clean pair of boxers.

"What time is it?" she asked.

He slipped between the sheets, into bed beside her, glancing at the digital clock. Without her contacts, she couldn't see it. "Ten," he lied, knowing she had been in bed by nine. The kids wore her out. She rarely knew what time he got home, nights he stayed out. Half the time she never even woke up when he crawled into bed.

"Oh." She exhaled dropping back onto her pillow. "Everything okay? You said you didn't have any appointments this evening."

"Paperwork." He fluffed his pillow and rolled onto his side. "You know, for Maria's Place. There's a lot of red tape to me getting paid. I told you it was going to be like this."

"I know," she sighed, already half asleep again. "It's just that . . . the kids and I, we miss you."

Paul lay there quietly, listening to his wife's breathing become more rhythmic. She was asleep again in minutes. He reached out to hit the alarm button and as he drew his hand back, he caught the hint of a familiar scent. Still there after showering with bacterial soap?

He knew it couldn't be. It was just his imagination. Just wishful thinking that he could smell her on his hands . . .

Chapter 8

The Daughter drew the flashlight beam over his body. *Sunday night,* she mused matter-of-factly. It had taken longer than she thought it would. Last night she'd come, thinking he would be dead for sure, only to find a feeble thread of a pulse. *Pig.*

But tonight he was definitely dead.

She touched his arm with the toe of her shoe. Stiff. That meant rigor mortis had set in. Would make him hard to move. But *The Daughter* knew it wouldn't last more than seventy-two hours. She'd seen it on *CSI.* She didn't watch much TV, but she liked investigative dramas, especially *CSI.* No matter what the critics said, she liked the one set in Miami better than Las Vegas. She liked the blond weapons expert. *The Daughter* didn't know anything about firearms, but she wished she did. She wished she could wear white jeans, big Dolce & Gabbana sunglasses, and frolic in the Miami sun, but that was never going to happen. She was a realist.

Drawing the flashlight along the length of his body, *The Daughter* wondered if it would safe to leave him here another two days until his muscles loosened up and he'd be easier to transport. She didn't know why it wouldn't be. In a week, no one had heard him. Found him. Her hiding place was ingenious. Hide things in plain view, she had learned that a long time ago.

Another two days. She wondered if he would become a smell issue in that amount of time. But it was relatively cool here. She doubted it would be. Certainly not enough to attract any attention. Who knew what a dead body smelled like, anyway? She certainly didn't, but she *was* curious. She knew a little bit about decomposition— from TV, too, of course. Apparently, following death, the flesh began to break down almost at once and bugs scurried in to feast and lay eggs. The organs began to rot. She liked the idea that Rob Crane's body would soon start to rot. Maybe even grow maggots. She didn't know any more about maggots than she did guns, but the idea of insects eating him from the inside out appealed to her.

Of course, she couldn't leave him here long-term. That would be totally unacceptable. His body needed to be found. His parents needed to bury him. What kind of person wouldn't allow a family closure? What would Delilah think of someone who would do such a thing?

The Daughter felt her cheeks flush with the thought of Delilah. She hadn't been in the papers or on the news for days, but she would be there again soon, wouldn't she?

"I have to run into the post office, the drug store, and the video store." Delilah rattled off her list as she slid the pickup into a parking space in front of the diner. Fast food still hadn't hit Stephen Kill, one more complaint on Callie's long list of reasons she hated the town and wanted to go home.

The thing was, Rosemary didn't want her back. Not yet, at least. Delilah had spoken to her the night before and it was now Wednesday. Callie had been here a week and a half and her sister hadn't said a word about sending the teenager home. When Delilah brought it up, Rosemary started gushing about how well things were going with her and Bruce, now that Callie wasn't there. Rosemary didn't seem interested in how things were going between her sister and her daughter; she didn't seem to be interested in anything beyond herself.

A part of Delilah was tempted to just put Callie back on the plane, pulling the same trick Rosemary had. She and Callie weren't getting along. Callie barely spoke, and when she did it was only to complain about her mother, her stepfather, her stepsister or brother, or her present "incarceration" as she called it. She was disrespectful when she could get away with it and just generally unpleasant to be around, not exactly the kind of atmosphere Delilah looked forward to after a long day at work.

Delilah was beginning to think she'd been kidding herself when she thought she could help. How was she supposed to help when Callie wouldn't even talk to her?

Delilah picked up a pile of rental DVDs off the seat of the truck and stuffed them into her leather backpack as she climbed out. "You want to go with me, Callie, or you want to go into the diner, get a soda, and wait for me there?"

"They only have Pepsi. I like Coke."

"Then have water," Delilah snapped. The minute she said it, she regretted her tone of voice. She sounded as bad as Callie. "Sorry," she said, doing a pretty darned good imitation of the teenager sulking as she passed her a five-dollar bill from the front pocket of her khakis. "Bad day, in a series of bad days at work."

It *had* been a really bad day. Johnson had gotten on her case about some paperwork she'd screwed up and later some of the guys had been pretty rough with their jibes. An order of printed public awareness pamphlets had come back with typos that were her fault. Then Rob Crane's parents had arrived, unannounced, at the station to see her about an update on the police search for their son. There had been tears from Mrs. Crane and a healthy dollop of guilt pushed on Delilah from Mr. Crane.

And it wasn't as if Delilah's personal life was going very well, either. She hadn't seen Snowden alone except Friday night when she'd stopped by his place just long enough to drop off some spaghetti she'd made. He'd wanted her to stay, wanted to make love, but she'd ducked out. She just had too much going on in her life and in her head. And now he was starting to get cranky with her at work—punishment for her imposed celibacy on him, no doubt.

"I hate shopping," Callie groaned, ignoring Delilah's apology as she snatched the bill. "Guess I'll get a stupid Pepsi." She kicked the curb as she stepped over it.

Delilah waited until Callie walked through the diner door before she headed for the post office. The service window was already closed, but she'd been out of stamps for almost a week. She'd have to use the vending machine. If she didn't get the bills in her bag mailed out, her electricity, phone, and cable would be off in a matter of days. Which, right now, didn't seem like such a bad idea. Callie would have to talk to her if there was no TV, no Internet, and no lights, wouldn't she?

Delilah climbed the brick steps. She didn't care what

Callie thought, she liked the small-town atmosphere of Stephen Kill. She liked the old fashioned "downtown" that only ran for three blocks on the same street. Besides the diner, the post office, a bank, a privately owned movie rental store, and the police station, there were small shops: a card store, a hardware store, a dry cleaners, a florist. Everything a person could want was right here. During the heavy summer season at the beaches, a girl never had to venture onto Route One and its madness if she didn't want to.

Delilah fed a five-dollar bill from her pocket into the vending machine inside the post office lobby and selected the number of stamps she needed. Nothing happened. She made her choice again, this time taking care to hit each button on the key pad precisely in the middle. It took three more tries before she finally gave up, hit the "coin return," and got her money back in quarters. No stamps.

"Great," she mumbled hiking down the steps, turning left, headed for the drug store. She'd either have to find the time to run by the post office in the morning or beg the new secretary, Mrs. Bartlett, to sell her a couple of postage stamps. Something she did not want to do if she didn't have to. She and fiftysomething Mrs. Bartlett didn't get along particularly well. Delilah had arrested her daughter a few months ago for a DUI, and Mrs. Bartlett had somehow held Delilah, instead of her thirty-five-year-old, living at home with two kids, deadbeat daughter, responsible.

Delilah finished her errands and twenty minutes later, walked into the diner. "Afternoon, Detective," Nateesha, owner of the diner, greeted from behind the cash register.

She was a tall, thin, black woman in her late forties with a glossy beehive hair do that had to be nearly a foot tall. Delilah liked her and her no-nonsense demeanor. Had liked her since the first day she walked in and Nateesha asked her if she'd lost her mind, applying to be the first female officer on Stephen Kill's police force.

"Just gonna be you, *Suga?*" Nateesha asked.

"Actually, I was looking for my niece." Not spotting Callie on one of the stools along the old-fashioned counter, she craned her neck, scanning the booths on both sides of the dining room, then the tables in the center.

A redhead, she reminded herself. *You're looking for a redhead.* Seeing Callie's beautiful, long blond hair cut shorter and dyed red had been a bit of a shock, but she was getting used to it now. In fact, she almost liked it on the teen; it certainly fit her personality.

"So tall." Delilah held her hand up just above her own head, still searching. The place was almost full, busy with Thursday evening supper. Chicken and dumplings special. She recognized most of the patrons, though with summer coming, they were already beginning to see a few tourists passing through on their way to the beaches. "Red pony tail," Delilah continued. "Green T-shirt, I think. I dropped her off a little ago. She was just coming in for a soda while she waited for me."

"That your niece, Detective? Mmmm hmmmm."

Delilah didn't know exactly what Nateesha meant by that sound, but she knew she didn't like it. She shifted her backpack on her shoulder. "My sister's daughter in from Georgia. She's staying with me for a little while." She offered a quick smile, feeling uncomfortable having to explain. "So you did see her?"

"I saw 'er, all right." Nateesha shoved the drawer of the old black cash register in and it dinged as it slid home. "Sat right there at the counter and ordered herself a

Pepsi. Then that boy with the nose ring come in." The woman placed one hand on her hip, swaying. She was attractive by any standard, with a knock-out figure and a remarkable rear end. Plenty of "junk in her trunk" as the song said.

"Had I known she was your niece, Detective, *I'd a* bounced his sorry butt *outta* here, told him to leave her be."

"She's not here, now. I don't see her." Delilah fought the panic that fluttered in her chest. "Who was she talking to? What boy with the nose ring?"

"Craig something. You know. Daddy did time a few years back for beatin' somebody with a baseball bat over in Laurel. His boy ain't no better. Got a nose ring"—she flared her nostril and pinched it—"some kind of flower tattoo on his arm, too." She patted her forearm.

"Craig Dunn?"

"That's it." She snapped her fingers, adorned with long pink curling fingernails she had done at a salon every week. "His momma took off years ago. Not that I blame her."

Delilah scowled. She knew Craig Dunn. Sixteen, maybe seventeen by now. High school dropout. Worked on and off for a local plumber. He was on a watch list for selling marijuana. So far, he hadn't been caught, but his name floated around the police station every once in a while.

"Did she leave?" Delilah stepped closer, putting her hand on the counter, knocking into a toothpick dispenser. "You see her leave with him?" She straightened the dispenser.

"Me? I didn't see her leave. I was back in the kitchen. Bunny," she hollered to a waitress headed toward the kitchen, a stack of dirty plates in her hands. "You see the two sittin' here a few minutes ago? Nice lookin' girl with red hair. That piece of crap Nose-Ring-Boy?"

"Both walked toward the bathrooms couple minutes ago." Bunny lifted her pudgy chin in the direction of the rear of the diner. "Didn't pay for their colas. Figured they went out the back. I told you we ought not to serve minors. Just like a bar." The waitress started toward the kitchen again, still rattling on as she disappeared into the kitchen. "Said it 'till I'm blue in the face. Not my place. Ain't my problem."

"Maybe she's in the potty, *Suga*," Nateesha offered sympathetically, ignoring her employee's grumpy diatribe.

"Sorry about the drink. It won't happen again." Delilah pulled out change she'd stuffed in her pocket at the drug store, laying down a crumple of one-dollar bills. "I promise you."

Quick as she could without bringing too much attention to herself, Delilah hurried through the dining room and down the back hall. The door that said "Ladies" was ajar, the light out. A one seater. She hurried past the men's room, also open. At the end of the hall was an entrance to the kitchen marked "Employees Only" and a heavy door with an illuminated "Exit" sign over it. She pushed the bar, swinging open the door.

The door opened to an alley that smelled of sour milk and newly cut grass. Straight ahead was a blue commercial dumpster. To its left, she caught a flash of bright green. A green T-shirt?

"Callie Marie Hollister," Delilah barked.

"You better go," she heard Callie tell someone.

By the time Delilah got around the Dumpster, Nose-Ring-Boy was hoofing it down the alley. "What do you think you're doing?" she demanded. "Were you buying pot from him?" She grabbed Callie's arm, watching the boy run, debating whether or not to go after him. She bet she could take him.

Callie yanked her arm free, looking at Delilah as if she'd grown a horn in the middle of her forehead. "No. What are you talking about? Why would you say that? We were just talking, is all." She drew the last syllable out as all girls born and raised in Georgia did.

"Talking. In an alley? Right." Delilah grabbed Callie's arm again, and this time, she didn't let go. "If I see you with drugs, by law I have to arrest you. You understand that, don't you?" She marched the teen around the corner and along the side of the diner, down the drive, toward the street. "And you get busted again and you'll end up in juvie."

"I wasn't buying any stupid weed," Callie muttered.

"Right. And that wasn't your weed the principal found in your locker, either, was it?"

"Yes, it was," she blurted aggressively. "I told the principal that. I told the cops. Mom. I told everyone!"

"I can't believe you would do this. I leave you alone for twenty minutes and you're making conversation with the neighborhood druggy. Your mother told me not to leave you alone. She told me you couldn't be trusted." They reached the sidewalk and Delilah led her diagonally across the street. "Get in the truck. Get in the truck before I swear to sweet Jesus, I—"

Delilah's cell phone in her backpack went off before she could finish her sentence, which was just as well since she didn't know what she was going to say. She didn't condone physical abuse, not under any circumstances. She certainly wasn't going to strike Callie. But that didn't mean she didn't want to . . .

Delilah released her niece's arm, going to the driver's side of the truck as she fished the phone out of her pack.

"Yeah?" She rested the phone against her shoulder, bending her neck at an unnatural angle as she found her keys and opened the door with the remote.

"Where are you?"

It was Snowden.

"I can't talk right now. Having a little crisis with my niece." She glared at Callie over the bed of the pickup. *Get in*, she mouthed. "Can it wait?" she said into the phone.

"It can't."

Delilah had been so wrapped up with Callie that she hadn't, until then, heard the tone in Snowden's voice. Her stomach did a sick little flip-flop. She knew that tone. "Sweet God," she whispered. "You found him."

"We found him."

Delilah yanked open the door and climbed in, throwing her backpack on the bench seat between her and Callie. "Where?" As she slammed the door shut, she pushed the key into the ignition. "Snowden?"

"Horsey Mill Pond. On Tatter Road."

The engine turned over and she threw the little pickup into reverse.

"Can you meet me there?" he asked.

"Yeah. Sure. Of course." She shoved the gear shift into drive and hit the gas. "I'll be there in ten minutes."

Hand trembling, Delilah hit the "end" button on her cell and dropped it onto the seat beside her. "I have to go to a scene."

Callie crossed her arms over her chest and threw herself back in the seat. "Take me back to the house. I'm not going with you to arrest any criminals."

Delilah gripped the steering wheel so tightly that her knuckles turned white. "You think I would leave you home alone after what I just saw?"

Callie stared straight ahead, slender jaw jutted out, lips pressed tight against her braces.

"No, you're going with me. You obviously can't be trusted. You've proven that."

Delilah, hearing echoes of Rosemary in her head, knew she was probably overreacting, but she couldn't help herself. All she could think of was Rob Crane and his poor parents. Snowden hadn't had to say so for her to know he was dead. She didn't know what she was going to find when she arrived at Horsey Mill Pond, but it was bad and the thought, even the remote possibility that something like this could happen to Callie, scared the bejeezus out of her.

"Drowned," Delilah said, watching the EMTs cover Rob Crane's grossly bloated body with a clean white sheet before lifting the stretcher from the pond's edge to carry him to the waiting ambulance. She couldn't take her eyes off him, not even after they had covered the body and the teen was nothing but a series of bumps and rolls beneath the pristine sheet on the narrow stretcher.

"We won't know until the autopsy comes back," Snowden answered.

"I understand it's not *official*, but look at him, you don't get to looking that way"—*looking that inhuman*, she thought—"without drowning first." She shook her head. "Poor kid. Probably screwing around on the bridge or something. Drinking. Fell in, maybe hit his head and never broke the surface again.

She stared at the water's lapping edge, trying not to think about the last body she had watched the EMTs load into an ambulance. Last summer, their mentally ill serial killer, Alice Crupp, wounded, had fallen into the very same pond, along the opposite shore, and drowned.

"Looked like maybe some trauma to the head." Delilah brushed the back of her head, not knowing why she felt the need to keep talking. "Hard to say, taking in the water factor. The bloating can distort the facts, but the ME will certainly be able to make a determination."

She watched Snowden take a step back in the trampled milk weeds and squint as he gazed west. She wondered if he was thinking about Alice lying dead in this pond, too. Sheer coincidence, of course. Alice had been wounded in a knife fight with Noah Gibson, had run from the police. There was no connection to her and the kid. None whatsoever.

Still a little creepy.

Delilah glanced in the same direction that Snowden was looking. The sun was bright and low on the horizon, still blazing through the pine and pin oak treetops, but the twilight shadows were pushing fast behind it. They would have to work quickly if they were going to collect any evidence before it got dark.

"We'll know soon enough. Autopsy will tell us cause of death," Snowden agreed, reaching out to brush her bare forearm with his fingertips before letting his hand fall.

There were people everywhere: town cops, state troopers, medical personnel. Up on the road, a news van had just arrived. In the midst of the commotion, Delilah appreciated Snowden's small, intimate gesture. He was trying to calm her. Trying to tell her she needed to compose herself and do her job. Follow the processes and try not to think too much. Not to feel too much.

He was right of course. All they knew right now was that Rob Crane was dead and that his lifeless, bloated body had been found in the pond by Todd Corkland, who had been fishing in his bass boat. They didn't know how Rob had gotten into the pond, what had killed him, or how long he'd been dead. Delilah tried not to extrapolate from what she saw, but it was hard. Good sense told her his body had not been in water eleven days. The kid looked bad, fish belly white, swollen, distorted, but the flesh was intact. A body didn't float in a fresh water pond with the all algae, bacteria, and fish eleven days and remain whole. Which meant he hadn't died the night he went missing.

The possibility that he had been alive when she had been actively searching for him last weekend made her want to upchuck in the bushes. Fortunately, she hadn't eaten in hours. Nothing in her stomach *to* upchuck.

She swallowed the sour taste in her mouth, trying to focus on the job she had to do and not her own emotions. "I got plenty of pictures with the department's new digital camera. I'll take Corkland's statement. I know he talked to Thomas when the first black and white arrived, but I'd like to hear the details myself. Tonight, while they're still fresh in his mind."

Snowden nodded, took one last look at the trampled area at the pond's shoreline where Rob's body had been, and then he started up the slight embankment toward the road. "News van's here. Marty Kyle, I'm sure. I better get over to the Crane's before she interrupts *Gunsmoke* for a special news report." He trudged up the path the EMTs had created through the weeds, walking as if his size fourteen shiny black shoes were made of cement rather than leather.

"You want me to go with?" she asked, following him. A mosquito lit on her forearm and she smacked it, squishing it in a smear of dark goo and blood.

"Nah. You talk to Corkland. See the guys search the

area for any evidence. Chances are he didn't go in this way, though. Thomas and Redden, on the scene first, were clear on the details. Corkland spotted the body from his boat. Called from his cell. Thomas was the first one down the bank. We made this path, trampled these weeds. It's all fresh."

"I'll tape off what I can. See what we can find before it gets too dark. We can come back at first light, do a full perimeter check of the pond."

"The bridge and the area under it, too," Snowden intoned.

They came to the ambulance at the top of the embankment. The EMTs and ambulance attendants were loading Rob's body. No one said anything.

Snowden glanced in the direction of Delilah's truck parked a quarter of a mile up ahead on the side of the road. "You didn't send your niece home with one of our guys?"

Delilah could make out Callie's form slumped against the passenger's side door, her face pressed to the window. She appeared to be asleep. "She's fine. She can't see anything from there. She's sleeping. Tired after a long day of sleeping."

"I don't want any media or cameras down there tonight. Have Johnson send a night shift car to sit here." He strode toward the cruiser stenciled with *Chief of Police* across the back of the trunk.

"Will do, Chief." Delilah wanted to run after him. To tell him how sorry she was that he would be the one to have to tell the Cranes. Even to offer to do it for him, but she knew her place and right now, it wasn't beside him.

Chapter 9

"I told Mrs. Bartlett I needed to see you almost an hour ago." Snowden spoke without looking up from his desk. He was wearing his new thick black reading glasses perched on the end of his nose. They made him appear scholarly. Imposing.

Delilah glanced at the door, debating as to whether or not she should shut it. It wasn't good for her to be in his office with the door shut too many times a day, but she really didn't need her co-workers hearing their boss chew her out, either.

In the end, she decided she wouldn't shut the door, but she hovered behind the chairs in front his desk just in case. "My fault, not hers. Sorry, Chief. I had that noon press conference."

"How'd it go?" He signed a document, flipped a page, signed again.

"How well could it have gone when there's nothing we can tell anyone, including the Cranes, except that he's dead? Our perky, spike-heeled Miss Kyle was brutal with her questions. I'm beginning to think she's got it out for me."

"Wet autopsy came back." He slid a pristine manila file folder across his desk.

Delilah swallowed, skirting the chairs to his desk. She picked up the file, opened it and began to scan the report, just hitting the highlights. She'd read the whole thing thoroughly when she got back to her desk. Then, if memory of the previous summer served correctly, she'd probably read it another twenty-seven times between now and midnight when she fell exhausted into bed.

"Cause of death, hypovolemia due to dehydration," she read aloud. For a second, she thought maybe the wrong report had been sent. Wrong victim. But Robert Lawrence Crane, Jr.'s, name was printed across the top. It was his report, all right. "Hypovolemia?" she said.

"I looked it up on-line in a medical dictionary. Reduction in blood volume—a common way to die of dehydration."

"He died of dehydration? How's that possible?"

"Keep reading, Detective." Snowden motioned impatiently, his attention still fixed on the paperwork under his nose. "ME's notes. She knew we were expecting a drowning."

Delilah's gaze flitted downward. She had to work on that, shooting off her mouth. Thinking out loud.

Absence of froth in airways, debris in lungs, or hemorrhages in the boney middle ears, she read. "He was dead when he went in the water?" she muttered numbly. "How long . . ." Stopping herself before she expressed another dumb-blonde thought, she scanned faster. It was only preliminary information—the full, detailed report would arrive in a matter of days with a case like this.

"Dead three days before he went into the water?" she read aloud. She looked at Snowden. "This doesn't make any sense. People—nineteen year olds—don't just die of dehydration. It takes . . . days."

He removed his glasses, set them on his desk and leaned back in his chair, rubbing his eyes. "Look at the tox report. In the back."

She flipped through several pages, for the first time realizing how sharp the writing was. It hadn't been faxed. It had been e-mailed as an attachment. The Stephen Kill police were, at last, stepping into the twenty-first century.

"Fine traces of GHB?" She glanced up again. She couldn't remember the exact chemical name, but she knew it was a "date rape" drug like Rohypnol. The thing was, if she recalled the details of her "drugs on the street" course correctly, it was one that could be made at home in any kitchen. "You think he could have been held against his will?"

"Possibly. No sexual assault, though. It's also possible he gave the drug a try at a party. Kids have been known to use it as another way to get high. Could have been an overdose and the kid went into a coma and lingered all week. Once he finally died, maybe his friends got scared, disposed of the body."

"I don't know about that theory." She knew he was just thinking out loud, but it didn't make sense to her. "People don't sit around and look at a dead body for three days before getting rid of it. Not even stupid, high, college kids."

"You're probably right, but I want you back on that party lead. If the friend can't tell you where the party was, we start going door to door in the neighborhoods. It's still early in the season. Someone might remember a drunken teenage bash."

"I can't believe he was dead before he went into the water," Delilah breathed. "It . . . it wasn't what I was expecting. You think someone *gave* him the GHB, gave him too much, he died eventually, and then they dumped him?"

Snowden reached for his glasses. "That would make it a homicide."

Delilah glanced at the clock. She wasn't even sure where to begin her investigation now. She only had a couple of hours before her shift was over. Having Callie here right now was the worst possible timing. Last summer, when she'd been investigating multiple homicides, she'd worked until she dropped each night, often ignoring the posted schedule and her days off. Now, she felt so divided, pulled in two directions, home and her job. It had never been this way for her before because there had never been anyone at home but her cat. "I . . . I was planning on taking off when my shift ended at four, but that gives me plenty of time to track down Jamey Pratt, who saw him last, as far as we know; I'll question him again. I've got something going on tomorrow morning, but I could work a couple of hours in the afternoon. It's just that I hate leaving Callie alone at home so much. I feel like I'm just asking for trouble."

"Don't worry about the weekend. We still need the full autopsy report. Do what you can today and we'll decide if we need to get some guys to pull overtime and go door to door." He lifted his chin in her direction, lowering his voice. "So how's that going, anyway? Your niece."

She lowered the autopsy folder to his desk, exhaling. "I told you about her and Craig Dunn. I'm beginning to think I overreacted. Maybe she wasn't lying. She still swears she wasn't trying to buy anything from him, just talking." She ran her finger along the edge of the file. "Not that I want her hanging out with him, but in all fairness, she's been pretty honest with what she's done in the past. At least with me."

"So you think maybe you're getting through to her?"

"Ahhh . . . I wouldn't go so far as to say that." She raised and then lowered her hands in exasperation. "She's not much of conversationalist. Mostly yeses and nos. Not volunteering in the way of thoughts or emotions. I feel badly for her, though. She really doesn't have anything to do here. No friends. School's out."

"I imagine that was what your sister had in mind when she sent her."

His mouth turned up on one side.

Delilah couldn't manage a whole smile, but she half grimaced, half laughed. "I'm not sure what to do with her and now it looks as if she might be . . ." She shifted her gaze to the pile of folders on his desk. "She might be staying a while. Maybe all summer."

"All summer?"

Delilah ignored his arched eyebrows. She knew what he was thinking. The same thing she thought every night that she climbed into bed alone. "Nothing has been decided."

He put on his glasses, sliding his chair toward his desk again. "She could do the same thing other teenagers do in the summer. Work."

She nodded. "A job. You know, I hadn't really thought about that. I just assumed she'd be going home in a few days."

"You could get her on an evening shift," he suggested.

She met his blue-eyed gaze and this time she couldn't help but smile. She could think of a dozen risqué retorts, none of which she could voice in Snowden's office at two thirty on a Friday afternoon. She picked the folder up off his desk and shook it at him. "I just might make that very suggestion to her. Thanks."

Delilah was almost to the door when Snowden spoke.

"Thank me later. Tonight . . ."

She looked back over her shoulder.

"Come tonight," he repeated quietly, watching her. "My place. Just for an hour."

"I can't," she whispered.

"I miss you," she heard him say as she walked out the door, into the hallway and back into the real world.

"A job?" Callie threw herself back on the seat, crossing her arms over her chest in her usual stubborn teen pose. "You've got to be *shittin'* me."

Delilah raised her hand off the wheel to point at the teen in warning. She had told Callie she wouldn't stand for inappropriate language and she decided she wasn't giving in. Not once. That was at least part of Callie's problem, she was discovering. Rosemary and Callie's stepfather, apparently, had strict rules, but they rarely had the time or the energy to enforce them. For instance, Callie did have a curfew, but when she missed it, her parents either pretended they hadn't heard her come in late, or threatened not to let her go out if it happened again. It did, but no one ever followed through on the threat.

Deaf ears and hollow threats were not Delilah's *modus operandi.*

"Sorry," Callie mumbled.

"Apology accepted." Delilah gave a satisfied nod as she pulled out onto the county road. It was eight forty-five Saturday morning. She'd dragged a grumbling Callie out of bed an hour ago, made her shower, and now they were on their way to Maria's Place where Delilah volunteered two Saturdays a month.

"Now, back to the job," Delilah redirected. "I think your Mom wants you to stay here awhile, soooo . . ."

"It's his fault." Callie frowned and stared out the window. "He's the one that doesn't want me there, the pr—"

She didn't finish the sentence, for which Delilah had to give her credit.

"A job would give you something to do," Delilah suggested. "Maybe help you meet some other girls. Make some new friends."

"I don't want any new friends," Callie grumbled. "I've got friends."

"And they're certainly fine friends. They're all about you, what's best for you, these friends who encourage you to disobey your parents. Encourage you to drink and smoke pot, knowing not only that it's illegal, but that it can harm you?"

They rode in silence for a full mile.

"I can't get a job," Callie blurted, surprising Delilah. The teen was actually attempting to continue a conversation.

"Why not?"

"I can't do anything." The admission clearly made her miserable.

"Sure you can."

Callie gave her one of those "you're an adult and you're an idiot" looks.

Delilah thought for a minute. You had to be quick on your toes with teens, she was learning. And honest. Without honesty, you weren't getting anywhere. Teens today grew up under the threat of nuclear war, with the nightly TV news images of kids getting blown up in the Middle East. The "everything's going to be all right and you can do anything you set your mind to" days were gone for this generation.

"Okay," Delilah said, regrouping. "So maybe you don't have any skills, but you've got a brain, don't you?"

Callie didn't reply, but she appeared to be listening.

"You can *learn* to do something. Someone shows you how to do a task. You repeat it."

"I'm not flippin' burgers." She looked out the window again. "I'm thinking about becoming a vegetarian."

Delilah had to fight hard not to laugh out loud. Last night they had ridden over to Rehoboth, eaten at a steak place, and then gone to a movie. Callie had consumed a piece of beef close to the size of her head.

It actually felt good to Delilah to smile. It felt good to be out, to be in shorts and T-shirt, driving in the sunshine. It had been a long week and yesterday had been a long day. After rereading the autopsy report several times, talking to Snowden again, she'd made the decision to ride over and tell the Cranes what they had learned, letting them know when the body would be released. It had been a difficult conversation, as hard as any Delilah had experienced in her career. Mrs. Crane had sobbed. Mr. Crane had been cold and angry, almost seeming resentful that she had told them the truth. That Rob had not drowned. Delilah knew this was a normal reaction for many people in their time of grief. The blame had to be focused on someone; she was just the closest person to him at the moment. That didn't mean it wasn't hard for her. Delilah had wrapped up yesterday by tracking down Rob's friend yet again, and, with a little muscle, gotten an approximate location of the party Rob had been headed to in Rehoboth Beach the night he'd disappeared. Jamey swore he didn't have an address. Just an idea of where. It was a six block radius, but at least it was a start.

Delilah glanced at Callie sitting beside her in the truck. She was pretty. Prettier than Delilah had ever been at that age. She already seemed to have grown out of that awkwardness girls hit in their early teens. Her face was slender, with high cheekbones and a sprinkling of freckles across her nose. With pale skin, the red hair actually looked cute on her. And she had the Swift eyes. Big and brown with long thick lashes.

"Well, you're in luck on the burger thing because there aren't any fast food places in Stephen Kill, as you have reminded me on more than one occasion."

"I have to get a job *here?* I can't go to the beach?"

Over my dead body, Delilah thought, an image of Rob's body floating in the pond where it had been when she arrived on the scene. "Nope. Sorry. You know I've got this case I'm working on. I can't be driving you back and forth to the beach. I get caught up somewhere; you are not wandering the boardwalk for hours waiting for me."

"Stupid guy. Guys are always doing stupid things. He was probably doing some kind of dare, jumping off that bridge or something, trying to impress his stupid friends."

"You think?" They had not released to the press the fact that Rob Crane had gone into the water dead. Not yet. Sometimes one of the best investigative tools of a police officer was withholding details from the public.

Callie shrugged. "Wouldn't surprise me."

Delilah pulled into the driveway past the big farmhouse and followed the gravel drive around to the back where volunteers parked.

"Can I just sit in the car?" Callie asked.

"Nope."

With a groan, she jerked open the truck door. "What

are we supposed to do for four hours? I don't have to talk to these losers or anything, do I? Anybody stupid enough to get pregnant these days . . ." Callie went on, following Delilah up the stone path toward the new deck.

"Morning, Monica." Delilah entered the office where volunteers checked in and checked out. "Don't you ever take a day off?"

"Seems to me, Detective, you've been known to work some long hours yourself." She pushed away from her desk, her office chair rolling on the plastic mat beneath it. "Who's this?"

Delilah gestured to Callie, leaning against the door jamb striking her favorite pose. "My niece, Callie. She's visiting from Georgia."

"It's nice to have you with us, Callie. I'm sure our girls will be pleased to see a new face. We don't have many teenage volunteers."

Delilah was afraid Callie would conjure a clever retort, but the teen kept her mouth shut.

"Well." Monica clasped her hands. "Go ahead and sign yourselves in. I've got a whole list of jobs, so you don't have to worry about not keeping busy." She picked up a yellow legal pad. "Callie, if you wouldn't mind, there's a laundry basket full of dish towels and assorted stuff in the kitchen. It goes down to the basement. Our laundry brigade should be down there now washing and folding. I'm sure they could use your help. We like to hang sheets out on nice days like today."

"Laundry?" Callie mouthed silently at Delilah.

Delilah grinned, giving her niece a little wave. "I'll sign you in. Go ahead, dear. Have fun."

"I hope you don't mind me bringing her." Delilah

leaned over the desk and added their names and check in time to the register.

"Of course not." Monica rolled her chair back under desk. "Let's see, we've got inventory in the bathroom cabinets, weed whacking around the trees in the front and side yards, or . . . cleaning up some old iron lawn furniture, getting it ready to paint." She looked over her cat-eye reading glasses. "What strikes your fancy this morning, detective?"

"It's too nice to be inside, but I'm not much for whacking weeds. How about the lawn furniture?"

"There's already a bucket ready with any tools you might need. In the back yard. You probably saw them when you were coming up the walk."

"So I just scrub them?"

"Not as easy as it sounds. You'll have to start with the metal brush. They must have a century of paint on them."

The phone rang, a little light blinked on the desk phone, and Monica reached for it.

"See you later," Delilah said as she went out the door.

"Good morning, Maria's Place. How may I help you?"

Callie stood at the top of the stairwell, looking down the steps, the laundry basket cradled in her arms. She'd been standing there at least five minutes . . . maybe a year. She didn't know why she was being such a chicken. What was the big deal? Go down. Leave the basket of dirty towels, come back up the steps, out the front door and to the truck. She could have a decent nap in before anyone knew she was missing. Then her aunt would carry on with her, flap her arms, go on about responsibility and trust and shit, and then they'd go back to the

town house and Callie could listen to music on her iPod.
By then Chrissy and Marissa would be out of bed. She'd
get to hear how the party at Tyler's house was. Who got
drunk. Who got laid. Who got dumped.

Callie studied the steep steps again as she lowered the
basket that was getting heavy in her arms. She could
hear voices. Girls who sounded to be her own age, which
made sense. Aunt Delilah said most of them weren't
even old enough to drive yet. How big a bummer was
that? Preggers without a license to drive to the store to
get milk and diapers and crap like that.

She pressed her lips together, wondering if she could
just leave the basket there on the landing and make a
run for it now.

She could . . .

But she didn't like the idea that she was being such a
coward. Her friends at home called her a chickenshit all
the time. She wouldn't put Jason's pecker in her mouth
no matter how much money anyone put up. She wouldn't
even look at the stupid, ugly thing. She didn't play the railroad track game either. The sound of the train, the vibra-
tions of the track under her Vans scared her. What was
wrong with them that they wanted her to do crap like
that?

Sometimes she thought some of her friends wanted to
die. Some definitely did. Like Chrissy. Chrissy was a
cutter. She made little cuts all up and down her fore-
arms, sometimes with a penknife she'd bought or an
X-acto knife she'd bagged from art class. Other times
she just scratched the skin with a pop-top until it bled.
But Callie didn't want to die. Even if her life did suck.

She heard laughter from the basement.

Sure. Maybe her life did suck, but not as bad as the
girls' down there.

Chapter 10

Callie picked up the clothes basket and took the first step down. After that, it wasn't that hard. At the bottom of the staircase, she followed the voices. There was kind of like a tunnel made from sheetrock that hadn't been painted, with bare bulbs screwed into sockets overhead to light the way. She went left, then left again. It smelled funny: damp, dusty, but with the definite scent of "Downy fresh" fabric softener.

The sheetrock tunnel opened up suddenly and she was in a big room with washers and dryers lined up along both sides and a long table that looked like a kitchen counter between them. The walls had been painted yellow and bright fluorescent lamps hung from the ceiling. Washers chugged and dryers turned rhythmically, the contents making muffled thumps as they spun.

One girl with a blond ponytail who reminded Callie of her friend Marissa turned and looked. Well, she didn't look exactly like Marissa because she had a big stomach and Marissa was skinny, way skinnier than Callie.

"Hey," the Marissa look-alike greeted suspiciously.

"Hey." Callie walked right over to one of the washing

machines and put the basket on top, acting like she knew what she was doing.

"Who are you?" the Marissa girl asked.

"Callie."

Marissa-girl looked Callie up and down. "You the new girl? The Sisters didn't say anything about another new girl. We were supposed to get one, but then I heard we weren't." She eyed Callie's abdomen with obvious distrust. "You're not showing much."

"I'm not pregnant," Callie scoffed. Then she felt bad for saying it that way. Like she was better than they were. Callie hadn't had sex yet, but most of her friends had. Chrissy'd already had an abortion, although it was all hush hush, even among their friends.

"I . . . I came with my aunt." Callie scuffed her flip-flop on the cement floor that had been painted gunmetal gray.

"A volunteer?" asked one of the other girls.

Callie shook her head, admiring the cool Led Zeppelin T-shirt stretched over her taut belly. "No. I just came with her." She shrugged one shoulder. "Nuthin' else to do. I'm visiting from Georgia."

"That's why you've got an accent," the third pregnant girl in the room said. She looked a lot like the other blonde who'd spoken first.

"I know," Callie groaned, trying hard not to draw out her vowels the way southerners did. "It's embarrassing."

"I'm Elise," the first blonde said. "That's Tiffany and Izzy."

"Cool shirt," Callie said, pointing to Izzy. She felt her face grow warm. She'd pointed right at her preggers belly. She hadn't meant to do that.

But Izzy didn't seem to be insulted. "Used to fit better." She tugged at the hem. "But thanks."

All four girls stood silent for a minute looking at each other. Callie wondered if that was her invitation to cut out, but just as she was about to turn away, Izzy dumped a load of whites on the counter in front of her. "We have to fold all these clothes, basket 'em, and carry 'em upstairs. You wanna help?"

Callie shrugged. "I guess." She walked over to stand beside Izzy and reached for a white sock.

Tiffany and Elise stood on the other side of the table, their backs to the washing machines, watching her. "Your aunt. Who's that?" Elise asked.

"Delilah Swift. You know her?"

"The detective?" Tiffany observed. "She's pretty all right."

"Yeah." Callie dug for a matching sock. "I guess."

"I like her. She just acts normal." Izzy shook out a pair of cotton white string bikini panties and checked the initial on the tag. "It's like some people who volunteer here, they want to give you some lecture every time they see you. Like you don't already know you screwed up. Or, some of the others, they pretend you're not carrying this basketball around under your shirt." She whipped the panties over her protruding belly. "Like you can ignore this? But Delilah, she doesn't act like it's a big deal. Not shocked or anything."

Turning the pair of socks one inside the other, Callie set them between her and Izzy and dug for another pair. "All she does is ask me questions. About my friends. About where I go when I'm home. What I do."

"So how long you going to be here? Probably pretty boring compared to Georgia," Elise observed, sounding snooty.

"I don't know. The town I come from's pretty boring,

too." Callie tossed another pair of socks on the pile. "I don't know how long I'll be here."

Elise smiled knowingly at Tiffany. "You don't know how long you're gonna be here?"

Callie shook her head.

"What? Your mom and dad ship you off?"

"Mom and stepdad. He's an ass," Callie added quickly.

The other three girls exchanged glances. "What'd you do?" Elise plied.

Callie looked up, not sure what to say, if anything.

"Don't pay any attention to Elise. Miss Know-It-All. She thinks she's the boss of the world and everyone in it." Izzy stacked panties. "Thinks she knows everything."

Callie looked at Izzy. She liked her. She knew it took guts to stand up to a person like Elise like that. Every group had one—an Elise, who called the shots—the one in her circle of friends was Patty. Patty Purnell. "I got arrested," Callie heard herself tell Izzy. "For having weed in my locker at school."

A buzzer went off behind Elise and Tiffany. Then another one. No one seemed to know what to say. The two blondes turned around to check the washers.

"You a pothead?" Izzy asked. She didn't sound accusatory as much as curious.

"Nah." Callie paired off two more socks, beginning to feel like she was playing a game of Memory like she'd played with her little stepsister. There were cards you laid face down, then you picked them up and tried to match them, like the hen to the hen, or the snake to the snake. She held a white shorty sock with a pink heel in each hand. "Mostly I was just holding it for friends. I'm not like a *dealer* or anything."

"Anyone else get arrested at school?"

Callie shook her head.

"Good friends," Izzy muttered.

"Yeah," Callie agreed. The girl in the Led Zeppelin shirt didn't have to say anything else for Callie to know what she was thinking. Same thing Callie, as much as she hated to admit it, had been thinking ever since she'd arrived in Stephen Kill and gotten away from Georgia. No one had stuck up for her when the principal called her to her office. When the cops came. Later, her friends had laughed about Callie being handcuffed. Callie had laughed with them at the time, but it really hadn't been that funny.

Callie grabbed a quick look at Izzy. "You like Led Zeppelin? I didn't know anyone else even knew who they were."

"Old school." Izzy nodded rhythmically, like she was rocking out.

"How about AC/DC?" Callie asked.

"I like all the seventies and eighties bands," Izzy said with enthusiasm. "Pink Floyd. Lynyrd Skynyrd."

"Hey, you two rock stars, help us with these sheets?" Elise called from the other side of the table. "New girl. You want to carry the baskets up? We have to hang them on the line because Sister Agatha says *the sunshine is good for our souls,*" she mimicked sourly.

"Sister Agatha, just wait until you meet her." Izzy started around the folding table. "She hums when she gets really pissed. She's what my Aunt Mary Lou calls *a real peach.*"

Callie carried first one laundry basket of wet sheets, then a second, up the steep basement stairs. Each girl then took one end of the baskets and hauled them through a huge area with couches and chairs, school lunchlike tables, and a new flat screen TV. Izzy explained, as they passed through, that was their new "family room" where they watched TV, did school work, had their counseling group sessions, and generally just hung out.

"Counseling?" Callie wrinkled her nose as they went out the back door, onto a deck and into a side yard where there were towels already fluttering on clotheslines in the warm breeze.

"Required, just like religion class." Izzy rolled her dark eyes. "Brad's the psychologist. That's what we call him because he sort of looks like Brad Pitt. Some of the other girls think he's cute. You should see Sister Agatha around him; she gets all giggly and stupid." She shuddered. "Me, he creeps me out. All wanting to be my friend and stuff. He always wants to know how we *feel* about things." Izzy dropped her end of the laundry basket next to an empty clothesline and flopped in the mowed grass. "Fat and stupid. That's how I feel. Fat because I'm pregnant, stupid because I was dumb enough to believe my boyfriend loved me."

Callie had to laugh. She fingered the clothesline. "Your parents . . . they kicked you out?"

Izzy looked away and the two of them watched a big man in khaki pants and T-shirt and ball cap pull weeds from a flower bed. "My mom's a big deal in our town. Real estate agent. On the board at the country club. She said a baby would ruin my life." She nibbled on her lower lip. "She said I could come home after I have the baby. After I give it up for adoption. All my friends at home think I got sent away to boarding school because I was doin' drugs. You know, sex, drugs, and rock 'n' roll." She waggled her eyebrows.

"Were you?" Callie asked. "Doin' drugs?"

"Nah. Just the sex and rock 'n' roll part." Izzy looked back at Callie.

Callie smiled. "At least your mom said you can go home. I called my mom the other night and she said she didn't know when I could come back." She pulled down on the clothesline and let it go, listening to the twang in the air it made. "I don't know what that means."

"Little less sitting, little more working, ladies," Elise hollered from the next clothesline over.

"All right, all right." Izzy groaned, starting to push herself up off the ground.

Without thinking about it, Callie offered her hand. When Izzy grabbed it, Callie felt kind of weird. She and her friends, they weren't the touchy kind. No holding hands or hugging like any of that crap some girls did. The strange thing was, helping Izzy up didn't bother Callie. In fact, it felt kind of good. Not in a gay, lesbian way, but in a . . . comfortable way. "Thanks." Izzy brushed the grass off her butt. "Hey, Mattie!"

A man in long pants and a ball cap turned around.

Izzy waved him over.

Callie and Izzy stood side by side watching as he slowly got to his feet and began to make his way toward them.

"That's Mattie. He works here. He's got something wrong with him. Sort of retarded or something," Izzy explained. "But he's nice to us. He helps us with our chores. He can't talk so he can't tattle. And he has a real ear for music. Someone said he plays a church organ or something, I don't know. But he likes Led Zeppelin." Izzy looked at Callie and grinned.

Callie grinned back.

The man named Mattie stopped a few feet from Callie and Izzy and waited.

"Come on, Mattie, we have to hang up sheets." Izzy grabbed a wet, pale blue sheet from the plastic basket and pushed it into Mattie's arms.

"Hey, no fair, getting Mattie to help," Elise hollered from behind the wall of a pink flowered sheet.

"She's just mad she didn't think of it first," Izzy whispered as she snatched a wet pillowcase out of the basket.

Delilah parked her butt on the wrought iron end table she'd been working over with a steel-bristled brush for the last hour and let out a groan. Monica hadn't been kidding when she said the furniture was badly in need of cleaning before it could be repainted. Delilah had to have scraped and brushed off at least six layers of various colors of paint, and while she had finally hit bare metal in some places, the grooves and crannies were going to take some more attention.

Delilah glanced up at the sun that was slowly rising in the sky. It wasn't quite noon, but it was getting close. She wiped her forehead with the back of her hand and reached for the water bottle Sister Julie had delivered earlier. She was ready for another.

She rose, emptying the last drop of cold water into her mouth. The bottles were kept in the cafeteria-size refrigerator in the pantry off the kitchen and volunteers were welcome to help themselves. Instead of heading straight for the kitchen, though, Delilah went in search of Sister Julie, thinking maybe she needed another, too. She'd said she was going to be repotting some plants behind the potting shed if Delilah needed anything.

As Delilah crossed the yard, coming around the side of the house, she glanced in the direction of the sheets flapping in the wind. Earlier, she had heard girls talking. She could have sworn she recognized Callie's voice, but she'd resisted the urge to go in search of her to see how things were going. Delilah knew Callie felt trapped in the house, especially since the incident at the diner. Here, Delilah felt as if she needed to give the teen a little space.

In the distance, Delilah heard the sputter of a small engine starting, then the steady hum of what sounded like a weed whacker. More volunteers had arrived a short time ago. Someone had apparently bit on Monica's bid to have the weeds trimmed around the trees.

Delilah approached the potting shed, a cute little out-building that had been moved onto the property from elsewhere last fall. "Sister Julie?" She stuck her head inside, but when she didn't see her, she headed along the side. She knew Sister Julie had to be around here somewhere. She'd just seen her five minutes ago walking in the direction of the shed, a huge red clay pot in her arms.

"Hey, Sister Julie, I was wondering if you wanted a bottle of—" As Delilah turned the corner of the shed, she saw Sister Julie drop something onto the ground, then grind it into the dirt with the ball of her foot.

It took Delilah an instant to realize what she'd just seen. The smoke dissipating in the wind was a dead give-away. "Hey, I was wondering if you wanted a bottle of water," she said, trying not to smile. Caught red handed. She'd caught the nun sneaking a cigarette. A filtered slim from the look of the butt in the dirt.

"Water, yes. Sure." Sister Julie exhaled the remainder of the smoke from her lungs. "Thanks."

Delilah watched the nun kneel on the grass in front of the big clay pot she'd carried over earlier, thinking to herself that Julie didn't seem much like a nun. It wasn't that Delilah didn't think she wasn't religious or anything. Nothing could be further from the truth; she seemed to be a truly giving, self-sacrificing, kind person. It was just that Sister Julie looked so different than people expected. Acted so differently. And she was never spouting religion the way some others did. She never came off as self-righteous or judgmental the way the other nun sometimes seemed. Maybe it was just Delilah or her own guilt, but Sister Agatha always made her feel . . . unclean.

"Don't suppose you've seen my niece around?" Delilah tugged on her short ponytail. "Redhead. Fourteen, no belly."

Julie laughed. "Actually, I have. I thought maybe she was with you. She looks like you."

"My niece," Delilah explained. "Guess I already said that."

Sister Julie looked up, squinting in the bright light. "She's visiting with you? How nice."

"Yeah. Well, sort of. It's not exactly voluntary on Callie's part." She rested one hand on her hip. "She's been in a little bit of trouble and my sister thought she could use a change of scenery."

Julie sat back, resting her hands on her knees. "Sort of the same idea we have around here, I suppose."

Delilah nodded. "Yeah. She's not a bad kid. She really isn't. She just . . . made some bad choices. Made some bad choices of friends, I think."

"It's easy to do at their age," Sister Julie observed. "You know, I don't how you feel about this sort of thing, but we have a great teen psychologist in town. Paul Trubant. You know him?"

"I think we've bumped into each other around town. Here maybe."

"He's very good. He volunteered here, still does. We've added him to our staff, part-time. I think his sessions with the girls, both individual and group, are really making a difference. You might consider taking her for a session or two."

"Maybe I will. I'll have to talk to my sister, of course. But I know they've talked about counseling before."

"It might be nice for your niece to have someone to talk to she doesn't see as the enemy. Because you know"—Sister Julie squinted theatrically—"we're all the enemy."

"I know I definitely am." Delilah glanced up. "So is my niece around or did she take off?" She said it only half jokingly.

"Nope. I think she's still around. She was hanging sheets with some of the girls." Sister Julie sat up on her knees again, picked up a bag of soil and dumped it into the pot. "I heard them saying something about sneaking Italian ices from the freezer before they went back to the chain gang. Or the sweat shop, or whatever it is they're calling our laundry room in the basement these days."

"Oh, gosh, I hope Callie isn't causing any trouble."

"Trouble? Certainly not." Sister Julie dug into the soft soil in the pot with a trowel. "I put the Italian ices right where the girls can see them in the deep freeze. We get a couple cases donated a month. Someone's got to eat all the watermelon-flavored ones. I don't care for watermelon flavor, do you?"

"Cherry. I'm a cherry Italian ice girl myself." Delilah turned to walk away. "I'll bring that water right back."

"Detective," Julie said softly.

Delilah turned back. "Delilah, please."

The nun nodded. "Delilah . . . if you wouldn't mind, I'd prefer you kept my little indiscretion to yourself."

It took Delilah a minute to even realize what she was talking about. She was thinking about Callie and the suggestion to take her to counseling. It really was a good

idea. If Delilah couldn't get the teen to tal
someone else could.

She gave a wave of dismissal. "No, I wouldn't say any
thing, of course not. Your secret is safe with me." She
walked around the potting shed. "Not to worry, Sister,"
she said softly under her breath. "I've got far bigger secrets than that one under my hat."

"Ready to roll?" Delilah asked Callie. They were standing on the back deck, Delilah having yet another bottle
of water.

"Um, actually, I was wondering . . ." Callie wiped at the
stained pink mustache over her lip. "If . . . if I could stay
awhile. Izzy wanted me to see her room and we just finally did get done putting all the laundry away."

Izzy stood next to Callie, awaiting the verdict.

The two girls were wearing almost identical jean shorts
and flip flops, both redheads, though Delilah suspected
Izzy's was natural. They were probably very close in age.

"Sister Julie said it was fine," Izzy piped in. "Please,
Delilah, can she? Just an hour or so?"

Delilah's impulse was to say *no*. She'd worked all week,
leaving Callie alone. Saturdays and Sundays were their
days to be together.

"Please?" Callie begged, clasping her hands together
in earnest.

"We're just going to hang out, I swear. How can I get
in trouble, Aunt Delilah? We're in the middle of the
sticks with a bunch of nuns watching us."

Delilah had to laugh.

"I just want to hang out for a while, you know. Make
new friends, like you said. And . . . and I know you could
use a break. From me, I mean," Callie said quickly.

Delilah's resolve crumbled. Callie was right. What harm could hanging out with Izzy for a couple hours do? And the idea of having a little time to herself was becoming more appealing by the second.

"I'm checking with one of the sisters, first," Delilah warned.

Callie gave a squeal of delight, high-fiving her new friend. "Yes!"

"Police officer." Delilah glanced up and down the narrow alleyway and seeing no one, banged on the back door again. "Open up. Police," she called in her best cop's voice.

The door opened and Snowden appeared barefoot in gym shorts and a T-shirt. "You know that's not funny," he grabbed her by the arm and pulled her into his laundry room. "Someone could have heard you."

She laughed as she let him push her up against the washing machine. "Sure it's funny. You do it all the time to me."

"Not nearly as often as I'd like to these days." He covered her mouth with his, kissing her until they were both panting hard.

"What are you doing here in the middle of the day?" He kissed her forehead, pushing her hair from her eyes. "Where's your niece?"

"I've got about an hour of parole before I have to go back to Maria's Place and pick her up."

He slid his hand into the rear waistband of her shorts. "An hour in bed. That works for me, Detective," he whispered in her ear.

She smoothed his cheek with her palm. "How about if I jump in your shower, and meet you in that bed in five

minutes?" She pulled away from him. She was su
and sweaty from working outside and even though sh
knew he probably didn't care, she did. "Just a quick
one," she promised, releasing his hand as she walked
away.

"It better be," he warned, turning around to lock the
back door.

And Delilah really had meant for it to be a short
shower, only when she got in the old style porcelain tub
with the showerhead built into the ceiling, the warm
water felt so good that she didn't want to get out. Every
muscle in her body, taut from the tough week at work,
seemed to be slowly relaxing. She couldn't get enough
of the soft water spray on her face.

Delilah heard the bathroom door open, then close.
She rested her palms on the old green tile, closing her
eyes as she leaned forward, letting the water spray her
back. "I'm coming," she called. "I swear it."

The curtain pulled away and Snowden climbed in,
naked, closing it behind him.

"Hey," she laughed, moving over to make room for
him in the small space. "I said I was coming."

He rested his hands on her shoulders and squeezed.
Against her will, Delilah closed her eyes and groaned,
leaning forward again. "Mmm, that feels good."

He kissed the back of her neck.

"That, too."

He continued to knead one shoulder, but slid his
other hand down her back, around her waist and
upward until he cupped one of her breasts.

"Definitely that."

His thumb flicked over her nipple and she pressed
her wet, bare buttocks and the small of her back against
his groin.

"Not hard to imagine what you're thinking about," she murmured, a warm ache spiraling upward from her belly.

He leaned over her, kissing her neck, her jawline. She rested her body against his, lifting her chin, turning her head one way and then the other, savoring the feel of his mouth on her wet skin. Having a lover over a foot taller made for some interesting acrobatics in bed sometimes, but there were definite advantages. Snowden was so much larger than she was that he seemed to be able to touch every part of her at the same time . . . seemed to be able to cover her with pleasure. Engulf her. Delilah had only had three previous lovers, but Snowden was by far the most giving, the most loving . . . and the most exciting.

She turned in his arms, slippery, warm, getting warmer by the minute. She lifted her chin to look up at him, his eyes half closed, his sensual lips slightly parted. She ran her palms upward over his hard, muscular chest. She'd never known a man with pecs like Snowden's. The man was like iron.

She pressed a kiss to his chest . . . stroked her tongue over one of his dark nipples. And although he was silent, she felt a groan of pleasure ripple in his chest. He kissed her again, hungrier this time. He was never rough with her, but always passionate. Intense. When they made love, he made her feel good not just physically, but emotionally.

"We could check out that bed of yours," she told him, sliding her hand over his hip, down his thigh.

"We could." His breath caught in his throat and he made a little gasping sound as she cupped his balls. "Or," he whispered, "we could stay right here."

She giggled, her voice surprisingly husky. For a by-the-book, never-take-chances, type-A guy, Snowden could be pretty adventurous in the art of making love.

Her cheek resting on his chest, she drew her hand down his muscular thigh, then upward, stroking him. "I don't know, pretty slippery in here. We'll feel silly if one of us breaks something."

His only answer was to slide his hand between her wet thighs. She didn't need any further convincing.

Bracing himself against the back wall, Snowden lifted Delilah into his arms. She threw her head back, gripping his shoulders as he thrust into her. The warm water streaming down her back mixed with the heat pulsing inside her and she groaned, realizing she was already close to coming.

"I've missed you," she murmured, a little surprised by how close she sounded to tears.

"I've missed you." He kissed her gently and then began to rock. She knew it couldn't be easy to stand on wet porcelain, keep her cradled in his arms, stay balanced, yet Snowden's motion seemed effortless.

He knew her so well. Knew her body better than she did. She tried to hold back, tried to relax and prolong the waves of pleasure just a little longer, but she couldn't.

Delilah cried out, closing her arms around Snowden's neck, pulling herself closer, him deeper, if that was possible. His release came only a pounding heartbeat later and she laughed, breathless, pushing away from him. "Put me down before you slip a disk."

Snowden's gaze locked with hers and his blue eyes seemed to be searching for something for a moment. Wanting something. Needing something more from her.

"Come on," she whispered, looking away, uncomfortable under his intense scrutiny. "Let me go."

He released her slowly, gently, easing her down until her bare feet touched the tub floor. She took a step back, tilted her head back and let the water wash over her head and stream through her hair. "I probably need to get ready to leave," she said, her eyes closed.

"You could pick her up, bring her back here, and I could make dinner for you both."

"I don't think so." She shook her head, keeping her eyes closed.

He stepped out of the shower and closed the curtain behind him without saying anything more.

Chapter 11

"Dr. Trubant. Hello."

Paul turned around, a bag of baby spinach in his hand. He knew whose voice it was; he was just surprised she'd speak to him in public.

"Hi." He smiled. No one was nearby; the closest person was an elderly lady fingering lemons in the next display counter over, but for appearance's sake, he had to be careful.

"How are you?" she asked, walking closer, a small grocery basket on her arm.

"I'm . . . I'm fine. Thank you." He reached for a bag of lettuce mix. It said "Spring Mix". He didn't know if that was the same thing as the "Field Greens" on Susan's list, but at this point, he didn't care. He just wanted to get the stuff she needed for her salad and get the hell out of there.

She moved closer, coming to stand beside him, reaching to touch a bag of iceberg lettuce on the shelf. "Nice day today, wasn't it? Nice day to mow your lawn?"

Paul felt the hair rise on the back of his neck. He had mowed this afternoon. Susan's sister and her family were

Hunter Morgan

coming for dinner and Paul always liked to have the yard looking nice when Sarah and Jim came. Sarah was a real estate attorney up in Dover. She had never liked Paul. Never seemed to think he was good enough for her baby sister.

Paul glanced over his shoulder. The elderly lady was slowly moving away from them, a single lemon in her cart. "You drove by my house?" He spoke under his breath, pretending to be reading the date on another prewashed bag of salad.

"The baby's getting so big," she said in the same hushed voice. "Did Susan get her hair cut? It looks different. Highlighted maybe?"

She hadn't just driven by. She had to have been watching him . . . Paul had known he would have to careful with her. Had known it was a bad idea, even worse than some of the others. He also knew that was one of the reasons he had been attracted to her in the first place.

"Kitten, I don't know what you're doing, but this isn't a good idea and you know it. You know the agreement. No contact in public." He laid his hand on the cart and pushed it forward a little, his heart pounding. Everyone in town knew both of them. The merest hint of rumor could hurt both of them; she knew that. They'd discussed it soon after they'd begun the affair.

She followed him to the next display. "You want me to meet you later?" she whispered.

"Can't. Family coming for dinner."

"I mean *after*." Annoyance tightened her voice.

"I . . . I'd like to, but I can't." He looked up toward the automatic doors as he heard the pneumatic sound of them opening. The father of one of his clients entered the store. His son was seeing Paul on a weekly basis. If he spotted Paul, he was bound to stop and say hello, maybe inquire into his son's progress.

"Oh, come on," she pressed. "Sneak out after Susan's asleep. You name the time. I'll be there. I bought new panties. You want a peek now?"

He pushed the cart to the next display, grabbing baby carrots and precut packaged mushrooms. He was shocked by her forwardness, by the personality that lay beneath the surface appearances. It didn't matter that she wouldn't really show him her panties standing in the produce aisle of the local grocery story.

Paul knew everyone had a different side, but Kitten's . . . "I can't," he insisted sharply under his breath. "But I'll make it up to you," he added quickly, always a little fearful of how she might respond to his rejection. Then, before she could reply, he made a sharp left with the cart, almost striking another, and rolled into the canned goods aisle.

Julie sat in the porch swing in the dark, touched her bare foot to the smooth floorboards and pushed off. Resting her head back, she closed her eyes, wishing she had a cigarette, and then feeling dutifully guilty. She'd already been caught smoking once today.

The swing moved forward and she felt the cooling breeze tickle her warm scalp as she leaned back as if on an amusement park ride. From the time she was a small child, she had always loved to swing. It was like floating, floating on a cloud, she always thought.

The front screen door squeaked and Julie opened her eyes to see Amanda dressed in pink baby doll pajamas standing hesitantly on the porch. She was barefoot, too.

"Hey," Julie called.

Amanda let the door close behind her, but continued

to stand there, staring out into the dark. The moon hadn't yet risen and Julie had shut off the front porch lamps, so the only light to illuminate the teen's face was from the blue vaporous security lamp high on a telephone pole in the side yard.

"You're up late," Julie mused.

"I know. I'm sorry. It's after lights out. Eleven o'clock is stupid, though." She dragged one bare foot in front of her as if doodling on the warped floorboards. "It's not like we have school tomorrow or anything."

"Eight A.M. mass."

The brunette lifted one thin shoulder and let it fall.

Julie could tell something was going on with Amanda. She didn't usually break, or even bend the house rules. "You wanna sit for a minute?" Julie asked, stopping the swing and sliding over to make room.

Amanda hesitated, glancing over her shoulder. "Sister Agatha—"

"Is probably in bed by now, where both of us should be." Julie patted the wooden bench swing. She knew she had to be careful about overruling Sister Agatha's rules with the girls and she was trying. Sweet Mary knew she was trying, but sometimes rules didn't apply. Sometimes, you just had to go with instinct. With your heart. "Come on. Join me." She closed her eyes and leaned back. "It feels great. It'll help clear your mind, help you relax so you can go to sleep."

Amanda padded barefoot to the swing, sat down, and Julie pushed off again. She tapped the girl's knee as they drifted forward, both lifting their feet. "So what's up? And don't tell me *nothing*, otherwise we'll be here all night and both of us will be in trouble over curfew."

Julie caught the barest hint of a smile on Amanda's pretty, but still juvenile face.

"I . . . I just keep thinking about that little boy. You know, in the paper. I . . ." She stopped, then started again. "I know you said I shouldn't worry, that those things don't happen very often, but . . ." She drew her hand over her large belly. "I just can't stop thinking about him, Sister Julie. What if . . . if something happened to this baby that I gave away? What if someone put him in a closet and he died? Wouldn't I be committing murder, then, too?"

"Ah, sweetheart." Julie slipped her arm around Amanda and gave her a quick hug. "The mother who put that baby up for adoption is in no way responsible for what the adoptive parents did. Those monsters did that to that child of their own free will and the sin is on their heads. There was no way for the birth mother to know."

"Exactly." Amanda's voice cracked with emotion as she hugged her belly. "If . . . if I kept this baby, I know no harm would ever come to it because I would protect it. I would protect it forever," she cried passionately.

Julie couldn't help but smile at the teenager's naivety. If only life was that simple. If only you could protect those you love by saying you would do so. "Have you talked with Dr. Trubant about this?"

She groaned and slumped back in the swing. "Yes. And he says all the right things, but he always does. It's like he says what he's *supposed* to say." They swung forward and she pushed off with her foot. "But he doesn't understand how I feel about this baby. About giving it away." She suddenly sounded tearful. "No one here understands because they've never done it. They've never had a baby taken from their bodies and handed over to strangers."

Unexpectedly, Julie's eyes clouded with tears and she looked away. She was surrounded by the sounds of a peaceful evening—the rustle of leaves on the trees that sheltered the house from the sun during the day, the scurry of some nocturnal creature along the old hedgerow behind her, the twitter of insects. This was why, most of all, she loved Maria's Place. Because here, she felt safe. Here, she prayed she could make others feel safe.

"I do know how you feel," Julie said softly, drawing her hands into her lap. She couldn't bring herself to look into Amanda's eyes. Even after all these years, she still felt the shame. She still felt the agony of what she had experienced when the nurse had carried her infant away. It was a pain as sharp as any knife could have been, twisting in her stomach.

"You can't possibly," Amanda argued. "It's not about knowing what's right or wrong." She grasped both sides of her head. "I know in my mind I should do it. For the baby. For my own future. For my family. But that's not how I *feel*, Sister."

"I know, Amanda," Julie said softly, reaching out to pat the teen's hand. "I know because I felt the same way when I was just your age."

Amanda looked at her for a moment. "I don't understand. You . . . you're a nun." She paused. "How could—"

"I wasn't always a nun." Julie smiled through unshed tears.

Amanda's eyes grew round, Julie's meaning seeming to sink in. "But you took a vow. I thought you had to be . . . you know, a virgin."

"I knew from the time I took my first communion when I was seven that I would be a nun. That God was calling me." Julie sat back. "I just got a little lost along the way. Or maybe not. Maybe it was all part of God's plan to help me understand what you're going through right now, Amanda. What all of you girls are going through."

"You had a baby and gave it away?" Amanda murmured, staring at her. "I just can't believe . . ." She looked down and then up again at Julie. "But you're so good, so . . . *pure.*"

Julie smiled sadly. "It was a long time ago. Not many people know. I had some problems." She lowered her feet to stop the swing. "My point here is that I do know how you're feeling right now, or at least I have a good idea. I worried about my baby's safety and happiness, too."

"You did?"

Julie nodded.

"And is . . . do you know . . ."

"I'm not supposed to know, of course," Julie whispered secretively. "But I've heard she's just graduated from college. And yes, she's very happy. Her parents love her very much."

"Wow," Amanda breathed, looking at her feet.

Even in the semidarkness, Julie could see that the teen's nails were painted hot pink. Pink had once been Julie's favorite color nail polish . . . a very long time ago, in a different life when she had been Terry, and not Sister Julie. Amanda reminded her so much of herself, sometimes. Maybe that was the reason for the confession. Julie hadn't spoken of the baby she'd given away in many, many years.

"And you know," Julie went on, trying to refocus the conversation on Amanda, "nothing is final until after the baby is born and the paperwork is signed. You still have some time to make your final decision. You don't have to put your baby up for adoption if you don't want to."

"Excuse me," Sister Agatha interrupted from the doorway.

Julie and Amanda both looked up at the same time to see a shadow of a figure standing behind the screen door. Sister Agatha opened the door and stepped out onto the porch, a white kerchief covering her head and a white robe over a long nightgown that Julie knew covered her from head to toe.

"I must beg to differ," Sister Agatha said sharply. "Amanda's parents have already made the decision. The child, when it's born, will be put up for adoption and Amanda will return home." She gave Amanda a stern look. "I believe you should be in bed, Miss?"

To Julie's surprise, Amanda didn't fly out of the swing. She looked up at the other nun, almost in defiance.

"Go ahead and go to bed," Julie whispered softly, giving her a gentle push.

Sister Agatha held open the screen door for Amanda, waiting until Julie heard the girl's footsteps on the staircase before she allowed the door to swing shut on its hinges.

"What do you think you're doing?" Sister Agatha demanded.

Julie looked up at her in darkness, wondering just how long Sister Agatha had been eavesdropping. Had she heard Julie's earlier confession? It wasn't so much that Julie cared what Sister Agatha knew, as how it could affect Maria's Place. Julie never wanted her past to impinge on the good being done here, in the house.

"The adoption papers have not *legally* been signed."

"There is a husband and a wife at this moment praying for that young lady's safety and health." Sister Agatha pointed in the direction of the screen door. "They are praying for the health of the baby God has seen to give them through that girl. You have no right to tell her she doesn't have to give up the baby. She does. She will!"

Julie rose from the swing. "Maria's Place provides a sanctuary for these girls who have no other place to go. No one to turn to. I can't lie to them, Sister Agatha. It would be wrong."

"It would be wrong for you to alter God's plan," she snapped, taking a wide stance in her scruffy slippers, as if she were some warrior preparing for battle.

It was on the tip of Julie's tongue to ask who Agatha was to think she knew God's plan for Amanda better than anyone else, but she swallowed the resentment knotted in her throat. She had been praying for patience with Agatha. For understanding. She needed to pray harder.

"I don't think Amanda is really considering keeping her baby," she said, facing Agatha. She had to hand it to the younger woman; she could be imposing, even in a bathrobe. "She just needs some reassurance. She needs to feel she has some control."

"Control is what she is obviously lacking. Had she been able to *control* her carnal desires, she would not be in this position today, would she?"

Julie studied Agatha's face that would have been quite pretty if it were not for the frown lines, wondering what had brought the nun to this place in her life. Where was the anger coming from? The bitterness? She must have had something terrible happen to her, a person so dedicated to God who could strike out this way. Julie tried to feel compassion for her, rather than be angry with her.

If she had controlled her carnal desires, the couple praying for her baby wouldn't have a baby to pray for, Julie thought, wanting to point out that sometimes bad things happened for good reasons. But she wasn't up for a fight; it was wrong of her to even consider picking one.

"We're both tired." Julie circumnavigated Sister Agatha to get to the door. "Let's talk about this at our meeting with Dr. Trubant on Tuesday afternoon, shall we? I think he probably has a better idea of Amanda's emotional state than any of us do, including Amanda."

"You can't continue to do this," Sister Agatha called after Julie. "To undermine me. To undermine our rules. I won't stand for it."

Julie went up the steps, ignoring Sister Agatha's threatening tone, thinking to herself that she might just have to sneak another cigarette.

The Daughter sat cross-legged on her bed, lying back on her pillow, listening to the night sounds that drifted through her open window. It was very late. She should be asleep. But she was too keyed up to sleep. Her mind wouldn't stop racing.

She sat up and reached over to her nightstand to pick up the new photograph she had lovingly cut from The *Wilmington News Journal*. She turned the pages of her scrapbook on her lap. Picking up a bottle of glue, she glued the new clipping on the next clean page. Smoothing it to be sure there were no bubbles, she inhaled the scent of the adhesive, taking a deep breath, closing her eyes, enjoying the way it made her feel just a little dizzy.

Opening her eyes again, she picked up her favorite pen.

My Dearest Delilah, she began.

> *I wish that I could express to you how proud I was of you this week. I know it must have been hard for you to tell*

*that boy's parents that he was dead. To stand in front of
all those cameras and tell the world you didn't know what
had happened to him. I wonder if that police chief you
work for appreciates you. Men never do, though, do they?*

*I wish that I could tell you in person how much I admire
you. I wish that I could at least be brave enough to send
you this letter. I think about you constantly and I wonder
if you think about me. I wonder if you even know I'm here.
But I am here, my love. I'm here and I'm watching you.*

Love,
The Daughter

Satisfied that she had expressed her true feelings, *The
Daughter* lovingly glued the letter into the scrapbook.
She wouldn't send it, of course, but maybe some day, she
told herself, she could read it to Delilah. Some day when
they were best friends who shared everything.

"Sister Julie. Sister Julie, wait up."

Julie turned around on the brick steps to see Marty
Kyle leaving the vestibule of St. Stephen's, the town's
Catholic church. She was dressed in a short, tight black
skirt and silky tank top with high heeled strappy sandals.
A little immodest for St. Stephen's early mass, but con-
siderably conservative for the reporter herself.

"Marty." Julie blinked theatrically. "I'm pleasantly surprised to see you here. Wasn't Father Seraducci's homily
inspiring?"

Marty slipped on a large pair of sunglasses, but not
before Julie saw the redness. She didn't appear to have
gotten any more sleep last night than Julie did.

"Frankly, I found it dull, which is why I avoid mass as
often as possible." Marty tucked the case for her glasses

into her slick black snakeskin purse and removed a tube of lipstick. "I'm here mostly for research. You told me you all come every Sunday, *religiously.*" She chuckled at her own joke. "I wanted to see for myself. All looking like vestal virgins, aren't they, lined up on the front pew, squeaky clean, not a streak of blue eye shadow in the lot?"

Julie prickled. "Is there something I can do for you, Marty? The girls and Sister Agatha are waiting for me in the van."

"I'm ready for that list of volunteers. Do you think *Monica* could find time to get it to me tomorrow? We just started editing what's already been taped. I'll get back to you once I'm ready for secondary interviews with you and your staff, but I want to go ahead and talk to some of your volunteers first."

"I can certainly see if Monica can get to that tomorrow." Julie turned away. "Have a nice day, Marty."

Marty smacked her lips, smoothing her lipstick. "Yeah, right, you too, *Sister,*" she murmured under her breath as she strode off in the opposite direction.

Chapter 12

"Are you okay? Are you sick?" Delilah leaned across the seat as Callie climbed into the police cruiser.

"I can't believe you came to get me in this thing again." Callie threw her purse and new blue smock down between them. "You know how I feel about it."

"Callie, it's the middle of the day. What's wrong? Your shift isn't over for another two hours." She studied the teen's face for any sign of illness. "I thought I was supposed to pick you up at five fifteen."

Callie crossed her arms over her chest and threw herself back against the seat. "I quit. I hated it."

"You quit?" Delilah exploded. "It was only your second day. You've worked a total of six hours. How could you know if you hated it?"

"I told you I didn't want to work in a drugstore. Mr. Lewinski wanted me to, like, stock nose spray and hemorrhoid cream and gross stuff like that."

"You were hired to stock shelves. What did you think you were going to stock in a drugstore?" Signaling, Delilah glanced in her rearview mirror and pulled away from the curb. "I have an interview in ten minutes." The final

autopsy report on Rob Crane had come back without providing any additional information on the young man's
death. The ME said there were traces of the drug GHB in
his blood, but that only indicated that he had not consumed any within a few days of his death. The autopsy
could not conclude what happened to Rob Crane between
the time he ingested the drug and the time he died.

With no real lead except the party Jamey said Rob had
been headed to, Delilah had been working every angle.
One of the guys in the department had actually managed to track down the location of the party in Rehoboth that Rob Crane was supposed to have attended.
A young lady named Betsey O'Connor had apparently
thrown the party. She and her father were coming in.
More than a week had passed since the college student's
body had been found. Delilah was praying like crazy the
girl would have information that would aid the police in
solving the case.

"You're going to have to go to the station with me,"
Delilah told Callie.

Callie looked over, her expression defiant. "I am *not*
going to the police station."

"Oh yes you are, young lady. You're going to go to the
station, sit in the break room, and wait for my shift to
end."

"I want to go back to the house."

"I can't take you back. There's not time. I can't miss
this meeting. Besides, the whole idea of the job was to
get you away from the Internet and out of the house."

Callie returned to her previous posture, arms crossed
over her small breasts. "I'll walk. I'm not sitting in the
police station like some criminal."

It was on the tip of Delilah's tongue to make a sarcastic
remark about how Callie ought to be comfortable at the

police station, considering her past experiences, but she squelched the impulse. Her mother has always used sarcasm as a way to communicate and Delilah knew for a fact it didn't work well with teens. Didn't work well with anyone, from her experience.

Delilah gripped the steering wheel, praying for patience. "I really wish you had given the drugstore job a couple more days. Mr. Lewinski was going to pay you well."

"He was a pervert."

Delilah glanced at Callie. As far as Delilah knew, Mr. Lewinski, in his early sixties, with wife, children, and numerous grandchildren was a model citizen. He served on the Chamber of Commerce board. He hadn't even been looking for help at his store, but had overheard Delilah talking at the Chamber about her niece needing a job and Mr. Lewinski had made the offer to hire Callie part-time to stock shelves.

"What do you mean he's a pervert? Did Mr. Lewinski approach you inappropriately?" Delilah found the idea difficult to believe, but in her line of work, she knew you never knew people as well as you thought you did.

"Did he?" Delilah repeated when Callie didn't respond.

"Not really," Callie finally agreed. "But he kept looking at me funny and asking me if I was cold and then he gave me that ugly smock thing to wear."

Delilah heaved an inward sigh of relief. "You need to be careful what you accuse people of, Callie. That's not something to joke around about." She glanced at her. "And I told you not to wear that tank top. Your bra straps are showing. The fabric's too thin. It's not appropriate for work. He probably didn't know how to say so, so he just gave you the smock to cover up with."

Callie frowned and looked at the window. "I told you the job was a stupid idea."

Delilah darted into the police station entrance on the street behind the old brick building and pulled into her parking space in the rear. "Come on, let's go. I'm going to be late." She grabbed her bag and slammed the driver's side door. "We'll talk about this later," she said over the roof of the car. "But I'm warning you, now. I'm not giving in this easily. You're going to get a job and you're going to do something this summer."

"And if I don't, what are you going to do?" Callie flung at her. "You going to do the same thing Mom did? Just put me on a plane?"

There was something about the way Callie said it that struck a chord in Delilah. For all the kid's bravado and talk of hating her mother and being glad to get away from her, she really was hurt by having been sent away. Maybe Sister Julie was right. Maybe some counseling would help. Delilah would suggest it to Callie again. When they were both in a better mood.

Marty sat in the driver's seat of her Miata glancing over the notes in her leather binder. She had decided to initially speak to half a dozen volunteers at Maria's Place and then pick one or two to interview on camera, depending on what they had to say. So far, she'd interviewed three and each one was duller than the previous. Marty was beginning to become frustrated. She really wanted the job in Baltimore. She just couldn't get a handle on what she wanted the Maria's Place piece to be about, what angle she wanted to approach it from. Sure, it was a feel good story; nuns taking in homeless pregnant teens, but *News Night* probably aired a couple dozen "feel good" stories a year. If Marty wanted this job, and she really did, the piece had to be different. And if it wasn't unique, she would have to make it unique.

After shoving her binder into her briefcase, she climbed out of her car and walked up the sidewalk to the quaint little story and half white Cape Cod in the middle class neighborhood of Sunset Farms in Stephen Kill. The postage stamp front yard was neatly mowed, the hedges trimmed, and flowers sprouted from flower boxes in the first story windows.

God, but Marty hated window boxes. They were so cutesy, it made her want to puke.

At the open door, her next interview waited eagerly, a kid on her hip. Jenny Grove, age twenty-eight. A part-time preschool teacher. Grew up in Delaware. Married. Two children. A dog. Welcome to small-town America. According to Monica's precise notes, Jenny didn't often volunteer her time at Maria's Place, but she baked desserts and delivered them regularly. Cupcakes were apparently her specialty. With pink frosting.

Marty forced a smile. "Mrs. Grove?"

"Yes, hi." The young brunette laughed nervously, shifting the child on her hip to the opposite side so she could shake Marty's hand. "This is CJ, Charlie Junior. He's twenty-three months. I have a daughter, too, but she's at my mom's. Ashley. She's five."

"How wonderful for you." Marty kept the smile frozen as she stood on the sidewalk in front of the door. She had met a guy who she dated occasionally for lunch and he had ordered a pitcher of margaritas. Hoping to get her liquored up enough for a little lunch nookie, probably, but Marty had passed. She didn't drink when she was working. As she looked at squeaky-clean, no make-up but mascara and lip gloss Jenny Grove, she was beginning to wish she'd taken Jeremy up on that drink. Wished she downed the whole pitcher. Wished she'd gone back to Jeremy's office that was closed for lunch, spread her legs wide in one of those dental chairs, and let him pound her good. At least then, she'd have something to think about while Jenny told her how important it was for people to help one another.

"Do you think I could come in?" Marty finally asked, realizing Jenny was still frozen in the doorway, smiling her pretty face off.

"Oh, yes. Gosh. Sure. I'm sorry. Come in. I made sweet tea. Or, I have lemonade. Or, apple juice," she sputtered as she led Marty through the front foyer. On one side was the living room; blue carpet, blue and rose furniture, country stenciling on the walls. Across the hall was a small den with a TV left on, a playpen, and a few scattered toys as well as an old couch and chair. This was probably the room they used the most in the house; the pink and blue room, Marty surmised was for "company," Christmas Day. So on. So forth.

Marty followed Jenny into the white and red kitchen.

"I hope this is okay." The woman tucked a lock of her shoulder-length hair behind her ear and let the child slide down until his little sneakers hit the vinyl flooring.

The little boy toddled off, headed for the dog bowls near the back door.

"Please, have a seat." Jenny indicated the small kitchen table. Placemats decorated with apples. A ceramic vase on the center of the pine table, filled with some kind of weedy fresh flowers. "I hope the kitchen is okay," she said cheerfully, obviously nervous. "I thought it would be comfy . . . you know. Homey."

Marty nodded vaguely. No, she didn't know what Jenny meant, but she didn't care. She was thinking about the dentist. She didn't like him much; he was a widower who talked too much about his dead wife. Some kind of guilt trip definitely going on there. But he was good in the sack. Would probably be good in the chair, too.

Marty sat down, lowering her briefcase to the floor cautiously, fearing something might be down there that would stain the new leather. It was a Coach. Expensive, even though it had come from an outlet store.

"Tea, lemonade?" Jenny asked, hovering near the counter.

"No, thank you. I have a couple more interviews to do today. We should probably get started."

"Right. Sure." Jenny hurried around the table. "Don't drink it, honey. No, no, CJ."

Marty eyed the little boy who was down on all fours, his mouth hovering over the dog bowl.

"He doesn't really drink the water," Jenny explained with a little giggle. "You know, one of those silly things your older sibling teaches you."

Marty flipped open her notebook. "So, Mrs. Grove—"

"Jenny, please."

"Jenny." Marty nodded. "Can you tell me what type of volunteer work you do for Maria's Place?"

"I bake. I'm a baker. I love to bake," she answered enthusiastically. "It's something I can do at night, you know, after the kids are in bed."

Marty scribbled *bakes at night* on the clean sheet of paper.

Jenny rattled on for another minute and a half before Marty interrupted. "So you deliver your baked goods?"

"Once a week, at least. Sometimes late." Shrug. Another giggle. "Sister Julie is so good about being flexible. She knows my schedule is crazy, what with work, the kids, my job. I just work mornings three days a week. St. Paul's preschool. Charlie, that's my husband, he works for a heating and plumbing company in town. His hours get crazy sometimes. You know, service calls. Sometimes I have to wait until he gets home after the kids are in bed to run over and drop off what I've made."

Marty noted that Jenny Grove delivered her baked goods, thinking that the chick probably baked pink cupcakes and delivered them at ten o'clock at night wearing flannel jammies and Coke-bottle glasses.

"The girls really like the treats," Jenny went on. "I mean, I know they shouldn't have too many sweets, being pregnant. You have to watch your blood sugar and your weight when you're pregnant. But a lot of people eat there. Not just the girls. The Sisters, the volunteers." Jenny clasped and then unclasped her hands, resting them on one of the apple place mats.

The little boy had wandered out of the kitchen. He was banging on something in another room.

"Can you tell me why you bake for Maria's Place?"

"Like I said. I love to bake, and a family of four, we can only eat so many cupcakes and cookies."

Marty smiled. "Yes, but I mean, why Maria's Place. Why give of your time, money, for *this* cause?"

"I . . . I don't know." She shrugged.

She was wearing a lavender T-shirt, khaki capris, and white sandals. Her breasts were small, but she had a decent figure for a girl who had popped out two babies in the last five years.

Marty waited. Cute, but apparently not a whole lot going on upstairs.

"Well, I guess because . . ." Jenny thought out loud. "Because I wanted to do something for someone else. It's important that we do for others. I . . . we, Charlie and I have been so blessed. Two healthy children. A good marriage. It's only right that we help those who are less fortunate than we are. I think it's what God wants us to do."

"So Maria's Place isn't a special cause, for you?" Marty checked her watch. "You didn't get pregnant as a teenager. Never had a sister or anything who gave up a baby for adoption?"

"No, no, no. Nothing like that." Jenny laughed, lifting her hands to flushed cheeks. "Mary Pettletown, who I work with at the preschool; she volunteers there. Does sewing. Mending, you know. Makes curtains. Does it in her free time. She has two kids, too. She was just telling me about Maria's Place one day and what a great charity it was. And they're so nice to their volunteers. Very appreciative. You know, they just had a big luncheon a couple of weeks ago. A ribbon cutting for the new addition. They——"

"I know. I was there." Marty glanced down at her notes. Jenny hadn't said anything more interesting than the last two interviewees, both women, one in her thirties, one in her fifties. They were all volunteering at Maria's Place because *it was the right thing to do*. No story there.

"Let's see." Marty tapped her pen. "Can you tell me——"

A loud crash and a baby's shriek shot Jenny out of her chair. She ran out of the kitchen, sandals clip-clopping. Sounds of the little boy crying, his mother soothing him came from the den. A minute later, Jenny was back, little boy on her hip. His face was bright red and wet with tears.

"I'm sorry. CJ was trying to stand on his fire engine instead of sit on it." She smoothed his dark hair and kissed his forehead. "And he had a little tumble. Didn't you, CJ?"

Tucking her notebook into her briefcase, Marty quickly got to her feet. She couldn't stand this a minute longer. She was heading back to the office. Maybe she could spend some time in the editing room if no one was using it. See if she could make some sense of the slop she had taped so far. And she still had to prepare for the evening newscast.

"Are you going already?" Jenny asked, obviously disappointed. "You . . . you don't have any more questions?"

"Not for now." The camera smile. "But thank you so much. If I have questions, I'll call." Marty made a beeline for the door. "I'll let myself out."

"Well, okay." Jenny stood there in the middle of the kitchen, holding her child to her breast. "Thank you. Have . . . have a good day."

"You're late."

"Ma, I'm not late." Snowden stood in his mother's laundry room and removed his black dress shoes. He hadn't gone home to change after work. If he had, he had been afraid he'd have ended up canceling on her again. "I told you I couldn't get here until eight. You didn't wait for me, did you?"

"Of course not. I know better than that."

He followed her into the old-fashioned kitchen that hadn't changed since he was a child. This had once been his grandparents' home, and it was the home Tillie Calloway had grown up in. The home where she had raised her illegitimate son.

"Eight o'clock is too late for me to eat. Too late for anyone to eat." His mother eyed him as she picked up a Corelle plate covered with plastic wrap on the counter and carried it to the microwave. It was the only appliance in the kitchen that wasn't avocado green. "I made your favorite. Chicken pot pie."

Snowden hated chicken pot pie. At least his mother's. Greasy chicken, overcooked potatoes, undercooked carrots. Some kind of soggy biscuit mix topping rather than a crispy crust. "I can heat it up myself. Why don't you sit down and tell me about your day?"

She slid the plate into the microwave, hit the key pad several times, hit "Cancel," and then a different sequence of numbers.

The timer on the display panel read 4:51. In five minutes, the pot pie would be a soupy mess.

He walked to the refrigerator. At least the carrots would be cooked. "You have a good day at work, Ma?"

"Got some new books in. Caught two kids sticking chewed up gum between the pages of Keats." She stood in front of the microwave, all five foot nothing of her, hands planted on her hips, watching through the little window. She always watched the food cook.

Snowden took a carton of off-brand orange juice from the fridge and grabbed a glass from the cupboard. He poured a full glass of the watery juice and walked to the table. His place had already been set. She had probably done it when she ate her own meal at five thirty.

"How was your day?" Tillie asked.

He sat down, eyeing the microwave. "It's probably done, Ma. It doesn't take long." He sipped his juice. "It was okay."

"Nothing more on that boy's death?"

The pot pie in the microwave was popping and sizzling. It was beginning to smell burnt. He wondered if the fire extinguisher he had bought her was still under the kitchen sink. "Ma, you know I can't talk to you about open cases."

She folded her arms over her chest still watching the

pot pie rotate. "Something fishy there. I knew it the day he disappeared." She shook her finger at the microwave.

There was no sense in Snowden arguing with her. She always knew things after the fact.

"You look into his father?" she asked. "He was always awfully stern with the boy. Always seemed disappointed in him no matter how high his grades were in school or how many races he won."

"You make that appointment to have the washing machine looked at?" Snowden reached for the newspaper folded neatly and left on the end of the ancient dinette table. It was the *Baltimore Sun*.

His mother, the town librarian, had never married. Her life, after her parents died, had been Snowden and her job. She was an avid reader and always read the papers. And not just the local rags. She read the *Baltimore Sun*, The *Wilmington News Journal*, The *New York Times*. She always saved the Sunday *Times* for him. He rarely got a chance to read it and it usually went out in his recycling, but he didn't have the heart to tell her.

"Washing machine's running fine."

The microwave finally beeped and she opened the door. Steam, the smell of chicken and burnt biscuit wafted through the air.

"Ma, you have to run it through the spin cycle three or four times or your clothes are soaking wet. You may need a new washer."

"Too expensive."

"I don't mind getting you one," he told her.

They had this kind of conversation often. Although her parents had left her comfortable, Tillie Calloway still lived as if she were an unwed mother trying to get by on her paycheck at the convenience store while she put herself through college. She was as frugal as anyone he had ever known.

Wearing flowered orange hot mitts, she carried the plate to the table, scuffing in her slippers. She set the plate down in front of him and he pushed aside the newspaper. She peeled off the plastic wrap and he stared at the gray mush, wondering if ketchup was in order.

"Want some bread?"

It would be white bread. Bought at the bread store where you could get two loaves for a dollar a couple of days after their freshness expiration date. "No, thanks, Ma."

"You should eat better." She dropped the plastic wrap in the trash can, returned the mitts to a drawer and took the chair across from him. "If you were married, you'd have a wife to cook for you."

He set his fork down without touching the pot pie and looked at her across the table. She kept her mostly gray hair cut very short. No make-up. T-shirt and sweat pants, and slippers. In the winter, it was a sweatshirt, sweat pants, and slippers. To work, she wore black polyester pants and some kind of flowered shirt, but at home, only sweats.

"Ma, could we not have this conversation, tonight? Just once, could I eat while we talk about something other than my failings?"

"Prickly tonight, are we?" She paused. "And don't be ridiculous. What's this talk about your failures? I'm proud of you, Snowden. You know that. I've always been proud of you. But it's time you started thinking about settling down. If you don't have children, you'll regret it someday. I'll guarantee it."

He picked up his fork and poked at a lump on the plate that was either chicken or biscuit. "I don't have time to date."

"That right?" She lifted a graying brow.

He looked at her, not sure how to interpret her tone of voice. Did she know something about Delilah? "What are you saying, Ma?"

"I'm not saying anything." She raised her hands, palms open to him, and let them fall. "I'm just thinking maybe you do have a little time to see someone. Maybe you just don't want to get my hopes up about grandchildren just yet."

Though he'd only drunk half of the juice, he rose from the chair, taking his glass with him. How could his mother know anything about him and Delilah? They'd been nothing but discreet. He'd never said a word to his mother about her. About dating anyone. "I don't know what you're talking about."

"You don't have to tell me about it if you don't want to. She's cute. I'll give you that. Smart. I like her."

He kept his back to his mother, reaching into the refrigerator. "You like who, Ma?

"You know. The one I told you for months you ought to ask out. That cute blonde. Detective Swift. I saw the two of you talking after the ribbon cutting at Maria's Place. You might be able to fool the guys at work, but you can't fool your mother."

Snowden was so surprised that his mother had suspected something and actually been right, that he let the juice fill to the top of the glass and start to spill over. Realizing what he was doing, he dropped the carton on the counter and reached for the dishrag hanging over the faucet.

He wasn't sure what to say. All he could think of was, if she knew they were dating, who else in the town knew?

* * *

Delilah was surprised to find Snowden at her back door. It was almost eleven. She was just getting ready to go to bed and read for a little while before she tried to go to sleep.

"Hey," he said softly. He was still in his uniform.

"What are you doing here?" She stepped out onto the back stoop, automatically scanning for snoopy neighbors.

He backed down the steps so that they were eye-level. "I just . . ." He looked down and then up at her. "I was on my way home."

Delilah tightened the tie on her robe, glancing over her shoulder. Callie was in the living room at the computer, probably oblivious to the fact that anyone was even there. "You can't come in, Snowden."

"I know. I just . . ." He looked down again.

"You should have called," she whispered.

He met her gaze. "Have you said anything to anyone? I mean, about us?"

"No. Of course not." She was surprised by his question. Surprised he would come by rather than call to ask. "What makes you ask?"

He lifted one broad shoulder and let it fall. "I had dinner with my mom tonight. She said something that made me think maybe—"

"She said something about you and me? Like she knew?" Delilah reached behind her and closed the door. "Like what?"

He rolled his eyes. "You know my mother. Always suspecting things. Always swearing she foretold some event after it occurs."

Delilah couldn't resist a little smile. "You think she knows about us? How did she say it? Did she seem to mind the idea?"

"Oh, no. She loves the idea of me dating anyone that could possibly produce a grandchild for her. She'd be totally irrational when it comes to understanding the complications here."

His words jumbled her already mixed bag of emotions. His mention of *complications* reminded her that this could lead nowhere; not that she thought about it often, because it wasn't an issue. They had never discussed any sort of future together because there was none. He was the chief of police and she was a detective under him. There could be no relationship. She had known that from the beginning. End of story.

But then he sounded so annoyed that it tickled her that even Snowden, the near perfect man, had to deal with a meddlesome mother. Delilah had to press her lips together to keep from smiling. "No," she said. "Of course I haven't said a word. Not to anyone. Certainly not to your mother."

He glanced left and then right. A dog barked in the cul-de-sac behind them. Her neighbors' back porch lights were out. Curtains were drawn. The lights were already out in most of the windows.

"She said she saw us at the ribbon cutting at Maria's Place. Saw us *together.*"

Delilah gave a little laugh. "We talked for about a minute before you sicced those reporters on me."

He drew his hand across his mouth as if to wipe away his smile. "Sorry. I shouldn't have come by. I just . . . I knew you hadn't said anything. I guess I just wanted to see you." He met her gaze again, steady this time. "See your pretty face."

That was sweet of him, Delilah thought. Very sweet. It really was too bad commitment wasn't an option. It was too bad he was her boss. Too bad he was half black and she came from a Southern family still harboring racial issues a century and a half after the Civil War. A crying shame, her granny would say.

"You should go," Delilah told him softly. "Callie's still up."

"That mean you're definitely not going to invite me in?" His tone was playful.

She crossed her arms over her chest. She liked him when he was like that, teasing, good-humored. She didn't see him often enough like that. His life didn't seem to afford it. The man was a serious guy. "No, I'm not inviting you in."

"And you won't leave your bedroom window unlocked for me?"

She laughed picturing him climbing over her rhododendron bush, in his uniform and hoisting himself through her window. "Go home, Snowden." She turned for the door, then back. "Oh, hey, did you get my message? I left it on your voice mail at work."

He was already on the sidewalk. He turned back. "What message? I had that thing to do at the Kiwanis Club tonight."

She nodded. "Right. I forgot. I finally got to talk to the girl who had the party. The party Rob Crane supposedly went to."

He nodded, giving her his full attention.

"We were right, of course. Parents were out of town. Underage drinking." She slid her hands into the pockets of her robe. "Anyway. He never showed up."

"He never went to the party at all?"

Delilah shook her head. "Nope. The girl was sure. The party was small, in the basement. Low key. No drunken brawls or jumping out the second story window into the pool. Guess that's why the Rehoboth cops were never called."

He looked down at the sidewalk, then up at her again. His face was cast in shadow. "So where does that leave us with the Rob Crane case, Detective?"

"It leaves us nowhere, Chief," she answered softly. "We've got a boy who somehow died of thirst and then was thrown in the pond. We've got a possible homicide and no leads."

The Daughter hadn't gotten up that morning planning to choose the next one. It was too soon. She wasn't even sure there *would* be a next one. If there was going to be, she knew she should wait weeks, months. And then, suddenly she was there. Right in front of her. Like an epiphany.

No, not *like* one. It *was* one.

When *The Daughter* had decided that Rob Crane had to die, she hadn't been on any sort of crusade. It had mostly been impulsive. He had angered her. Pretended to be someone he wasn't in the newspapers, on TV, overshadowing Detective Swift. But now, watching the next one, everything seemed to be falling in place in *The Daughter's* mind. She had never felt as if she fit in anywhere until she had come to Stephen Kill, and she had often wondered why.

Was this why? Had this been her purpose all along? Had all her past experiences led her to this point in her life?

It was certainly possible.

As *The Daughter* watched her next victim, she felt her cheeks flush and her pulse quicken. Then she consciously reined in her emotions. She couldn't allow herself to think about the pleasure it had given her to hear Rob Crane beg for water. Beg for his life. She couldn't allow herself to wonder if this one would beg, too. That was how people made mistakes. You saw it all the time on the news. People couldn't keep their business to themselves. Couldn't keep their emotions . . . their desires in check. But not *The Daughter*. She was smarter than all of them. She didn't think. She didn't feel. She just studied the woman, letting the plan fall into place.

Chapter 13

Julie hung up the phone and sat for a moment, her fingers finding the Benedictine crucifix she, like all nuns of her order, wore, even if they set aside their habits.

How dare she! was her first reaction when the bishop had spoken. *How dare she go over my head! How dare she bring negative attention to Maria's Place in the Diocese that still did not fully support a project left solely to nuns, especially a nun with such a checkered past as her own.*

But as Julie's fingers rubbed the ridges of her crucifix, she began to calm. She forced herself to calm down and replace her anger with logic. Sister Agatha had not called the bishop out of malice; he had made that clear in their brief conversation. He had said it was only a courtesy call and that he had no true concerns. He knew she and Sister Agatha could work out their differences.

Sister Agatha had called the bishop because she had believed it was what was best for the girls, Julie told herself. And in all fairness, the sister had first brought her grievances, on more than one occasion in the last few months, to Julie. But Julie had been too busy to really listen to her.

Or she had merely disagreed and pushed Sister Agatha's concerns aside. Pushed Sister Agatha aside.

And it wasn't right.

Still, she wished Sister Agatha hadn't contacted the bishop. She wished Sister Agatha had made it clearer just how upset she was.

So now what?

What did she say to Sister Agatha? How could they resolve their differences, as the bishop had assured her he knew they could? Julie obviously had to speak with her. She considered tabling the conversation for a day or two, letting her emotions settle, her thoughts jell, but putting Sister Agatha off had probably caused much of the tension between them in the first place. There was only one thing she really could do.

Taking a deep breath, Julie rose from the desk chair and walked out of the office and down the hall. She found Sister Agatha sitting at one of the big tables beside Lareina in the family room, reading quietly to her from an old Catechism book.

It was Julie's belief that young people responded better to some of the newer teaching programs the Catholic Church offered, but it was from Psalms and the word of God was the word of God, she reminded herself.

When Sister Agatha saw Julie approach, she finished her sentence and looked up.

"Could I speak with you when you have a minute?" Julie asked, finally releasing her crucifix and tucking it inside the neckline of her Nike T-shirt.

"Certainly. In the office?" Agatha pulled the corners of her mouth back in a placating smile.

She knew what this was about. She'd been waiting for the bishop's call. Julie felt her anger heating her cheeks again. "How about out on the back deck?" she countered, strolling toward the French doors. "It's beautiful outside this evening."

All the girls except for Lareina, who was with Sister Agatha, and Katy, who was lying down with a headache, were gathered around the wide screen TV watching an ancient rerun of *The Fresh Prince of Bel Air.* The girls laughed along with the laugh track and Julie smiled to herself, glad to know they could laugh at such silliness, considering their situations.

"You *wanna* watch with us?" Belinda called to Julie, tossing a kernel of popcorn into her mouth. "This is a funny one. Will Smith gets this job, only he's really bad at it. I've seen it before." She dug into a big plastic blue bowl on the couch between her and Tiffany for more popcorn.

"Maybe in a few minutes." Julie opened the door, stepping out onto the deck and into the warm, humid evening.

Sister Agatha followed Julie outside a moment later. She closed the door behind her and stood waiting. Julie took her time before she spoke. "Beautiful crescent moon tonight," she remarked, pointing into the dark sky, glad Sister Agatha had not flipped on the deck lights as she usually did. "We should talk to the girls about moon phases. Maybe borrow a telescope."

"You spoke to the bishop," Sister Agatha said.

"Yes." Julie continued to study the tiny sliver of moon hanging low on the horizon, just above the treetops of the woods beyond the rear of the property.

Sister Agatha shifted nervously behind Julie in her squeaky leather shoes.

"I wish you would have come to me before you spoke to the bishop," Julie said.

"I didn't speak to him. I sent him an e-mail. The

bishop appreciates e-mail. And I warned you several times about this matter before I felt compelled to inform him of the situation."

"And what is the *situation,* Sister?" Julie turned to her, hating to abandon the glorious sight of the moon for Sister Agatha's sour face.

"This home is not being run as it should be. Rules are lax, enforcement even laxer. We're not spending enough time in spiritual training." The nun cupped her hands together as if making a presentation or singing an operetta. "Volunteers are given free rein of the property and the girls, bringing in questionable influences. What we have here is a potential disaster. All the hard work, the dedication to the Lord's work, could all be for nothing if we end up in a lawsuit with one of these girls' parents. You know very well the diocese cannot afford any more lawsuits right now. Not of any nature."

Julie studied Agatha for a moment. Though it was dark on the deck, light from the TV flashed through the glass, backlighting the nun in her knee-length habit, black stockings, and utilitarian shoes. "The bishop said that you believe you would be better suited to run this house than I am."

Sister Agatha stood her ground. She hummed under her breath. "I did."

"How can you say such a thing?" Julie took a step closer. "Sure, I may be a little lax with the girls. I certainly don't always lead by the best example, but I *understand* these girls in a way you never could. I *feel* what they're feeling." She pressed her hand to her heart. "I know on a level that you can't possibly what they're going through right now."

Sister Agatha said nothing.

Julie crossed her arms over her chest. "Is this about

what you overheard that night Amanda and I were talking on the front porch? Is this about me and my worthi-
ness in your eyes?"

"I don't know what you're talking about. I do not
listen in on private conversations."

"You most certainly do," Julie said curtly, taking another step.

Sister Agatha slid one foot back, watching Julie. Seeming almost fearful of her, suddenly.

"You listen in on private conversations," Julie accused.
"You don't think I don't see you sneaking around? You
think the girls don't see it?"

"You have no right to make such allegations," Sister
Agatha flared.

Julie nodded. "You're right. I don't. Your indiscretions
are between our Lord and you. But what is between you
and me is this house. This house that I built." She
pointed at the deck, taking yet another step closer. "This
house that was my dream. *Is* my dream. And I won't
allow you . . . I won't allow *anyone* to come between me
and this house. These girls. Do you understand me,
Sister Agatha? Do you understand what I'm saying?"

"No," Sister Agatha snapped. "Actually I don't know
what you're saying. Are you threatening me, Sister Julie?"

"I'm warning you," Julie said softly, looking into her
pretty, cold eyes. "I'll try to work on my enforcement of
the rules we've set down for the girls. I'm willing to look
at any religious curriculum you believe would benefit
them. I'm even willing to adjust the weekly schedule to
include more religious training, but I will not shut out
our volunteers. I will not remove these girls from the
love this community has to offer. And *you*, Sister, *you* will
bring your concerns to me in the future. You will not
attempt to usurp my position, not with the girls, not with

the community, and certainly not with the bishop. Not ever again, or *you*, Sister, will find yourself elsewhere, far from Maria's Place and these girls."

"Is that all, Sister Julie?"

Agatha's response caught Julie off guard. Julie knew she had stepped over the line and expected Agatha to call her on it. Julie hadn't meant to lose her temper. This wasn't how she had wanted to leave this issue between them. She didn't want to be a bully.

But maybe it was better this way. If this was what it took to protect her girls. To protect this house.

"Yes. That's all," Julie said softly. Then she turned to see the moon again, her back to Agatha, so that the nun did not see the tears that welled in her eyes.

"Hi, honey, sorry I'm so late." Charlie leaned over Jenny's shoulder and kissed her on the cheek. "Had a heat pump that just wouldn't play right."

"That's okay. Kids and I had a nice evening. We rode bikes down to Mom and Dad's for homemade ice cream. We worked on plans for the picnic on the Fourth. We're taking potato salad and shish kabobs. Daddy says for you to bring your lucky horseshoes." She closed the women's magazine she'd been reading and rose from the kitchen table as he sat down in his chair. "CJ fell asleep on the bike on the way home. I put him to bed with chocolate ice cream still smeared all over his face." She laughed as she took the plate of baked ziti from the refrigerator and popped it in the microwave. While it hummed and spun, she removed a cereal bowl of salad from the fridge, drizzled a little dressing on it, and carried it to the table.

"Thanks, hon. Hear anything else from that reporter?" Charlie leaned over to remove his steel-toed work boots.

"Nah. It's only been a few days. She said she'd call if she had any more questions."

"So is she coming back with the cameras and everything? Are you going to be on TV?"

The microwave beeped and Jenny pulled out the plate, gingerly removing the plastic wrap, trying to keep from getting burned by the steam. "Who knows? She was a little weird." She carried the plate to him, setting it down on the placemat where she'd left a fork and knife and napkin. "I told you, she didn't really seem to be all that interested in what I had to say."

"Well, I'm interested in what you have to say." He grabbed her hand and pulled her into his lap.

Jenny laughed and pretended to want to get away, but she didn't really want to. It was just in fun. She threw her arms around him and gave him a big smack on the mouth. "Eat." She got up. "Want iced tea or water?"

He slid up to the table. "Water's fine. What smells good in here beside the ziti?"

"Banana nut crunch muffins. I had some squishy bananas." She dropped ice into a glass and walked to the sink. "I hated to see them go to waste."

"I get any of these muffins or are they all for the pregnant girls?"

She eyed him. "Not like you need more muffins, buster."

He patted his stomach and then stuffed a forkful of ziti into his mouth. "Great, honey. But you already knew that. I swear, you've got to be the best cook in town."

She carried the water to him. "I left some muffins in the breadbox. I was thinking I might run the others over to Maria's Place, if you don't mind."

"Now?" He glanced at the clock on the wall that was shaped like an apple. "You sure? You don't want me to run them over in the morning?"

"Nah, I thought it would be nice if they were there for breakfast tomorrow. You have to get up early enough as it is." She drew her hand across his shoulder. "You sure you don't mind? I won't be gone long."

"'Course not." He took another bite. "I'll wait up. You wake me up if I fall asleep on the couch?" He waggled his eyebrows suggestively.

"You bet." She grinned, grabbing the cardboard box covered with plastic wrap sitting on the counter. It was one of those that cases of soda or beer came in and it was perfect for transporting muffins and cupcakes. A nice man at the local liquor store up the block always saved them for her. Jenny took him muffins or cookies in exchange.

"Don't forget your keys," Charlie called as Jenny sailed out the back door.

She stepped back through the door, grabbed her keys and purse off the counter, and headed out again. "Be right back."

Jenny didn't run into anyone at Maria's Place, but the back door was still open and the lights were still on in the kitchen. She left the box of muffins on the counter, without a note, as she often did, and then headed back out into the dark driveway. As she climbed into her mini-van, her flip-flop caught on something and she looked down. When she looked up, someone was standing right next to the open door.

"Oh, hi." Jenny pressed her hand to her pounding heart. "You scared me. I didn't see you."

"I was wondering. Could you give me a ride into town?"

Jenny looked at her. At the house. She thought she saw someone pass by the kitchen window. "Sure. I . . . I guess so," she said, a little surprised by the request.

It was so easy that *The Daughter* almost laughed out loud. Jenny Grove never saw her coming until it was too late. Even when *The Daughter* startled her, even when Jenny seemed to know it was odd to be asking for a ride into town at this time of night, the woman never suspected a thing.

The Daughter chatted with Jenny all the way into town. Asked her about her kids. About her husband. *The Daughter* complimented her on her baking. Asked about her vacation plans now that school was out and she wouldn't be teaching preschool again until September. The young woman was so gullible. So . . . *nice*. It would be hard for many people to believe she was a monster. A fact *The Daughter* knew to be a fact.

"I'm sorry. Where did you say I was taking you?" Jenny asked as they entered the city limits and slowed down to the posted twenty-five miles per hour.

The Daughter named a garage off Main Street that she knew had an unlit parking lot. It would make the whole process more efficient. Even though *The Daughter* already had a complete explanation of why she needed a ride to the garage, Jenny was polite, she didn't even ask.

The Daughter had contemplated several ways to subdue the woman who made cupcakes, taught preschool, and pretended to be a good person, but in the end, she just went with simplicity.

"Could you wait a sec?" *The Daughter* asked, climbing out of the minivan. "It's so dark out here."

"Sure." Jenny put the minivan in neutral.

Getting out of the vehicle, *The Daughter* pretended to

trip. "Oh," she cried, dropping her bag as she went down on both knees.

"Oh, gosh. Are you okay?" Jenny jumped out of her door and ran around the front of the van, through the headlights, and into the shadows of the passenger's side.

The Daughter moved her hands under the edge of the van, pretending to look for something. "My keys. How clumsy of me."

"Here, let me help you." Jenny dropped to her bare knees. She was wearing shorts and a T-shirt.

The Daughter lifted the heavy flashlight she'd pulled out of her bag and gripped it tightly. As Jenny leaned over, *The Daughter* struck her as hard as she could on the back of the neck. Jenny dropped to the dirty pavement. *The Daughter* had been ready to hit her again, but it apparently wasn't going to be necessary. Jenny lay perfectly still, face down, unconscious. *The Daughter* had read on the Internet where to hit a person and it worked!

The Daughter reached for her open bag, found the pill bottle using the flashlight, and removed one capsule. She rolled Jenny onto her back, and Jenny's mouth opened slightly. *The Daughter* pulled open the capsule, dumped the powder into Jenny's mouth, and clamped it shut. It was stronger than the dose she'd slipped into Rob's beer. This would give *The Daughter* the time she needed. By the time Jenny started to come around from the blow to the head, the GHB would be absorbed into her bloodstream. *The Daughter* knelt, pulled the colored handkerchiefs from her bag, and tied a yellow one around Jenny's mouth to gag her. Then she rolled her roughly onto her stomach again, yanked her hands behind her back, and tied her wrists together with a lime green one.

The bandanas worked perfectly. And to think, they had been two for one at the dollar store.

"I was just about to call you." Johnson met Delilah at the rear door the officers used as an exit and entrance into the station.

"I'm not late." Actually, she probably was late. She'd overslept, then roused Callie to try to get her to come to work with her, maybe walk up and down Main Street and submit some job applications. Callie had not been open to the suggestion and they'd ended up arguing over the teen's habit of staying up so late.

"If you're not fifteen minutes early for your shift," Johnson said drolly, "you're late, in my book."

Delilah strode down the hall. "What can I do for you, Sergeant?"

"Got an MIA mom this morning. I thought you'd want to talk to the husband."

"An MIA?" she asked, not really expecting an answer. Johnson talked like that, sometimes, as if he was still in the military's Special Forces. "Another missing person? You have got to be kidding me."

He followed her down the hall. "Woman's only been missing a few hours, but the husband's beside himself. Apparently she ran out on an errand last night. He fell asleep on the couch, didn't wake up until he heard the baby crying this morning."

"Who is it?" Delilah's mind was going a mile a minute. Rob's disappearance hadn't been solved. But there couldn't be a connection. A college kid. A wife and mother. She fought the fear that crept in her blood. "The husband in the interview room?"

Sergeant Johnson nodded. "Name's Jenny Grove.

Twenty-eight years old. Two kids, part-time preschool teacher."

Jenny Grove. Delilah vaguely recognized the name, but she didn't know from where. She couldn't put a face with it.

Johnson pushed a file into her hand. "Husband's name is Charles, but he goes by Charlie. Holler if you need something."

Delilah strode into the interview room, fighting that feeling of déjà vu. Less than a month ago, she had met Mr. and Mrs. Crane here. A second missing person in Stephen Kill in one month. The words kept echoing in her head. *How was that possible?* God, she prayed the woman ran off with the butcher.

"Mr. Grove." Delilah entered the room, extending her hand. "I'm Detective Swift."

A man stood up from the chair at the table and offered his hand. He was wearing a wrinkled khaki workman's uniform: pants, a short-sleeve button-up shirt with placket pockets. His embroidered name tag said A-1 Heating & Air and below it, Charlie, in red script. "Nice to meet you, ma'am. I've seen you. On TV, I mean. In the papers. Those murders last year." He half smiled, almost shyly, as if he thought he was in the presence of a celebrity or something.

"Please. Have a seat." She indicated the chair he'd just risen from. She took the one across from him and opened the file. It was a missing person's form. Completely blank. She'd get address, phone number, so forth in a few minutes. "I understand your wife didn't come home last night? Jenny, is it?"

"No. Yes. I mean. Yes, it's Jenny. Jennifer Lynn Grove. She was there when I got home late after work. But then she went out and didn't come back."

"So you saw her last night when you arrived home from work?"

He nodded. "She was waiting up like she always does. Kids were already in bed. She said she was just going to run some cupcakes or something . . ." He shook his head, looking down at his hands that were clean with neatly trimmed nails. "No, it was banana nut muffins. I smelled them in the kitchen."

"She took them somewhere last night, after you got home?"

"She does that, sometimes. To Maria's. You know, where those nuns keep the pregnant girls. She likes to bake and she drops the stuff off after I get home from work so she doesn't have to haul the kids out. You know, car seat, booster seat. They can be a handful."

"What time was that?" she asked.

"Ten thirty-five." He rubbed his eyes with his fingers. He was an average-looking man. Five-ten, maybe. Stocky build. Brown hair that was a little shaggy. "I looked at the clock," he said. "I offered to run them over in the morning, but she wanted to do it herself. Said she wanted the girls to have the muffins this morning."

She noted the time. Making a banana muffin run at ten thirty at night after the kids were in bed seemed a little odd to her. Was this a case of a woman giving her man a line, making up some excuse to get out of the house at night? He said she did it regularly. Maybe she had a boyfriend. This angle was looking good, and Delilah felt her shoulders relax a little. "Anyone see her leave. To take the cupcakes?"

"They were muffins," he said. "Definitely muffins. I don't know. Our neighborhood is pretty quiet. I . . . I woke up this morning on the couch. I fell asleep waiting for her, I guess, and I didn't wake up until the baby started crying."

"And that was when you realized you hadn't seen your wife all night?"

He nodded.

"And you checked the house?"

"I checked the house. Then the carport. The van was still gone. She took it last night. We just have the van and my service truck. I called her mom, but she hadn't seen her. Then I called Maria's Place and I talked to the Sister. She said the muffins were there. Right on the counter where Jenny left them." He clasped his hands and then unclasped there. "Where do you think she could be, Detective? I thought about calling the hospital. Seeing if there was an accident. But she had her purse. Her driver's license was in her wallet. Someone would have called me, right? If she had been in an accident and was hurt and couldn't call me herself?"

Delilah was making notes. The husband seemed genuinely concerned, but emotion wasn't that hard to fake. "You said the Sister saw your wife last night?"

"No. I guess no one saw her, but the muffins were there this morning. She does that. Just slips in, leaves stuff on the counter."

"And this was Sister Julie you spoke to?"

He shook his head. "Sister Agatha. I called at twenty-five after seven. I knew that was early, but I couldn't figure out where Jenny was. I didn't know who else to call after I talked to her mom."

"And then what did you do?" Delilah glanced at the clock. It was ten after nine.

"I . . . I got the baby up. And our daughter. I called my mother-in-law again and she came over to stay with the kids."

"And what time was that?"

"Eight, I guess."

"And you came to the police station, what? Nine?"

He glanced at the clock. "A little before that."

"What did you do between eight and nine, Mr. Grove?"

"I—" He looked at her. "Why are you asking me that? You think I—you think I have something to do with this?" He pressed his hands to the table, the veins rising as he tensed.

"I'm just trying to get a time line, Mr. Grove. I'm required to follow certain procedures. Right now, mostly I can only ask questions because she's an adult missing less than seventy-two hours."

"You can't look for her for seventy-two hours?" he demanded.

Delilah reached across the table, stopping short of touching him. "I didn't say that, Mr. Grove. What I'm saying is that I have to establish a time line. I have to know what her normal habits were. How you got along. If she's done this before."

He slumped back in the chair. "I don't understand why we have to do all this. I'm telling you, something's wrong." He ran his fingers through his hair. "Something's happened to my Jenny."

Half an hour later, Delilah was at her desk making phone calls. She spoke with Jenny's mom who was still at Jenny's house. Then she called her own home to speak to Callie. There was no answer; she'd probably gone back to sleep. Then she called Maria's Place. Sister Agatha wasn't available to speak, but Monica said she would return her call as soon as the Sister was out of her meeting. Delilah tried her house again. Still no answer. Then she decided to run out to Maria's Place and personally speak to Sister Agatha. On her way out the door, she asked Johnson to send out a message over the radio to be on the lookout for the Grove's light blue 2002 Dodge Caravan.

Sister Agatha was still in her meeting when Delilah arrived. The girls were all having an art lesson on the back deck, Monica explained. With school out for the summer, regular classes had been suspended, but the Sisters thought it was important to keep the girls busy. Delilah was welcome to wait in the Sisters' office, or wander around as she pleased. Monica offered coffee, then excused herself when Delilah declined.

Standing in the family room, watching the girls through the French doors as they listened to the local high school art teacher, Delilah used her cell phone to dial home again. It was almost eleven. As it rang, she turned to see Mattie McConnell slowly making his way across the room with a broom. "Hey, Mattie," she called.

He didn't look up.

"Good day for sweeping, Mattie," she said, still listening as her own voice came on the line. The answering machine.

He glanced at her. Nodded. She felt badly that he was uneasy around her. Though nearly a year had passed since the murders the previous summer, he had been a suspect and actually been arrested as a result of her investigation. She didn't know how much he understood about what had happened or even if he knew it was his mother who had killed those people.

"Callie. It's Aunt Delilah," she said into the phone when her answering machine beeped. "Would you call me on my cell?" She hung up, watching Mattie push a broom, head down, eyes locked on the hardwood floor.

Delilah turned at the sound of footsteps and a male voice. It was Paul Trubant coming down the short hallway that led to the offices in the new addition.

"Detective." He smiled broadly, offering his hand. He was good looking; dressed nicely in khakis, a well-fitting polo shirt the color of eggplant and deck shoes without socks. His smile was infectious.

"Paul," she said.

He held her hand just an instant longer than he should have. But he had been that way since she met him last fall. She guessed most psychologists were. He was a little too touchy-feely for her taste, but seemed like a nice guy. Had a nice family, and she understood from Sister Julie that he was doing great work with the girls here.

"The Sisters should be out in a second." He hooked a thumb in the direction of the offices. "Just reviewing our cases."

Delilah nodded, glancing in the direction of two female voices in an obviously heated conversation. She couldn't make out what they were saying. "Ah, hey," Paul said, obviously sharing her awkwardness. "Sister Julie mentioned—I hope you don't mind—that you have a niece staying with you. She said she'd been in a little trouble and you were considering getting her some counseling." He pulled a leather business cardholder from his back pocket and removed a card, offering it. "I'd be happy to see her. You know, for an evaluation. The initial consult would be free. I could talk to her, just see if maybe there's something I can do for you guys. For her."

Delilah looked down at the card in her hand. "Well, she's not exactly keen on the idea."

He laughed. "Who is?" He slid the cardholder back into his pocket. "But honestly, a lot can be done with counseling at this age, at this juncture in young people's lives. Before the issues get too serious. Think about it." He pointed. Winked.

She half smiled. "I will. Thanks," she called after him as he crossed the family room.

A door opened down the hall and Delilah moved away from the glass doors when she saw Sister Agatha appear.

"Sorry to keep you waiting, Detective Swift." The nun, dressed in her habit, which was certainly not that severe, appeared severe all the same compared with Sister Julie, bringing up the rear, in khaki capris and a turquoise T-shirt and Keds sneakers.

"Good morning, Detective," Julie sang, passing by. "Iced tea, Sister?" Whatever disagreement had passed between her and Sister Agatha, she didn't seem to be carrying any resentment.

"No, thank you."

"Detective?"

"No. Thanks."

"Get the detective a banana muffin, Sister," Agatha called after her. "She probably hasn't eaten this morning." She looked her up and down. "She probably doesn't eat most mornings."

Delilah smiled, not sure what to say. "I hope you don't mind if I stopped by. The muffins were actually what I wanted to ask you about. I understand that Jenny Grove brought them by last night?" She removed her note pad and a pen from her jacket pocket.

Sister Agatha hustled to a table and began to straighten a pile of magazines. "She did. Ten forty-five, perhaps eleven." She turned a stack of magazines on end, tapping them on the table to line them up.

"You saw her?"

"No, Detective. I heard her. I was saying my prayers. Mrs. Grove comes and goes, leaving little packages on our counter at least once a week." Her voice sounded taut. "Is there a problem, Detective?"

Delilah wasn't sure how much to say. "We're not sure," she answered. "About the deliveries. You said she brings baked goods by a couple of times a week?"

"Sister Julie insists we leave the kitchen door unlocked between six A.M. and eleven P.M. Volunteers are free to come and go as they please during those hours." Sister Agatha slapped the magazines down and reached for another pile.

"And . . . is that a problem, Sister Agatha?"

"Certainly not." She looked up. "Should it be?"

The nun was younger than most people realized, probably only a couple of years older than Delilah. And pretty, almost. At least around the eyes. "I'm just trying to pinpoint Mrs. Grove's whereabouts last night."

"Has something happened?" The nun's brow drew taut across her forehead.

"No. I don't think so." Delilah glanced in the direction of the teenage girls on the deck. One was passing out sheets of white paper. Another, pencils from a box. She looked back at the nun. "At least, we hope not."

Sister Agatha crossed herself and whispered something.

"You said you were saying your prayers when you heard Jenny Grove come into the kitchen with the muffins."

"That's correct. My room is over the kitchen. I hear everything, Detective."

"But you didn't see her, so you're not sure she was the one who delivered them."

"Well, no, I didn't see her, but who else could have brought them?"

Delilah made a notation. "You said the doors are locked at eleven. Did you lock the doors last night?"

"It was my turn. After prayers, I came down, got a glass of water, locked the doors and turned out the lights."

"And what time was that?"

"No later than ten fifty-five," Sister Agatha responded. "We wake at five A.M., Sister Julie and I. To prepare for our day before the girls rise."

"And did Sister Julie see . . . or hear Jenny drop the muffins off last night?"

Sister Agatha scooped a handful of paperclips off the table into her hand. "I believe you'd have to ask Sister Julie that."

"Ask Sister Julie what?" The nun appeared almost as if on cue.

"Jenny Grove. The muffins. Delivered last night. Did you see or hear her?" Sister Agatha questioned, dumping the paperclips into an old white vitamin bottle that was labeled *paperclips* in permanent marker.

Sister Julie held up two muffins wrapped in a paper towel. "No, sorry. I went to bed early. I must have been dead to the world." She looked from the nun to Delilah. "Why? Is something wrong? Is Jenny okay?"

Delilah tucked her pen and notepad into her pocket. "Her husband's reported her missing," she said quietly. "She hasn't been seen since last night when Mr. Grove says she left her house to bring the muffins here."

"Oh, my," Sister Julie murmured. "You don't think he did anything to her, do you?"

"Why would you say that? Do you know something about their relationship I should know?"

"No. Certainly not. Jenny has mentioned several times

what a wonderful man her husband is. How understanding." She pushed the muffins into Delilah's hand. "Eat, Detective. It sounds like you're going to have a long day."

Delilah didn't really want the muffins. In fact, the smell made her a little queasy. Maybe it was just the fact that a young mother of two had now been missing over twelve hours that was upsetting her stomach. "Thank you," she said. "And thank you, Sister Agatha. I'll let myself out."

"I hope you find her safe and sound," Sister Julie called after Delilah.

"We'll pray," Sister Agatha said. "The girls. All of us. We'll pray for her safe return."

Delilah wasn't off the front porch steps when her phone rang. Muffins in one hand, she answered her cell with the other, hoping Callie had finally dragged herself out of bed. It was the station, according to the caller ID, though.

"Johnson here."

"Yes, sir."

"Tried you on the radio."

"Talking to the nuns, sir."

"They found the minivan. Parked behind The Pit."

"A bar?" Delilah asked, halting on the newly laid brick sidewalk.

"No sign of forced entry. It was unlocked. Purse and cell phone inside. Keys in the ignition."

Just like Rob Crane's vehicle, Delilah thought.

Chapter 14

At a little after two P.M. Delilah walked into the cubicle that served as her office in the station's bullpen to find Callie sitting in her chair, typing on the computer keyboard. "What are you doing here?" she asked the teen. "I've been calling you for hours."

Delilah reached into her desk drawer and pulled out a pack of saltine crackers the diner provided with their take-out soups. Her stomach was queasy again. She hadn't been able to eat the banana nut muffins Sister Julie had given her this morning. It had just seemed too weird, considering the circumstances.

Delilah glanced at the display of sneakers on her computer's monitor. "And get off the Internet. You can't shop on a computer at a police station. We're not authorized for that kind of Internet access."

Callie's fingers flew across the keyboard. She looked cute today. Short shorts, tank top, red hair braided, with a ball cap pulled down low over her eyes.

"How did you get here?" Delilah asked, stuffing a cracker into her mouth.

"I walked."

"Callie, that's three miles."

The teen shrugged. The tops of her shoulders were pink from the sun. "You said I needed to get off my butt and get some exercise. You also said you wanted me to check out jobs on Main Street. I thought you'd be glad to see me."

"Get out of my chair." Now Delilah was dizzy. Close to puking. She'd gone to The Pit and seen the abandoned minivan. She'd helped collect evidence. There was no sign of Jenny Grove anywhere. No one had heard from her. Gone. Vanished. Just like Rob Crane.

Callie got up.

Delilah shrugged off her jacket and slipped into her chair.

"You okay, Aunt Delilah?" Callie grabbed the last cracker in the cellophane package. "You're looking kinda green."

Delilah closed her eyes for a minute. "I'm fine. I just . . . a woman disappeared last night. A woman who should not have disappeared." Delilah's closest guess, so far, was that Jenny had dropped off the muffins, bet on hubby falling asleep on the couch the way he did every night, and headed for the bar. They couldn't find anyone who had seen her at The Pit, but that would take several nights of questioning patrons. And who was to say she went inside at all? What if she'd met someone in the parking lot?

"You think she drowned like that boy?"

"Rob Crane didn't drown, Callie. Someone threw his body in the pond after he was dead."

"Wow," Callie breathed. She looked down at Delilah. "So is it okay? If I walk up and down Main Street and see if anyone's looking for help?"

Delilah eyed her. "Why are you being so cooperative all of sudden? I thought you didn't want a job."

Callie frowned. "Internet's down at your place. I called the cable company. They said it would be up again in a couple of hours. Can I get some money to stop at the diner? I talked to Izzy this morning on the Internet before it went on the fritz. She said she and some girls were going for sodas later. Fridays they go shopping, go to the library and boring stuff like that."

Delilah spun around in her office chair so that she was facing Callie. She was feeling a little better with the crackers in her stomach. "They invited you to join them?"

"Please. It's not a big deal." Callie put out her hand.

Delilah reached into the pocket of her jacket and pulled out a couple of dollars. "I saw that psychologist I was talking to you about. I'm going to make an appointment for us to go in."

Callie dropped her hand to her hip. "*Us?*"

"Well, you. I thought maybe you could just go once. See how it goes?"

"I'm going to miss Izzy, Aunt Delilah." Callie thrust out her hand again.

Delilah slapped the bills into her palm. "Two hours and you're in this chair, and not shoe shopping on the Internet."

"What am I supposed to do here? Stare at the walls?"

"You could try reading a book. You get them at that library place."

Callie rolled her eyes and flounced off.

"You be here in two hours," Delilah warned, "or I'm coming after you. In a squad car. Bubble lights flashing and siren blaring," she hollered after her.

As Delilah crumpled the empty wrapper package and dropped it in the trashcan, Snowden leaned over one of the half walls of her cubicle. "Sounds like you're getting the hang of this teen parenting thing."

"Yeah. I'm doing great. Bribery and threats."

He came around the side, entering her office. "Worked with me when I was her age."

She would have smiled, but she was too tired. She didn't know what was wrong with her. She could barely keep her eyes open and she'd gotten plenty of sleep last night.

"Tell me where we are with the Grove case," Snowden said.

She groaned, leaning back in her chair. "We're nowhere. We've got nothing. An abandoned van with the purse and keys still in it and no sign of the woman. I swear, Chief, it's like déjà vu, like the Rob Crane case all over again, except that the two have no connection whatsoever that I see, so far, other than that they both lived in this town and walked upright."

"Nothing in the vehicle?"

"Like a note? Blood?" She shook her head, opening her drawer to look for more crackers. "We dusted for fingerprints, but the minivan was covered with them. And mostly kids' prints. My guess is that she wasn't abducted from that car."

"You said earlier on the phone that no one saw her drop off the muffins at Maria's," Snowden thought aloud. "Do we know, for a fact, that she was the one who did drop them off?"

"You mean did the husband do it to cover his tracks?" she asked, following his line of thought. "No evidence of foul play, at least not so far. It appears to me as if she walked off, just like the kid." Finding no crackers, she pushed the drawer shut. "Of course, if I was going to murder my spouse, I'd make it look like he left me."

He raised a dark eyebrow.

"That cheating husband of my sister's? Had he been my man, he'd have found himself in the bottom of a swamp with alligators nipping on his toes and a trail of evidence leading out of state a mile long."

He stared at her, seeming surprised.

"What?" she asked, suddenly defensive. "I don't like cheaters."

He smiled out of the corner of his mouth. "Any suggestion she *was* cheating? Or he was?"

"Not so far. He seems genuinely torn up about her being missing. Parents seem nice. Supportive. I talked to the three of them together and separately. Nothing seemed to be out of place. They're all scared to death."

Both were quiet for a moment, lost in their own thoughts.

"So what's your next move, Detective?"

She looked up at him. She could feel the strain between them, like a small electrical undercurrent crackling just beneath the surface of the conversation. It wasn't just having Callie around and not being able to have sex. It was about their secret. About having to pretend all the time. It was beginning to get to both of them. She could see it on his face, feel it in the pit of her stomach.

"Well, officially she's not a missing person yet, so there's not a whole lot we can do. Check area hospitals. Talk to neighbors. Friends. See if there's something about Jenny Grove that her family doesn't know about." She met his gaze, fighting the feeling she had that this wasn't going to turn out any better than the Rob Crane case. "Or something about her husband Jenny didn't know."

* * *

Jenny woke to find herself curled up in a ball on her side, her cheek pressed into the dirt. When she opened her eyes, she was in complete darkness. "Is anyone there?" she croaked, trying to pick up her head.

But a wave of nausea washed over her and she rested her head on the ground again. She vaguely remembered retching. Throwing up. She was thirsty.

She didn't know where she was. How she had gotten here.

Where *here* was.

Terror coursed through her as she tried to make her brain work. *Think.*

She remembered the smell of the banana muffins in the van. The lights of the kitchen at Maria's Place. Then she drove home . . . didn't she?

Her head throbbed. Bits and pieces of memories pulsed in her mind like the flash on a camera going off. Charlie at the kitchen table. CJ asleep in his crib, mouth smudged with chocolate ice cream. She was out of trash bags . . . Riding in the dark in the van. Going home. No . . . not home.

Jenny remembered getting out of the van in the dark. Dropped keys on the pavement. Then her head exploding in pain.

Oh, God . . . She'd been abducted. Like one of those women she'd seen on Oprah. The ones who were raped. Tortured. A sob rose in her throat. *Charlie . . . her babies . . .*

Jenny knew she had to get up. Had to try to find her way out, but she was scared. What if he was there? The man who had abducted her . . . What if he was listening? Waiting for her to wake up.

And she was so sick to her stomach that she didn't know if she could even sit up right now.

Please God, she murmured silently, pulling into a

tighter ball, the ground rough under her cheek. *Please help me.*

"I can't," Paul whispered into the phone. "It's Saturday night. My kids," he said lamely. He was going to have to end this. He knew it. It was just so hard. And she was such a nice person. A little mixed-up, maybe. But a good person.

"But I need to see you," she murmured. She sounded different than usual. She wasn't making demands or threatening with ultimatums. She seemed . . . sad. "Please, Paul. I wouldn't ask if I didn't need you."

He glanced in the direction of the kitchen as he leaned over to pick up a Cookie Monster stuffed animal. It squeaked when he squeezed it. Susan was cleaning up after dinner. He could hear her loading the dishwasher. He had offered to help get the house organized. Get the kids to pick up their toys, throw a load of clothes in the washer. He and Susan had talked about going for a walk together as a family, maybe into town to get ice cream. Or, Susan had suggested, they could make their own ice cream with the hand crank ice cream maker they had found in the garage earlier, when cleaning it out.

"Please, Paul," she whispered in his ear.

"Is . . . is everything okay?" He retrieved several plastic building blocks from under the edge of the couch. "Are you all right?"

"I wouldn't call you on a Saturday night if I was all right, would I?"

He glanced in the direction of the kitchen again, his resolve wavering. She had never called needing him like this before.

"Paul?"

"I . . . I have to run out to the grocery store. I can meet you there," he said, not trusting himself to agree to meet her at the office. Not on a weekend. Weekends were family time. It was strictly off limits. He knew he had a problem . . . a sexual addiction . . . but he'd always been able to keep it under control. He kept it that way with rules, the same way he taught his clients. And one of the rules was never on weekends.

"Only to talk." He headed down the hall to get his keys. "And just for a minute."

"Around back," she said. "There's employee parking."

"Kitten—"

"So no one sees us," she said, her voice filled with concern. "We have to be careful, Paul."

He hung up, grabbed his keys, and walked back through the house, into the kitchen. Pauly toddled behind him. "Hey, hon, I'm going to run out and get that cream and sugar to make the ice cream," he said to Susan as he headed for the back door.

Susan looked up from pouring dish detergent into the washer. "Oh . . . okay. I hadn't realized we'd decided."

"The kids will think it's fun. Making ice cream the way we did when we were kids." He brushed his lips across her cheek as he passed her. "I'll get a bag of ice, too. Anything else?"

When he stopped at the back door, his son caught the cuff of his khaki shorts. "No, no, sweetie. You stay here with Mommy." When he unclasped his son's hand, the toddler burst into tears.

"You don't want to take him with you?" Susan scooped Pauly into her arms. "Car seat's still in your car."

"Be faster without him." He wrinkled his nose. "I think I'm smelling a stinky butt, anyway."

Susan lifted the little boy into the air, poking her nose in the direction of his shorts. "I don't smell anything."

"Be right back," Paul sang, closing the storm door behind him.

He drove to the grocery store and followed the fire lane around back. He pulled into a parking space in his Audi and just as he started to open the door, the passenger door swung open.

"Kitten," he said, startled. He didn't know where she'd come from or where she'd parked.

She slid in beside him. "Thanks so much for coming."

He looked around. There was no one in the parking lot. It was dusk and the shadows from the rear of the brick building fell over the car. "What's up?" he asked. "I really can only stay a minute."

"I just needed to see you," she breathed, climbing over the parking brake.

Before Paul could stop her, she had straddled him, pulling up her skirt, seating herself on his lap.

He caught a flash of white panty between her bare thighs and his pulse quickened.

She pressed warm kisses to the crook of his neck. "You missed me, didn't you? I knew you were missing me."

"Kitten, please." Paul halfheartedly tried to push her away. Trying not to think of the glimpse of panty he had caught. How it must be damp by now . . .

It was a weekend. He told himself. *She was off limits.*

She pulled up his polo shirt, running her hands over his chest.

"Kitten—"

But she wasn't listening to him. She wouldn't.

She lowered her head to take his nipple between her teeth and bite down just hard enough to send a shock . . . a ripple of pleasure through him.

She ground her hips against his, taking his mouth with hers, forcing open his lips, thrusting her tongue. Hungry for him. Needing him. Almost in a frenzy now, she yanked her shirt over her head, throwing it onto the seat beside them, thrusting her breasts into his face.

She grabbed his hands, guiding them over her breasts. "Squeeze them," she insisted in his ear.

He squeezed.

"Harder," she insisted, moving rhythmically on his lap, massaging his hard-on with her crotch.

She threw her head back and he caught one nipple between his lips and sucked hard.

They were right there in the parking lot. Anyone could have seen them. It was wrong. A weekend. Paul knew he was out of control.

He greedily took her other nipple. Bit down.

She squealed. Pain. Desire. It all mingled.

She leaned forward, her hair falling around her face. She yanked at his belt buckle, popping the button, easing down his zipper. With the aid of her hands, he sprang out of his wrinkled boxers. Hard. Pulsing.

Her hands were so warm. So capable.

Paul groaned, closing his eyes, feeling as if he was going to explode.

She lifted up, pulling her panties aside. He could smell her, hot and wet for him. He was surrounded by the scent of her. The heat of her. The car was hot now. Cloistering.

She sank into his lap again. Onto him.

He reached around her, gripping the steering wheel, trying to hold back.

"Say it," she demanded, nipping at his earlobe, his chin. Rocking back and forth, taking him deeper. "Say it. Say you wanted me. You've wanted me all day."

When he didn't answer, she halted her movement. Paul moaned.

"Say it," she ordered.

"I . . ."

She lifted upward.

"Wanted you . . ." he moaned.

She sank down again.

"W . . . wanted you all day."

She slid upward and then down again.

"Wanted you—"

"When you were with your wife," she whispered in his ear.

"When I was with my wife."

She rewarded him by reaching down, back, behind her, squeezing his balls.

Paul grunted out. She slammed into his lap, once, twice. The third time he exploded inside her. She grasped handfuls of his shirt. Screamed.

His eyes flew open as he looked out the windows. No one was there. Thank God.

She grabbed her shirt off the seat, pulled it over her head and climbed out of the car on the driver's side. Leaving the door open, him exposed to the warm summer air, she strode in front of the car, dragging her hand along the hood. "Better hurry up, Paul. Susan's waiting for those groceries."

Delilah stood in the aisle of the drugstore and stared at the shelf. It was Saturday night and Jenny Grove had now been missing four days. So far, like the Crane case at this point, they had nothing. There had been no word from her and no additional evidence found. Delilah was still working on interviewing neighbors, friends, co-workers, but with the Fourth of July long weekend, she still had several people to talk to on Monday when folks got back in town.

Nothing, just like with Rob Crane. The words kept bouncing around in her head. Delilah kept telling herself that Rob's disappearance and subsequent death had nothing to do with Jenny Grove's disappearance. It couldn't. They didn't know each other. Had no mutual acquaintances. He had never babysat for her. She had never taught his Sunday school class. There was no connection.

But what if there was?

Miserably, Delilah drew her attention back to the shelf in front of her. Cops weren't supposed to have personal lives at times like these. Delilah knew that. But cops' lives didn't know that. Jenny Grove wasn't the only thing missing right now.

She put out her hand, making herself clasp the white box tastefully decorated in pale yellow and green. She wouldn't dare touch the brand in the pink and blue box.

"Aunt Delilah?" Callie came around the corner, swinging a red shopping basket on her arm.

She startled Delilah so badly that Delilah almost dropped the box.

"Could I get some lip gloss?" Callie asked, reaching for a stick of deodorant. "I gave mine to Izzy."

Delilah set the box back on the shelf as if she'd accidentally picked up the wrong one. She grabbed a box of tampons. *Nothing like the power of positive thinking.* "That's fine. Get whatever you want. Need anything here?" She gestured to the feminine products as she walked away. "Meet me at the front counter."

Delilah's heart was pounding so hard that she had to pause in the next aisle to get her breath. She was hot and dizzy, despite the air-conditioning blasting in the new

store in the shopping center off Route One. She'd purposely stopped here tonight after seeing the movie with
Callie so that she wouldn't run into anyone she knew.
She'd hoped Callie would just stay in the truck as she
usually did. No such luck tonight.

Delilah would have to run back over to Rehoboth another day this week. Of course she didn't know what day
she could do that. Monday she had interviews for the
Grove case and Callie had her first appointment with
Paul Trubant. She probably couldn't slip away until
Tuesday. By Tuesday, surely her period would have
started.

She couldn't be pregnant.

She closed her eyes, standing in the middle of the
paper goods aisle, feeling weak in the knees. *Please God,*
she prayed silently. *Don't let me be pregnant. Not again.*

Chapter 15

"I can't believe you're making me do this," Callie groaned, slumped in the waiting room chair. "I can't believe you're making me do this at *nine o'clock in the morning.*"

Delilah flipped a page in a health magazine, not really reading, just pretending to. She'd hardly slept all weekend. No one had heard from or seen Jenny Grove. The only good thing that had happened was that one of Jenny's colleagues, another teacher at the preschool, was back in town and Delilah was meeting her at noon in the classroom they shared.

A door opened and Delilah and Callie both looked up. Paul Trubant had stuck his head around the corner. "Muriel, could you send in my next victim."

Callie groaned and slumped further back in her chair. The receptionist smiled and leaned over the counter that served as her desk and work space. "You can go ahead in now, Callie. Don't pay any attention to him. His jokes are always that bad."

Delilah tried to smile, setting down the magazine and rising. When she'd talked to Rosemary about Callie seeing a therapist, her sister hadn't seemed to care one way or the other. Delilah hoped she wasn't making a mistake, forcing Callie into this. She gestured for Callie to get up. The teen dragged herself to her feet. "You want me to come in?" Delilah asked.

Trubant looked at Callie, then at Delilah. "Nah, we'll call you if we need you. I just thought Callie and I would get acquainted today. Nothing too hard core."

"Go on," Delilah whispered under breath, giving Callie a little push.

Callie took her time crossing the nicely decorated teal and brown waiting room.

"Don't worry. She'll be fine," Trubant assured Delilah as Callie passed through the doorway into his office. "Give us half an hour, maybe. That'll be plenty for today." Delilah nodded, easing back in the cushy chair. He seemed nice. Easy going. She hoped Callie would like him. Trust him. Maybe open up to him a little. She reached for the magazine again, glancing at the clock on the wall and then flipping open to a page outlining the new guidelines for healthy eating.

Trubant closed the door behind him and turned to Callie. "Have a seat wherever you like. Table or one of those chairs." He pointed toward an area sort of set up like a small living room.

"What? You don't have one of those couches I'm supposed to lay down on?" she asked, letting him know with her tone of voice that she was in no way here voluntarily.

He laughed.

Callie plopped down on the edge of one of the denim chairs. He sat on the end of the matching couch, a coffee table thing between them. "You want a Diet Coke?" he asked, picking up a can off the table.

She shook her head. "Saccharin kills lab rats."

"Which is why they don't make most diet sodas with

saccharin anymore." He lifted the can as if toast her and took a drink.

Callie watched him. Izzy didn't like him, which immediately made him suspect. Like some of the girls at Maria's Place said, he was sorta cute in an old guy *kinda* way, but she could definitely tell that he thought so, too. Just like Izzy said.

"So," he said.

"So," she repeated.

"You can call me, Paul, or Dr. Trubant, whatever you're most comfortable with." He sat back, crossing one leg, propping his ankle on his knee. He was wearing boat shoes without any socks. "Okay if I call you Callie?"

Okay if I call you butthead, she thought. She shrugged and looked away. "I guess." On the far side of the room, he had a big desk with lots of photos. Wife. Kids. Him on some kind of sailboat in one picture. Lots of bookshelves. Lots of books. Filing cabinets. On top of one of them was a big, ugly gold trophy with a medallion that announced *World's Best Dad*.

She guessed that was where he kept all his records. There was probably stuff about Izzy in there. If Callie said a word, there'd probably be some kind of report on her in there, too.

"Listen, Callie, I know you don't want to be here. Most of my clients don't want to be here, at least not at first. But why don't we give it a try, see how things go? I really can help you feel better. Maybe get some things straight in your head."

She tried to read some of the titles of the books on the shelves, but she was too far away. She could just spot words like *adolescence* and *teen* and *psychology*.

"Let's start with something easy," he went on when she didn't answer him. "Tell me about your aunt."

She frowned, shifting her gaze to him. "You want to know about Aunt Delilah?"

"You're staying with her, right? Been there a few weeks?"

What was up with this? He knew the deal. "Yeah. My mom and stepdad basically kicked me out of the house."

"And your aunt offered to let you stay with her?"

Callie was again surprised by his question. She had thought that from there, they would certainly launch into why her mother had kicked her out. Why she was smoking weed. Why she was friends with people she didn't really like; who didn't really like her.

She looked right at him. That usually made adults uncomfortable. They usually looked away. He didn't.

"She didn't exactly offer to let me stay," Callie told him, still staring. "I don't even think she knew I was coming until after my mom made me get on the plane."

"But it's okay?" he asked, running his hand over the arm of the couch, straightening the little square piece of matching cloth that kept you from actually getting the couch dirty. "Staying with your aunt?"

"It's okay. Better than being home right now, I guess." She looked at the little table next to the chair she sat in. There was a box of Kleenex—for when she *opened up* to him and started bawling, no doubt. *Like that was going to happen.* There were also some cute little *Bendables* guys in a can that had been decorated with colored yarn. Probably made by one of his juvenile delinquents he called clients.

"You get along?"

She picked up a *Bendables,* one with jeans and yellow hair painted on. She moved his arms straight out. "I guess."

"You guys talk much?"

Callie pulled the *Bendables'* legs out so he looked like

he was doing a jumping jack. "Sometimes. She's pretty busy, being a cop and all. She's working that case, you know. The missing teacher. When I first got here, she was looking for that college guy they found in that pond. She saw his dead body and everything."

He reached for his soda can again. "Does your aunt do things other than work?"

Callie studied the doll in her hand for a minute thinking it kind of looked like Trubant. Blond hair. Goofy look on its face. She stuck it head first into the can and took another one. "What do you mean? Like does she throw pots on a potter's wheel, run marathons?" She smiled to herself, having no idea where that came from, but thinking it was pretty funny for off the top of her head. She had never thought of herself as being funny before but Izzy said she was. Maybe Izzy was right.

"Do you guys go out and do things like ride bikes, see movies? Does she invite friends over? Go out on dates?"

He threw that last question in so casually that most girls would have let it go right over their heads, but not Callie. Callie was smart and she was good with people. She understood people a lot like her Aunt Delilah did. That was something no one knew about her.

Trubant liked her Aunt Delilah. *Liked her* as in *wanted to screw her.* She could hear it in his voice. She could see it in the way he relaxed his face, pretending it wasn't true.

So Izzy had been right. He was a horny bastard. *World's Best Dad? Yeah, right.* Callie smiled to herself and made the *Bendables* in her hand twist backward like it was going to do a somersault. Callie had been able to do backward somersaults when she was kid. She'd taken gymnastics classes and been pretty good. Then she'd had to stop the classes when her mom married *Loser #2* and popped out her baby brother. Then there was no money for gymnastics classes for Callie. No time to take her. No interest in going to her exhibitions.

"I haven't seen my aunt go out with anyone. She sticks pretty close to home when she's not working. You know, that whole guilt thing about leaving me home alone all the time when she's supposed to be helping me get straightened out." Callie was careful not to look up at him. Afraid she might laugh. "But I think she does have a boyfriend, but it's a secret."

"And what makes you say that?"

He was definitely interested.

Callie made the brown-haired dollette do a somersault on the arm of the denim chair. "She gets phone calls," she said, pretending to really be into the toy. "You know, the kind where she goes to the other end of the house or even on the back porch so I can't hear what she's saying. It's gotta be a guy." She thought about telling him the guy was an undercover FBI agent or something, but decided that might be a little over the top.

"Could be work related," Trubant commented.

"Nah, it's a guy," Callie said, knowing full well she was taunting him.

"That bother you?" He leaned forward. "Your aunt having secrets, Callie?"

"What do I care?" she asked, starting to get bored with the game. She threw the *Bendables* back into the cup, looking up at Trubant. "So are you going to ask me about getting busted for the weed, or is that for next session and the next eighty bucks?"

"You sure you're going to be okay?" Delilah pulled up to the curb in her police cruiser to let Callie out on

Main Street. Barbara Finch, the owner of the card and gift shop, had agreed to let Callie come in and try out working as a salesclerk, just in the middle of the day, during her busy time. It had been Callie's idea that Delilah drop her off at the diner to get a late breakfast after the session with Trubant, and then Callie would walk down to Barb's Cards for her three-hour shift.

The teen had agreed to meet Delilah at the station later when Delilah would take a late lunch and run her home. It was actually a pretty good plan, which was what worried Delilah. Was Callie up to something? She was being awfully agreeable this morning, especially after being forced to attend the counseling session.

"I'll be fine. *Sheesh,*" Callie moaned, getting out of the car, tugging her flowered cotton purse after her.

"You better not be meeting Craig Dunn," Delilah warned, leaning over so she could see Callie's face.

"*Pul-lease,*" Callie scoffed. "Izzy says he's a loser. He like hits his little sister and stuff."

"Just the diner, the card store, and then the station, okay, Callie? I'm really stressed out. I don't have the time or the fortitude to chase you down today."

"Go to work. Catch some bad guys," Callie said as she closed the door.

Delilah waited until the teen walked through the diner door before she pulled away from the curb and headed for St. Paul's. She was quite sure her sister wouldn't approve of giving Callie a second chance at the diner like this, but Rosemary wasn't here, was she? By putting Callie on that plane, hadn't she effectively given up her parental control for a few weeks? Hadn't she wanted Delilah to be the one to make the decisions?

At the church that housed the preschool where Jenny had worked, Delilah pulled up to the brick wall of the old churchyard, cut the engine, and sat for a second. Her thoughts were flying in a hundred directions; Callie's appointment this morning, Snowden not calling all weekend, Jenny Grove's husband's teary gaze when she had told him they had no leads, the still unsolved death of Rob Crane.

And then there was the little issue of the fact that her period was now a week late. Stress could do that to you. She'd read it in some women's health magazine or something. But stress didn't do it to *her*. There was only one thing that did it to *her*.

Delilah checked to be sure she had her notepad and a pen in the pocket of her sage green linen blazer and got out of the car, locking it behind her. She found her way with no problem through the narthex and down the stairs into the basement of the community building. She'd been here last year when investigating the "Sin Murders," then twice since then to give presentations to different citizens' groups that met there. When she knocked on the open door of the third classroom on the left, a cute redhead in her midthirties popped her head out from under a table that was only knee-high.

"Mrs. McGovern?"

"Detective." She backed out from under the lime green wooden table, bumping into and knocking over a yellow chair. "Bunny rabbit cookie cutter. I've been looking for it everywhere." She held up the pink, plastic object. "The church is getting ready to clean the carpets while school's out for the summer, so I wanted to make one last sweep of the room and make sure everything was picked up." She walked around the table and pulled out a chair. "Would you like to sit down?"

Delilah would have preferred to stand rather than sit on one of those little preschooler chairs, but Alicia had already sat down. It was good detective work to make interviewees comfortable. If Alicia McGovern could make herself at home in a chair only eight inches off the ground, Delilah could.

"Thanks so much for seeing me today," Delilah started off. "I know you said you just got back in town after vacation."

"We went to the Outer Banks with my in-laws," Alicia explained, setting the plastic cookie cutter down on the green table. "It was nice, but you know, *still with the in-laws*," she said, her tone suggesting they could be difficult. "I was shocked when we got back into town yesterday morning and heard about Jenny. I still can't believe it. I called her house. I didn't get to talk to her husband, but I talked to her mom and they're all pretty upset, I guess. I guess you would be. Guess we all are." She looked up. "And the police still have no idea where she is?"

Delilah pulled out her notebook. "We're doing everything we can, which is why I wanted to talk to you. We're talking to all her friends, neighbors, family members, co-workers. Sometimes something comes up that can seem insignificant and yet help us find a missing person."

"Do you really think she just left? That was what her mother was telling me. That that's what the police believe."

It was not what anyone at the station thought, but no matter how unlikely, it was an issue that had to be addressed with a family in a missing person's case. It was Delilah's personal belief that if a woman did decide to just walk away from her life, her husband, and her children, she wouldn't leave her purse. She wouldn't leave her keys in the ignition of her unlocked car, either. And she'd have prepared in some way. Packed clothes. Taken money. Left a note. *Something*. But Delilah was trying to keep an open mind. Sometimes people did just walk away, although it was rare that that someone was female, in her twenties, and a mother of young children.

"Do *you* think she would leave town without telling her family?" Delilah asked.

"Leave those kids? Goodness no. Not ever. A person would have to kill Jenny to get between her and ..." Realizing what she'd just said, Alicia's voice trailed off.

"How long have you known Jenny?"

"Four years. That's how long she's been teaching here. She came highly recommended from a preschool in Millsboro."

"And would you say you're good friends, you and Jenny?"

"Well, we don't get together at each other houses very often, if that's what you mean. Or talk on the phone evenings or anything." She met Delilah's gaze. "But I would say we're good friends. When my mother got cancer and died last year"—she fiddled with the cookie cutter—"Jenny was so kind to me. She was so good about covering for me when my mom was in the hospital, then with the funeral and everything."

"So would you say you were close enough to confide in each other?"

Alicia didn't answer at once. "Yeah," she said finally. She looked up. "I guess we did confide in each other."

"Can you think of anything Jenny might have said to you recently that might be able to help us find her?" Delilah kept eye-contact with Alicia. "Did she drink? Do drugs? Have a gambling addiction? Maybe a troubled marriage? Did she get unusual phone calls? I know school has been over almost a month, but did anyone ever come by here to see her that shouldn't have been here?"

"No. No. None of that." Alicia shook her head. "Jenny

was a good person. A caring person." She stood the cookie cutter up on end in front of her. "I can't believe something like this could happen to her."

"Do you think something *has* happened to her?" Delilah pressed.

"Well, what else could it be?" Alicia's eyes clouded with tears. "I'm telling you, she would *never* have left her children."

Another dead-end, Delilah thought, trying not to be disappointed. She closed her notebook. "I won't take up any more of your time, Mrs. McGovern." She took the long trip upward from the minichair. "I do ask that if you think of anything that might be of consequence, any little thing that could help us find Jenny, that you call me." She set one of her business cards on the tabletop. "You have a nice day, Mrs. McGovern."

Delilah had almost reached the door when she heard Alicia McGovern speak.

"Detective," she said softly, her voice full of emotion.

Delilah turned back.

Alicia's tears were spilling from her eyes. "There is one thing I thought of. It . . . it was years ago. It probably has nothing at all to do with this, but—" She picked up the cookie cutter again, looking down at it. "Jenny, she had an affair. Like I said, though, it was years ago. It was a time in her life when—" She halted, looking down at her hands in her lap.

Delilah walked back to the table, this time taking one of the little chairs next to Alicia, rather than across from her.

"It's okay. Take your time." Delilah brushed her fingertips across the woman's forearm. "Can I get you something?"

Alicia shook her head. Sniffed. "I'm fine. Really. I just,

I just feel so bad, even mentioning it. She and Charlie have been getting along so well. Ever since they had CJ. Jenny had made herself content. She really did love her husband."

"How long ago was the affair?"

"I . . . I don't really know when it started, but when she and Charlie decided to have another baby, she ended it." Alicia looked up, teary eyed but no longer crying. "That was almost three years ago."

"Did her husband know?"

Alicia shook her head. "No. Most definitely not. Jenny didn't want to hurt Charlie any more than she already had. It . . . it was with a married man. They . . . they were both married. Jenny said a confession to cleanse her own soul wasn't worth the pain she would cause others. I think the guy stayed with his wife, too."

"And do you know who it was?" Delilah asked softly.

"No." Alicia pressed the cookie cutter between the palms of her hands. "Jenny never said and I never asked. She knew it was wrong. I don't even think she really wanted to do it. I think he kind of . . ."—she glanced up—"you know, made a fuss over her. Flattered her. Told her how beautiful she was. How smart she was. She and Charlie had been married long enough that I don't think he was saying those things anymore."

"You said she was the one who ended it."

Alicia nodded. "I think it only lasted a couple months. Two, maybe three. She was a wreck the whole time."

Delilah was trying to think clearly, logically, trying not to be shocked. This apple pie, all-American mom had been cheating on her husband and her husband hadn't known? None of her friends or neighbors or family had known? Did that really happen in small towns like Stephen Kill? She almost laughed aloud, realizing what she was thinking. She and Snowden had been having an affair for almost a year and no one suspected, as far as she knew. Except maybe his mother, and they couldn't be sure with her. As Snowden had said, sometimes she was just a good guesser.

"And did he—the man—take the breakup okay?" Delilah asked, forcing her thoughts away from her own personal problems and back on Jenny's.

"I don't know. I suppose. He didn't really have a choice, I guess. How big a fuss could he make?"

"And you're sure you have no idea who it was?" Delilah asked, giving her time to think. "Or maybe at least where she met him?"

"No. I'm sorry."

"It's okay." Delilah rose from the little chair. "Thank you so much for sharing this with me. I know it had to be hard."

"I promised her I would never tell." Alicia's gaze shined with welling tears again. "She only told me because I kept asking her over and over again what was wrong. I said I would never tell."

"You did the right thing," Delilah assured her.

"Do you think . . ." Alicia studied her hands for a moment and then looked up at her. "Do you think this man could have something to do with Jenny's disappearance? Even after all this time?"

"I don't know," Delilah said, walking toward the door. "But I'm going to find out."

The Daughter sat in the dark on the hard dirt floor, her back against the little door. It was quiet on the other side. Had been since she got there. Last night when she'd come, Jenny had still been whimpering. Too exhausted to call out anymore, but whimpering. Mewing. Kind of like a dying kitten.

The Daughter would have felt sorry for a dying kitten. She did not feel sorry for Jenny Grove.

So now it was done. Over with. Nothing to do but the clean up. Last night, hearing her on the other side of the door had made *The Daughter* feel good. Powerful. Vindicated. But tonight, tonight it was so quiet. The air so cool and still down here that she felt nothing, really. No happiness. No relief. Not even any remorse. Just nothing.

It wasn't supposed to be like that, was it?

The Daughter exhaled, straightening her legs out in front of her. She had a flashlight beside her, but she didn't turn it on. Didn't need it. She was used to the insects, the occasional rodent that scurried by. She was used to the dark. She had grown up in the dark.

She directed her thoughts to something more pleasant. She wondered what Delilah was doing right now. Was she lying in the dark, asleep, or was she awake? Was she staring at the ceiling, wondering where Jenny was? Worrying?

The Daughter didn't want Delilah to worry. It really was a conundrum she'd created here, she had realized over the last few days. She was doing this for Delilah. Championing her, in a way. But *The Daughter's* deeds made life harder for Delilah and that was unfortunate.

The Daughter didn't want Delilah to feel bad.

Maybe she should write her another note. Actually send this one. Anonymous, of course. Just tell her how proud she was of her. How proud all of Stephen Kill was of their own, home-grown heroine, defender of retarded people and dogs.

The Daughter rose in the darkness and slid the ancient iron bolts back, one at the top of the door, one at the bottom and swung it open. Jenny was lying there right in front of her. Now *The Daughter* did pick up the flashlight, but she waited until she was inside the tiny room before she clicked it on. One had to be careful. It was late at night. No one was around, but you could never be too safe. She didn't want any busybody neighbors seeing light, nosing around. Those *Bread Ladies*, they were pretty nosy.

Pushing the door shut with her knee, *The Daughter* moved the beam of light from the toes of her own shoes to the lifeless form at her feet. Jenny had been a pretty girl, but she was ugly now. Ugly in death.

The Daughter set the flashlight on the ground and leaned over to pull off Jenny's sandals, then her shorts, making a pile. As she methodically went about her task, she composed her letter to Delilah in her head.

Dear Delilah, she would start, leaving out any endearments. That was too dangerous. Might seem weird to Delilah, not knowing who it came from. Not knowing how much *The Daughter* loved her.

I am writing this letter to tell you . . . The Daughter thought, pulling off Jenny's panties, *just how proud we are of you here in Stephen Kill.*

And before *The Daughter* knew it, Jenny was ready to go, and the letter was set in her head. Now all she had to do was write it down and mail it.

The mailing part was going to be hard, *The Daughter* knew that. But she had to do it. She had to do it for her Delilah.

Chapter 16

"So what did you find out about Jenny Grove's affair?" Snowden asked from behind his desk.

"Nothing. I found out absolutely nothing." Delilah rubbed the back of her neck, knowing she sounded irritable. Not meaning to be. She was just so darned frustrated. Frustrated with this case. With her sister. With Snowden. With herself, most of all.

Delilah was aggravated that she hadn't been able to make any progress in her investigation. That she was letting the relationship between her and Snowden fizzle out right in front of her eyes. That she wasn't able to be there for Callie, the way she should. Never had been. And what was going on inside her head that made her unable or unwilling to buy an over-the-counter pregnancy test? Did she really think this problem was going to go away?

Delilah forced herself to refocus. Snowden was waiting. "No one knows anything about this affair, except the other teacher, apparently."

"You spoke to the husband?"

She shook her head. "I was hoping I wouldn't have to."

"Detective," he said sharply. "It's been—"

"*A week.* I know that. And with every passing day, it's less likely we'll find her alive. Don't you think I know that, Snowden!"

His gaze darted to the open door. Someone hurried by in the blur of a gray uniform.

She groaned and dropped into the chair in front of his desk. "I'm sorry. I apologize," she said, louder. "That was out of line, Chief. I was hoping I wouldn't have to ask Mr. Grove if he was aware his wife had an affair with a married man."

Snowden watched her over the rim of his reading glasses.

"Guess it has to be done now, though." She rose to go, then turned back. "But what if Mrs. McGovern is mistaken? What if . . . I don't know . . . There's a problem between her and Jenny? What if she made it up to make Jenny look bad?"

"Do you think she made it up?"

Delilah walked out of Snowden's office without answering him.

The red light flashed on Marty's phone. An incoming call. She was tempted to ignore it. Damn, but she wanted a cigarette. She hadn't had one in over three months and she still wanted one as badly as she had the first day she quit.

The call was probably Joe, the station's manager, again. He called at least twice a day. Once, threatening to fire her for her latest infraction: late or missed morning meeting, treating the employees with disrespect. He had a whole litany of complaints. His other call was always to ask her out. Well, to ask if she would screw him.

Dates were tricky with two kids and another on the way. Apparently, pregnant wives could be demanding, and they didn't put out.

Marty didn't like screwing married men. Not ones with pregnant wives, at least. And Joe was a pig. She'd had sex with him a couple of times and it had always been all about him. About getting *his* rocks off. The man couldn't even spell foreplay.

The phone continued to flash. In a second, her voice mail would pick up. No secretary. Not even an assistant.

Maybe she needed to ask Joe for an assistant. Maybe she'd trade him ass for one.

The voice mail didn't pick up. The phone system in the dinky station wasn't working. Again.

She lifted the handset to ear. "Marty Kyle."

"Miss Kyle?"

"Yes?" *What, was this guy some kind of idiot?*

"Hey, this is Patterson Loredo with *News Night*."

Patterson Loredo? Marty sat up in her chair. The senior editor from the news program. The guy she'd sent the interview tape to last week. "Yes, hi, I'm sorry." She laughed. Light. Sexy. "Got a million people talking to me at once. Nice to speak with you Mr. Loredo, what can I do for you?"

"I just got out of a meeting. We had a look at the piece on the school for pregnant girls you sent us, and I have to tell you, we were impressed." He chuckled. *"I* was impressed, Miss Kyle."

"Great. Well, thank you." She tried to sound humble, yet eager at the same time. "Maria's Place really is incredible to see. What the sisters, what *the community*," she added, "is doing for these teenagers is phenomenal."

"We completely agree with you. What we were wondering,

is if you'd be able to expand the interview to a full twelve-minute piece. We'd like to air it."

She slid to the end of her rickety chair, imagining a corner office with windows, a leather executive's chair and cherry desk. Two assistants. "Does that mean I have the job?" she blurted.

He chuckled. "It means we'd like to see some more of your work. Often, Miss Kyle, we find that while reporters from small stations such as your"—he paused and she heard him shuffle papers—"WKKB are able to pull off five-minute news stories, they don't translate well to the longer medium."

She didn't know if she should be flattered or insulted.

"So, are you interested?" Loredo asked on the other end of the line.

It only took Marty an instant to snap out of it . . . snap back into it. "Yes, I am, Mr. Loredo. Should we make arrangements for a personal interview? I'd love to meet you. Meet your staff."

He cleared his throat. "Actually, I think the way *News Night* would like to proceed from here, Miss Kyle, is that we'd like to see the expanded piece. Then we'll talk. Does that sound good to you?"

It didn't sound good to Marty. In fact, the idea sucked. "Perfect," she said into the receiver, smiling because she knew a smile could be conveyed over the phone.

"How about two weeks? Do you think you can manage that? Once we see it, we might be ready to sit down at the bargaining table. We may have an open spot in late August and we've discussed airing the story then, should we think it appropriate."

Marty wanted to argue. She wanted to suggest that if she joined their staff now, she could use their crews to finish the piece. Use their equipment which had to far outshine the crap at WKKB, but she could tell by Loredo's tone of voice that the conversation was over.

She forced the smile again. "I'll get to work and be in touch soon. Thank you, Mr. Loredo. You have a great day."

Marty hung up the phone, rocking back in her chair. *Great*, she thought. *Now I've got to go back and talk to those damned nuns again.*

"Was I aware my wife what?" Charlie Grove demanded hotly.

Delilah glanced in the direction of the family room where Jenny's mother had taken the children *so the nice detective could talk to daddy.* The TV was pretty loud. Cartoons. But not loud enough to muffle Charlie's voice in the cheery apple motif kitchen.

Delilah had known this conversation wasn't going to be easy, but she hadn't known it was going to be this hard. She felt so bad that she wanted to crawl under the kitchen table with the scattered Cheerios that crunched under her shoes.

"I'm sorry, Mr. Grove. I apologize for even having to bring up this subject, but we have to cover all our bases. Your wife's been missing a week and no one has heard from her. I don't need to tell you that the situation is grave."

He rubbed his eyes with the thumb and forefinger of one hand the way men did. "You said she was having an affair?" he asked, much quieter.

The cartoons in the other room got louder. *Dora the Explorer.* Callie sometimes watched it on the Cartoon Network. Delilah could hear the character was saying something in Spanish about a lost duck.

She returned her attention to Charlie. She could hear the emotion in his voice and she had to fight not to allow his pain to seep into her.

"With who?" He sniffed and wiped under his nose with the back of his hand. "God, I thought that was all behind us." He looked up at her. "Who was she with? How do you know?"

Delilah studied his face carefully. "You mean you did know she had had an affair?"

"What are we talking about, here? Just lay it straight out, Detective. What do you know that you're not telling me? Did Jenny run off with some other guy? Did she leave us?" he demanded. "Me and the kids?"

"No. I . . . I don't know, Mr. Grove. I don't think so. It was just that in talking with people, I learned that your wife may have had an affair."

"You mean a while ago?"

"Were you aware your wife was seeing someone else?"

"Not now, she wasn't. Everything was fine. We were fine. That was years ago."

"How many years ago?" Delilah questioned.

"I don't know." He grabbed a dishrag that hung on the kitchen faucet and began to drag it along the clean counter. "Before CJ was born. We were going through a rough patch. But she got counseling. We decided to have another baby and everything was fine." He kept his head down. "I know she wasn't seeing him again. I would have known."

"Mr. Grove," Delilah said gently, "we have no reason to believe your wife was having an affair with anyone when she disappeared. The information I received was about Jenny's past."

He sniffed and looked up. "So she wasn't cheating on me again?"

"Not to our knowledge, and I believe we've done a pretty thorough investigation."

He rubbed under his nose again with the hand that held the dishrag. "I would have known," he repeated, more to himself than to Delilah. *"I would have known."*

"You said your wife had counseling. Was this marriage counseling?"

"Not really. I mean, I would have gone. Jenny said it was about her, not about me or us. It was about old stuff. Things she'd never gotten over, from her past, you know? She said she loved me."

"I'm sure she did, Mr. Grove." Delilah paused before continuing. "Can you tell me who counseled her?"

"Why do you want to know? I don't want old stuff dragged up. Jenny wouldn't want that."

"I'm just trying to reconstruct the last few weeks. Last few months. Perhaps she was seeing her counselor again. It might be helpful to talk to him or her. Not about specifics. That's not allowed, Mr. Grove. But at this point, anything, anyone who's had contact with Jenny in the last few weeks might be able to help us find her."

Delilah felt guilty for using those last words. For offering a glimmer of hope when she knew very well hope was getting dimmer by the hour.

"It was that guy in town with the office in the old insurance place. Dr. Trubant. He was real nice. Nice to both of us. Real supportive about us making our marriage work." Charlie returned the dishrag to its place on the sink. "Is that all you wanted to talk to me about, Detective? 'Cause if it was,"—he hooked his thumb in the direction of the family room—"I *wanna* get back to my kids."

* * *

"This was fun, Callie. Lunch together. We should do this again." And Delilah meant what she said. Although she hadn't been up to eating much after her conversation with Charlie Grove, the last forty-five minutes of talk of lip gloss and *American Idol* had been a needed respite. "I'm glad you could join us, too, Izzy." Delilah glanced at the two teens sitting across from her in the diner booth, then at her wristwatch. "But it looks like I have to get back to work, and so do you, Missy," she directed at Callie. "Can I give you a ride somewhere, Izzy?"

"No thanks, Detective Swift. I'm going to walk down to the library. Meet some of the other girls. There's this reader's book club thing." She shrugged one shoulder. "It's kind of dumb, but it's one of the activities in town we're can always get Sister Agatha to bring us in for."

"I see," Delilah said. "What about Sister Julie? Does she drive you places, too?"

"Well, Sister Agatha likes to keep a tight rein on the van keys." Izzy sucked up the last of the Coke in the bottom of her plastic glass. "And Sister Julie is really busy a lot now. I guess since they added that national hotline, a lot of people want to talk to her. You know, about the program."

Callie slid out of the booth, dragging her bag along with her. "Um . . . I thought I'd go with Izzy, if you don't care, Aunt Delilah. To the, you know, book club thing."

Delilah smiled with surprise. Despite Callie's protests to the contrary, maybe her first counseling session had been worthwhile. The teenager certainly hadn't expressed any desire to do anything so productive as to join a readers' club before.

"Sure, that would be— Wait, what about work?" Delilah interrupted herself. "I thought you said this morning that you had to go back. Isn't Mrs. Finch expecting you?"

Izzy stared over her belly at the linoleum floor.

Callie slung her slouch bag over shoulder, avoiding eye contact with Delilah. "I . . . um . . . I *kinda* quit."

"You *kinda* quit?" Delilah exploded.

Callie cringed, looking around. "Could you not be so loud?"

Delilah snatched up the bill and slid out of booth, marching up to the cash register. "You've had the job two days. Why would you quit after two days?"

Callie crammed a stick of gum into her mouth. "Can we talk about this tonight and like not embarrass me in front of Izzy and the whole town?"

Delilah accepted her change. "Thanks, Nateesha." She waited until she was out on the street to speak again.

Callie just stood there on the sidewalk, shoulders slumped, gazing into space, chomping on her gum.

Delilah was tempted to march the teen down to the station. Make her sit the rest of the day in the break room. Then take her home and chew her out some more.

But what good was that going to do? What problem was that going solve? How was that going to improve communication between the two of them? And it wasn't as if it were normal for members of the Stephen Kill police department to bring errant teens to work with them. Delilah wasn't in a position to be written up right now.

"All right," Delilah said, trying to remain in control of her anger. "You go with Izzy to the library and then you come back to the station. We'll talk about this tonight."

"Sure." Callie was off like a shot down the sidewalk, Izzy hurrying behind her. "Thanks, Aunt Delilah. See you later!"

* * *

Delilah stood beside Snowden on the trampled, grassy bank of Horsey Mill Pond and stared at the nude body of Jenny Grove. She lay face down, arms spread wide, leaves and bits of twigs caught in her long brown hair, floating on the water's surface like a spider's web. Her flesh was wrinkled and pasty, almost entirely devoid of color except for the tiny orange butterfly tattoo on her right buttock.

"When I asked her husband about identifying marks," Delilah said softly, "he never mentioned the tattoo."

"Probably hoping we wouldn't have to know."

Delilah let out a shuddering exhalation and turned to the EMTs who waited patiently at a respectful distance from the crime scene.

"We done with the photos?" Delilah asked Snowden.

"Lopez took plenty."

She nodded to the two men in the navy blue jumpsuits and stepped out of their way. "Come on down, guys. Let's get her out of here."

She and Snowden stood off to the side while the men wearing rubber boots carefully lifted the body, placing it on a stretcher. No one spoke until Jenny Grove's face was covered with a white sheet.

"Not a mark on her body. She hasn't been in here long, but she's been missing nine days," Delilah said under her breath. "What makes me think the ME is going to tell us that Jenny Grove died as a result of dehydration?" Tears filled her eyes as she looked up at Snowden. She made no attempt to hide them or wipe them away. "Two naked bodies of missing persons show up in the same pond in a month's time. We're kidding ourselves if we try to see this as anything other than what it is."

"Yeah," he agreed stoically. "Another serial killer in Stephen Kill."

Chapter 17

"Thank you for coming, Detective," Charlie said as she passed the open coffin where he stood vigil. His eyes were teary, but considering the circumstances, he appeared to be holding up well.

She squeezed the hand he offered her, but said nothing. What was there to say? All the sorries on earth couldn't bring Jenny back. They couldn't change the circumstances of her death.

Delilah released Charlie's hand and moved on. She barely glanced at Jenny's body, no longer nude, lying face down in the stagnant pond as she had last seen her, but now in a bright blue sundress, nestled in a bed of white satin. She always heard that people looked like they were sleeping when they lay in caskets. Delilah had to disagree. Jenny didn't look like she was sleeping. She looked like she was dead.

Delilah took a deep breath, but didn't feel as if she was getting enough oxygen into her lungs.

The funeral home was stifling, the sweet odor of the mountains of flowers nauseating. Delilah walked as quickly away from the white coffin as the line of mourners in front of her would allow. She had come, she had paid her respects, and now she needed to get of here before she threw up or passed out.

She scanned the crowd, looking for Callie, who she had insisted attend with her. Callie had protested, arguing that the entire custom of laying a dead body out to be viewed was barbaric. Callie fumed that didn't even know the woman. What Delilah hadn't said was that she needed Callie tonight. Needed her to be here with her.

The teen had begrudgingly agreed to go, if there would be dinner out afterward. Bribery, once again, had been Delilah's parenting tactic.

Delilah wiped her brow with the heel of her hand. She was sweating in her dress uniform. Her armpits were itchy and sticky in the starched polyester. She tugged at the narrow black tie at her neck that felt like a noose. *Why didn't someone turn up the blasted air conditioning,* she wondered as she scanned the crowd.

The whole town had shown up for Jenny's viewing: the congregation at St. Paul's, the parents of her preschool class, friends, relatives, all the people who had known her as a volunteer through Maria's Place. Outside the small, family-owned funeral home, there had been news cameras and reporters. Delilah had spotted Marty Kyle, dressed in a white linen suit of all things, interviewing teary-eyed mourners before they entered the building.

Maria's Place. *Of course.* Delilah's mind flitted from one thought to the next. *The girls were all here. That's where Callie probably was, with the girls.*

Delilah moved from one room to another, rooms usually partitioned off with wooden folding doors, but which had been opened to accommodate the large crowd. She spotted a nun's black wimple beyond a knot of middle-aged, chubby women in tight flowered dresses.

"Detective Swift." Cora Watkins, one of the notorious *Bread Ladies*, grasped Delilah's arm and held her fast, stopping her forward momentum through the crowd.

"What a tragic day for Stephen Kill," the woman in her late fifties or early sixties declared tearfully. "My sister Clara and I were just saying how much this reminded us of the funerals last summer. Those poor souls. Murdered so hideously."

Delilah nodded, gazing back into the throng of men and women dressed in their Sunday best, milling, talking in hushed tones. She'd lost sight of the nun's wimple.

"Whoever killed Jenny killed that nice young man, too? Didn't he?" Cora asked, lowering her voice. "Come, Detective, you can tell us. We knew Jenny well, Clara and I. We were neighbors."

Jenny's neighborhood was at least a mile from where the sisters lived in a residential area in the old part of town. Cora and Clara Watkins had not been listed on the pages of names provided by Charlie Grove as friends or acquaintances. "You know I can't discuss an open case, Miss Watkins," Delilah said, feeding her the party line as she tried gingerly to extricate her arm from the woman's iron grip.

"She was dead before he put her in the water, just like that nice boy. We already know all about it, Clara and I." She and her sister nodded in unison.

With Rob's death, the police department had kept that detail from the press for some time, but eventually it had leaked out. The ME's initial report on Jenny had only come in that morning. It had been Snowden's decision to allow Delilah to reveal at the noon press conference that Jenny had died of renal failure due to dehydration and her body disposed of postmortem. He hoped, he had told her, that those details might lead to someone coming forward with information. Surely someone had seen something suspicious in the week Jenny had been missing. Missing, but alive.

The thought of her alive, held somewhere against her will, made Delilah's stomach flip-flop.

Like Rob, according to the ME, Jenny had been alive for at least five days before she died. She had died of kidney failure due to lack of hydration. Her body had been in the water approximately two days. As with Rob, there were trace amounts of GHB in her bloodstream. But Jenny had not been a teenager, and it was highly unlikely a mother on her way home from delivering cupcakes had experimented with illegal drugs. The most logical deduction was that someone had kidnapped Jenny, held her against her will, and allowed her to die of thirst. Like Rob, she had not been sexually assaulted.

Bile rose in Delilah's throat and she pulled her arm ungracefully from Miss Watkins's grip. "You'll have to excuse me, ladies," she murmured.

By the time she reached the far end of the room where the girls from Maria's Place were gathered, Callie standing in the midst of them, Delilah was feeling light-headed. She hadn't eaten all day. No wonder she felt awful.

"Callie," she said.

"Aunt Delilah. Izzy wants to know if I can go have pizza with them."

Callie was so exuberant that Delilah brought her finger to her lips to shush her.

Monica, who stood among them, hid a smile with a tissue balled in her hand.

"Aw. Sorry." Callie lowered her voice. "Is it okay? Can I go with them? They're going to Grand Slam. We were going to play air hockey while we waited for the pizza and stuff."

The thought of having to go back out to get Callie later was more than Delilah could bear. All she wanted to do right now was go home, get into her PJs and eat a bowl of ice cream. "I don't know, Callie," she said softly.

"Please, Aunt Delilah." The redheaded teen clasped her hands, bouncing up and down on her toes.

"I've had a long day. I really just want to go home and—"

"Please, please. You said I need to get out more. Make friends. I found friends." She gestured to the knot of girls in various stages of pregnancy.

Had it not been for the circumstances of the day, Delilah might also have had to hide a smile.

"You look tired, Detective," Monica intervened. "I was going to join them and then go home. Callie could ride over in the van with the Sisters and the girls, if you'd like. I don't mind bringing her home afterward if that would help."

Several of the teenage girls looked at Delilah expectantly.

She caved. What harm was there in Callie having some pizza with some girls her own age? So what if they were all pregnant and ousted from their homes? From what she could gather, these teens were still a better influence than those Callie had considered her friends back home.

"Okay, go have pizza." Delilah raised her hands and let them fall. "But you'll have to run out to the truck and get my purse. I didn't bring money in with me."

"My treat," Monica offered.

"You really don't have to do that."

"Sister Julie!" Izzy bubbled as the nun joined the group. "Detective Swift says Callie can come with us for pizza. Monica's going to take her home. It's all set. That's okay, right?"

"That's fine, dear." Sister Julie turned to Delilah. "We won't keep her out late." She reached out to touch Delilah's arm. "You look as if you could use a break, Detective. I know these last few days have been hard on you."

Delilah met Sister Julie's gaze and was so struck by the compassion she saw in her brown eyes that a lump rose in her throat. *What was wrong with her?* Afraid she might start to cry, she just gave a nod to Sister Julie and walked away, pressing a kiss to Callie's cheek as she passed.

For once, Callie didn't push her away.

"See you later. Be good."

Delilah was almost out the door, almost free of the heat and the oppressive bodies when she heard Snowden call to her.

"Detective."

She waited for him. "I was on my way out." She felt perspiration trickle from her temples down along her jawline. The scent of calla lilies was so strong in her nostrils that she had to fight not to gag.

"Me, too. I'll walk out with you," he said in his captain's voice.

Half-way down the brick steps, Delilah swayed. He caught her elbow.

"You okay?" he whispered.

"I will be, if I can just get out of here," she answered from between clenched teeth.

"Where's your niece?"

"Going out for pizza with the Sisters and the girls. Monica Dryden's going to bring her home later."

They walked down the sidewalk, past Marty Kyle and her news van. "Detective Swift, if you could—"

Delilah held out one hand to the reporter. "Not tonight, Miss Kyle."

"Chief Calloway—" She thrust the mike in his direction.

"You've had the department's statement for the day, Miss Kyle. Have a good evening." Snowden hurried down the sidewalk, placing gentle pressure between Delilah's shoulder blades.

In the dimly lit parking lot, he took Delilah's keys from her hand and opened her truck.

"It was just so darned hot in there," she muttered, yanking the knot of her tie down, sliding into the driver's seat.

Snowden leaned in, one hand on the steering wheel. He smelled so good. So safe. If she was the kind of woman who would swoon, he'd be the man to make her do it.

"You sure you're okay?"

She pressed her lips together and reached for a half empty water bottle on the seat. "A little light-headed is all. The smell of the flowers, they get to me."

"When was the last time you ate?"

She looked at him, taking a sip. "Snowden, are you serious? Can you really eat yet, after seeing her floating in that pond like that? Seeing both of them?" She closed her eyes for a moment, swallowing another gulp of water. "I don't know if I'll ever be able to eat again."

"You have to eat," he said firmly. He glanced over his shoulder. People were entering the parking lot. He stood up. "You all right to drive home?"

"Fine." She grabbed the door and slammed it shut, nearly catching the tails of his dress uniform coat.

Two blocks from the funeral home, Delilah looked up in her rearview mirror to see the police cruiser still following her. She didn't know if she should be annoyed or grateful.

She pulled into her cul-de-sac and parked in front of her town house. Snowden pulled in behind her. On the front porch, as she slid her house key into the lock, she looked back at him. "You shouldn't be here," she said tiredly.

"I want to make sure you're okay. That you get something to eat."

"I'm fine," she insisted.

He followed her into the house and flipped on the entry hall light. Closed the door behind them. Locked it.

She looked at the door knob.

"Get out of your uniform," he told her, striding past her, down the hall toward the kitchen.

She was too tired, too overwhelmed, to argue. In her bedroom, she changed into a T-shirt and an old pair of boxers that had once belonged to one of her brothers. If Snowden was expecting sexy lingerie, he wasn't getting it tonight. In her bathroom, she splashed her face with cold water and brushed her teeth. Even after she rinsed her mouth with mouthwash, she could still taste sour bile in her throat. The taste of death.

Walking back down the hall, Delilah smelled a familiar, sweet starchy scent. "Waffles?" she asked, pleasantly surprised.

Snowden, having shed his uniform jacket and left it hanging neatly over the one of the antique dining room chairs at the table, stood at the counter. Apparently he intended to stay a few minutes.

He opened the door of her toaster oven and removed four waffles, previously in a box in the freezer. "I actually can cook, but all I could find in the fridge was some yogurt, one egg, and three bottles of Gatorade. Your freezer and cupboards aren't any better." He pushed a plate into her hands and poured syrup on the waffles. No butter. He knew how she liked them.

Knew how she liked a lot of things . . .

She smiled to herself, thinking obviously she was feeling better.

He grabbed his own plate. "Table or couch?"

She groaned and rolled her head, trying to relieve the stiffness in her neck. "Couch. Definitely."

He handed her his plate. "There's OJ. I'll bring you some. Go eat while they're semiwarm."

She had barely enough time to settle on the couch and tuck her bare feet beneath her when Snowden walked into the living room, carrying two glasses of orange juice. He set them down on the old steamer trunk she used as a coffee table. "This all you're going to eat?" she asked, handing him his plate. "Two measly waffles?"

"I said we needed to eat. I didn't say I felt like eating."

Half smiling, half grimacing, she cut off a piece of waffle with her fork and pushed it into her mouth. Surprisingly, it tasted pretty good.

They ate in silence, but it was a comfortable silence. In a way, it felt weird to be alone with him here in the house. It had been weeks. More than a month since they had been here together alone. But it also felt good. It felt right.

Licking his fork of the last drip of syrup, Snowden set aside his plate and reached for one of the glasses of juice. "Better?" he asked.

She nodded. She hadn't been able to finish the second waffle, but it definitely felt good to have something in her stomach. "That was pretty awful," she said, setting her dirty plate on top of his. "I don't know why it bothered me so much, seeing her in the coffin. You know, after seeing her in the water, but it did."

He sipped his juice and set it down. "At the scene, you had to be a cop. You can't expect to be one twenty-four–seven."

Thinking on that, she sipped her juice. "Now that we've got the ME's report, I'm not even sure where to start. My mind is racing in a hundred directions, but mostly I come back to thinking I can't believe this is happening again. Then I start wondering if we got it right last summer? Are we sure Alice killed those people?"

"We're sure. We have her diaries. There's no indication that these two deaths had anything to do with Alice Crupp's death. Alice was stabbed in the struggle with Noah Gibson. The ME's report stated clearly that she drowned. She drowned, Delilah. Jenny and Rob didn't drown."

"I know." She squeezed her eyes shut. "I know. I know, I know. It's just a coincidence that Jenny and Rob ended up in the same pond Alice ended up in, right?"

"Right," he answered gently. "Alice drowned of her own accord. No one dies of dehydration of their own accord."

"Or dumps their own body into a pond, naked, after they're dead."

They were quiet again. She glanced toward the closed blinds over the window. "You should go. Someone might see your car.

"Considering the circumstances of the week, I think for once, people's minds won't be in the gutter." He slid his hand across the couch, taking hers. "Last night I was at Lopez's for three hours."

"House calls, Chief?"

"He just needed someone to talk to. Seeing bodies like

that, it affects us all. Just in different ways." He squeezed her hand.

"You know, Snowden, you're entirely too understanding for a man in your position. You really need to be more Neanderthal-like." She rubbed his hand with hers, marveling at the differences in their skin tones.

"I'll work on that." He lifted her hand to his mouth and pressed a kiss to her knuckles.

Tears welled up in Delilah's eyes unexpectedly and she crawled across the couch, her arms out to him.

He drew her into his embrace. "Shhhh," he breathed, kissing the top of her head.

She leaned into him, his freshly starched shirt rough against her cheek. "I feel so inadequate. I'm not up to this job. I can't do this. I can't help these people," she cried against his chest.

"Shhhh," he soothed. "Of course you can. You're being too hard on yourself. I wouldn't give you this assignment if I didn't think you could do it. If I didn't think you were the best *man* or *woman* in the department to do it."

She opened her eyes to look into his. The palest, most mysterious, warmest blue eyes she had ever known. "You mean that, don't you?"

"Am I just saying it to get into your boxers?" he whispered, brushing his lips across her forehead. "No. I wouldn't do that, Delilah. You know I wouldn't." He kissed her again. "Although, I have to admit I could use a little peek inside those boxers right now."

She lifted her chin, drawing his head down to her mouth, her lips wet with her tears. She was laughing and crying at the same time. Her fingers found the white buttons of his crisp uniform shirt, then the dark, short curly hair on his bare chest.

Snowden covered her mouth with his and they kissed greedily. She welcomed the thrust of his tongue, as they shared the taste of orange juice and maple syrup.

He shrugged off his shirt.

She grasped the bottom of her T-shirt and pulled it over her head, flinging it. Callie wouldn't be home for at least another hour. The pizza place would be packed on a July night. There was no need for them to hurry, yet they both seemed to feel an urgency she didn't understand.

Snowden pulled the bobby pins that held her blond hair up in a knot and fanned her hair over her shoulders, running his fingers through it until it fell in a curtain around her face. "You have the most beautiful hair I've ever seen on a woman," he whispered in her ear.

She slipped her arms around his neck and leaned back, her breasts aching for his touch. She looked down, watching through half-closed eyelids as his dark hand cupped her small, pale breast. Her nipple grew hard under the pressure of his fingertips and she leaned back further, drawing his head down.

She turned in his lap, resting her head back on the headrest of the couch. His mouth was hot and wet on her nipple and she arched her spine. She ran her hands over the well-defined muscles of his shoulders, pulling him closer, needing to feel his skin against hers.

Teasing one nipple with the tip of his tongue, he drew one hand over her bare inner thigh.

Delilah grabbed the elastic waistband of her boxers and started to pull them off but Snowden pushed her hand away. "Shhh, it's okay," he murmured in her ear. "Let's take our time. Let me make love to you, Delilah."

Tears filled her eyes again and she covered her face

with her hands. "I don't know what's wrong with me," she whispered. "I'm sorry."

"Don't be." He drew her into his arms, holding her against his bare chest. "We don't have to do this right now. Not if you don't want to."

"No. No, I want to." She sat up, throwing her arms around him, clinging to him. "I need to . . . to feel alive, Snowden." She opened her eyes, fearing he would think her foolish.

But there was no judgment in his eyes. Her tears welled again and she touched her lips to his. His kiss was gentle, at first, tender, but as she pressed her bare breasts to his chest, his breath came quicker. He pushed his tongue into her mouth. She moved against him, in his lap, savoring the feel of his hard groin against her buttocks.

She tore her mouth from his, dizzy, panting for breath and pushed away from him, getting to her feet. She hooked her thumb in the waistband of the old boxers and this time he didn't protest. He watched through hooded eyes.

Naked, she bent over and pulled off his shiny shoes and his black dress socks and discarded them. She leaned over to unfasten his belt buckle and her hair fell around her face so that she couldn't see him watching her. He raised his hips, allowing her to pull off his dress pants and boxer briefs. Throwing them aside, she smiled, almost shyly, pressing her hands to his bare knees as she started to kneel.

"Oh, no you don't." He caught her hand and pulled her into his lap again. "We're not in a hurry," he teased. "You have somewhere you need to be?"

She laughed and they kissed again. She moved her hips against him, her heart pounding, pulse racing. He kissed the crook of her neck, her bare shoulder, the tip of her chin, sliding his hand gently in and out between her thighs.

Delilah moaned, moving against his hand.

Time seemed to stop and start again. The living room, the couch, the dead woman and Delilah's failures slipped away until there was nothing and no one but Snowden. She and Snowden, moving, first together with the tide, then against it as the motion intensified. Deepened.

Every nerve in Delilah's body seemed to quicken, all the synapses in her brain firing at once. She was overwhelmed by the taste, the smell, the sensation of him deep inside her.

She resisted the inevitable. She wanted to share this closeness with him just a little longer. But she couldn't hold back. And he, too, was so close.

Delilah threw her arms around his neck and thrust her hips hard against him, crying out before the motion was complete. Snowden's entire body tensed, every muscle seeming to shorten at once. He grunted. Exhaled.

She let out her breath with his. Exhausted. Relieved. And fell forward, dropping her cheek to his broad shoulder, holding him inside her, trying to make the moment last just a while longer.

Snowden kissed her sweaty neck. Said something she didn't quite catch.

She closed her eyes. She knew they should get dressed, just in case Callie ended up coming home early. But she stayed in Snowden's arms, hoping he could hold the world at bay for just another minute.

* * *

Delilah picked up the envelope, looked for a return address, and seeing none, frowned and tossed the white vellum sheet of stationery and envelope onto a pile of papers on her desk. "Fan mail" as the guys in the station liked to call it. She had received a lot of it during and after the *Sin Killer* cases last summer. Letters from every-day people, mostly locals, praising her for her work in the department. Her contribution to keeping Stephen Kill's streets safe. When the story had gone national, she'd even received letters from people living in other states. Along with the thank-yous, she even got a couple of marriage proposals, mostly from mothers looking for "a nice young woman" for their thirty-something—and-still-at home—sons.

But those letters always came to the station. This one had been in Delilah's personal post office box. That was odd. And no return address. But what was really strange was that the letter hadn't been signed. She glanced at it again as she reached for the cup of coffee she'd stopped for on the way to work. She wondered if she should show it to Snowden.

But to what purpose?

She didn't want him to think the letter spooked her, even if it did, a little. After all her crying last night, which embarrassed her this morning in the bright fluorescent light of the office, she didn't know if she was ready to face him.

She'd be better off getting back to work on the Grove and Crane cases. Now that there was no doubt that they were linked, she needed to review every detail in the files and begin cross-referencing them. Initially, she hadn't thought there was any connection between the two, not until they were both victims.

Serial killers didn't kill randomly. That was something

she had learned last summer. Even if she couldn't see the connection between Jenny and Rob, the killer could. And if she was going to catch him, she was going to have figure out what it was. Fast. Because he would strike again. Probably had killed in the past. Was now on a hot streak. Something else she had learned last summer when researching serial killers.

Her mind drifted back to the previous summer. To Alice and her drowning in Horsey Mill Pond. The Crupp drowning had no connection with her present cases. She knew that. It was just a weird feeling.

An investigation had no time for weird feelings. Cops didn't have time for them.

She grabbed the "fan mail" and the envelope and tossed both into the trash can under her desk and flipped open Jenny Grove's file.

"You don't have to drive me to my doctor's appointment." His mother crossed her arms stubbornly over the black purse in her lap. "I can drive myself. I've been driving myself to the doctor my whole life."

"Ma. You've been having dizzy spells. Your blood pressure medicine probably just needs to be adjusted, but you shouldn't be driving if you're dizzy. You wouldn't want to have an accident."

"I feel just fine. I don't know why I agreed to go to the doctor in the first place," she grumbled. "I should be at work. I don't like to miss work."

"You're not missing work, Ma. You have a nine-fifteen appointment with Dr. Carson. You'll just be a little late."

"I don't like showing up late. It shows bad work ethic."

Snowden exhaled through his mouth, trying to rechannel his frustration. He didn't know why his mother was irritating him so much this morning. She wasn't acting any differently than she normally did. She'd grumble about going to the doctor, but she would go. And even though she would go on about his diagnosis and treatment, she'd do as she was instructed.

He just felt out of sorts today. He was worried about the case, of course. A second serial killer in his town only a year after the first. How long would it be before the attorney general's office was looking his way? He'd already had a call from the FBI. A woman out of the Philadelphia Field Office, Special Agent Cahill. She said she had seen a memo go by on her desk suggesting a kidnapping might have taken place in Stephen Kill. She was just offering a hand if he needed it.

So how long before the FBI would be at the station door if they didn't find this guy quickly? Not that he didn't have the greatest confidence in Delilah. He'd meant what he said the previous night about her being the best officer for the job. There was something about her, about her instincts, that made her better at investigating than the average cop. Certainly better than him. He was a paper pusher. He looked good in the uniform. Was a by-the-book man, which was good for a chief of police, but Delilah, there was something special about her.

Something special about her . . .

He thought about the night before, making love on her couch and he unconsciously brushed his hand against his mouth. He could still taste her.

He didn't know what was going on between the two of them, but there was certainly a lot of tension. Tension that had been there before, but had gotten worse since the niece arrived. It wasn't just the logistics. He certainly missed the sex, missed her, but he felt as if she was brushing him aside. Brushing him off emotionally. Distancing herself.

He'd said something the night before that he hadn't meant to say. Spoken in the heat of the moment.

The thing was. She hadn't responded. Hadn't said a word.

This morning, he woke up feeling foolish. Who was he, a half-black illegitimate policeman in a little pissant town to think a white woman like Delilah Swift could ever love him?

Chapter 18

"Rosemary, listen to me." Delilah glanced in the direction of the dark living room, lit only by the glow from the computer monitor. Callie was seated in the office chair, engrossed in her IM messages popping up on the screen. The teen still stayed in contact with some of her friends in Georgia, but she had also added names to her "buddy list," girls from Maria's Place, Delilah suspected.

"I think you and I need to talk about this some more," Delilah said into the phone, walking down the hall toward the bedroom. "Maybe Callie and I should fly down this weekend and the whole family should sit down together."

"There's nothing to talk about," Rosemary responded firmly. "Bruce wants to move back in. He wants to make our marriage work, but he says he can't deal with *her*. Not right now."

Delilah pushed her hair out of her eyes, walking into the bedroom, sitting down on the edge of her unmade bed. It was only eight o'clock, but she could have climbed under the duvet and slept for a week. "Rosemary, this just isn't a good time for me right now. I told you about this case I'm on. I can't be here with Callie like I should be. I'm working overtime every night. I have to bring work home. I'm just thinking that maybe she'd be better off at home."

Delilah heard the rumble of a male voice in the background. Someone was obviously talking to her sister, but she pressed on, feeling more desperate by the moment. She really, *really* didn't know if she could handle this right now. Even without the murder cases . . . "Now that school's out," she said into the phone, "I know Callie could help you with the kids. She really is a terrific—"

"Look, Delilah, it's time for the kids to have their baths. Bruce rented a movie and we want to watch it together. He's been so romantic these last couple of weeks," she whispered into the phone. "It's like we're dating all over again."

"Rosemary, you're not hearing anything I'm saying." Delilah threw herself back on the bed, staring up at the ceiling fan. "I really think—"

"Coming, hon," Rosemary called, her voice muffled and then she spoke into the phone again. "Gotta run, Sis. Thanks bunches." She made a smacking noise as if throwing a kiss. "Talk to you soon."

It took a moment for it to register in Delilah's mind that the click she heard on the phone was Rosemary hanging up on her. She stared at the phone like an idiot and then hit the "off" button.

"She said *no*, didn't she?" Callie said, her voice seeming to come out of nowhere. "I can't go home."

Delilah sat up.

Callie stood in the doorway in a pair of sweatpants rolled down over her hips, braless, in a tank top. They'd both changed into their PJs before making a dinner of

spinach salad together. They actually had fun talking. It
had looked to be a nice evening . . . until Rosemary called.

"Callie, she didn't say—"

"She doesn't want me. You don't want me. Maybe I
should get pregnant, at least then I could move in with
Sister Julie." She crossed her arms over her chest.
"She'd take me in, I guess."

Delilah closed her eyes for a minute. "Come here,"
she said, patting the mattress beside her.

Callie remained in the doorway.

"Come on," Delilah said quietly. "Sit here and talk to
me. I'm not trying to get rid of you."

"It *sounds* like you're trying to get rid of me." Callie
crossed her arms over her chest, but she came toward
the bed.

"The truth is, I kinda like having you here. I'm not so
lonely anymore. But what I'm trying to do," Delilah said
honestly, "is what's best for you, Callie. I do worry that
I'm not here enough for you. That you're alone too
much."

"I don't want to go home if she doesn't want me."
Callie dropped onto the bed beside Delilah. "I mean,
maybe she's right. Maybe I shouldn't be there . . . right
now. Bruce is such an asshole, anyway."

Delilah had to bite back a smile. Bruce *was* an asshole. "Callie—"

"I know. Inappropriate language. I'm sorry." Her thin,
tanned shoulders slumped. "It's just hard to live somewhere where people don't want you. Where they ignore
you unless they're yelling at you." She looked quickly at
Delilah, then looked away. "I mean, maybe you're not
here a lot, but when you are, at least you talk to me."

Delilah stared at the phone she still held in her hand. "I
don't feel as if we're talking about the things we ought to

be talking about, though. I don't feel as if I'm helping you, Callie. And that was the whole point of you coming here."

"Well . . ." Callie seemed to be searching for the right thing to say. "You *are* sending me to that stupid shrink. That's doing something to help me."

Delilah looked at her. "You think it's helping?"

The teen grimaced. "Nah, but at least you're trying." She fiddled with the hem of her shirt. "And it's nice to have someone to talk to when you're here, even if it is about dumb stuff." She looked up again, this time meeting Delilah's gaze. "If it's about me being here alone all the time, maybe I could get a job. Could I stay, then?"

"You've had two jobs, Callie. You quit both."

"So maybe they weren't the right jobs."

Delilah couldn't resist a smile. "You serious? You'll honestly try?"

"If I do"—Callie narrowed her eyes—"do I have to keep seeing that shrink?"

"Yup."

Callie pressed her lips together, thinking. "But you won't put me back on a plane?"

"We have to think about you going home eventually. School starts again in September. But it's only mid-July. You get a job, we'll back off your mom, give her some space, and we'll see how things go."

"Thanks, Aunt Delilah."

Callie gave her a quick peck on the cheek as she bounced off the bed and for the first time since the teen arrived, Delilah felt as if she had done something right.

"Marty, so nice to see you again. I guess congratulations are in order." Julie waved the reporter into the new staff office that was already beginning to pile up.

"I'm going to run into town and do those errands," Monica said, rising from behind her desk, one of three in the room. "Is there anything I can do for you or get you in town, Sister Julie?"

Julie turned to Monica who had grabbed her purse and a satchel of mail and was already on her way out the door. "Just pick up Izzy and her friend, Callie, at the library. I already checked with her aunt and she's going to stay for supper tonight."

"I'll probably stay through supper, too." Monica halted in the doorway, her hand on the doorframe. "Mrs. Santori is making enchiladas. I can run Callie home on my way, if that will help out Detective Swift."

"That's nice. I'll have Callie call and check." Julie gave a wave as she turned her attention to Marty who had taken a seat in a metal folding chair in front of Julie's desk. Leather chairs matching the desk chairs had been donated and ordered from an office supply company, but they hadn't yet arrived. "So, you're expanding the piece," she said, pushing aside a stack of letters Monica had left for her to read through.

The reporter leaned back in the chair, watching Monica as she went down the hall. "I didn't get much of an interview out of her," she said.

"I told you she was shy."

"Even shy people aren't usually shy once they get in front of a camera." Marty shifted her attention to Julie. "What's her story? She wouldn't really give me any background info. Just talked about what a good deed for society people were doing here. How much she loved the girls. So on and so forth." She leaned forward. "And what's with the scar on her arm?" She touched her own slender, tanned forearm. "It looks like a burn or something."

"Marty." Julie pressed her hands to her desk, leaning

toward the reporter. "You know very well that if my staff doesn't want to share personal information, I'm not going to share with you."

Marty exhaled, reaching for her notebook in her leather bag beside the chair. "It's my job to ask these kinds of questions."

"I understand that." Julie continued to smile.

"Okay." Marty looked to her notes. "I just need a little bit more background on how this house came about. Let's see . . . you always wanted to help girls like these. You became a nun, convinced the church of the need, and became the director. You started out with a couple of girls and an old farmhouse. At what point did you begin hiring permanent staff like your mysterious assistant, and creepy penguin woman . . . Sister Agatha." She looked up, her pursed pink lipsticked mouth twitching with amusement at her own joke.

This wasn't the first time Marty had made a derogatory remark about Sister Agatha. Julie knew very well that the nun probably wasn't the kind of person the reporter would like, or even understand, but she sensed hostility in Marty's voice that seemed out of place in a supposedly impartial interview.

"At first, the Archdiocese sent different nuns on a rotating basis to help me out. We hired Monica when our funding and our need increased." Julie sat back in her own chair. "Tell me something, Marty. Didn't you mention once that you attended Catholic school?"

Marty tapped her pen on her knee. "Kindergarten through my senior year of high school."

"Me, too. And were you happy with your education?"

"Hated every minute of it," Marty said coolly. "I always found it odd that women who had chosen not to be mothers, women who obviously hated children, would want to be nuns. Want to teach children."

"Because we chose not to be mothers doesn't mean we hate children. What makes you think that?" Julie sensed not just anger, but pain in the reporter's statement.

"Come, Sister, this interview isn't supposed to be about me, now is it?" Marty chuckled warmly, moving her pen to begin taking notes. "Back to Maria's Place's success. When you first started, how were you able to convince parents to send their daughters to you, sometimes all the way across the country?"

Julie talked to Marty about how they had made their presence known through the Catholic Church and how they had miraculously found girls, just through word of mouth. Julie spoke of God's hand in bringing the girls to her but was careful not to sound too preachy, knowing she would quickly lose her audience. She and Marty went over a couple more topics, made an appointment for another taped interview later in the week, and in less than an hour, the reporter was packing up her fancy leather briefcase.

"Thanks again for taking time from your busy day," Marty said, rising from the chair, unfolding her long, suntanned bare legs. "I know *News Night* will love this longer piece. Once it's released, you'll have more girls wanting to come here than you'll know what to do with."

Julie smiled, finding Marty's implication bittersweet. She wanted to provide a haven for pregnant girls with no place to go, but, at the same time, she wished there was no need for Maria's Place at all. She wished no teen had to find herself pregnant and alone.

"So the piece will be done soon?" Julie rose, but

didn't walk around her desk. She had been a little upset that the reporter had turned the piece over to the news station before letting her see it, and even suspected she might have purposely *overlooked* getting the tape to Julie. But the matter did need to be addressed.

"You had said when we first started this whole process that I'd be able to see it before it was aired," Julie reminded her. "I know you were in a rush to submit it to the news show, but I'd still like to see it. *Before you present your final piece.*"

Marty glanced over her shoulder and the look on her face, though it only lasted an instant, made Julie think the woman had never intended to allow Julie to see it beforehand, if she could help it. Julie waited, deciding she would have to be firm on this matter. So much for her unfounded suspicions . . .

"A week, you think?" Julie asked sweetly.

"Tops. I'll let myself out." The reporter gave a wave.

Julie walked around her desk, wondering what it was that Marty didn't want her to see in the new program or what she thought Julie would think was questionable. Lost in her thoughts, she nearly ran directly into Sister Agatha, who had to have been right outside the door.

"I don't care for her," Sister Agatha said under her breath, turning to watch as Marty cut across the family room, headed for the front door.

"Why, Sister, what makes you say that?"

"I don't trust her," Sister Agatha hissed. "I don't think she should be left alone with the girls. I don't think any of us for that matter"—she looked Julie up and down— "should be alone with her. A darkness hangs over her." She crossed herself. "I can't explain it, Sister. Just a feeling."

"Why, Sister Agatha, if I didn't know better, I would think you were looking out for me."

"We're all God's children, Sister Julie," Sister Agatha said, brushing by her, entering the office. "I pray for both your souls."

"I'm going to drop you off and then go to Maria's," Rachel said, lifting her foot off the gas pedal as she entered the town limits and the speed limit dropped to twenty-five miles an hour. "I'll pick up Mattie, swing by Antonio's for pizza, and pick you back up on the way out of town."

"He's been there all day again today?" Noah asked. "You don't think he's making a pest of himself, do you?"

"I'm sure Sister Julie would say if there was a problem. Last time I talked to her, she said he was doing great. He worked hard and the girls liked him." She looked over at Noah in the passenger's seat of her Volvo station wagon. "Probably take me about an hour. That be long enough for your meeting?"

"That'll be fine. I just hate making you do this." Noah watched out the window, not really looking at anything in particular. Though it was early evening, it was still light out. Hazy from the heat of the day. "Still driving me around after over a year."

"Better than me having to hear about you driving that lawn mower around town like some crazy guy."

He met her gaze and couldn't help grinning. He loved Rachel, he loved her so much that it hurt. And it hurt him, even after all this time, that she was still paying the price for his DUI and the deaths he had caused. But she kept such a good attitude. She was so forgiving that Noah was finding that he could forgive himself. Just seeing her smile always made him smile. "Hey, it's not a lawn mower, it's a lawn *tractor*, and I'll have you know I get around just fine on it," he told her, refusing to allow himself to get maudlin over the fact that he was a forty-two-year-old male without a driver's license.

"Two more months and it will all be over. You'll have completed all your classes, paid your fines, and be driving again."

"God willing," he said.

She reached out to cover his hand with hers. "I'm proud of you, you know. Some people said you wouldn't make it when you got out of prison."

"Said *we* wouldn't make it," he mused aloud.

She pulled up in front of the Moose lodge and braked.

He climbed out of the car and leaned over to kiss her mouth, closing his eyes, letting his lips linger over hers.

"See you in a bit," she told him.

He waited until she had pulled away before walking up the sidewalk and entering the building. He took the stairwell down, thinking to himself what a cliché it was, AA meetings being held in basements.

He entered the room where men and women were still milling around, just beginning to take their seats. Noah headed straight for the coffeepot the way everyone else did, and grabbed a white Styrofoam cup.

"Ah, I see you're going for the decaf, too."

Noah turned to the woman behind him. "Sister. Good to see you. You want one?"

"Please."

"Ladies and gentlemen, if you'll take your seats, we'll go ahead and get started."

Noah passed the nun the cup of coffee, and took his own, looking for a chair in the middle. As he sat down, he let the events of the day fade from his mind and focused on the speaker's words and his own battle to continue to remain sober.

"I'm Paul," the man behind the podium said. "And I'm an alcoholic."

Chapter 19

"I've got a one thirty with a city councilman," Snowden said to Delilah, glancing at his watch. They were standing in the hallway of the station just behind the glass "fishbowl" where the dispatcher and receptionist worked in a secure office with bulletproof glass walls. The visitors' lobby was in plain view from the hall, through the thick glass. "Give me the bullet," he continued. "Where do we stand on the cases?"

"I'm trying to cross-reference friends, family, even people the two victims might have both come in contact with like store clerks, the mail lady, anything," Delilah said, a file of info she had printed off the Internet perched on her hip. "It's crazy because Rob and Jenny had nothing in common, but as soon as you open the gates to who they came in contact with locally, that no longer holds true. They used the same video rental store, bought slushies in the same convenience store, frequented the same grocery store. They came in contact with the same store clerks, city garbage men, you name it."

"Small town," he mused. "Big pool of potential suspects."

"Just as before," she told him. "The other angle I think

we need to look into, although I hate to cause any more pain for the family, is exactly who Mrs. Grove had the affair with."

"There was no sexual assault in either case."

"I know. Neither case appears to be sexually motivated, but why did the killer strip the bodies naked? Is that about sex," she said, thinking aloud, "or is it about stripping them of who they are? I'm thinking I might call Dr. Trubant. See if he could give me any insight." Out of the corner of Delilah's eye, she saw the lobby door open and Callie walk in. The girl waved. Delilah lifted her chin in greeting and then focused her attention back on Snowden. "That okay with you, if I discuss the cases with him?"

"I don't have a problem with it, as long as you keep it professional. Obviously you can't reveal any information the press hasn't already given out."

"Not that there's a lot of info to give."

"You'd be talking to him more about the human mind, in general, rather than these cases?" Snowden continued.

Delilah's gaze drifted from Snowden's face to the lobby again. Callie was hopping up and down, waving her arms to get Delilah's attention. "Exactly," she said. "I think I know what direction I should be going with my profiling, but I was wondering if Dr. Trubant might be able to offer some insight in a direction that I haven't gone yet."

"Go with your instincts, Detective. Just be careful not to reveal any more details than necessary," Snowden continued, unaware of the teenager's antics beyond the glass walls behind him.

Delilah raised a hand at her side, trying to inconspicuously signal Callie to chill out for a minute. Couldn't she see Delilah was talking to her boss?

"Speak in generalities when you can," Snowden said. "I'm sure Dr. Trubant understands the importance of confidentiality in these—" He halted midsentence, turning around to look through the glass.

Callie was now trying to tell Delilah something by speaking with exaggerated mouth movement.

A smile tugged at the corner of Snowden's sensual mouth. "Detective, I believe your niece is attempting to tell you something."

"I know. I saw her." She shifted the file of papers under the other arm. "Sorry, Chief. She can wait." Delilah looked up at him. "Go ahead with what you were saying."

"No. I've got to go anyway. You don't need me on this. You're right on track." He turned away to walk down the hall. "Let me know when you know something. I want to hear it from you before I hear it from that reporter on the evening news."

"Yes, sir." Delilah waited until he was halfway down the hall, then buzzed the door into the lobby and walked out to join Callie. "What are you doing here?" she admonished. "I thought you went to the library. You said you could keep yourself busy for a couple of hours. I told you, hon, I can't have you here every day. This is a police—"

"I got a job," Callie interrupted, grabbing Delilah's free hand. "I got a job!" She hopped up and down in her rhinestone lime green flip-flops.

"You did?" Delilah squeezed her hand before releasing it. "Where? I know you said you were going to check Burton's, but I thought you didn't want to sort nuts and bolts all day."

"Not the hardware store. I went to the library, just like I said I was going." The teen began to bounce again. "I got a job at the library. Miss Calloway hired me."

"You're kidding!" Delilah managed a certain degree of excitement in her voice. *You've got to be kidding*, she thought. *Callie working for Snowden's mother? That had to be a disaster in the making.* "What . . . what are you going to do at the library?"

"I don't know." Her red ponytail swung back and forth. "Whatever she wants me to do. She hired Izzy, too. She can't pay us much, but she said we could check out six books at a time instead of three, and she wants us to read some books for her to tell her if they'd be good to add to her teen shelves. Isn't that cool? The librarian wants to know what *I* think about a book?" Callie bubbled.

"You're right, that is pretty cool. You could have just called me."

"I could if I had a cell phone like I told you I needed." She lifted a thin brow. She'd asked Delilah twice in the last week about adding a cell phone onto Delilah's account. So far, Delilah wasn't going for it. Even if Callie promised to pay her share each month, even if the phone could be used anywhere in the country to call anywhere, she just wasn't sure if Callie was ready for the responsibility.

"Anyway," Callie went on, snapping her hand at her wrist. "I'm not *officially* starting until Monday, but Miss Calloway said I could hang out today; she's going to show me around and maybe I could learn how to put books away. There's a lot to it, you know. If a book's not put away right, people can't find it."

Callie was so excited that Delilah couldn't help but be excited for her, but all she could think of was that the teen would be working with Snowden's mother, who she knew from what he said, could be nosy. Even interfering. How was she going to tell Callie to keep her mouth shut, without telling Callie why?

"So it's okay, right? Miss Calloway says that even though she only wants me to work four hours a day and Izzy can't come until one because she has *religious training* in the mornings,"—she rolled her dark eyes—"I can still come in the mornings when you go to work and just, you know, hang out, and read. I might even get to check people out or something if Miss Calloway is really tied up or something." She gazed eagerly into Delilah's eyes. "So?"

Delilah knew she couldn't say anything but *yes*. The fact that she was secretly dating the librarian's son was her problem, not Callie's. Delilah didn't even know for sure if they were exactly dating anymore. "Of course." Clasping the file, she raised her hands. "Sure. A job at the library? What parent could argue with that?"

"Thanks. I gotta go." Callie spun around and rushed for the door. "I'm off at five but I'll wait for you on the library steps. I told Izzy we could usually take her home so she doesn't have to call for the van." As she pushed open the heavy door, she looked back. "That's okay, too, right?"

"Sure."

Callie grinned. "I knew it would be. Izzy was afraid to ask, but I knew you'd be fine with it. It's not like you really have a life or anything." She gave a wave. "See you later, Aunt Delilah."

Not like I have a life? Delilah said to herself, signaling to the receptionist in the fish bowl to buzz her back into the hall. "I have a life," she muttered under her breath. "Sort of . . ."

"Thank you for seeing me on short notice, Dr. Trubant." Delilah offered him her hand in the doorway of his office.

She had called thinking she could make an appointment for early next week, but his receptionist had put her on hold, then come back on the line to say the doctor had had a cancellation that afternoon and he could see her at four fifteen. The timing was perfect. She could talk to Dr. Trubant, pick up Callie by five; they'd run to the post office and the dry cleaners and eat at a reasonable time tonight. She'd have to take work home, but she and Callie could make dinner together, go for a walk on the beach in the State Park at Cape Henelopen, which the teen seemed to enjoy. Then, when Callie settled down at the computer, Delilah could adjourn to her bedroom where she could spread out the mind-numbing photographs of her victims and try to make sense of the crimes.

"As I think Muriel told you on the phone, I had a reschedule. I'm just glad you called today. Next week is booked solid." Trubant stepped aside. "Come in. Make yourself comfortable. Can I offer you a Diet Coke? Water?"

"No, I'm fine, thanks." She took in the office as he closed the door behind her and ushered her toward his desk.

He had what appeared to be a small dining room table in one corner of the room, as well as a separate seating area with a couch and chairs and a coffee table. He probably saw clients in both places, she imagined. Floor to ceiling bookshelves lined one wall, filled with books and photographs. Mostly textbooks. There were three large black file cabinets flanking another wall. Two additional doors. One probably leading out of the office into the rear parking lot, the other a private restroom, she assumed. His large oak desk was situated in front of three windows, trimmed with stylish drapes and wooden blinds. There was an impressive brown leather executive's chair behind the desk and two smaller matching arm chairs in front of it. The doctor appeared to be doing pretty well for a hometown psychologist.

"Please, sit." He walked around his desk, motioning for her to take one of the two smaller chairs.

As she sat, she scanned the photos on his desk. Three kids. A pretty wife. Several shots of him; one on the teak deck of a decent sized sailboat, another in front of the Eiffel Tower, another near the Coliseum.

One of Callie's complaints after her second session with the psychologist had been that he was conceited. She could see how Callie might think that: the fancy office, his expensive Ralph Lauren polo, the photographs of him on the ritzy sailboat, in France and in Rome. But what did Delilah care how he spent his money and his free time? He came highly recommended by Sister Julie, and after only two weeks Callie's attitude really had seemed to improve. She was talking more. She had found a job on her own initiative.

Delilah shifted her thoughts from personal to professional. "I didn't really want to go into details on the phone with your receptionist," she said, studying his handsome, suntanned face from across the desk. Callie said the girls thought he looked a little like Brad Pitt and she could see the resemblance: shaggy blond hair, craggy good features, winning smile. But he wasn't her type. She liked tall, broad-shouldered men. Men who didn't have their hair cut at a professional salon.

"What I'd like to talk to you about are the homicides that recently took place here in Stephen Kill," she continued, removing her notebook and a pen from the pocket of her navy blue linen jacket. "I have to preface this conversation, of course, with an understanding between us that you won't share any of this information. With anyone."

"Of course." He straightened the family photograph closest to him. "I'm sure I don't have to tell you, Detective, I'm very good at keeping secrets." He smiled, almost flirtatiously. "My clients depend on it."

She glanced at the photograph he was adjusting, not quite sure how to interpret what he had said. Was he suggesting he knew she had secrets? That he, himself, had things to hide? Or had he simply been referring to the people he treated? The picture on his desk had been taken in the sand dunes along the nearby shoreline by a well-known local photographer. Each member of the family was dressed identically, but casually, in khaki shorts and white polos. His wife's name was Susan, Delilah recalled. She'd met the woman briefly at the Maria's Place annual picnic fund-raiser the previous year. An event that was coming up the following weekend; she'd forgotten all about it in all the confusion of her life right now.

She looked across the desk at the psychologist. "I know most of the details of the deaths are public knowledge. What the newspapers and TV haven't covered, our cops, EMTs, and neighbor's dogs have told."

He chuckled.

"But just the same," she went on. "I'd ask that you not share this conversation with anyone else. I'd prefer no one even knew I'd been here."

He leaned back in the leather chair, smiling. "What can I do for you, Detective?"

He really was full of himself.

She didn't smile back. "I'm trying to create a profile of our killer."

"So you do believe it was the same person?"

"There can always be a copy cat killing," she said, "but you rarely see that this early on."

"You mean with a serial killer."

Delilah hated even to use that term, but she nodded. "As you know, both the body of Rob Crane and Jenny Grove were disposed of in the pond, after their deaths. Both naked. None of their clothes have been found. I've been doing some reading, but I was wondering what you, knowing what you do about the human psyche, would make of that."

He put his hands together, tenting them, elbows on the arms of his chair. He brought his index fingers to his lower lip, taking his time to respond. It was such an exaggerated motion that Delilah thought it a little silly. What was he doing, impress her? Wasn't it enough that she had brought Callie to him? That she was asking him for help with the case?

"Well," Trubant started slowly, "the dumping of the body is simple; I'm sure you already know what that is, Detective. It's as if our killer is literally disposing of the persons as if they were nothing. Refuse."

Delilah jotted down his key words. She joined the word *body* with an arrow pointing to the *trash*.

"Now, the naked part, that's interesting." He used his index fingers to point at her, his hands still clasped. "There was no sexual assault, I believe."

"No. No evidence on either body."

"Your killer's not a sexual predator. This is about something else," he said, taking his time. "By removing a victim's clothes, one objectifies the victim. Robs the victim of his or her power. It's analogous to death, a great leveler, if you will, Detective." She jotted down *objectifies the victim.* "Could he also have done it to remove trace evidence?"

"He certainly could have. You know, I was reading an article an FBI agent had written about serial crimes and he was saying that today's criminals are very clever."

A cell phone, probably in his desk drawer, rang. Trubant ignored it, continuing to talk. "These criminals watch TV; shows like *CSI* and those crime-scene docudramas on Discovery Channel and the like. The author said killers are learning how law enforcement tracks them, what they need to do to protect themselves. They're wearing gloves." The phone stopped ringing. "Shaving their body hair. Rapists are using condoms."

She gritted her teeth. Everything he was saying was true. She knew it was true, and that meant that not only was this killer smart, but he was a planner. He wasn't some mental case who was hoping to get caught; he was a vicious killer who meant to get away with murder.

"What about keeping victims hostage? Letting them die of dehydration? If you wanted to kill someone, why wouldn't you just kill them? Why risk getting caught by keeping them alive until they die of complications of thirst?"

Trubant leaned forward, hands on the desk. He wore a heavy gold class ring with a clear stone. She couldn't make out the college name. "It's punishment of some sort. The killer has suffered, at the hands of his victims, or at least he *perceives* that they are responsible for his suffering, so now, he wants them to suffer."

"Where would you keep someone for a week while they died slowly?" she asked, still almost in disbelief, although she knew that was exactly what had happened.

"Think about it logically rather than emotionally. All kinds of places to keep someone, Detective. The trunk of an abandoned car, a freezer in your garage, drilled with air holes. Hell, I've got a great little room in my

basement where we store paint, drain cleaner, other poi-
sons away from our children. It's padlocked. If you
locked me in that dark, windowless room, my neighbors
would never hear me scream, especially if you drugged
me first, then I went a couple days without water."

His words made her shiver. Nothing he had said came
as any surprise. It really wasn't anything she hadn't
thought of before, but just hearing someone say it out
loud made her stomach queasy. She could only imagine
the suffering, the terror Jenny and Rob had endured
before succumbing.

As Delilah looked down at her notebook, the cell
phone in the desk rang again. "Go ahead," she said, not
looking up at him, wanting to give herself another
minute to digest what he had just said.

"My voice mail will pick up," He dismissed it with a
wave.

The phone kept ringing.

"It might be your wife," Delilah offered, trying to
lighten the conversation. "You'll be in trouble if you
don't pick up that milk on the way home."

He opened the center drawer and removed a cell
phone. He glanced at the screen on the front, hesitated,
and then flipped open the phone. "Hey."

Delilah thought she heard a female voice and she
smiled to herself. *And who said she wasn't a good detective?*

She glanced around the room again, trying to give
him a little privacy without either of them actually
having to get up.

"Listen, hon, now's not a great time," he said.

Delilah spotted the bendable doll toys Callie had mentioned. Her eyes settled on the three filing cabinets
again. They were expensive, with locks. He had to have
a pretty good sized clientele list to need room for that

many files. That, or he was hoping that one day he'd have that many.

The woman spoke for a moment and then Trubant said. "How about if I call you right back?" He paused long enough for his wife to say something. "Nope. Be done here in a few minutes and I'll call you right back. Promise."

She said one thing more and he hit the end call button. "Sorry."

"Not a problem. I think we're about done here, anyway. You know, one of things I have to figure out is how these two victims were connected. Did you know either one of them?" The minute she said it, she realized it really wasn't a fair question. She already knew he had counseled Jenny, but she wasn't sure how he felt about volunteering his client list.

"I knew both of them, I'm sad to say." He leaned back in the leather chair, tenting his hands again. "I counseled both of them."

"I see." That one took her by surprise. The Cranes hadn't said anything about Rob attending counseling. "Actually, I think Jenny's husband might have mentioned some counseling a couple of years ago. Had you seen Rob recently?"

"Nah. He was here toward the end of his senior year. Just some teenager issues. Parents, grades, girlfriend. He was a great kid." He shook his head. "Sad. They were both great human beings. Jenny was one of those people with a really kind heart. She was always doing things for others."

Delilah closed up her notebook and stood up. "I know I might be crossing over the line here, but I know Jenny had an affair a few years ago. I don't suppose you could tell me who she had that affair with?" she asked, not terribly optimistic.

He smiled. "I really can't. If I knew, I couldn't. I'm sorry, Detective."

"No, no. It's all right. I understand." She fingered her pen inside her pocket. "Thank you for your help."

"You're certainly welcome. Please, feel free to call me again. I'll do anything in my power to help you find this monster." He stretched his hand over the desk and shook hers.

"Go ahead and call your wife back," she said with a wave as she headed for the door. "I'll let myself out."

Paul waited until he heard the outside waiting room door close before he pulled his cell out of the desk drawer, hit a recall button and it dialed the last number dialed in.

"I really wish you wouldn't do that," he said, keeping his voice down. Muriel never walked in without knocking, but he didn't want to take any chances.

"I only wanted to say *hello,*" she said.

"I'm working, Kitten. I can't talk on the phone when I'm working."

"You can't talk on the phone when you're home, either. When *can* you talk to me, Paul?"

He exhaled, sitting back in his chair, running his hand over his head. "You . . . you told me you weren't looking for a relationship. I thought we were very clear what this was."

"Just fucking," she quipped.

"Just sex." He hated the way she said that word. The way it made him feel. "Just fun. Those were your words. We were just getting together to have fun."

"And are you?" she asked. "Having fun?"

"You . . . you know I am." He glanced in the direction

of the door to the waiting room. He could hear Muriel moving around. Locking the front door. Picking up magazines, straightening the waiting room before she went home for the day. "Of course I'm having fun," he murmured into the phone. "You're a lot of fun, Kitten."

"I don't like how you say that. Are you seeing someone else?" she demanded.

"No, no, of course not. What would make you think that?"

"Because you better not be," she warned. "I don't do that. You might, but I don't, so if you're with me, you don't do it either. Is that clear, Paul?"

"There's no one else, Kitten," he said with a little laugh. And there really wasn't. Not right now. *Not exactly, at least.* He rarely saw Marty any more. She was too busy with her career and this opportunity that had sprung up with the news show in Baltimore. She almost never called him.

There was a knock at his office door. He lowered the cell phone, putting his hand over the mouthpiece.

Muriel popped her head around the door. "Headed out. You need anything?"

"Nope." He gave her a quick smile. "Have a good weekend. Enjoy the game tomorrow. Tell Stewart to hit a home run for me."

"Will do."

Paul waited until she closed the door before he brought the phone to his ear again.

"What are you doing?" she said.

"What am I doing? I told you. I'm at work."

"I mean, what are you *doing*?" Her last word was husky.

Paul felt a rush of heat in his face and in his groin at the same time. *God. What was wrong with him?* Just the sound of her voice gave him a hard on. "I don't know," he whispered into the phone, cradling it with his chin so he could unzip his pants. "What are you doing?"

"Wait a minute," she breathed.

He heard a door close.

"What am I doing?" she said into his ear. "I'm sliding my hand into your pants."

He groaned.

"You want to know what I'm doing now?"

"Yes, Kitten," Paul panted, wishing he was there. Wishing he had his camera. "Tell me what you're doing now . . ."

Chapter 20

"So how was your day, ladies?" Delilah asked the two girls sitting in the back seat of her cruiser. "Been there a whole week and you haven't quit yet, Callie?"

"Very funny," Callie called over the seat. "Today was fun, right, Izzy? We started cleaning out the media storeroom and there's all kinds of cool junk in there. There're these tubes of film that load into this old projector and it puts pictures up on the wall. We watched this movie about forest fires. It was pretty fun."

"Pretty crazy," Izzy chimed in.

Delilah looked up at them in the rearview mirror. "Are you talking about *film strips?*"

"Yeah. That's what Miss Calloway said they were called," Callie said excitedly. "I guess they used to use them in schools and stuff in the old days before there were computers and PowerPoint."

Delilah loved the references to "the old days" which, to her niece, meant anything pre-VCR, cable television, and cell phone service.

"Thanks for taking me home, Detective Swift." Izzy

half groaned, half laughed. "*Home.* I can't believe I just called Maria's *home.* You know what I mean."

Delilah glanced at her in the rearview mirror. "You're certainly welcome, Izzy. How long have you been there? If you don't mind me asking?"

"Nah, I don't care. I came in April. My baby's due September seventeenth. I'll go back to Cleveland some time after that, I guess. Back to my old school. I'll be a junior. Sister Julie has been helping me keep up with my French, even though they don't really teach it at Maria's Place."

"Izzy says she can teach me," Callie piped up. "I can already say thank you in French. *Merci en Français.*"

The girls giggled. Delilah smiled at Callie being silly. She'd seemed like such a serious girl when she'd gotten off the plane six weeks ago. It was nice to see her acting like a fourteen year old.

"I like French," Izzy said. "I want to go to Paris some day. Maybe when I graduate from high school or something. That's where all my friends think I am; my mom told everyone I went to France to go to school for a semester."

"Like people believe that," Callie groaned.

"Yeah, right. I know," Izzy agreed. "But, whatever. I didn't care. I might as well be in France. My boyfriend dumped me. My best friend moved to California. Mom said she and Herbert, that's her husband, weren't raising a baby. And I want to go to college. You can't really take a baby to college," she said almost wistfully. "Soooo . . . somebody in my church told us about this place. And here I am," she finished off matter-of-factly.

Delilah felt her chest tighten with emotion. She felt badly for Izzy, and yet she was impressed. The teen sounded so mature. She sounded like a young woman who'd had some bad things happen to her, but who was determined to make out all right.

"Hey, Aunt Delilah, we were wondering, Izzy and I, if maybe I could stay for a while. Sleepovers aren't allowed, but Izzy says she's sure it would be okay if I stayed for dinner and helped get ready for the fund-raiser tomorrow. We have gallons of lemonade to make. They make it with lemons, not frozen out of a can. Do you think you could come back for me at ten?"

"Please?" Izzy asked. "Or maybe, I could see if someone could bring her home."

"Please?" Callie repeated.

"I thought you wanted to call your Mom tonight." Delilah signaled and pulled onto the road that led out of town.

"She probably won't even be there. She and Bruce will be out on a date or something." Callie made no attempt to cover her disdain.

Delilah wasn't really up to talking to Rosemary either.

"Okay," she said, looking at both girls in the mirror. "But I don't want you making a pest of yourself."

"Callie's no problem," Izzy insisted. "Sister Agatha says it's good for us to have friends like Callie. You know, good girls who do what their parents tell them to do. Who don't break curfew and get good grades in school."

Delilah arched her eyebrows.

Callie must have caught the motion in the rearview mirror because she laughed. "Of course, we didn't tell Sister Agatha why I was *really* in Delaware."

Izzy giggled with her. "She definitely would not have okayed it, then."

"You just better behave yourself," Delilah warned. "If you deceived Sister Agatha into thinking you're an angel, you're going have to live up to the reputation now."

"You're funny, Aunt Delilah. You're a lot funnier than my mother."

Delilah didn't know if Callie had meant that as a compliment, but she took it as one.

Half an hour later, Delilah had dropped off the girls, picked up her dry-cleaning, and stopped at the post office for her mail. She had actually contemplated running over to Route One to one of the drugstores to buy a pregnancy test; she had a couple of hours to herself before she had to pick up Callie. But at this point, it seemed like a waste of the ten bucks. In a few weeks, she'd need to make an appointment with an OB.

She groaned to herself, flipping through her mail. Electric bill, junk mail, phone bill, junk mail. Her life was falling apart before her very eyes. She couldn't have a baby. How was she going to tell Snowden? What was he going to say?

And who had killed Rob and Jenny? Why, after all the hours of investigating, had she been able to come up with nothing but more questions?

This morning, the ME had finally gotten back to her about the Alice Crupp autopsy she'd done the previous summer. The ME, once again, confirmed drowning as the cause of death. She had based her conclusions on the information provided, primarily by Delilah herself. So why couldn't Delilah just let it go? Why couldn't she stop thinking about Alice and Jenny and Rob, all floating in the same pond, and start figuring out what the heck she was going to do with the mess she'd made of her personal life?

Headed back down the brick steps of the post office,

still flipping through her mail, Delilah nearly collided with Cora Watkins.

"Sorry," Delilah muttered, stopping short, dropping half the mail on the step below her.

"Detective Swift, how nice to see you. Getting your mail, I see." Cora leaned over to help Delilah retrieve the envelopes and advertisement flyers.

"Yeah. Thanks. Sorry. Not paying attention where I'm going, I guess."

"I know you must have a lot on you mind, Detective." Cora straightened up, handing Delilah the stack of envelopes. "Clara's gout's flared up so I'm running all the errands. Busy. Busy. Busy," she said, seeming to have no intention of stepping aside to let Delilah pass.

"I know. I was doing the same thing. Errands," Delilah said, trying to make the effort to make conversation. There had just been a meeting the other day at the station to discuss public image. How important it was for the people of Stephen Kill to believe in its police force right now. They needed to make the extra effort to be friendly to the citizens of the town, offer an air of confidence and reliability. "On my way home, now." She took a step sideways.

Cora inched in front of her. "Well, you're ahead of me, Detective. I still have to get the mail and go to the market. Already been to the library. That's your niece working there, isn't it? The pretty redhead—not the *expecting* one."

Delilah began to restack her mail in her arms, wanting to get it to the car without dropping it again. "Yes, my niece Callie is the redhead."

"Nice girl. Chatty."

"Yes. Thank you. Well, I better be on my way." Delilah stepped left.

Again, Cora stepped in front of her. "Nice girl. Friendly, but you know," the older woman lowered her voice to a stage whisper. "She really does need to be careful about what she says in this town. Some people are such scandal-mongers." She flapped a chubby hand. "Not that I would ever repeat such things, but—"

"I'm sorry." Delilah looked Cora eye to eye for the first time. "What do you mean? What did Callie say to you?"

"Just teenage girl talk. They can be so ornery at that age." The older woman laughed in obvious delight.

"Miss Cora, what did my niece say?" Delilah demanded directly. She could feel her cheeks growing hot, anger welling up inside her.

"Oh, my." Cora brought her hand to her rouged cheek. "I wouldn't want to get her into any trouble."

Delilah glared.

"We . . . we were talking about boyfriends. You know, girls that age, they start liking boys. And somehow . . . I don't know how, we got on the subject of older girls"— Cora looked up through her lashes—"adult women and boyfriends." She hesitated.

"Yes. Go on."

"And, well . . . your niece mentioned Chief Calloway." Cora went on faster than before. "I'm quite sure she didn't mean it the way it sounded, but—of course I would never say a thing, Detective."

Delilah held her gaze, unsmiling. "No. I know you wouldn't Miss Cora, because you know how gossip can ruin a woman's reputation, especially in a town like Stephen Kill. Especially a single woman with a high-profile job like mine is right now."

"Yes, yes of course, Detective." Cora sucked in air, her cheeks puffing out, and then exhaled. "I would never say a word." She touched her pink lips with her fingertips.

"But I'm glad we ran into each other. I knew it wasn't true. It couldn't be true. You know, him being . . . *you know.*"

What? Tall? Delilah wanted to say. Delilah had half a mind to call the old biddy on her bigotry. But she was too angry. Too angry with Cora. Too angry with Callie. She was even angry with Snowden.

"If you'll excuse me." Delilah took a big step right and hurried down the steps. "Have a good evening."

"You, too, Detective," Cora called after her, turning to watch Delilah go. Waving as if she were the prom queen. "Say hello to that nice niece of yours. Tell her Miss Cora enjoyed chatting with her at the library."

Delilah got into her police car and dropped the mail on her lap, slamming the door shut with more force than necessary. For a moment, she just sat there, gripping the steering wheel with both hands.

How could Callie have done such a thing? And where had she gotten the idea that Snowden was her boyfriend? The girl had barely ever seen them together and never in any way but in a professional context.

But Callie worked for Snowden's mother . . .

Snowden had said a few weeks ago that his mother had asked him about Delilah. Asked if they were dating. Had Tillie said something to Callie? If she had, why hadn't Callie mentioned it to Delilah? What would have possessed her to have gossiped with a nosy busybody like Cora?

Delilah had half a mind to turn the car around and go back to Maria's Place. Drag Callie out of the house and ask her what the heck she thought she was doing. Did the teen have any idea of the magnitude of her actions? Did she have any clue what a big mouth Cora Watkins was? Everyone in Stephen Kill would be talking about the chief of police and his detective by Sunday morning church. Sooner if tomorrow was sunny.

But then, Callie was only fourteen. Maybe she should have known better. But even if she didn't, Tillie certainly should have.

So now what did she do? Go to Tillie?

No. Tillie was Snowden's mother. She wasn't Delilah's problem, she was Snowden's. And she was going to tell him so.

Delilah grabbed the mail from her lap to toss it on the seat. As she picked it up, one of the envelopes caught her eye. It was smaller than the business size envelopes in the pile. Stationery size. White. Neat square printing in black ink on the address line. No return address.

She recognized the envelope at once. It looked just like the one she had received more than a week ago.

Delilah fingered the smooth vellum paper. She told herself she shouldn't even open it. She should just toss it in the trash.

But she couldn't.

Dropping the rest of the mail on the seat beside her, she dug at the corner of the rear flap with her fingernail, opened a corner and tore open the envelope. She pulled out a piece of plain white stationery that was identical to last week's. A news clipping fluttered from inside the folded paper. Delilah picked it up.

It was a black and white photograph of Delilah at the door of City Hall. It had been taken last week to accompany an article on the murders that had appeared in the *News Journal,* one of only two daily papers in the state. She stared at herself in the photograph for a moment, then released the clipping and let it flutter to her lap.

Who would send her a picture of herself?

Sure, you might send a photograph of someone you

knew who had won an award, or received a commendation. But you didn't send news clippings to people investigating a murder. It was odd. No, it was odder than odd. It was weird.

A shiver crept up her spine. It was hot and close in the car, but suddenly she felt cold and clammy.

Delilah unfolded the piece of stationery.

My darling, it read.

"My darling?" she read aloud in disbelief. This was getting more bizarre by the moment.

> *I thought you might like this. You're doing such a fine job of the investigation. Don't be so hard on yourself. You're doing your best and your best is all any of us expect from you.*
> *Take care.*

Again, the note was unsigned.

Delilah grabbed the news clipping from her lap and threw both pieces of paper on the floor of the car on the passenger's side.

It's nothing, she told herself as she crammed the key into the ignition. At least it was nothing compared to the immediate problems at hand.

The minute Snowden opened his back door, she walked in, brushing past him. "We have a problem," she said.

He closed the door behind her. He had changed out his uniform into running shorts and a T-shirt and his running shoes. He hadn't been out on his run yet, though. He must have just been getting ready to go. "What's the matter? What's happened?"

"I'll tell you what's happened." Delilah turned in the laundry doorway to face him, pointing an accusing finger. "I'll tell you what's happened. Your mother has been talking to my niece."

He looked at her, his brow creasing. "Callie works for my mom at the library, Delilah. I imagine she talks to her every day."

"I mean about us," she spat, tapping her chest, then pointing at him again. "You and me."

"What? Are you sure?" The look on his face told her he didn't believe her. "Why don't you come in? You look beat. You want something to drink?"

"No, Snowden. I don't want *something to drink*. I want to know what your mother said to my niece. Because whatever she said, Callie repeated it to Cora Watkins and now it will be on the evening news."

He looked at her for a minute and then drew his hand over his mouth, down his chin. He did that when he was unsure of himself in a situation. "What did Callie say Mom said?"

"I didn't talk to Callie yet! She's with Izzy at Maria's." Delilah threw up her hand and walked into the neat, small kitchen.

The house, on one of the quiet streets in town, had been built in the 1940s, but he had done quite a bit of remodeling, especially in the kitchen. The house still held all of its old charm, but he'd totally modernized this room with stainless steel appliances and a rich, dark marble countertop.

"Okay, calm down."

"Don't tell me to calm down," she flared. "I've never said a word about you to Callie. There's no way she could have known unless your mother told her."

"Unless my mother told her *what?*" Snowden rested

his hand on the end of the countertop. "She doesn't know anything. She never saw or heard anything. I told you, it was just her wishful thinking."

"Well, obviously it's more than that." Delilah spun around, presenting her back to Snowden. Her head hurt. She couldn't think straight.

She'd meant to bring home the autopsies of Jenny and Rob and Alice to compare them side by side. She just couldn't get the picture of Alice Crupp floating in the weeds of Horsey Mill Pond out of her head. Maybe it was mere coincidence. But maybe it wasn't.

She turned back to Snowden who was now just standing there, looking at her. "Well?" she said.

"Well, what?"

He had a tone about his voice that annoyed her even further. "Are you going to call your mother and ask her what she said to my niece?"

"No, I'm not going to call my mother and ask her anything. Not at least until you talk to Callie."

"Fine. So this is my problem?"

"Delilah, you're being unreasonable. You—"

"Unreasonable? I'm being *unreasonable*? Why? Because I want you to keep your job as the first black police chief in the county? Because I don't want blabbermouths like Cora Watkins going around town saying you and I are dating when I don't even know if that's true?" she demanded. "Because I don't know."

He did it again. Ran his hand across his mouth, down his chin. She wished he'd stop doing that.

"I don't know what we're doing here, you and I." She gestured to him and then to her. "Do you?"

"No, I don't know, Delilah." he said quietly. "This last month or so, you've been pretty preoccupied."

"Preoccupied?" She laughed, but she didn't think it

was the least bit funny. "Snowden. We've buried two people in that graveyard in the last month."

"I know."

"We've got some nut case who drugged them, kidnapped them, and held them prisoner until they died of thirst."

"I know, Delilah."

"You know? You *know*? I'm lying awake nights, trying to figure out what these two victims have in common when they have nothing in common." She threw up her hands. "And I've got my fourteen-year-old niece who my sister apparently no longer wants to raise." It was on the tip of her tongue to spill it all. To tell him that she suspected . . . no, *knew*. That she was pregnant with his child, but she couldn't do it. She just couldn't. "Preoccupied," she repeated. "I would say I was. What's the matter, Snowden? Am I not giving you enough attention? You not getting enough lovin'?"

He reached out to her, but she waved him away.

"Delilah, please."

"No." She shook her head ducking around him, going for the door. "I can't do this, Snowden. Not anymore. Not the sneaking around. Not the watching every word I say in the station. Every move I make." She turned in the laundry room to face him, her hand on the back door. "I don't know what we're doing here, but whatever it is, I think we need a break." Delilah turned around and walked out the door, a part of her hoping he would follow.

He didn't.

Chapter 21

By the time Delilah reached home, she almost felt normal again. She'd been so upset by what Cora had said, by the letter, that she'd gone off the deep end with Snowden. She knew she'd behaved irrationally. He was totally right and she was totally wrong. But she was still totally confused.

Back at the house, she changed into shorts and a T-shirt. She made herself scrambled eggs, then she sat on the end of couch, ate her dinner, and stared at the cordless phone on the end table. She wanted to call Snowden and apologize. Even if his mother *had* said something to Callie, which she didn't know to be true, it wasn't Snowden's fault.

But she had never been good at apologies. And by the time an hour had passed, by the time she had gotten up the nerve and had rehearsed what she was going to say, she didn't know if she wanted to call.

Why hadn't he called her?

Why had he let her walk out the door, knowing she was that upset? So upset that she was acting crazy, saying crazy things. Talking crazy. Snowden should have known this wasn't like her. He should have known something was wrong.

She sipped a glass of fat-free milk, still staring at the phone. Was this Snowden's way of telling her he was no longer interested in going out with her, or whatever it was they had been doing? Was he tired of the sneaking around, too? Had he just been too much a gentleman to say so? Had this been his plan all along, to let her be the first one to say the relationship wasn't working?

In which case, did she want to tell him about the baby? Did she want him to share in the decisions she was going to have to make? And when he offered gallantly to marry her? Did she really want him if he didn't want her?

The more she thought, the more confused she became. Before Delilah knew it, it was time to pick up Callie. She was ten minutes late. The teen was waiting out front, swinging on the porch swing with Izzy and another teen. The girls waved when they saw Delilah pull into the driveway.

Callie jumped off the swing, ran down the steps and hopped into the car. "See, I was waiting outside for you so you wouldn't even have to come to the door in your PJs," she said proudly.

"I'm not in my PJs," Delilah muttered, following the drive around to the back parking lot where she was able to turn around.

Callie looked at her, in her gym shorts and old T-shirt.

"Okay, so maybe I am." Delilah pulled out on the paved road and headed east toward town.

"I helped get ready for the picnic tomorrow. Did you know they're going to have bands and games for kids, and an auction, and all kinds of cool stuff?" Callie asked. Then, seeming to realize she sounded way too excited, she altered her tone. "'Course there's not much for us to do, Izzy and me and the girls, *except work*."

"Izzy and I," Delilah corrected.

Callie screwed up her face. "No, I think I was right the first time."

Delilah felt herself stiffen and she forced what she hoped was a smile. "Izzy and I."

"No." Callie shook her head. "Sister Agatha said the 'proper use of the phrase is Izzy and me.'" Mischief twinkled in the girl's eyes. "And I'm sure she's right, Aunt Delilah. She has a direct line to God, or something."

Headlights approached and a white passenger van passed them. "Hey! That was Monica." Callie turned in the seat to wave. "You see her? She's really nice. She doesn't say much but, she's nice."

"What's she doing, coming back so late from town?"

"I don't know. Probably doing something for Sister Agatha; she's really bossy. Monica works like twenty hours a day or something." Callie settled in the seat again. "Sister Julie says there's no way they could pay her for how hard she works."

Callie leaned against the door, elbow on the sill, propping up her chin with the heel of hand. "Amanda's been worried about putting her baby up for adoption. We were talking about it tonight while we were squeezing lemons." She was quiet for a minute. "It's not so bad, when you think of it, though. Being adopted. Having parents who really want a kid—aren't just stuck with it."

Something in Callie's voice made Delilah's chest tighten. It had to be a hormonal thing. Why else would she be close to tears for at least the third time today?

"Your mother loves you, Callie. She wanted you."

"I guess."

"She does. She did. And your brother and sister love you. And your grandparents and I love you." She looked at her in the darkness, the glare from the headlights on the pickup reflecting off the road signs, illuminating Callie's pretty, serious face. "I probably love you more than anyone, kiddo."

The teen turned her face toward Delilah. "That's the nicest thing anyone's ever said to me in my life."

After that conversation in the truck on the ride home, Delilah hadn't had the energy or the desire to bring up the whole subject of Snowden and his mom and what Callie had said to Cora Watkins at the library. Delilah and Callie were in the truck at nine the next morning, headed for Maria's Place, when Delilah finally decided this was as good a time as any to address the issue.

Each year, since its inception, Maria's had held a fundraiser, inviting everyone in the town. Local bands played outdoors on a makeshift bandstand, there were carnival games and pony rides for kids, food booths, and a silent auction, all proceeds going toward the maintenance of the house. It was a festive day that everyone in town looked forward to each year; a day of sunshine and fun where neighbors and family could meet and everyone could go home feeling as if they had done something good for society.

She'd gotten pulled into the whole volunteer thing, and to be honest, she dreaded it. But now, she was glad. It had been fun, and taking part in the festival and contributing to the cause had made her feel a part of Stephen Kill in a way she wouldn't have for a long time.

"Hey, Callie," Delilah said casually, glancing at the teen sitting next to her.

"Uh, huh?" Callie flipped down the visor and checked the mirror to make sure her eyeliner wasn't smudged.

"I had an interesting conversation with someone yesterday. Miss Watkins. Do you know her?"

Callie pursed her lips and plucked a lip balm from the pocket of her jean shorts. "Which Miss Watkins? Fat, nosy chick or her sister?"

"Callie!"

The teen popped the cap and began to apply red lip balm that had a distinct cherry odor. "I'm just saying . . . she's kind of chunky. But they both ask questions every time they come into the library. The fat one asks stuff about everyone. She asks about you."

"Which is exactly what I wanted to ask you about." Delilah stole a quick glance in Callie's direction. "Did you say anything to her about me having a boyfriend?"

"No. Well . . . she's asked me like every time she's been in. She came Friday, then Wednesday, then Friday again. She checks out VCR tapes because she says the rental store people are nothing but thieves, renting out movies to old people when they can borrow them for free at the library.

It certainly sounded to Delilah like Cora. "She's asked you about me and what? Dating?"

"Sort of. I guess. Like she wanted to know if guys come to the house and like, you know, spend the night and stuff."

Delilah knew she should be shocked, Cora asking such personal questions, making such implications, but she wasn't. After the murders last summer, the secrets of the town she had learned, she knew better than be surprised by anything anyone did or said.

Callie flipped the visor back up. "Miss Calloway was the one who said something to me about Chief Calloway thinking you were cute or something. I think Miss Cora was being snoopy because we were on one side of the bookshelves, Miss Calloway and I, and Miss Cora was on the other side, only I saw her nose sticking between the books." She slid the lip balm tube back into her pocket. "*Kinda* weird, huh?"

"You didn't tell Cora Watkins that I was dating Chief Calloway?"

"Nope."

"So why'd she tell me you did?"

"I don't know. Maybe because of what she overheard Miss Calloway say? I think Miss Calloway was hoping I'd say something to you, you know, like about how her son likes you, maybe. Maybe Miss Cora just got things confused."

Delilah looked at Callie, not sure whether to believe her or not. She'd not caught the teen in a lie since Callie arrived, but before that Callie had certainly told plenty to her parents and anyone willing to listen.

"Callie, this is really serious. Chief Calloway is my boss. I'm . . . he and I are not allowed to date. It's against station policy."

Callie looked at her, her plucked brows knitting. "So *do* you like him? I mean, I didn't say anything to his mom or anyone else, but he does call a lot. From his house and his cell phone."

"How do you know that?"

"Caller ID. It's all stored in the phone. I told you, I fixed that new phone you have in your bedroom. You just hit that arrow." She demonstrated, pretending to operate a phone in her hand. "And the numbers pop up with the names."

"You've been checking to see who calls me?"

"No." Callie looked away. "Well, I was looking to see if someone called me."

"Callie, you have not been talking to Craig Dunn on the phone, have you?"

Callie looked at her as if she was nuts. "No. It was some guy from home. He said he was going to call me." She shrugged and looked away again. "Not that I really care any more. He's a jerk. I haven't even checked since I started working at the library. I've been too busy."

Delilah exhaled, feeling a little better. "So you're sure you didn't say anything to Miss Cora about me and the Chief?"

"No. I just checked out her movies and let her talk. I didn't say anything to anyone." Callie looked back at Delilah. "Oh, but I did say something to Dr. Trubant."

"What? He's married." She looked over the steering wheel, then scowled at Callie.

She shrugged and pulled the lip balm out of her pocket again. "So? He still has the hots for you."

Delilah spotted someone rolling up behind her at the stop sign and was forced to turn onto the county road.

"I said, I thought you had a boyfriend but it was a big secret."

"You shouldn't have done that."

"It's no big deal. He was just acting all, you know, like Mr. Good Looking or something. Izzy says he's like that with women all the time. Sister Agatha thinks he's cute."

Delilah didn't know what to say.

"I know. She's a nun. That doesn't mean she can't *think* some old guy is cute." She turned in the seat to face Delilah. "Did you know Sister Agatha is younger than Sister Julie? I thought she was really old, like forty or something."

At almost thirty years old, Delilah was just beginning to appreciate age and how quickly it crept up on you.

"Okay, back to Dr. Trubant. Did you mention Chief Calloway in that conversation?"

"No." Again she made a face as if Delilah was crazy. "Why are you asking me all these questions? Do you like him?"

It sounded so high school. Of course, why wouldn't it? She was having this conversation with a fourteen year old.

"Okay." Delilah shook her head as if that could somehow clear the issue in her mind and Callie's. "From now on, please don't discuss my personal life with anyone. Not your counselor, not Miss Calloway, not the cute guy at the counter in the video rental store."

"Why would Pete care who you like?" Callie asked.

Delilah burst into laughter.

Delilah and Callie checked in at the volunteer table under one of the big silver maples on the front lawn at Maria's and Callie took off to find Izzy and her new friend Lareina. The girls of the house were in charge of the homemade lemonade stand and had apparently painted big signs to hawk their wares this year. Callie wanted to get the signs up before guests began to arrive.

Delilah was assigned to the silent auction table. Additional volunteers would join her and give her a break as the day went on, but she was in charge of receiving the donations and making the signs for the silent auction items that people would bid on using their assigned number. Later, she and her helpers would collect the money. There were over a hundred auction items, ranging from a plate of homemade brownies to a gift certificate for a week in a condo in Barbados, so Delilah had her work cut out for her, just getting organized.

Not that she minded. Callie had been insistent that they stay all day and help clean up in the evening, so

Delilah knew she was there for the long haul; she was just as happy to be busy. Besides, from the auction table in the backyard under the trees in the roped-off parking lot, she could see everything and everyone. It occurred to her as she checked in a basket of hair products and a coupon for two free appetizers at a beach restaurant that this would be the perfect opportunity for her to study the good citizens of Stephen Kill.

From the profile of the killer she'd created, she had concluded that he was probably local. That he had known or known of Rob and Jenny and their habits. For all Delilah knew, the killer might be there today, drinking lemonade, sharing a picnic lunch with neighbors, or even dropping off an item for auction. Killers who murdered close to home were careful to appear to be model citizens, Delilah had learned from researching FBI files. They were well-known and well liked in their communities. They were Cub Scout leaders, Sunday school teachers, and volunteers for local charities.

Delilah looked up from the sign she was making with a black Sharpie and gazed out over the well-trimmed lawn and blacktop parking lot. Members of a country and western band were unloading their instruments from the back of a pickup truck and stacking them on the bandstand. Several men were hooking up the generator to start the large, blow-up amusements that would be set up in the meadow, and a handful of women were on ladders stringing red, white, and blue banners in the trees overhead. So many people. So many people she knew. None of them appeared, to her, to be suspects. But neither had Alice Crupp.

Delilah bowed her head and went back to writing the sign. If she was going to catch this killer before he struck again, she was going to have to look at the people around her with a more critical eye. She was going to have to look at each and every one of them as a suspect.

"Detective?"

Startled by a female voice, Delilah looked up.

It was Marty Kyle, smartly dressed in white linen knee-length shorts, a turquoise T-shirt and matching white linen jacket. She was wearing cute, strappy turquoise sandals that made her long, thin tanned legs look even longer and thinner. She made Delilah feel short and plain.

"Good morning, Marty, you're out and about early."

She dropped a white wicker basket on the table in front of Delilah. "Some giveaways from the station." She reached in with a manicured hand, picked up several plastic items and let them fall back into the container. "You know, key chains, rulers, stress balls, crap like that. People like them. Oh, and there's an envelope in there. Gift certificate for two for a dinner cruise out of Ocean City. For the auction."

Delilah fished the envelope out of the basket. "Thanks. I'm sure we can use them."

"Certainly, Detective."

Delilah added the envelope to a pile of gift certificates she'd already collected and went back to her sign, but Marty didn't go away.

"So," she said, running her French-manicured fingernail along the edge of the red and white checked plastic tablecloth. "Anything new on the investigation?"

Delilah didn't have to ask what investigation Marty was talking about, but she was tempted. Hadn't Marty been in this business long enough to know this wasn't how the give and take between the media and the police worked?

"Nothing new that I can tell you, Marty."

Marty chuckled. "It's my job to ask, Detective."

"And mine to keep my mouth shut." Delilah smiled sweetly and reached for another piece of poster board. "How's your piece on Maria's going?"

"Great. The news show wants it."

"So I heard."

"We're wrapping up today. I want to get a couple pans of the festivities and then I'm submitting it." She straightened the white basket in front of her. "You know, I interviewed Mrs. Grove. She died before I had a chance to go back and film her."

Delilah looked up, her interest tapped. "Did you?"

"I could wring my own neck for not taking a film crew along with me that day." She posed, one hand on her hip. "But how did I know she was going to get kidnapped and murdered, right?"

Delilah looked at her, saying nothing. To this point, she had assumed the killer was male. Most were, as many as 98 percent, but Alice Crupp had not been a man. Perhaps she needed to broaden her vision. Marty was certainly odd. She had an overblown sense of self that was classic in serial killers who held their victims prisoner before killing them.

"Say, didn't you also interview Rob Crane? Back in May, maybe, just after he returned home for the summer? I remember seeing just a clip of him on the evening news, but that was you interviewing him, wasn't it?"

"Second time, actually. I interviewed him the spring before when he finished first in regionals in some swimming race. He was a handsome young man," Marty said. "Well, I'll let you get back to your work. Have a nice day, Detective."

"You too, Marty."

Delilah watched her walk away.

"Two more baskets for you, Detective." Monica walked

up behind her, setting them on the table. "Gosh, look at all this stuff. You need help?"

Delilah looked over her shoulder at Monica and then all the baskets and loose items like golf clubs and coolers of soda beginning to stack up on the tables. "I think I'm supposed to get some help later. I know you must have plenty of jobs to do."

Monica chuckled. "Phone's ringing off the hook this morning, the blow-up jolly slide is missing a power cord, but the rental store swears they sent it, and Sister Julie has misplaced yet another set of keys to the van. Oh, and Belinda was having contractions this morning; turned out to be false labor. She's due the same time as Amanda." She pushed a lock of brown hair that had slipped from the neat bun on the back of her head. "But today isn't really any crazier than most days around here, Detective. If you need help . . ."

It was the most Delilah had ever heard Monica say at once. "Nah, I'm fine." Delilah waved her away with her Sharpie. "I can tell you what you can do for me, though."

"What's that?" Monica turned to her.

She wore no make-up, a shapeless T-shirt, and knee-length jean skirt. But she was pretty, Delilah thought, pretty in a clean kind of way. "Could you send my niece over with a cup of lemonade as soon as they get set up? I think we'll be running a tab today."

In the distance, Delilah heard someone calling for Monica through the kitchen window. It sounded like Sister Agatha.

"Ever seen a nun with her panties in a twist," Monica whispered to Delilah behind her hand.

The comment was so unexpected from her that Deliah had to laugh.

Monica turned away. "I'll send Callie with the lemonade," she said over her shoulder. She waved toward the open kitchen window. "Coming, Sister!"

For the next two-and-a-half hours, Delilah checked in auction items, made signs for them, and set them out on the tables. Rachel Gibson joined her at ten thirty and the two women had worked side-by-side, chatting as they went. By the time the farmhouse and the surrounding yard were filled with people and the band was playing its first set, they were finally caught up. Deliah fell back into one of the two lawn chairs Mattie McConnell had just delivered.

"Thanks, Mattie," Delilah said.

"Thanks, Mattie," Rachel echoed, dropping into the chair beside her.

"He seems to be fitting in well," Delilah observed, watching the man lumber away, lawn chairs tucked under each arm. "My niece, Callie, has made a couple of friends here so she's been around a lot lately. She says the girls like him."

The previous summer, evidence had pointed to Mattie and he had been arrested for the sin murders. At the time, Delilah had truly believed he might have been responsible. Now, watching him deliver chairs to various booths, she wondered what she had been thinking. The man could barely communicate; he didn't have a violent bone in his body. What could possibly have made her believe he was guilty?

"He has a good heart," Rachel said, smiling as she watched him offer a chair to another volunteer. "He's a lot of help at home, too. With my daughter, Mallory. And now, with another on the way . . ."

Delilah looked at Rachel. "You're pregnant? Rachel, that's wonderful!"

Rachel had dated Snowden for a while before Delilah

had moved to Delaware, and when Delilah had first been attracted to him, she'd been a little jealous of the green-eyed beauty. But since she had gotten to know her better, since she had seen how much Rachel loved her husband, any jealousies had long faded.

"When are you due?" Delilah asked, genuinely excited for her.

Rachel grinned, running her hand over the slight swell of her stomach. "Christmas. Noah and I wanted to wait a few months before we told anyone, you know, me being so old." She laughed. "But I'm starting to get fat now, so we thought we could probably tell people. Noah's been a blabbermouth all week. I didn't think anyone in Stephen Kill hadn't heard the news."

Delilah couldn't help but think of her own situation. Noah Gibson was thrilled his wife was going to have a baby. Who would be thrilled for Delilah? Certainly not her mother and father. Not Snowden. She looked down at the trampled grass beneath her feet. "That really is exciting." She got up suddenly from her chair. "Hey, you don't mind if I take a break, do you? Going to run to the ladies' room. Get some more lemonade. You want some?"

"Sure, why not?" Rachel started to reach into the back pocket of her shorts.

"I'll get it." Delilah walked away. She felt as if she needed a breather, needed to get away from the ambiguity poking at her. It wasn't that she wasn't happy for Rachel; it was just that she was sad for herself.

Delilah used the restroom inside the house, washed her face and hands, and by the time she stepped into the rear hall, she was feeling better. It was hot outside. She hadn't slept well the night before. The chance to stretch her legs had done her a world of good.

As she started down the hall toward the family room to the French doors that led into the backyard, she heard raised voices. Female voices.

Delilah halted, curious. She couldn't make out what was being said, but the disagreement sounded heated. She stepped back into the hall that led to the office in the new addition. She thought she heard Sister Julie's voice and . . . Was it Sister Agatha? She didn't believe she had ever heard Sister Agatha raise her voice since she'd come to Maria's last fall.

"Ah, Detective, there you are." Paul Trubant appeared in the archway leading from the old house into the new addition. "Rachel Gibson said I might find you here. You have a minute? I thought we could take a walk."

Delilah looked at him. She could still hear the two women, but they were quieter. They might have heard Paul's voice in the hall. She thought about what Callie had said about him asking who Delilah was dating. Was the teen right? Did he have a thing for her? "A walk?"

"To talk about your niece." He lowered his voice. "The girls." He glanced around as if looking to see if anyone was present. "They tend to take up for each other. Carry tales. I know Callie's gotten to be good friends with some of them. I thought we could take a walk outside, just to be sure we're not overheard."

Delilah looked back down the hall, still curious as to what two nuns would be arguing over. "Um . . . sure," she said, looking back at Paul. "Let's go out the front so Callie doesn't spot us from the lemonade stand. Otherwise, we'll both be in trouble."

Chapter 22

"I'm not budging on this issue, Marty," Julie said firmly, holding the remote control to the TV in her hand. "And I don't appreciate you raising your voice that way to me. I laid out the ground rules before the interviews ever started. You agreed to my stipulations."

Marty stood in her smart, white linen suit, between the small TV on the table and Julie. "You can't even see her face." She gestured in the direction of the still photo on the screen.

"I can tell who it is and that means her family, her friends, everyone else will recognize her."

"You don't seriously think it's a secret, why any of these girls left or were sent away from home, do you?" Marty demanded.

Julie looked down at the remote in her hand. Marty should not have shouted at her, but Julie shouldn't have shouted back either. It was totally inappropriate. "It doesn't matter," she said quietly, setting the remote down on Sister Agatha's desk. "What matters is that we promised anonymity and that extends to news programs I've allowed to be filmed here. You have to take this clip out. You have to take it out, or I'll revoke my permission for you to use any of my or my staff's interviews and then I will call the producers and inform them that you no longer have my permission to air those interviews."

"You don't understand how badly I want this job," Marty said, her voice surprisingly thick with emotion. "I *need* this job. I need to get away from here. I need to make a fresh start, Sister Julie."

Julie studied Marty for a long moment. Her face was so pretty, pretty enough to be a model's, but pain, emotional pain that Julie sensed ran deep, shone in the woman's eyes. "Why is this story important to you?" she asked.

"It's not." Marty turned slightly to stare at the still photo on the screen of Izzy and Amanda leaning over a flower box, planting zinnias. On the tape, the girls only appeared for an instant, and it was shot from an angle that didn't really capture their faces, but it was shot of them just the same. Marty had apparently allowed her cameraman to shoot the domestic scene one morning when she'd come to interview Sister Agatha while Julie was out.

"Did you have a baby?" Julie said gently. Marty's suffering was so apparent on her face that Julie could feel it in her own heart. "Did you have to give up a child?"

"You don't understand."

"I probably do, better than you realize." Julie hesitated, considering the ramification of saying anything more to a reporter. But Sister Agatha knew. She assumed the bishop did. And surely all the girls in the house knew because there were never secrets between them.

Julie fingered her cross. Maybe it was time she started telling her story. Maybe, then, at last, she could leave her own pain in the past where it belonged. Maybe by voicing that pain, she could help others. "I understand," she said, her voice growing strong, "because I gave up a child."

"What do you mean?" She stared at her for a second, then understanding passed over her angry face. "You had a baby? A nun?"

"Before I became a nun. I was a teenager, just like these girls." Julie took a step toward her. "If you want to talk about this. About what happened to you, we can. Now. Later. Whenever you're ready to talk, I'm ready to listen. I think you need someone to listen, Marty."

"Don't be ridiculous. If I need psychiatric counseling, I'll pay for it." Marty hit the stop on the VCR and popped out the tape. "I'll take the girls out. They don't add anything, anyway." She strode past Julie to the door. "Anything else, *Sister?*"

"Please don't leave like this, Marty. I'm not doing this to harm your career. It's about the girls. Two separate issues." She paused and then started again. "You know, if you'd tell me, maybe I could help you," Julie offered.

"You can't help me. I had an abortion when I was sixteen." She jerked open the door. "No one can help me, Sister. No one can help anyone. No one can help anyone but themselves. "

Julie followed Marty, but she hurried down the hall.

Monica stood off to the side, just outside the office door, her gaze downcast. "Oh, dear," she muttered, clearly embarrassed. "I was looking for you. I didn't know if you wanted to put some of the cash in the safe." She produced a large manila envelope, fat with bills.

Julie looked, wondered how much Monica had heard. Wondered if she owed her some sort of explanation. "Monica," she said gently.

"It's okay." Monica pushed the envelope into Julie's hand. "You don't have to say anything, Julie."

Before Julie could say anything more, Monica was gone.

Paul scooped his son out of the grass, walking away from the petting zoo set up in a small, fenced in area near the garden. Pauly fussed, opening and closing his little hands, wanting to pet the baby goat again, but Paul lifted him to his shoulders and the toddler was mollified at once.

"There we go, attaboy. Look how tall you are now. What a big boy." Paul glanced over his shoulder. He'd been avoiding Kitten all day, but it had been hard. He'd caught her several times following him, watching him. This seemed to be a game to her. A dangerous game. An hour ago, she'd actually walked up to Susan and spoken to her.

Paul couldn't imagine what she was thinking. Actually, he could. She called him on his cell phone earlier. She had said she was in the house, that she could see him. She wanted him to meet her in one of the upstairs dormitory rooms. When he'd refused, she'd become angry.

It was time to get out of here. Time to go home. He and his family had been here for hours. No one would think anything of his going home now. A man had to get his young children to bed early on a Saturday night to make church in the morning, didn't he?

Balancing Pauly on his shoulders, Paul walked around the back of the house, weaving his way through the crowd. The summer fund-raiser had always been well attended, but this year it seemed as if half the county— half the state—had come. There were easily four hundred people milling around the old farmhouse, and it seemed as if the crowd had never died down all day.

"Should we go find Mommy, Pauly?" Paul asked his son, holding both of his chubby hands. "Where's Mommy?" He walked around the house to the place where they had left their blanket, picnic basket, diaper bag, and other belongings beneath the huge lilac bushes. The blanket was gone, as was everything else.

"There you are," Susan said.

Paul could tell he was in trouble. "Honey." He turned around, spinning Pauly. The toddler laughed.

"Where have you been?" she demanded, her voice tight. "I've been looking for you for the last hour." She reached up to her son and he threw out his hands.

Paul lowered the little boy into his mother's arms. "We've been around. We walked down to the pond to feed the fish. We went to the petting zoo."

She eyed him, her tone cool. "You've been with someone, haven't you?" she whispered.

"Susan, honey." He gestured to their son. "I don't know what you're talking about. I've had Pauly with me."

Her face remained stern. "Didn't stop you from picking that girl up on the boardwalk that night," she accused.

He looked around. There were people milling around the front yard, coming in and out of the house. The remaining Bread Ladies, the sisters Cora and Clara, sat on old aluminum lawn chairs on the porch, watching, listening, no doubt, to every word they could hear.

"Honey, not here," he said quietly. He didn't know what had gotten into her. Had she seen him speaking to Kitten at the lemonade stand earlier? She couldn't have. She'd been taking the girls to the bathroom when he'd run into Kitten there.

Then he wondered if Kitten had said something to

her. Why else would Susan be this upset? It had months since they had even discussed his indiscretions. As far as he knew, she thought that had all ended when he went back to AA.

"Let's go home. We'll talk there."

"I don't want to talk," she said. Pauly patted her face and she pushed his hands down. "I want to go home, take a shower, and go to bed, Paul. I just want to go home," she said, her eyes filling with tears.

"Then we'll go home, honey." He reached out to rest his hand on her hip and guide her across the front lawn. "Where are the girls?"

"I told Annie she could use her last ticket to try and win a goldfish. Chloe took her. I told Chloe to meet us at the car."

"Perfect end to a perfect day," he said as they walked across the yard. It was growing dark and someone had strung lanterns in the tree overhead so that they cast patches of pale light in the trampled grass. "Here, let me carry him. He's getting so heavy." Paul took the toddler from his wife's arms. "We get home," he said, "and I'll get everyone bathed and in bed. You have your shower and go to bed. I'll take care of everything. You look beat."

"I am," Susan agreed, the tightness easing from her voice.

Paul dropped his hand on his wife's shoulder and kissed her temple. Out of the corner of his eye, he spotted someone standing under the big tree watching them.

She just wasn't going to be happy until he broke it off with her, was she?

"So, you having a good time?" Delilah patted the spot beside her on the wooden bench and looked up at Callie who had just walked out of the house. "Want to sit down?"

"Sure. I guess so. For a minute. Then I *gotta* go. Sister Agatha is like this crazed woman. She wants things cleaned up before they're like even dirty." Callie pulled the elastic from her pony tail, leaned over, gathered her red hair, secured it with the elastic again, and then stood up.

"I'm glad she's putting you to work. It's good for you." Delilah gazed out over the backyard from the haven she'd discovered between the potting shed and a stone bird bath. The auction items had all been paid for and she had been relieved of her duties an hour ago. Now she was just hanging around, waiting for Callie, trying to enjoy the evening.

The bandstand, the makeshift dance floor on the parking lot, and the carnival booths were lit with lanterns and twinkle lights strung in the trees, but the bench, off to one side of a grassy area, sat in shadows. From here, Delilah could watch people without being detected.

Callie dropped down on the bench. "It's been *kinda* fun, I guess. I get all the heavy work, of course because nobody else is supposed to lift heavy things," she said, sounding full of importance. "But the really heavy things, I make Mattie lift them."

"I know the Sisters are happy to have your help." Delilah patted her knee.

Callie leaned back on the bench. "So," she said casually, "what'd Dr. Trubant have to say about me? He think I'm crazy?"

"What?" Delilah looked at the teenager beside her.

"I saw you talking to him earlier today. Acting all secretive. You were talking about me. I could tell."

Delilah considered denying it, but she could tell by the

look on Callie's face that there would be no point. The girl was too intuitive. "No, he doesn't think you're crazy. In fact, he thinks you're pretty with it for a fourteen year old."

"Pretty *with it*?" Callie wrinkled her freckled nose, that closely resembled Delilah's. "What's that supposed to mean?"

"It just means you've got good sense."

"Apparently not good enough sense to keep from getting caught with my friends' weed in my locker," she mused sarcastically.

Delilah looked at her in the semidarkness. "Question is, are you smart enough not to do it again?"

Callie watched a toad hopping in the grass under the birdbath. "I know it was stupid and I know this is no excuse, but Mom makes me crazy. She . . . she doesn't listen to me. She never wants to hear what I have to say."

"So you've been drinking, smoking marijuana, and skipping school to get her to listen to you?"

Callie was quiet for a minute. "I don't know. Sounds kind of stupid when you say it like that."

Delilah had to smile to herself. She'd certainly done her share of stupid things when she was a teenager.

"So . . . he didn't say anything too bad?" Callie pressed, kicking out one foot and then the other.

"Nope. We didn't talk that long about you, actually. He said you were doing great."

"Great enough that I don't need to go any more?" the teen asked hopefully.

"Not that great."

Delilah saw Callie smile.

"There you are. I've been looking for you all day." Snowden stepped into the privacy of the shadows of the potting shed. "Hi, Callie."

"Hello, Chief Calloway," Callie looked up at him as if considering him in a new light. "How are you tonight?"

Delilah felt heat rise in her cheeks, knowing very well what the teen was up to. She just prayed Callie didn't say anything too embarrassing.

"Fine, thank you. I hear from my mother that you're an excellent librarian's assistant," he said with a casual smile. "Maybe you ought to think about library science when you go to college."

"Maybe I should." The teen popped up off the bench. "I better go. I'm supposed to be helping Tiffany and Yolanda take down some tables. Catch you later, Aunt Delilah." Callie sneaked a quick glance at Delilah, a silly little smile tugging at the corner of her pink lip-balm saturated mouth.

Delilah gave her a "get-the-heck-out-of-here" look and the teen skipped off.

Snowden sat down on the bench beside Delilah. He wore a pair of khaki cargo shorts and a navy polo. He stretched out his long legs beside hers. "You been avoiding me today?" he asked quietly.

She gazed out at the group of men and women, aged four or five to probably eighty-five, doing the twist to an old fifties song the band was playing. "Not really," she said. "I've just been busy. I took care of the auction table most of the day."

He nodded.

Both watched the dancers for another minute or two in silence until he spoke again. "You want to talk about last night?"

She looked down at her own short, pale legs next to his long, dark ones. "Not really."

He exhaled and was silent again.

They continued to watch the dancers and it occurred

to Delilah that to any casual passerby, they would appear to be two co-workers or just neighbors chatting. They didn't look like lovers who had made a baby together. She swallowed the lump that rose in her throat.

"I've been thinking about the case today," she said. It was funny that it was easier for her to contemplate a serial killer than her own personal life. "I was thinking we should broaden our pool of suspects."

"Meaning?"

"We've assumed we're looking for a male."

"And you think we could have a female killer?" he said, almost incredulously. "Again?"

"I know. I know, it's highly unlikely, according to statistics."

"Especially when a kidnapping was involved. This isn't the same as last summer. Alice Crupp ambushed her victims. She killed them where she attacked them and left the bodies."

She raised one finger. "But drugs were probably used in these kidnappings. You drug someone with GHB, you can get them to walk on their own, or at least it's a lot easier to move them around."

He put his hands behind him, resting the heels of his palms on the edge of the bench and leaning back. "Then there's the matter of moving the bodies after death. Rob weighed a hundred and sixty pounds."

"I could probably move a hundred and sixty pounds," she observed thoughtfully. "If I wanted to badly enough."

"Have anyone in particular in mind?"

Delilah thought about the conversation she'd had this morning with Marty Kyle. The reporter had interviewed both victims. That was certainly not evidence enough to seriously suspect her, but it was a common thread between the two victims. Certainly as significant as them having the same clerk at the minimart. And then there was the fact that Paul Trubant had counseled both victims. He wasn't female, obviously, but maybe she should consider him, as well.

"No," Delilah said to Snowden. "No one even on the radar, really. It's part of what's making me so crazy. I keep thinking he . . . or *she's* right here." She gazed out at the crowd, looked at him and back at the dance floor again. She needed to tell him about the second letter she received. She'd been thinking about it off and on all day. She supposed this was as good a time as any.

"Listen, I wanted to tell you. This probably has nothing to do with anything, but I got a weird piece of fan mail yesterday. Mailed to my personal P.O. box."

"Weird in what way?"

"I'll bring it in on Monday and let you see for yourself. There was a clipping of me, a photo. And it says something about me doing a great job on the case . . . but, it's not signed. She hesitated. "And this is the second unsigned letter I've received from the same person in the last couple of weeks."

"Second?" He turned on the bench to face. "Why didn't I know about the first?"

"I didn't think it meant anything. It didn't seem that odd at the time, so I tossed it."

"You shouldn't have done that."

"I know that now, but Snowden, I got a lot of these letters last summer. It just didn't occur to me . . ." She sighed.

"Bring it to me."

"I will," she said.

He was quiet again and then Delilah felt his hand on hers. "Delilah, we need to talk. I—"

"Please," she whispered under her breath, looking

straight ahead, afraid to look at him for fear of what she might say. What he might say. "I can't do this right now."

He removed his hand and she immediately felt a loss. She crossed her arms over her chest, taking care not to touch him. It had been a hot day, temperatures in the mid-eighties, but after the sun set, it had really begun to cool off. She had goosebumps on her arms and legs. Probably a little sunburn. That was what was making her chilled now.

"I don't feel like we can end, this way, Delilah. I don't know what happened. What I—"

"Just let it go," she interrupted. "For now." She rested her palms on her thighs. "Let's find who did this. Get this out of the way. Maybe I . . . I can think clearly then. Maybe then we can both figure out what we want."

He made a sound as if he was going to say something and then stopped himself. He rose from the bench. "Guess I'll head out."

"Good night."

The Daughter watched the exchange between the police chief and Delilah, a little concerned. They had seemed to be in a serious conversation. *The Daughter* hadn't seen him chastise her, but it was obvious that Delilah was upset. *The Daughter* didn't like to see her upset.

She didn't like the police chief, either. She didn't like the way he seemed to hold himself above others.

The Father had been that way. Thought he was smarter. Better than others. Better than *The Daughter*. He had used his size, his strength, to control *The Daughter* as well as *The Mother*.

In the end, his size and strength had meant nothing. It meant nothing to the fires of hell that had licked his body as he screamed to escape the burning car that would not set him free. That *The Daughter* would not allow to set him free.

The police chief disappeared into the crowd gathered around the dance area and *The Daughter* looked back at Delilah sitting alone on the bench. She looked tired. Sad. And *The Daughter's* heart ached for her. Perhaps the police chief didn't appreciate Delilah, didn't value how good she was, what a fine officer she was, but *The Daughter* appreciated her. She wished she could walk over to the bench, sit down and comfort Delilah. Wished she had the nerve.

But the time wasn't right.

Tonight was not the night. Tonight was the night to watch. To remain invisible. A *need* was beginning to pull at *The Daughter's* mind. She had not thought consciously about the next; she had not allowed herself the privilege. The pleasure. But all the same, the possibility was there. She felt it nudging. Heard it scratching.

Flirtatious laughter caught *The Daughter's* attention and she turned to see Marty Kyle sitting on the edge of a picnic table beside the bandstand, her pretty little feet propped on the bench seat. Lights twinkled over her head in treelike stars in the nighttime sky, casting a glow over her blemish-free skin. She threw her head back, tossing her perfect blond hair. She was talking to a man she should not have been talking to that way.

Didn't Marty know you weren't supposed to sit on the table? It was very rude. Very unladylike.

The Daughter watched the reporter with disdain. Perhaps she was pretty in the face, but she was an ugly woman inside. A woman who deserved to be punished.

But then, there were so many who deserved to be punished, weren't there?

Chapter 23

"Thank you for meeting me here so late, Sister Julie." Marty cupped her hands around the white coffee mug, seeming not-at-all to be her usual confident self. She stared into the depths of the black coffee. "I know I must have surprised you. My call. After the way I acted the other day, I was afraid your assistant wouldn't even put me through."

A lamp hung over the diner booth, casting a sharp circle of illumination on the center of the table. In the less harsh edges of the light, Marty's face somehow seem softer to Julie than usual. She was still attractive, but tonight, without the make-up, in jeans and a black T-shirt, she barely appeared to be the same cool, polished woman who appeared each night on the local news.

Julie wondered if she has misread Marty from the beginning. She, of all people, knew that no one was truly who they appeared to be.

"I'm glad you called." Julie dropped a plain-Jane tea bag into the mug of hot water the waitress had placed in front of her. At ten thirty on a Wednesday night, and only a half hour before closing, the diner was deserted. Not even the tired, overworked owner was to be seen. "I'm afraid I didn't handle the situation very well in my office Saturday."

"No, it's okay. I behaved poorly." Marty poured some sugar from the dispenser on the table into her coffee. "I wanted my piece to be just right. I wasn't thinking about the girls. All I was thinking about was myself and getting the story right. I *really* needed the job."

"It was still wrong of me." Julie pressed her hand to her forehead. "I don't know what I was thinking, cornering you like that, piling my own confession on you." She tugged on the tag of her tea bag, dunking it in and out of the hot water. "What I was trying to say . . . it didn't come out the way I meant it."

"Yeah. You really caught me off guard." Marty gave a little laugh of disbelief. "A pregnant nun. Phew. I don't know what I was expecting, but that wasn't it."

"Well, as I said, I wasn't a nun then. I was a scared kid." Julie fished the tea bag out of the water with her spoon and wrapped the string around the bag, squeezing all the liquid from it. "I guess it's the whole reason why Maria's Place was conceived. I had no where to go when I was sixteen and pregnant. I don't know if you want to use that information in your story. I'd certainly like to talk to my bishop first about it, if you do."

"No. Don't need it. The story's a wrap. I worked all night Saturday night. Overnighted the tape Monday. I got the call a couple of hours ago." Marty brought the coffee cup to her mouth. She wasn't even wearing lipstick. "They not only want my piece, they want me. I'm hired as one of their new feature reporters."

"Marty, that's wonderful!" Julie reached across the table to grab her hand. "Congratulations."

"I start right away. I think I'm moving to Baltimore this weekend. My cousin has a lead on a sublet. Haven't decided yet if I'll put my condo in Rehoboth up for sale or hang onto it." She shrugged and stared into her coffee cup, almost seeming shy to Julie now. Certainly humble. "Maybe I should wait. See how I like the show. See how the show likes me."

Julie watched Marty for a moment. She'd always been good at reading emotions on people's faces. Marty was happy. She was scared. She was regretful. But Julie also saw hope in her eyes. "I'm glad you called me," she said. "Glad you wanted to share this with me."

"Actually, you're the first person I called. After my boss. To tell the asshole I quit." Marty glanced up. "Sorry, Sister."

Julie gave a wave of dismissal. "Can't say I haven't used a curse word on occasion, myself."

They both laughed and Julie waited for the laughter to subside. Sipped her tea. "Listen, about what you told me. About your abortion."

Marty groaned. "I don't know what was wrong with me. I didn't mean to shock you or anything. Not that you don't know people . . ." She let the sentence trail off, not seeming to really know what she wanted to say.

Julie tried to choose her words carefully. "Marty, you should talk to someone about this. I don't mean to get preachy, but you need to seek forgiveness from God. From yourself. You need to get some counseling."

"Tried that." She gave a laugh that was void of any humor. "I'm embarrassed to say I ended up on the doctor's couch, but not the way I should have been." She looked at Julie, waiting for her disapproval.

Julie took another sip of tea. "You're moving, making a fresh start. Why not find a new therapist? Find a church, Marty?"

"You make it sound so easy."

"It isn't. I realize that. Finding people you can trust is hard work, but you could do it. I know you could."

Marty tipped her coffee cup and took a last sip as she slid out of the booth. "Listen, I hate to run on you, but I have a zillion things to do." She reached for the check the waitress had left on the table. "I'll get this."

"Please." Julie covered the piece of paper with her hand. "Let me."

"Well, thanks." Marty lifted the strap of her purse onto her shoulder. "I just wanted to tell you about the job. And let you know that I took out the shot of the girls. I'll let you know when it's scheduled to air."

"We'll be looking forward to it." Julie smiled up at her. "Take care, Marty."

The Daughter stood in the shadows at the corner of the diner and watched through the windows as the two women said their good-byes and the reporter walked away from the table.

The Daughter's heart pounded with excitement.

She had been watching her for some time. In her heart, she had known what had to be done. Saturday night, her thoughts had simply been confirmed. She had to die for what she had done to her child.

Delilah lay on her bed, her head propped on a pillow as she stared up at the ceiling fan. Around her were piles of papers; printouts from FBI and psychology websites. She had a book on profiling and copies of the files and photos of the two murders. Plenty to read. Plenty of info to take notes on and instead she was watching the ceiling fan blades spin.

She had turned the anonymous letter in to Snowden Monday morning. He had looked at it and agreed it was strange. He had also agreed that it was probably nothing. Perhaps even a joke. Kids were out of school; it was late July. They were beginning to get bored. It might have been written as a prank. He said he would hang onto it, just the same, and if she got another one, she was to hand it over to him immediately. It had barely been admonition, but it had annoyed her just the same. Snowden had said he still had confidence she could crack this case, but she wondered if that confidence was now waning.

There was a knock at her open door. "Aunt Delilah?"

Delilah sat up, feeling as if she'd been caught playing hooky. She closed the nearest manila file, filled with horrendous photos of the Horsey Mill Pond crime scene. "Yeah?"

"I just wanted to see if you wanted some ice cream." The teen stood in the doorway. "I was going to get myself some before I went to bed."

"Sure." Delilah stacked files. "Ice cream would be good."

Callie continued to stand there.

"So what have you been doing?" Delilah asked, taking the cue. She had learned that Callie would never come right out and say she wanted to talk, but she offered definite hints when conversation was what she was seeking. Delilah just had to be smart enough to see them.

"Nothing. Reading. I called Mom on my cell to see if it would work, you know, and not charge me because she has the same phone service. The phone's really cool, Aunt Delilah. I can't believe you got it for me. I'll pay you every month, I swear, I will."

Delilah had noticed in the last few weeks that Callie

was losing her accent. She no longer sounded as if she was from East Jesus.

"That's nice that you called your mom. She have anything to say?"

"Not really. Usual stuff. She said I got a letter. I have to go to court in September." She ran her hand down the doorframe molding. "She was talking about school. About me transferring to some church school." She looked down at her painted toenails. "It's expensive. I kinda feel bad about her paying for it because I screwed up. I don't think I'm going to like it there."

"Won't know until you give it a try, will you?" Delilah asked cheerfully.

"I guess not. I do think she's right. Even if my old school would let me back in, maybe it's not a good idea if I go." She continued to avoid eye contact. "Which kind of made me wonder . . . made me think, I don't know, maybe there's somewhere else I could go to high school." She looked up at Delilah with big brown eyes. "Like maybe here?"

"Here?" Delilah asked.

"Wait. Wait. Before you say no." Callie rushed across the room, both hands out to Delilah. "Mom said it would be all right."

"You asked your mother?"

"She agreed it might be a good idea."

Delilah was going to *kill* Rosemary.

"She said I should ask you. Let you think about it." Callie sat down on the edge of the bed. "Aunt Delilah, I really like it here. I like my friends."

"Honey," Delilah said gently. "You keep forgetting that Izzy can't stay. None of those girls can stay. They're all going home, once they have their babies."

"I know," Callie groaned. "So I'll make new friends. I

already met this girl, Marci, at the library. She's going be in tenth grade, too. And she's not pregnant. She's never even had a boyfriend. She goes to Stephen Kill High. She asked me if I played field hockey. I did in middle school, you know. Mom made me quit because there were too many practices and she couldn't drive me, with the kids and stuff."

Delilah looked away. Callie was serious about staying. And honestly, maybe Stephen Kill High School was a better choice. Whatever Delilah was doing, she seemed to be getting through to Callie in a way Rosemary couldn't.

A teenager and a baby?

Delilah had to be out of her mind. Just the idea that she would keep the baby was crazy. But a baby and a teenager? There was no way she could be a cop and a single mother to two kids.

So maybe she couldn't be a cop anymore.

She let the idea settle in her head. It wasn't the first time she'd thought about it. The truth was, she'd become a cop because her brothers were cops. Because they said she couldn't do it. And she liked being a cop, at least she liked part of it. But the part she really liked was the people. The criminals. The victims. Just plain old citizens she came in contact with each day. She liked figuring them out. Her undergraduate degree from Georgia State was in psychology. If Paul Trubant could be a psychologist, why couldn't she? He'd gone to school nights to get his master's degree and then his doctorate. He certainly wasn't any smarter than she was.

"Will you at least think about it?" Callie asked, breaking into Delilah's thoughts. "Please, Aunt Delilah." The teen put her hands together as if in prayer.

Callie could certainly be dramatic when she wanted to be.

"I don't know, Callie," she said honestly. "I guess I can think about it. We can talk about it. With your mother," she emphasized.

"That's all I'm asking, just think about it?" Callie leapt off the bed. "I'm going to get the ice cream. You want anything else?"

"Nope." Delilah began to stack her files and printouts and place them in a cardboard storage box on the floor beside the bed. Callie brought her a bowl of chocolate-chip ice cream and slipped out of the room calling good night. The teen was so happy that Delilah was unsure how to tell her that she was afraid that mothering a teenager was just too much responsibility for her to handle. She certainly would be overwhelmed in about six months.

How could Rosemary have encouraged Callie without speaking to Delilah first?

Delilah ate a few bites of her melting ice cream, sitting cross-legged on her bed. She looked at the phone on the nightstand. Her sister would still be up. She was a night owl.

She punched the memory dial on the handset and rested the phone on her shoulder, spooning in another mouthful of ice cream.

"'Lo?"

"Rosemary, how could you talk to Callie about attending high school here before consulting me?"

"Oh, hi, Delilah, how are you darlin'?" her sister asked sweetly.

"I was fine before Callie came into my bedroom and asked me if she could go to high school in Stephen Kill. Before she told me you had already agreed to the idea."

"Well, I did say it might be a good idea. I also told her that she would have to talk to you about it."

"Rosemary," Delilah sighed, setting the bowl down on

the nightstand. "You're missing the point, here. Now you've got her hopes up. I can't . . . I don't know that I can keep her long term. I . . . I still have these murder cases and—"

"I'm coming, sugar pie," Rosemary sang into the phone. Delilah doubted the comment was intended for her. "Rosemary—"

"Delilah, it's late. Bruce doesn't like me on the phone this time of night. It's our time together. I know you can't understand that, you not havin' a man yourself, but . . ."

"Oh, no, you're not doing this tonight," Delilah warned. "You are not avoiding this subject. We're not tabling it for another day which will turn into another week. We have to make some decisions here, Rosemary."

"You're absolutely right," Rosemary snapped. "We do. And it's high time some of us started taking responsibility for ourselves, isn't it, Delilah? Now, I have to go. You want to send her back, you go right ahead. You put her on a plane. Daddy says he might be able to pitch in and we can send her to some kind of boarding school. I'm not having her here. I'm not having her ruin my marriage. I know I told you a long time ago that I could do this, but I can't. I'm not strong like you. I never was. I just can't do it anymore."

Delilah heard Bruce's voice in the background. She didn't wait for Rosemary to say anything else. She just said good night and hung up.

Her first impulse was to cry. Her second was to call Snowden. Instead, she unloaded the box of files, spread them out on her bed again, and got back to work.

Julie woke sometime in the night. At least she thought it was night. She was surrounded by darkness. She pushed up off the hard floor that was not a floor at all, but the ground. "H . . . hello?" she called out, her voice trembling.

Where was she? How had she gotten here?

Her head pounded. The back of it . . . She ran her hand over her hair and felt a sticky warmth. She could smell its sweet, cloying scent. *Blood.*

She remembered the odd call from Marty. It had been late. She'd been watering the tomato plants by the light of the security lamp out back. The party. The auction. Marty's tape with the shot of the girls.

No. Julie hung her head, trying to think clearly. The fund-raiser hadn't been today. That was days ago. Today was . . . Wednesday.

Nausea rose in her throat. Her head hurt so badly, she thought she might be sick. She ran her hand through her hair again. The skin was split open. It was still bleeding, but not heavily. It was so dark that she couldn't see anything, but she could feel the dampness of the blood. Blood on her shirt. Now on her hand.

Sister Agatha had brought her the cordless phone in the garden. She remembered that the tomato plants were getting so tall that the girls would have to check each plant carefully to be sure they were getting all the ripe fruit.

Julie remembered what Marty had said about having an abortion. She remembered meeting her at the diner. They had been alone. The cup of tea had tasted good after a long day.

They had parted on good terms.

Hadn't they?

Julie remembered walking to her van. She'd had to park in the back because the curb had been roped off. Wet paint, or something.

Marty had been waiting there for her at the diner when she arrived. She had been there a while. On her second cup of coffee she had said. She had seemed so happy about her new job. About moving.

Julie had walked out to the van in the dark.

She had heard someone behind her just as she reached the driver's side door. "Marty?" she cried hoarsely, lifting her head up, pushing herself to a seated position.

Her head swam. The nausea rose again and she gagged and vomited. Tears filled her eyes but she did not cry. She wiped her mouth with the back of her hand and felt along the ground with her hands. Had she fallen in the parking lot?

But the parking lot was paved. This was dirt. Hard-packed. Funny smelling.

"Hello," she cried. "Is anyone there?" Her voice seemed to echo around her and though she couldn't see, she sensed she was in a room. A very small room.

Julie had never liked enclosed places and she shivered, feeling her way forward again, crawling. Fighting panic. "Hello? Hello!" Her fingertips found a solid edge along the dirt . . . a wall? She rose to her feet and felt blindly with both hands, slapping her palms against the wall as she followed, making a turn, following another wall. *She was trapped. Someone had hit her in the back of the head. Kidnapped her.*

She fought the terror that suddenly gripped her chest. She was breathing, in and out, but she didn't seem to be able to get any air. Hyperventilating . . .

All her life, Julie had read descriptions of hell, but never once had it been a small, dark room.

* * *

"I don't care what Sister Agatha says," Izzy hissed in the dark dormitory room on the second story of the old farmhouse. The only light illuminating the four beds lining the wall was the security lamp in the backyard, casting a feeble glow through the curtained windows, and a night-light near the closed door. "I think someone should call the police. And if she won't do it, we should."

"Shhhh. She's going to hear us and then we're going to be in so much trouble." Yolanda, in the twin bed beside Izzy's, leaned back and pulled the sheet up to her chin. "I think we should just do what Sister Agatha says, say our prayers and go to sleep. Sister Julie will be home by the time we wake up in the morning."

"Go to sleep? How can you sleep when Sister Julie is missing?" Tiffany whispered from the next bed over.

"She isn't *missing*. She just isn't home yet."

"*Dios, amio*," Lareina prayed from her bed on the far side of the room. Her wooden rosary beads clicked. "I think you're right. We should call the police. Sister Julie would never leave us."

Yolanda lay still in her bed. "But what if she's just *out*?"

Izzy glanced at the digital clock on the nightstand between her bed and Yolanda's. The bright red letters glared. "At one o'clock in the morning?"

"Ah, *Dios*, where could she be?" Lareina moaned.

"Shhhhhh." Yolanda popped up in the bed, still clutching her sheet to her chin. "Sister is going to hear us and we're all going to be in trouble and it's going to be your fault, Izzy. It's always your fault when we get in trouble."

The door opened and Yolanda fell back in her bed, pretending to be asleep.

It was only Elise, dressed in pink babydoll pajamas

which Izzy kept telling her looked stupid with her big baby belly.

"We're all going to be in trouble for what?" Elise demanded, dropping down on Izzy's bed. "What'd you do now? Steal some of Sister's Julie's cigarettes again?"

Izzy pulled up her feet to make room. "We're talking about Sister Julie. Yolanda thinks we should just go to sleep and she'll be here when we wake up in the morning, but I think the senorita's in denial. I think we need to call the police. Something's wrong. Something's happened to Sister Julie and if Sister Agatha won't call the police, someone else has to."

"Maybe Sister Agatha knows where she is." Elise shrugged, scooting back on Izzy's bed until her back rested against the wall. "Maybe she's somewhere she's not supposed to be," she whispered conspiratorially, "and Sister Agatha is just trying to protect us from the truth. Spare Maria's Place the shame of a nun gone off the deep end. Sex, drugs. Rock 'n' roll. You know the routine, Izzy."

"Elise!" Izzy kicked her in the calf. "You're not even funny."

"You know, Sister Julie's an alcoholic," Amanda entered the dark dorm room, followed by two more girls. "Maybe she's at a bar."

"Sister Julie is not an alcoholic," Pam defended, pushing Yolanda over to make room for herself in Yolanda's bed.

Someone closed the door again.

"She is, too," Yolanda insisted. "She told me."

"You're such a liar, Yolanda," Elise complained. "Who would believe anything you said? You told us that you lived in Beverly Hills and your mom and dad were plastic surgeons and they had their own show on E!"

"So," Yolanda whispered loudly. "She *is* an alcoholic. She told me herself. She goes to AA and everything, just like my mom and my Aunt Carmen."

"So maybe she's at a bar?" Belinda asked. "And Sister Agatha is covering for her? Maybe Sister Agatha doesn't want us to know Sister Julie fell off the wagon."

"No, wait, I know," Tiffany offered triumphantly. "She's out on a date."

Izzy grabbed a pillow and threw it at her.

"Hey, maybe she's out on a date with Dr. Trubant. Maybe she's screwin' his brains out as we speak," Tiffany suggested.

Izzy threw her last pillow at the girl.

"Did you see him flirting with her on the front porch Saturday?"

"*Pul-lease.* Brad flirts with everyone." Elise pulled up her bare feet to sit Indian-style on Izzy's bed. "Even with Sister Agatha. Did you see them—"

"You guys are such idiots," Izzy interrupted. "Sister Agatha wouldn't protect Sister Julie. She hates her guts. She thinks she should be in charge here." She looked at the clock again. "Like Sister Julie always tells us, use your heads, ladies. It's one o'clock in the morning and Sister Julie isn't here. As long as you've been here, has she ever been out until one in the morning?"

"What could have happened to her?"

"I don't know, but it can't be good," Izzy admitted. "I'm telling you, we need to call the police."

"You call the police and Sister Julie is somewhere she's not supposed to be and you'll get her fired," Amanda warned.

"Excommunicated," Lareina breathed.

"Better than being dead!" Izzy climbed out of bed. "That's it. I'm using the hall phone. I'm calling 911."

"That's right next to Sister's door." Yolanda tugged at her sheet, pinned down by the girls sitting on the edge of her bed, and tried to climb further under. "You'll be grounded until your baby is born."

"I don't care."

As Izzy headed for the door, Elise caught her hand. "Wait," she whispered. "I have a better idea. I know who we should call."

Chapter 24

Callie was dreaming she was at an Eric Clapton concert. She and Izzy had front row seats and he was playing the best guitar riff, ever.

Only . . . it didn't quite sound right.

She woke up suddenly, realizing the sound of the guitar solo wasn't in her dream; it was coming from somewhere in her dark bedroom. Her new phone, in its charger beside her bed, was ringing the Clapton ring tone she'd downloaded.

She looked at the clock beside her bed. One fifteen in the morning. Who the heck was calling her at one fifteen? She hadn't given Jessica or any of those dorks in Georgia her new cell number. Her mother better not have.

Callie grabbed up the phone, afraid it might wake up her aunt in the next room. "Hello," she whispered.

"Callie, it's Izzy. I've called you like three times."

"Izzy? What's wrong? You okay?" Callie reached for the lamp beside her bed, switched it on, and squinted in the bright light.

"Callie," she whispered, "we got a problem here."

Callie listened to everything Izzy had to say. By the

time her friend had spilled the story of the missing nun, Callie was out of bed, pacing. "Izzy, you have to call the police."

"But what if she's just out or something?"

"Yeah, and what if the serial killer has her and is driving away with her this minute?"

"Callie, please," Izzy groaned. "Sister Julie is like the nicest person in the whole world. I mean, she's been nicer to me than any other adult I've ever known. I can't rat her out if she's out at some bar or something."

"She wouldn't be at a bar."

"She might. Yolanda says she's an alcoholic and she goes to AA."

Callie was getting scared now. "You have to tell."

"What about Sister Agatha?"

"What about her?" Callie dropped down on the edge of her bed, leaning over, trying to think. She sat up and pushed her hair out of her eyes. "I don't know. Maybe she *wants* something bad to happen her. You know she hates Sister Julie. She wants to get rid of her so she can be in charge there."

"I don't know," Izzy whispered. "I was thinking the same thing, but it sounds pretty crazy."

"Izzy, please," Callie begged. "Call the police. Let me call them or . . . or at least let me wake up my Aunt Delilah. She'll know what to do."

Izzy was quiet on the other end of the line.

"Izzy?" Callie said.

"I don't know! I don't know!" Izzy moaned. "I don't want Sister Julie to get in trouble, but I don't want anything bad to happen to her, either."

Callie could tell that her friend was crying now. "You said she went out and she didn't come back. Tell me where she went and me and Aunt Delilah, we'll check it out."

"Wait a minute," Izzy said into the phone.

There was whispering.

"Okay." Izzy came back on. "She got a phone call tonight. Lareina saw Sister Agatha take the phone out to the garden. Then, Amanda said she saw Sister Julie in the kitchen. Sister couldn't find her keys to the van. When Amanda found them in the dining room, Sister Julie said she'd be back in an hour."

"So she couldn't have meant to go too far," Callie questioned.

"I don't think so."

Callie tried to think fast. "But no one knows who she was meeting?"

"No. At least none of us," Izzy said. "Maybe Sister Agatha, or Monica, but none of the girls know."

"Okay," Callie said. "I'm going to hang up now, but I'll call you back."

"No, you can't! Sister Agatha will hear the phone ring. We're on the stairs."

"Then, call me back on my cell in five minutes. Okay?"

"Okay," Izzy whispered.

Callie hung up the phone and bolted for her bedroom door.

Snowden had the phone in his hand by the second ring. "Chief Calloway," he said as clearly as if he had been wide awake rather than sound asleep.

"Snowden, it's Delilah." Her voice sounded stiff.

"You okay?" He swung his feet over the side of the bed and switched on the bedside lamp. "What's the matter?" He looked at his alarm clock. It was two twenty-five.

"I'm fine," she said, her voice strained. Odd. "I have Callie here in the car with me."

"Something wrong with Callie? She in some kind of trouble?" He was already on his feet, searching for the shorts he'd worn the evening before.

"No, Chief. Nothing like that. We're fine, Callie and I, but . . ." She took a breath. "Sister Julie might be missing."

"Might be?" He dropped his shorts on the floor and went to his closet. He pulled a pair of gray uniform pants from a hanger and stepped into them, cradling the phone on his shoulder.

"Long story. I'll tell you everything once you arrive. I've got Smith and Tattersaw here in a car, and Williams on his way out to Maria's Place, but I think you need to come now. We're at Nateesha's diner. In the back parking lot."

Snowden was so relieved that Delilah was okay that he wasn't quite thinking clearly, as he tried to switch gears. Tried to think about his job. About Sister Julie and not about how badly Delilah had scared him when she called. He'd been afraid she was hurt. In danger.

He couldn't remember having ever been afraid for anyone like this before.

"Let me get dressed," Snowden said into the phone. "I'll be there in ten minutes."

"I'll be right here, Chief."

No matter how many crime scenes Snowden attended, he'd never get used to the ominous, rhythmic pulse of the emergency vehicle lights. The sober faces of his cops. His officers always knew what their jobs were; he never walked in on a scene to find them standing around with their hands in their pockets. They were always taking photographs, collecting evidence, talking to witnesses. But it always seemed to him as if time was moving in slow motion.

He drove up Main Street, turning into the driveway that led to the rear of the diner. He could see the blue flashing lights reflecting off the surrounding buildings even before he made the turn. Delilah approached his car as he pulled in behind her cruiser. A set of spotlights had been set up, running on a noisy gas generator. The lamps illuminated a white fourteen-passenger van that read Maria's Place in block letters along the side.

"Detective," Snowden said as he climbed out of his car, placing his hat on his head. He noted at once that she was dressed in jeans and a T-shirt and sneakers. Civilian clothes. When she'd left her house, he guessed she hadn't expected to end up here. His gaze strayed to her car. Her niece was sitting in the front seat, watching them through the rearview mirror. He met Delilah's gaze.

"One of the girls from Maria's called Callie about one fifteen. Said she didn't want to get anyone in trouble, but she was concerned because Sister Julie wasn't home yet. And no, she never stayed out late."

Snowden tried to concentrate on what Delilah was saying and not on her. Not her worried brown eyes or the slight Southern drawl he could still detect in her voice, especially when she was tired or upset. He didn't think about how much he missed her or how close he was to telling her the hell with them all. If they couldn't be in Stephen Kill together, if they couldn't both keep their jobs, they'd go elsewhere. He thought about telling her he loved her.

Instead, he listened, processing her summation.

"Apparently she had gone out sometime after ten, but had been expected back within the hour. I left my house thinking I'd drive to Maria's. Possibly find her broke down or something. When she wasn't between here and there, I started cruising the streets looking for the van. Found it here."

"You brought your niece along?" he questioned.

"The girls from the house called her. They trusted Callie. I thought she should go with me. Besides, it's the middle of the night. I wasn't that comfortable leaving her alone."

"What kind of details you get about where Sister Julie was going? Why'd the van end up here?" He lifted his chin in the vehicle's direction.

"I spoke with Sister Agatha on the phone. She wasn't pleased the girls had contacted me, but she was cooperative enough. I think she's concerned, should this go down ugly, about bad publicity affecting Maria's."

"She have a reason to be concerned?" He glanced at the white van. Officer Tattersaw was dusting the inside of the vehicle for fingerprints. Smith was taking photos with a digital camera. "Our nun up to anything nuns shouldn't be up to?"

"We didn't really get into that over the phone." She glanced in the direction of her car. "I got the feeling all the girls were there in the room listening to the conversation. I thought I should talk with her face to face."

The teenager was still watching them.

"What's your gut instinct?" Snowden asked Delilah grimly. "Our guy strike again? She been kidnapped?"

"I want to walk out onto the street."

He followed her.

"I think it's a definite possibility," she said. "A woman in her thirties who doesn't come home. A nun who doesn't miss curfew. The abandoned vehicle. Possibly some blood on the pavement, but very little."

"Keys? Purse?"

"On the seat of the van. Looked as if they had been placed there."

They walked down the blacktop driveway, through the dark, out onto the streetlamp lit sidewalk. "Appears the city was doing some painting or something yesterday." She indicated the yellow tape blocking off the parking spaces on both sides of Main Street in front of the diner. She looked back at the dark windows. "If she was here, someone must have seen her." She checked her wrist-watch. "Staff will be coming in by five. I think I'll go out to Maria's, talk to Sister Agatha, and be back here when the diner opens."

"When the guys are done here, I'll have the van towed and send our patrols to cruise the streets. Get Johnson to call the morning shift in early. If she has been kid-napped, we have to move quickly, Detective."

"If he did take her, she's still alive, Chief," Delilah said staring at the darkened diner windows.

"If he follows the MO," he agreed.

"That means we have a little time." She started back up the driveway. "I just hope we have enough."

"I knew something like this was going to happen," Sister Agatha said.

"You knew?" Delilah sat at the table in the center of the brightly lit kitchen. The clock on the wall read four twenty-five.

"It was only a matter of time." The nun, dressed in a habit, her hair hidden under her wimple, reached for the tea kettle on the institutional size stainless steel stove. "Can I make you some tea, Detective?"

"No, thank you."

"I'm going to make myself some tea," Sister Agatha said, seeming to be moving on autopilot.

It had been Delilah's experience that often this was how people responded in times of emergency. Some fell apart, but most just kept doing whatever it was they normally did. She thought about Jenny Grove's husband cleaning off the kitchen counter while discussing his missing wife.

"Can you tell me why you knew Sister Julie would go missing?"

"I didn't mean I knew she'd disappear." She flipped the lever on the kitchen sink faucet and watched water pour into the spout of the teakettle. "I just meant that something bad would happen. To her."

Delilah waited.

"You know, she wasn't what she appeared to be," Sister Agatha said. "Not what you expected of a daughter of Christ."

"How so?"

"Shall we say, she *had a past*?" The kettle full of tap water, Sister Agatha carried it back to the stove. "She had bad habits."

"What kind of past? What kind of bad habits?" Delilah was almost afraid to hear what the nun had to say. She had liked Sister Julie. Did like her.

She wasn't ready to think of her in the past tense. Not yet.

"Did you know Sister Julie drank?"

"She drank?" Delilah's job was to remain neutral in her interview, but she couldn't keep the shock out of her voice.

"Well, she said she hadn't had a drink in years. Never even partook of the blood of Christ in communion," Sister Agatha said, as if that, in itself, was a sin. "She attended AA sometimes."

"Regularly?"

"No. Just occasionally." The nun turned the gas flame on under the teakettle. "But she'd been going lately, once, twice a week." She turned to face Delilah. "Temptations come and go, Detective. I suppose she was in a temptation phase. I don't know. We never discussed it."

Delilah made a note in her notebook to check out the AA meetings in town. She didn't know how much information she'd get out of anyone. Meetings were considered private. Nothing anyone said was ever supposed to leave the room. But it was worth a try.

"When I spoke to Amanda when I came in, she said she saw Sister Julie before she left the house. That it was at least ten o'clock and that she said she was meeting someone. Do you know who she was meeting?"

"Monica had answered the phone but she was trying to finish an e-mail for me before she left for the evening. I carried the phone out to Sister Julie in the garden myself, but no, I don't know who she spoke with."

"I'll need to talk to Monica as soon as possible," Delilah said.

"I've already called her in." Sister Agatha removed a blue coffee mug from a cupboard. "You certain you won't have tea, Detective?" She went on without really waiting for a response. "I expect Monica will be here any minute. She was very upset when I called her. She and Sister Julie were close, I think."

Delilah noted that the nun spoke as if the woman wouldn't be returning. She recalled the argument she'd heard in the office Saturday afternoon.

The teakettle rattled on the stove burner. Then it began to whistle.

"I knew you would want to talk to her. Monica." Sister Agatha dropped a tea bag into her cup.

"You said you thought the two were close. You don't know?"

She shrugged one shoulder. "Monica is introverted. She doesn't say much around me. All business. A hard worker. But she obviously liked Sister Julie. Everyone liked Sister Julie."

Again, past tense.

"And you didn't?"

"I didn't say that." Sister Agatha lifted the teakettle from the burner, turning off the flame. "Sister Julie was easy to like. She had that kind of personality." She poured boiling water into the mug. "You know exactly what I mean. You saw it. You liked her."

Delilah thought Sister's Agatha's comments were odd. But then she had always thought the woman was odd. There was no reason for her to expect anything any different from her. "Back to Sister Julie and this phone call. You took the phone to her and then what?"

"I went upstairs. Some of the girls were throwing water in the bathroom earlier while washing up and brushing their teeth. I'd gone back upstairs to be sure it had been cleaned up."

"Did Sister Julie tell you she was going out?"

"She came upstairs. There was still water on the floor and I had given one of our young ladies a mop. I was overseeing the completion of the cleanup. Sister Julie said she was going out, but that she would be back shortly. It was my night so it wasn't necessary that she provide any further explanation."

"Your night?"

"We take turns overseeing evening prayer. Making sure the girls get to bed at a decent time."

"So basically Julie had the evening off?"

"Something like that." Sister Agatha carried her mug to the table and sat down across from Delilah.

Delilah waited until the nun was settled in her chair. "Did you and Sister Julie have a disagreement Saturday?"

Sister Agatha looked up. "What do you mean?"

"I mean an argument."

The nun blew across the surface of the steaming mug. "I don't believe so."

"In the office."

Sister Agatha shook her head. "No. Definitely not."

"Hmmm," Delilah mused. "I heard voices when I walked into the house; I believe they were coming from the office. Someone was having a disagreement with Sister Julie. I assumed it was you."

"You assumed incorrectly, Detective." She sipped her tea. "Do you think she's been kidnapped? I was wondering, because I'll have to make a full report in the morning to our bishop. Someone will have to take immediate charge of Maria's Place. It's only logical that that person be me, Detective."

Chapter 25

"I don't mind skipping today's session." Callie tipped her chin, letting her hair fall over her face. She still hated riding in her aunt's cruiser. Hated being gawked at. And there were plenty of gawkers passing by as they sat parked in front of the shrink's office.

Callie was supposed to have gone Monday, but Trubant's secretary had called and postponed until today. Callie was going to be pissed if she had to go today and then again Monday. "I can just go to the library now. Then you don't have to worry about me the rest of the day."

"Thanks for getting back to me," her aunt said into the cell phone at her ear. "Can you hold on for just a second?" She lowered the phone. "Go to your session, Callie. I have to pay for the appointment whether you show up or not, so go."

"This isn't my regular day. He's the one who changed it."

"It doesn't matter. The appointment was made."

Callie considered arguing further, but she could tell by Aunt Delilah's voice that the counseling session wasn't up for negotiation today. Callie felt bad for her. Everyone was upset about Sister Julie being missing, but it seemed like her aunt was taking it personally. Callie didn't know that she and Sister Julie were good friends or anything, but it was like her aunt thought she was responsible for everybody in the town. Everything that happened to them. Aunt Delilah hadn't come right out and said she thought the killer had kidnapped Sister Julie, but Callie wasn't stupid. She knew, in all likelihood, the poor woman was going to end up floating in Horsey Mill Pond. It was just a matter of time.

"Wait for me inside the office," her aunt ordered. "I don't want you waiting on the street. I don't want you walking to the library, alone. Now, go. I have to take this call."

"I'll see you in a little while." Callie got out of the car and took the sidewalk up to the door. She entered the waiting room and waved to the receptionist. Dr. Trubant came out for her before she had a chance to read the whole article in the magazine about the cost of cosmetic surgery. Callie was a little bummed as she set the magazine down and followed the psychologist into his office. She was wondering how much a boob job would be since she was severely lacking in that department. "So how've you been?" Dr. Trubant asked.

They took their usual seats. He sipped a Diet Coke. She reached for the can of *Bendables*.

"Freaked," she told him. "I really like Sister Julie. I can't believe she disappeared. I know that nut job has got her."

"Pretty scary stuff, I know," he said, not sounding like he really thought so. "I understand you went out looking for Sister Julie with your aunt last night."

"I have been sitting at the station since five this morning. One of the cops took me home a little while ago and waited outside while I took a shower and got dressed."

She shook the can of *Bendables* making them dance inside, but she didn't take any out. "Aunt Delilah is like afraid to let me out of her sight. I guess she's afraid I'm next on the creep's list, or something."

"You afraid you might be?"

She shrugged, putting the can back. "Not really. I mean what are the odds? Stephen Kill is a town of three thousand, if you include the people living in the sticks. It's probably more likely Mrs. Carpenter will run me over on the sidewalk." She looked at him. So far he hadn't reacted to anything she said. "You know her. The old lady with the oxygen tank who drives the Caddy. I saw her run two red lights last week and she always parks two tires on the sidewalk in front of the library when she comes to check out her steamy romance novels. " She narrowed her gaze. "You know, Dr. Trubant, there're a lot of sex scenes in those books. You wouldn't think Mrs. Carpenter would have it in her."

"You think about death a lot, Callie?"

He hadn't bitten on the Mrs. Carpenter subject or the trashy novels. She arched an eyebrow. "No. Should I?"

A phone rang. The sound was muffled. It had to be a cell phone in his desk.

He ignored the phone, smiling at her. "I'm supposed to be the one asking the questions. Remember, I'm the one getting the big bucks."

It was an okay joke, but she didn't laugh. She wasn't in the mood to play his games today. She was worried about Izzy. Izzy was really upset about Sister Julie. Callie had talked to her three or four times this morning and she'd cried every time. Callie had wanted to go over, but Aunt Delilah wouldn't let her. She said that Sister Agatha and Monica had enough to worry about right now; they didn't need Callie.

The phone in the desk drawer began to ring again. Callie looked at Dr. Trubant, at the desk, and back at him again. "You going to answer that?"

"I'll check my messages later." He set down his soda can and reached for his leather portfolio where she knew he jotted his notes about her. "Did you talk to your mother this weekend?"

"Yeah." Callie picked at her blue nail polish.

"How'd that go?"

"Fine. She likes me fine as long as I'm more than three hundred miles away from her."

"You don't think your mother likes you, Callie?

The cell phone began to ring again.

"I don't know." Her gaze shifted from the desk, and its invisible ringing phone, to him. "I think she just can't deal with me. Like, now that I can think for myself. She liked me fine enough when I was little and I did what she said. Wore what she said. Said what she told me to say. Now . . . it's like she doesn't know what to do with me, anymore."

"Do you think—"

A knock on the door interrupted him. It opened. "Sorry, Paul," the receptionist said. "You've got a call. She won't leave her name, but she says it's urgent."

Callie watched him. He seemed flustered as he got up off the couch, which amused her. He always played everything so cool. She wondered what was up with the megaphone calls.

"Could you excuse me for just a second, Callie?" he asked. "I apologize for the interruption."

"Line two," the reception called before closing the door behind her.

Dr. Trubant sat down in his big leather chair behind

his desk and picked up the phone. "Hello, Dr. Trubant speaking."

Callie got out of the chair and wandered over to the dining room table and chairs in the corner of the office and picked up a brochure on Attention Deficient Disorder someone had left there.

"I'm with a client," Trubant said into the phone. He paused. "That was why I couldn't pick up. I'm in a session."

Callie dropped the brochure back on the table; she didn't have ADD, but she was pretty sure both her half brother and half sister had it. They couldn't do anything for more than about five seconds before they were hopping off to do something else. All the Hawaiian Punch and Fruit Roll-Ups they ate. That was her theory.

"I can't talk," Trubant was saying.

Callie walked in front of the wall of bookcases, dragging a finger along the shelves. Besides all the books, there were more framed photos, mostly of Trubant, pictures, and stuff his kids must have made for him. There was a clay pot that looked like a coiled worm. A fake stained-glass window of tissue paper. Some other junk.

Trubant needed to bust out his dust rag. Either that or *Muriel* needed to stop shopping on the Internet and get her big butt in here and do it.

"No, no I don't believe I have any open appointments today," he said into the phone. "I *can't*." His last words sounded weird. Like something was going on that he didn't want Callie to overhear.

She passed the bathroom door and the one he had told her led into the back to a hallway. She'd once read somewhere about shrinks always having an escape route planned, kind of like they taught you in school during fire safety week. That way, if a client flipped and whipped out a gun or a machete, the doctor would have a way to get out.

Callie halted in front of the big, black filing cabinets. Trubant was whispering now.

Interesting, she thought. She'd have to tell Izzy about it later. Izzy would have all kinds of crazy ideas about who Trubant was talking to and what all his whispered comments meant. Callie's guess was that it was a girlfriend. She'd seen Trubant at the picnic at Maria's with his wife and kids. She'd also seen him flirting with half a dozen women throughout the day. He cheated. She knew he did. She could tell by his body language when he talked to other women.

Callie studied the blank tags on the file cabinet drawers. Nothing was labeled. They had locks. She had seen a set of keys on the bookshelves behind a papier-mâché mask one of kids must have made.

Callie looked in Trubant's direction. He had turned his back to her and he was still whispering. She rested her hand on the drawer. She really wasn't that big a snooper, but she was curious about his files and what he was saying about her. There were no file cabinets in Muriel's cubby—everything had to be here.

She pulled and the drawer began to glide out.

"Please," Trubant was saying insistently. "I'll have to call you back." He swung back around.

Callie let go of the drawer.

He looked at her.

Caught.

"Callie, those files are private. It's actually against the law for you to open that drawer."

"They've got locks on them. You ought to actually lock them if they're so top-secret," she said defensively.

He walked around the desk, returning to the couch. "I do. At night."

He gestured to her chair. "You want to sit down again and we'll continue."

Callie dropped into the chair, surrendering, at least for the moment. "Sure, Paul," she said, leaning back, arms on the chair. "What's on your mind?"

"Hey, Chief." Delilah walked into his office, checking his clock as she entered. She only had ten minutes before she had to leave to pick up Callie. She didn't want to be late. She had instructed the girl to stay inside the office, but she wasn't taking any chances. Not with Sister Julie missing. Not when she still couldn't figure out how this screwball was choosing his victims.

Snowden set aside what he had been reading, removed his reading glasses, and shifted back in his chair. "What have you got?"

They were both grim.

"Well, the waitress who served three cups of coffee to the woman waiting for Sister Julie said she didn't recognize her. Of course, she also said she'd left her glasses home on the counter yesterday. All she could tell me was mid-thirties. Blond. Jeans. T-shirt. Didn't see either of them drive up or drive away, but that was because—"

"No open spot out front," Snowden finished for her.

"Exactly. And no one else came into the diner except one woman who picked up a quart of chicken salad. Spoke to her and she didn't remember anyone being in the diner at all. The waitress says Sister Julie and this woman she met sat in a rear booth. You've been in there. You can't really see those booths well from the cash register." She exhaled, trying to keep her thought processes going and her emotions at a minimum.

"I talked to Sister Agatha and Monica again a little while ago. Separately this time." She hovered behind the chairs in front of his desk. "I almost had the feeling when I first questioned them that one was covering for the other, but I couldn't be sure. Sister Agatha kept repeating the need for privacy at Maria's. Both claim they didn't know who had called. Apparently, there are different phone lines and numbers at the house. There's one private line designated for the personal use of the nuns, employees, and volunteers. It's unlisted. The only people who should have it are people who it's been given to."

"But if there's a hundred active volunteers right now," Snowden intoned.

"Everybody's got it." Delilah rested both hands on the back of one of the chairs. She was still having bouts of morning sickness, but there was no rhyme or reason to when it came or went. Morning. Afternoon. Evening. On an empty stomach. On a full stomach. She knew from experience she just had to ride it out.

"So . . . I've requested a trace on that phone line. We'll have the numbers received and dialed for the last week"—she glanced at the clock again—"in about half an hour."

"Fingerprints?"

"Tattersaw picked up a few. It'll be easy to rule most of them out. Sister Julie required that anyone who worked at Maria's have a background check and be printed. We'll even have her prints, but I'm not expecting any earthshaking news. There were no prints in the other cases."

"Gloves," Snowden murmured.

"There were lot of prints in the back, but they most likely belong to the girls. Shoot, Callie's are probably back there. We'd have to have permission from their parents to print them so I hesitate to do that."

"You think one of them could have something to do with this?"

Delilah frowned. As preposterous as the idea sounded, she knew they needed to think outside the box. Consider every possibility, no matter how remote. It was the only way they were going to have a chance of being able to find the nun before she was dead. No one would ever have dreamed soft-spoken, well-liked Alice Crupp heard voices in her head commanding her to murder people in the town who had committed sins, so a teenaged killer probably wasn't as far-fetched as it might sound.

"It's not likely. If they were going to hire someone to kidnap anyone, it would be Sister Agatha." She half-grinned, half-grimaced. "Not too many Sister Agatha fans in the house. In the town, for that matter."

"Okay."

She was quiet for a minute, thinking about the argument she had heard in the office at Maria's Saturday. Sister Agatha denied she had had an argument with Sister Julie. Had she been lying to cover herself? Had the two nuns had it out? Delilah had heard from Callie who had heard from Izzy that Sister Agatha made no bones about believing she was better suited to the job of director of Maria's Place. The women apparently had disagreements regularly. Could Sister Agatha have done something to Sister Julie? Maybe made it look as if Rob and Jenny's killer had kidnapped her? She'd certainly been eager to call the bishop this morning about having herself put in charge.

If Sister Agatha was capable of doing away with Sister

Julie, Delilah extrapolated, could Sister Agatha have been responsible for the other murders? She *had* known Jenny Grove.

But not the kid.

Delilah rubbed her temple. She needed to eat something or her blood sugar would soon plummet. She was starting to move beyond *looking outside the box* to plain craziness.

"So that's where we are now," Delilah said. "I'm going to find out who called and who Sister Julie met. I'll talk to that person." She started for the door. "I was also wondering if we didn't need to consider . . ." She halted, and then started again. "Posting a twenty-four watch around the perimeter of Horsey Mill Pond."

They were both silent for a moment, both thinking the same thing, she knew. If the maniac who had killed Jenny and Rob had taken Julie, or followed the same MO, then the stakeout would be about body recovery. It might mean catching the bastard, but it would mean giving in. It would mean giving up hope of finding Julie alive.

"Let's wait another day or two," Snowden said softly. "I think we've got a little leeway."

Delilah only nodded.

Leaving Snowden's office, she returned to her desk, grabbed her bag, keys, and a pack of saltine crackers and headed for the back door. As she stepped into the parking lot, two reporters shoved microphones into her face.

"Detective Swift!" It was a woman in her early twenties who occasionally did bits of the evening news at WKKB.

No Marty Kyle, which seemed odd to Delilah. The reporter hadn't attended the press conference this morning, either.

"Just a couple of quick questions," said a young man

whose name she didn't know, but she recognized as a reporter for a Salisbury station.

Bright camera light shined in Delilah's eyes. She was tired. Worried. Annoyed. She didn't have time for this crap right now. She'd already given a statement this morning and if she didn't hurry, she was going to be late to pick up Callie.

"Where are we in the investigation, Detective Swift?" the eager young woman from WKKB asked. "Do you believe the same person who abducted and murdered the two locals has also abducted Sister Julie?"

"We know the passenger van driven by Sister Julie was found abandoned behind the diner," the young man barged in, knowing he only had a couple seconds to get a piece to run on the noon news. "Have you discovered the identity of the mystery person she was meeting last night?"

"Now, if we knew who the mystery person was, would it be a mystery?" The flippant remark slipped from Delilah's mouth before she had time to think. It was completely inappropriate. The Stephen Kill police didn't need her getting smart with reporters. Not right now.

The woman cut in front of him. "Sister Julie has now been missing more than twelve hours. Do you believe with each passing hour, it's less likely she'll be found alive?"

"I don't have answers to your questions," Delilah said, looking straight into the cameras. "But what I do know is that Sister Julie is alive out there somewhere and someone knows where she is. That someone, perhaps, is confused, angry, suffering, and my heart goes out to him or her. But he or she has to understand that this is not the way to solve these issues."

"Are you saying that if the kidnapper was to set the nun free, punishment would be lighter?"

"I'm saying we can help. It's not too late." She looked down and then up again. "But Sister Julie must be freed. Alive. Today." She looked at the reporters. "That's all I have to say. Now, if you'll excuse me."

Back in her chair forty minutes later, Delilah removed a yellow highlighter from a drawer and began to scan the phone numbers on the printout. The last incoming call the night before was at nine forty-seven, concurring with Monica and Sister Agatha's estimation.

The call had come from Dr. Paul Trubant's office.

Chapter 26

"But, Paul, you canceled him last week." Muriel frowned. "It's not good for business."

He stood in front of his receptionist's counter, wanting to kick it. He kept his face impassive. "Could we reschedule?"

"Not for today. You're already double-booked at four; you have a five and you're supposed to be at Maria's Place at six. The Klines are no-shows half the time. You said to double-book during the Klines' hour and pray Roberta's forgotten again."

He wasn't going to let her make this his problem. "Muriel. I don't care what you do. The police obviously need my help. I'm going to speak with Detective Swift and then I'm going to catch up on my notes." He walked through the doorway into his office. "I'll see my next appointment at two when you get back from lunch. Show the detective in when she arrives."

He closed the door and leaned against it. Detective Swift hadn't said why she needed to speak with him, today, as soon as possible, but he knew it wasn't about

Callie. That could have been done over the phone and they'd just discussed her *progress* the other day.

There wasn't a thing wrong with Callie that a little maturity and parental guidance wouldn't solve. She didn't really even need to be in counseling, except that Paul needed the money. Hell, the girl had more common sense, more intuition, more people skills than most of the mentally healthy adults he knew. She certainly had it all over him. The teen had him figured out; he could see it in her eyes, hear it in the careful words she chose.

He took a deep, calming breath and walked to his desk. *Maybe the detective just wanted some assistance with her profiling,* he told himself, taking his chair. He didn't imagine a lot of that kind of police business took place over the phone. She'd come in person before when she'd wanted his help.

But it hadn't sounded on the phone as if that was all she needed. This had something to do with Sister Julie's disappearance. She'd sounded too official during the phone call, which made him uneasy.

He was afraid for Sister Julie, for the unspeakable crime that could very well have befallen her. But he was also afraid for himself. He wasn't exactly in a position for close scrutiny. He had known for some time he'd been playing with fire. That his impulses were getting out of control. Addiction worked that way; it didn't matter if it was gambling, drugs, alcohol, or sex. It sneaked up on you. Little infractions. Justifications. Then suddenly you were back in the middle of it again.

Eighteen months ago, Paul had found a good psychiatrist in Baltimore. Maybe he needed to see him again.

Paul heard Muriel speaking in the waiting room. A slightly lower-in-pitch voice followed. A knock at the door and Detective Swift walked in.

"Thanks for seeing me, Paul," she said casually. *Almost too casually.* She was attempting to make him feel comfortable. A psychological technique he knew all too well.

"Have a seat, Detective." He indicated the chair near his desk.

Muriel closed the door behind her.

"What can I do for you?"

"I'll stand. This'll be quick. I know you're busy." She opened a small notebook, glancing over it at him. She was a petite, slender woman, but she held herself well. Despite the pale lipstick and sassy blond hair, she almost appeared intimidating right now. "As you know, Paul, Sister Julie is missing."

"Yes. We're all shocked. Frightened. I talked with Sister Agatha this morning and she invited me to come for dinner tonight; give the girls some time to talk through this."

"What I needed to ask you about was a phone call you placed from here to Sister Julie last night at approximately nine forty-five."

For a moment he sat there flabbergasted. He was home last night with Susan. He couldn't have placed any calls from the office.

"Did you call Sister Julie last night?"

"N . . . no. Are you certain the call came from here, Detective? The office was closed. I was at home all evening." *Thank God,* he thought.

"This is one of your phone lines, isn't it?" She read a number.

"Yes. That's our number, but no one was here last night, Detective. Dear, that's disturbing." He averted his gaze. *Who the hell had been here last night? Had Kitten thought he would change his mind and meet her, after he had told her he couldn't?* Susan had seemed to be getting suspicious lately. He was trying to be careful. Trying to . . . ease off.

But Kitten hadn't said anything this morning on the phone about waiting for him last night. He was certain he hadn't agreed to meet anyone else here. Who else had a key? "Your secretary, maybe?" Detective Swift questioned.

Paul looked up. "I can ask her, but she never comes in after hours. Single mom. She's a busy lady."

"Anyone else have access to the office?" she pressured.

"Ah . . . the cleaning lady has a key. Connie Santori." She was Consuelo Santori's daughter, a sometimes drug addict, but she cleaned well most of the time and she was cheap.

"Was last night one of her usual cleaning nights?"

"No, it wasn't." Paul tried to take his time in responding to her questions. Meanwhile, his mind was running double-time.

He doubted Connie had been here. Who else had a key? Susan had gone out for milk, but that had been earlier in the evening, hadn't it? He couldn't say for sure what time she'd come back into the house. He'd fallen asleep in his La-Z-Boy after the kids were in bed. It had been after midnight when he'd gotten up and gone to bed. *Could Susan have been at the office, snooping around? God . . . that would be a disaster.*

"Paul, I'd like her name and number. I'll speak to Muriel on the way out to be sure she didn't stop by to pick something up. Can you think of anyone else who would have the key? You rent the building, don't you?"

"I do." He looked to her. "That would be upsetting. To think the Realtor allowed keys to get into someone else's hands."

Detective Swift glanced around his office. "So, you're

saying someone who didn't have permission to enter the office might have been here last night. Was anything disturbed this morning?"

If it was Susan, he didn't want the police involved. No matter what she'd found, he could talk her through it.

Except that she'd poured him a cup of coffee this morning on her way out the door to meet friends for a day at the state park and she hadn't behaved as if anything was wrong.

"Nothing seems to be touched." Paul glanced around. "We don't keep any money here, Detective. I can't imagine why anyone would break in. Or why they'd call Maria's Place."

"Were all the doors locked when you entered the building this morning?"

"The back was. I unlocked it myself. I suppose it's possible, though, that Muriel left the front door unlocked last night. Accidentally, of course. She's always in a hurry when she's leaving. She's been known to forget to switch the message over on the answering machine, leave lights on. You know, that sort of thing. She's a good employee most of the time, though, and she is trying to raise her son on her own. Deadbeat dad." He rolled the pen on his desk. Detective Swift was making him nervous the way she kept watching him. "I suppose she could have forgotten to lock the door."

She was silent for a minute. He didn't like silences. He resisted the urge to speak.

"That's all I have for right now," she finally said. "It's just that this phone call led Sister Agatha and Monica to believe Sister Julie was meeting the caller."

"I can't imagine who it could have been," he told her. "But in light of this, do you think I should have the locks changed on the doors?" He got up, and walked around his desk, adjusting the glass shade of the pharmaceutical lamp. "Maybe put a lock on my outside phone line box. People do that, you know, plug a phone into the outside jack and make charge calls, prank calls."

"We haven't had a problem with that in the area, as far as I know, but it's a possibility," she said. "If I were you, I'd definitely change the locks, and get a padlock on the outside box."

"Let me tell Muriel to get you those numbers."

"Great. And if you don't mind,"—she looked up him—"I'll talk with her a second alone."

"Mind? No, of course not." He offered a quick smile, opening the door for her. "Muriel, get the detective the phone numbers she needs and answer any questions she has, will you?"

Muriel looked up at him from her work station. "Sure, Paul, of course."

"I won't tell you to have a good day, Detective," Paul said. "Considering the circumstances, I wouldn't think that would be possible. Unless, of course, you were to find Sister Julie."

"Thanks for your help." She reached out and shook his hand, taking him by surprise.

"Call me if you need anything else," he said, heading back to the relative sanctuary of his office.

Delilah was outside on the sidewalk just a couple minutes later. She slid behind the steering wheel, started her car, and sat there letting the air-conditioning blast in her face. What was going on here? She'd known it wasn't Paul Trubant who called Sister Julie because both Sister Agatha and Monica had said the caller was female. But Paul had acted oddly; seemed nervous. Was he covering for someone?

The secretary had said she had not been at the office

last night. She'd been at a kid's pizza party with her son and then taken a group of boys home to her house for a sleepover, so she had witnesses. She also claimed she didn't forget to lock the door last night; she said she'd unlocked it herself this morning after arriving just behind her boss, who had used the rear entrance.

So, the question now was who had made the call? Why had it come from Paul's office, and why had the caller wanted to talk to the nun?

The Daughter set the VCR to record the news at noon and again at six thirty and eleven even though most likely, most of the segments would be repeats. There wasn't much coming out of the police department. The traitorous nun had only been missing twenty-four hours.

She watched the morning press conference on her tiny TV and noted how tired Delilah looked. *The Daughter* was concerned. She wondered if Delilah was eating enough, getting enough sleep.

The detective gave the usual briefing, which was pretty much lacking in any details. It was the way it was done. Reporters asked a couple of stupid questions. Delilah repeated most of her replies more than once, which irritated *The Daughter.* But Delilah remained patient, confident. It was why she was so good at her job. She looked great in the slacks and jacket she'd had Callie bring to her from her house when Officer Lopez had run the teenager home for a shower early that morning.

The Daughter fast-forwarded the tape to the noon news and discovered, to her delight, a new interview of Detective Swift. It was Megan Carmel from WKKB and appeared to have been taken in the rear parking lot at the police station. The reporter wasn't very good; she lacked charisma, but it didn't matter because the star of the moment was Delilah.

The Daughter held her breath, listening. The reporter jabbered for a minute and then came Delilah's sweet, melodic voice.

"I don't have answers to your questions," she said, looking right at *The Daughter.* Seeming to *see* her.

"But what I do know is that Sister Julie is alive out there somewhere and someone knows where she is," she continued. "That someone, perhaps, is confused—"

Confused?

The Daughter hit the pause button, thinking she must have misheard. She played it again.

"That someone, perhaps, is confused," Delilah repeated.

The Daughter felt a pang of resentment. "I'm not confused," she told the Delilah on the screen. She replayed it again, letting her go on further this time . . .

"—Angry, suffering, and my heart goes out to him or her. But he or she has to understand that this is not the way to solve these issues."

"Not a way to solve these issues?" *The Daughter* wondered allowed. What was Delilah talking about? Why was she saying these things on TV?

Didn't she realize how badly a loved one could be hurt by her words?

"Are you saying that if the kidnapper was to set the nun free, punishment would be lighter?" the reporter asked.

The Daughter couldn't take her eyes off the screen. She couldn't believe what she was hearing. She was completely blindsided. How could Delilah have so misunderstood her? Misunderstood their situation?

"I'm saying we can help. It's not too late."

The Daughter watched as Delilah lowered her gaze and then looked directly at her again, through the lens of the reporter's camera.

"But Sister Julie must be freed. Alive. Today."

"I can't let her go, Delilah," *The Daughter* said. "What are you talking about?" She tried to stay calm. "You know we can't let her go. She has to be punished."

The Daughter paused the tape again, staring at her sweet Delilah on the screen. It was all a misunderstanding. She took a breath, another, forcibly calming herself the way she had when she was little and *The Father* threw her into the closet. Into the soundless darkness.

"All a misunderstanding," she told herself aloud. But a misunderstanding that had to be corrected at once.

The Daughter stopped the VCR tape and scooted over to the far side of her bed, opening the nightstand drawer to remove her stationery. She planned to visit the nun later, but first she needed to write to Delilah.

Friday night, Marty sat in her Miata parked in front of a Baltimore restaurant. She'd been invited to join some of the reporters and staff from *News Night*.

For hours she'd been debating whether or not she should call Detective Swift. She hadn't heard about the nun's disappearance until late afternoon because she'd unplugged her TV the day before in anticipation of her move. She'd been ignoring the messages on her cell phone and landline, thinking her ex-employers were just trying to lure her back to work at that dinky, flea-bitten station. She'd spent all day yesterday deciding what to take with her and what to leave behind. It wasn't until Marty had run into a minimart for cigarettes, deciding to take up smoking again to lose a little weight, that she'd overheard a news bulletin and discovered Sister Julie had been missing for two days.

Eventually, the detective was going to find out that it was Marty who had met the nun at the diner, if she didn't already know. Marty had been afraid to check her cell phone voice messages for hours. It was better to tell her herself, she thought. There was no way she wanted to jeopardize this job opportunity. Some of the things that Sister Julie had said the other night had really hit home.

Emotion tightened her throat. She couldn't believe Sister Julie had been kidnapped. What kind of sick son-of-a-bitch kidnapped and murdered nuns? And Marty knew that was where this was headed. She knew it.

She sniffed and picked up her phone and keyed operator assistance. Within two minutes, she was connected to the Stephen Kill police. She learned that Sergeant Detective Swift had already gone home for the day. Of course she had; it was after nine. Marty told the desk sergeant or whoever the hell he said he was that it was urgent she speak to Detective Swift as it concerned the missing nun. He tried to get her to agree to talk to some other local yokel cop on duty, but Marty refused. She gave the pissed off cop her cell number and he said he'd pass her message on to Detective Swift. Less than five minutes passed before Marty's cell was ringing.

She finished applying her lipstick before answering the phone. She hadn't done anything wrong. God, for all she knew, she could have been the next victim instead of Sister Julie. Still, she was nervous. She really did want to move on with her life; get a fresh start. She didn't want to carry any pall into the office, come Monday morning.

"Detective Swift," she said. "That was quick."

"Miss Kyle, I understand you might have some information regarding Sister Julie?"

Marty got out of her car, closed the door, and leaned against it. She lit up a cigarette. "I've been incommunicado for a couple of days," she said into the phone. She inhaled deeply, speaking as she exhaled, trying to keep her voice even. What she had to say was incriminating enough. She didn't want this woman thinking she felt guilty over anything. "I didn't know Sister Julie had disappeared. I got a new job. I'm moving to Baltimore. Immediately. I'm already here."

"I wondered why I didn't see you at the press conference yesterday," the detective answered evenly.

"Yeah, I quit. They weren't too happy at the station. They walked me to the door with a box of my crap."

"I understand you have some information regarding the case?"

"Well, I don't, but . . . I do. I understand you're looking for anyone who might have seen Sister Julie Wednesday night." Against her will, tears filled Marty's eyes. The nun had been nice to her the other night, even after that trick Marty had tried to pull over on her with the shot of the girls in her piece. This was a shitty thing to happen to her. "I saw her. I mean, I met her Wednesday night in Stephen Kill."

There was silence for a moment on the other end of the line. "You met Sister Julie at the diner and you're just now coming forward?" the detective demanded.

"Yeah. Like I said, I've been out of touch. I didn't know anything about this until . . . until a little while ago." Marty inhaled the cigarette smoke deep into her lungs. Through the windows of the bar, she could see people moving around. Laughing. Talking. Even if there was a madman less than a hundred miles away, life was continuing inside the bar. On the block. In the city. "We had coffee."

"What time?" the detective asked.

"She arrived about ten thirty. I left after fifteen, twenty minutes. I went back to my place to pack."

"Did you see her get into her van, Miss Kyle?"

Marty dropped the cigarette, only half smoked, on the sidewalk and ground it out with her pale green sling-back. "I left ahead of her. She stayed to pay the bill."

"Where were you parked?"

"Behind the diner. The street parking was taped off."

"Was the white van Sister Julie drives in the parking lot as well?"

"Yeah. It was." She couldn't have missed it. It was a big white passenger van with Maria's Place written on the side panel.

"Miss Kyle, I'm going to have to ask that you come in," the detective said.

"I . . . I moved. I'm not in Rehoboth anymore. I start work here, Monday," she said. If she had her way, she'd never go back to Sussex County again.

"I'll do my best to work around your schedule. I can meet you tomorrow if you like, but you have to come to the station," she said firmly.

Marty opened her car door, grabbed her keys and her purse off the seat. She slammed the door shut. "I guess I can come back tomorrow. Get another load of stuff." She'd hired a moving company. Her apartment would be emptied and loaded into a truck Wednesday, but she'd barely been able to fit enough clothes for the next week in her car.

"What time is good for you?"

Marty glanced in the direction of the bar. She didn't plan on going home with anyone tonight. She was going to try hard not to make that mistake again, but she was certainly planning on tying one on. "How about three o'clock?"

"At the station," the detective said.

"Can do." She locked her car and followed the sidewalk up to the front door of the bar.

"Do you have a number where I can reach you?"

"This cell is fine, but I'll be there, detective. I don't have anything to hide," Marty said, trying not to be angry. The woman was just doing her job. She gave a little laugh. "I called you. Remember? I'll see you tomorrow."

Chapter 27

Delilah paced the floor in Interview One, waiting for Marty Kyle. She was thirty-five minutes late and Delilah was beginning to fear she wasn't going to show up.

The minute Delilah had gotten off the phone with the reporter last night, she'd called Snowden, repeating the conversation and questioning aloud Marty's responses. She wondered if she'd made a mistake in not asking for the reporter's whereabouts in Baltimore and sending the local police to pick her up. What if she'd done more than just meet Sister Julie for coffee?

It was odd that the reporter would make the decision to move to another state the day the nun disappeared. But then, Marty had called her, volunteering the information as well as informing her that she had been the woman in the diner. If Marty knew something, or had played any part in the disappearance of Sister Julie, would she have called the police and offered the information?

Last night, thinking on her feet, Delilah had made the decision to allow Marty to come into the station on her own terms, but she had not asked about the phone call from Dr. Trubant's office. Potentially significant or incriminating information was far better obtained face to face. But maybe Marty hadn't been the person who had called just before Julie left Maria's Place. Maybe the phone call from Trubant's office wasn't, in any way, related to the case.

Fortunately, Snowden had agreed with her on all points and listened patiently for an hour while she went over what her strategy should be with the reporter and what other direction her investigation should be going, in case this lead turned out to be nothing.

Delilah glanced at the clock on the wall. Three forty.

She plucked at the fabric of her polo shirt under the armpits. She was sweating despite a heavy dose of antiperspirant/deodorant that morning. Snowden had agreed she should conduct the interview alone. If Marty did have something to do with Sister Julie's disappearance, they didn't want to spook her. He had, however, come into the station and was cooling his heels in his office.

The sound of footsteps in the hallway had her turning toward the door in relief.

"Detective," the sergeant called, pushing open the door fully to allow the woman ahead of him to enter the room.

"Thanks, Bobby."

Delilah was at once taken aback by Marty's appearance. Wearing no makeup, her hair pushed back with sunglasses, in a T-shirt, capris, and flat sandals, she barely resembled the cool, polished professional she presented at press conferences and on the nightly news.

"Sorry I'm late, Detective. Bay Bridge was backed up something fierce."

Delilah must have stared a moment too long because the reporter gave a little laugh. "I know. I don't look like what you think I look like. My disguise," she explained, opening her arms wide. "I clean up well, don't I?"

Unsure of how to respond, Delilah now understood why no one at the diner had recognized the reporter. If she'd looked like this, she might not have either, and she'd shared at least a dozen conversations with her in the last year.

"I want to thank you for coming in," Delilah said. "I'm sorry to have had to ask you to drive all the way over on a Saturday."

"Needed a few more things from my place, anyway." She tossed her purse on the small table between them and they both sat down. "I don't suppose I can smoke in here?"

"Not hardly." Delilah opened her portfolio to a clean legal pad. "We're talking to everyone who spoke to or saw Sister Julie Wednesday, so—"

"Detective, if you don't mind, let's just cut the bull. It's Saturday and you don't want to be here any more than I do. And believe it or not, I want you to find Sister Julie as much as you do." She looked down at her French-manicured nails. "She was kind to me the other night."

"So you met her at the diner about ten thirty?"

Marty nodded. "We didn't talk long. I told her about my new job and that I was leaving the area and we discussed some . . . personal things."

"Personal between the two of you?"

Marty avoided eye contact. "No. Personal as in a personal issue I had that Sister Julie knew about. She . . . was counseling me, I guess you could say."

Delilah scribbled a couple of notes, not sure where to go from here. From the emotion in Marty's voice that she was trying hard to hide, Delilah believed she was being truthful. "You didn't argue?"

"No. She was very encouraging. She suggested I seek professional help and then she wished me luck." Marty looked up at her. "I left the diner first. I had a million things to do at my place. I offered to pay the bill for the coffee. She insisted she would pay it. I walked out of the diner, down the driveway, to my car, and drove away."

"When you left the diner, to your knowledge, was Sister Julie still inside?"

"As far as I know. She was nursing a cup of tea. I just figured she was enjoying the quiet. House full of teenagers? That would certainly make me nuts." Marty sat back in the chair.

"Was there anyone else in the diner?"

"People eating? No. The waitress was still there. At least one other person, because I heard them banging pots and talking in the back." She thought for a minute. "A guy, I think. And I heard someone come in, a customer to pick up take-out, but I couldn't see her from where we were sitting."

It was exactly the information Delilah had obtained from the diner's staff. She tried not to be disappointed. She didn't know what she'd been hoping for, but this wasn't going anywhere. "And you're sure the van was there when you left?"

"Positive." Marty laid her hand on the table. "What about the cook and waitress? Did they see the van when they left?"

Delilah set her pen down. She was the one who was supposed to be making the inquiries, but she knew it was in Marty's nature to ask questions. Delilah decided to go with it. One of the techniques of good witness interrogation was allowing the witness to offer information freely. Maybe Marty would offer additional information in her quest to get an exclusive on the story. "Neither drove to work that day. One has a suspended license, the other shares a car with a family member. Both left through the front doors, locked up together, and were picked up." It wasn't anything the newspaper hadn't already printed, complete with an interview of the cook.

Delilah shifted in her chair. She wanted to get all the details of the meeting before she asked about the phone call. "Let's go back. You made arrangements to meet Sister Julie when?"

"Saturday. At the fund-raiser. We talked about my . . . the personal matter," Marty went on. "And we agreed to meet Wednesday night, somewhere neutral, to talk about it some more."

Delilah studied her carefully for a moment. Marty had responded immediately, no hesitation. People telling lies didn't usually do that, at least not without a lot of practice. "You didn't call Sister Julie at Maria's Place Wednesday night?"

"No. Why do you ask? We were meeting late because of my work." She shrugged. "Turned out I quit that day so I guess it was a moot point, but we'd already made the arrangements."

"And you don't want to share with me what it was specifically you spoke of?" Delilah pushed.

Marty met her gaze. "Not if I don't have to, Detective. It had nothing to do with Sister Julie. It was about my past and not anything I want on public record, if I can help it. "

"You know, you've interviewed Rob Crane, Jenny Grove, and Sister Julie."

"I know who I've interviewed. Are you saying I'm a suspect, Detective?" Marty sounded more amused than anything else.

"I need to know if you can offer any insight into

what the first two victims and Sister Julie might have had in common."

"You mean other than that they lived in a town in the sticks of Southern Delaware? Nothing comes to mind."

Delilah glanced down at her notes, not appreciating Marty's sarcasm, but knowing from interviews with her that it wasn't out of character. She jumped back to a previous subject. "So you didn't call Sister Julie Wednesday night around ten?"

"I did not. Why do you ask? Again."

"As I said, I'm trying to track down who Sister Julie saw and talked to."

Marty leaned forward on the table, palms down. "So she got a call that night and you don't know who called her?"

Delilah suddenly felt as if she was on the defensive, not the way she wanted the interview to end. "Marty," she said, meeting and holding her gaze. "What you and I have said here today is part of an ongoing investigation. Sister Julie is still missing. It would be unethical of you to use any information for your own personal gain."

"I know that, Detective." Marty reached for her purse. "What kind of person do you think I am? I told you. I want to see Sister Julie alive and safe as much as you do." She lowered her purse to her lap. "Do you have any more questions, Detective? I have a real estate agent meeting me in half an hour at my place."

"That's all for now." Delilah closed her notebook. "I know I can reach you at the same cell number."

"Sure. Or the *News Night* offices. They're in the book."

Delilah pushed a small pad of paper and a pen across the desk. "Put down the address where you'll be staying."

Marty wrote a Baltimore address in loopy cursive and got up from her chair.

"I'll walk you out." Delilah escorted her to the lobby and walked back down the hall to Snowden's office.

He looked up from his desk.

Delilah propped one hand on her hip. "She says she met Sister Julie at the diner, but left her alive and well. She says she didn't call Maria's that night, though. Says the arrangements were made ahead of time."

"You believe her?"

Delilah rubbed the back of her neck. "I don't know."

Marty strode down the brick sidewalk, unlocked her car door, and climbed in. She started the car, switched the air conditioning to high and took a pack of cigarettes from her purse. "Jesus," she whispered.

Her hand shaking, she lit up.

How the hell did the police know about a phone call she'd made from Paul's office? They'd done a phone trace, of course.

Stupid idiot. How could she have been so careless? How could she have been so lazy that she couldn't walk out to the car and use her cell phone, after she rifled his office looking for the keys to his file cabinet? Or a pay phone?

Because, of course, she didn't have the ability to predict the future. She'd had no idea the phone call would matter because she had no idea Sister Julie was going to disappear.

Fortunately, the police couldn't determine who had called from his office. Fortunately, she was used to thinking fast. Lying smoothly.

She smiled to herself. She might be sweating, but Paul had to be shitting his pants. Surely the police had contacted him by now, asking about the phone call made after hours. Maybe they'd even talked to his wife.

She pushed the cigarette between her lips, trapping it, and pulled away from the curb.

So now what did she do? she wondered. *Take her chances or call Paul and tell him she wanted the photographs?*

"Hel . . . hello?" Julie called, thinking she heard something behind the wall. The door.

She had discovered, by using her hands, there was some sort of door, flush in the wall. No hinges, though. No latch or handle of any sort. "Is someone there?" She paused, lifting her head off the ground . . . listening.

"M . . . Marty, is that you?" she croaked. She thought of the hot tea she'd been drinking at the diner with the reporter. Wished now that she hadn't left any in the cup.

Now she didn't hear anything. Wasn't sure if anyone was there or not. If anyone had been there. If there even had been any sound.

Her mind drifted.

Amanda's due date was coming up. She was worried that she'd not adequately counseled her. Worried the girl wasn't absolutely sure she wanted to give her baby up for adoption. Sister Agatha would push Amanda to give up her baby.

Sister Agatha . . .

Julie lifted her head again. She thought she heard the nun's voice. Criticizing her. Judging her.

But it could have been in her mind.

Julie was pretty sure she had been hallucinating earlier. She had been talking with her grandmother. *Seen* her grandmother. Her grandmother had been dead for years.

Julie picked up the empty plastic water bottle beside her and brought it to her parched lips. She didn't know where the bottle had come from. It had appeared with just a few sips of water that she had sucked down greedily.

Something startled Julie. Movement maybe. She sat up, unsure if her eyes were open or closed. Of course it was impossible to see anything in the darkness.

She rolled onto her back, thinking hard about the voice. It had come with the bottle of water.

Or had the voice brought the water?

She wondered how her tomato plants were faring in the August heat. It was hot in here, though not as hot as one would think a black box would be. Which made sense, of course. You wouldn't make hell so hot it would kill you. That would end your suffering prematurely.

Her fingers found her Benedictine crucifix and she tried to pray, but no words of supplication would come to her lips.

"I'm sorry," she mumbled, lying flat on her back, her arms spread wide. She heard the plastic bottle fall. Roll.

"Why? Why did you do it? Why did you give away the flesh of your flesh?" the voice demanded.

"I'm so sorry. I'm so sorry."

"The pain I have suffered because of you. Pain you inflicted upon me because of your weakness of the flesh."

Julie squeezed her eyes shut. *It's okay, Amanda. You have time. Of course your baby will be safe. The church screens all prospective parents. They'll be able to care for your baby in ways that would be difficult for you to care for it.*

Julie didn't know if she was saying the words out loud or if they were just running through her head.

She wondered if Elise had found her iPod. It had been missing for days. Julie secretly suspected that Sister Agatha had taken it.

Julie wished she had a cigarette. A gin and tonic. She touched her cross again, shamed by the thought. She'd been sober all these years and yet at this moment she could remember perfectly the coolness and bite of the drink.

She turned her head toward the wall, thinking she heard the voice again. Whose voice was it? She *knew* the voice.

She closed her eyes, her whole body convulsing in sobs. Except that there were no tears. She knew she had to pray for the voice on the other side of the wall, for what they had done to her, but still the words wouldn't come to her. All she could remember were the words she and her grandmother has spoken together, years ago. Hours ago.

"Hail Mary, full of grace," Julie croaked. "The Lord is with thee."

"Blessed art thou among women, and blessed is the fruit of thy womb, Jesus," *The Daughter* said from the other side of the door.

The Mother had taught it to her and oddly enough, as much as *The Daughter* hated Sister Julie, she found a strange sense of comfort in speaking the words with her. "Holy Mary, Mother of God, pray for us sinners now, and at the hour of death."

The Daughter drew her knees up to her chin, wrapping her arms around them, tears sliding down her face. All these years, and still the pain was there. Searing.

"Amen," she and Sister Julie whispered together in the darkness.

Chapter 28

"*Whatcha* doin'?"

Startled by Callie's voice behind her, Delilah closed the screen on the computer monitor with a quick click of the mouse. "Hey, what are you doing up so late?" She spun in the office chair.

"Saw the living room light under my door." Callie plopped down on a stool beside the chair at the computer desk. She'd dragged it there earlier in the evening to get Delilah to look at the web site of the local high school. She'd been running a hard-hitting campaign for the last week, taking every opportunity she could to try to convince Delilah to let her stay for the school year. School started in three weeks so there wasn't much time left to make the decision.

"What you looking at on the computer?" Dressed in gym shorts and a T-shirt that appeared to be from Delilah's drawer, the teen pulled her knees up to her chin, balancing effortlessly on the stool.

"Nothing. Internet shopping," Delilah lied. "I was thinking I needed some more push-up bras."

She'd actually been looking over the graduate courses

in psychology offered at various colleges within reasonable driving distance. By her calculations, she was about nine weeks pregnant. She had plenty of time still before she would begin to show, but fall classes started in a month. If she was going to seriously consider a career change, she had to begin to make plans.

"Think you could buy me one, too?" Callie placed her hands on her breasts. "Not that I even have much to push up."

Delilah smiled, reaching out to push hair out of the teen's eyes. Callie had gotten much better in the last few weeks about physical contact. She still didn't want much in the way of hugging and kissing a la Swift family style, but she didn't shrink away when Delilah touched her any more.

A strange tenderness washed over Delilah as she studied the girl's sleepy face. "Couldn't sleep?"

Callie wrinkled her nose and shrugged, noncommitting. She'd dyed her hair the day before, and even though it was still red, it was now a reddish blond and far closer to her natural color. "I guess. I was thinking about Sister Julie."

Delilah shut down the computer. It was one thirty in the morning, time both of them should be in bed. "What were you thinking about?"

"It's been more than a week and no one's found her. That can't be good."

"No, it's not," Delilah admitted. There was no reason to lie to her.

"I just think it's really sad. She was such a good person; she helped so many people and now . . ." Callie paused and then went on. "Elise and Tiffany were talking today about the body patrol."

"The what? Come on." Delilah lifted her chin in the

direction of the kitchen. "Let's get some ice cream and then hit the sack. What body patrol?"

"You know. The cops, cruising the pond. They're just waiting for someone to chuck Sister Julie's body in the drink and nab him. It means you're not looking for her anymore."

"That's not true." Delilah flipped the lights off in the living room and walked into the kitchen. Her nausea was greatly improved, but had been replaced by nonstop hunger.

Callie followed.

"So you're not staking out the pond?"

"We are." Delilah grabbed the rocky road ice cream out of the freezer and set it on the counter, thinking to herself that if the teenagers at Maria's knew they had twenty-four hour watch on the pond, who else did? "But that doesn't mean we're not still looking for her, still following leads," she said, sounding more sure of herself than she was.

"But I heard you talking to Chief Calloway last night." Callie got two spoons from the drawer and an ice cream scoop. "You said your leads weren't leading you anywhere."

Delilah was clearly going to have to be more careful about her phone conversations. She *had* told Snowden that. Right now, her only remote possibilities of suspects in Sister Julie's case were Marty Kyle, Sister Agatha, and possibly Dr. Trubant. Marty Kyle because she was the last one to see the nun alive and Sister Agatha because she'd an obvious beef with the Maria's Place director. The bishop had confirmed complaints levied against Sister Julie by Sister Agatha on several occasions in the last six months. She added Paul Trubant to the list simply because the phone call had come from his office and he had known both victims, as well as the missing nun.

Delilah took two bowls from the cupboard over her head. "We have a few leads."

"Like what?"

"I can't *tell* you." Delilah slid the bowls across the counter to the teen.

"So you don't have any."

The teen was half right. She had no real leads, but she did have some unanswered questions that could possibly lead to leads. The phone company had reported that it was possible that someone could have tapped into the phone lines on the exterior box at Trubant's office, so there was no way to know who had called from there. If she could figure out who had called, she had a feeling she'd be one step closer to Sister Julie.

Delilah had also discovered the day before, after chasing down a city employee on vacation in the Finger Lakes, that not only had there been no painting done on the street or sidewalk in front of the diner a week ago, but that the city wasn't even responsible for putting up the tape that had prohibited parking. There was a good possibility that the tape had been put up by the killer to guarantee Sister Julie would park in the rear of the diner, where she was less likely to be seen getting in and out of the van. But who had known she was meeting Marty that night at the diner? Marty said she told no one because of the personal nature of the conversation. Sister Agatha claimed that not only had she not known where Sister Julie was going that night, but was still in the dark as to who had made the late-night phone call. Unfortunately, the tape had been removed Thursday by a city employee, thinking an error had been made in a work order. Delilah had a photograph of the tape, but the evidence was gone.

"Aunt Delilah?"

Delilah looked up at her niece. Obviously she'd missed something.

"I said, do you think she's dead?"

Delilah reached for the ice cream scoop. "I don't know, honey. I hope not."

Delilah hadn't had a chance to pick up her mail in three days. The minute she pulled the stack out of her mailbox, she spotted the white envelope. Identical to the last two.

The last thing she needed, right now.

She set the mail, including the white vellum envelope addressed to her in neat, handwritten block letters, on the seat of the police car and drove to work. She slipped on a latex glove to carry it into the station. Another officer was in with Snowden so she sealed the envelope, unopened, in an evidence bag and did what every woman nine weeks pregnant did in this situation. She went to the bathroom.

By the time Delilah had gone back to her cubicle for the evidence bag, Officer Thomas had vacated Snowden's office. She knocked on his doorframe.

He waved her in and grabbed several sheets of paper off his printer.

"Guess what I've got," she said, approaching his desk.

"I can't imagine." His tone was testy. He'd tried a few days ago again to talk to her about their breakup, but she'd refused to have the conversation. She just couldn't do it yet. Not with Sister Julie missing, Callie pressing to have her records transferred, and a bladder that suddenly seemed miniscule.

She tossed the evidence bag on his desk, not in the

mood for his dry humor this morning. "Use gloves. I haven't opened it yet."

"I'm aware, Detective, of procedure for items in evidence bags." He stared her down while opening his top right drawer and removing two large blue latex gloves.

"I just picked up my mail, but I haven't been to the post office since"—she quickly calculated—"Monday, I think. Maybe Saturday."

"Postmarked Saturday," he observed, studying the envelope through the plastic bag as he snapped on one glove and then the other.

She watched as he slipped on his reading glasses and removed the envelope. He used a letter opener to carefully lift its adhesive flap. The piece of vellum he unfolded matched the letter she knew he had in a file, as well as the letter she'd tossed in the trash weeks before.

She waited while he read it silently.

"Well?" she asked when she thought he was taking too long to tell her what it said. After all, it had been addressed to *her.*

"We might have a problem, Detective." There was no mistaking the dread in his voice.

"I'm listening."

He took a breath, exhaled, and began to read aloud. *"Dearest Delilah, I was disappointed to hear what you said on the evening news and wanted to explain myself. Wanted you to understand."* He paused and then went on. *"I am not confused. I am not mentally unstable. I know exactly what needs to be done."* He paused.

"Go on," she urged, sitting down in the chair in front of his desk.

"New paragraph," he said. *"Please don't take this personally, my darling. Please understand that this must be done and in no way reflects on your ability to do your job. No one is better*

than you are," he read. *"No one is more beautiful . . .
more pure."*

"Sweet Mary," she muttered.

"Yours always," he finished with distaste in his voice.
"The Daughter."

"The Daughter?" she questioned.

Leaving the letter opened, he slid it and the envelope
back into the evidence bag, sealed it, and slid it across
the desk toward her. "I think we might have a note from
our killer, Delilah."

The Daughter sat in the cool darkness, her back against
the door, her knees drawn up. She was in a melancholy
mood today. Had been all day. She had come here,
thinking it would cheer her up. She had hoped to talk to
Sister Julie, but though she was still breathing, she was
unresponsive.

The Daughter felt a pang of some emotion she couldn't
quite identify. Sister Julie had been nice to her. She had
seemed like a good person. But she had not been. How
ironic it was that the reporter was such a mean, spiteful
woman, and yet she had done the right thing. She had
ended her child's life; protected it. Marty deserved to be
punished for all the mean things she said and did, but
that wasn't up to *The Daughter. The Daughter* had been
wrong even to consider it. A person certainly didn't deserve to die just because she was callous and unkind.

The Daughter's thoughts drifted back to Sister Julie.
She was disappointed in the nun. Even after twelve days,
Sister Julie still didn't seem to understand. Wouldn't
admit that she had been wrong and *The Daughter* had
suffered for it. Adopted children all over the world suf-

fered because of her and would continue to suffer as *The Daughter* suffered still now.

The Daughter hugged her knees, drawing into a tight ball. She had been afraid she might run into a problem with police patrolling the pond, but it had been easy enough to solve. Her idea of supplying the tiniest amount of water, laced with GHB she'd bought in Wilmington, had worked out just fine. The mouthful or two of water each day kept Sister Julie alive and the drug kept her passive. Not that *The Daughter* thought anyone would hear her cry out; no one had heard the other two. But it was always better to be safe than sorry. Once the police gave up the twenty-four hour watch, and she knew, eventually, they would have to, she would dispose of the body.

Better safe than sorry. That had been what *The Father* had said about the locks on the closet door. *The Daughter* would never have left without permission, but he locked it anyway.

She closed her eyes, beating her chin rhythmically on her knees. She had a lot on her mind. Maybe that was why she was not enjoying this as much as she had hoped she would.

She was worried. It was a strange position she had put herself and Delilah in, and she hoped it wouldn't affect their relationship. The relationship they would have one day. That was why it was important to *The Daughter* that Delilah understand. That was why she sent the note. She had thought about going to her house and telling her in person. Or calling her on the phone. But *The Daughter* wasn't ready for that. Not yet.

She banged her chin hard against her knees, feeling the pain and the comfort that went hand in hand. "Bad, you're bad, Sister Julie," she whispered, the way she had

once whispered *bad Father, bad Mother.* "Bad," she repeated. *Must be punished. Time out. Dark. Time to think.
Time to contemplate bad behavior.*

Of course, *The Daughter* knew that no matter how long
Sister Julie lay in there, she would never come to see the
error of her ways. Just as Rob Crane had never admitted he had been wrong to abandon his girlfriend and let
her go to college in a different state and give his baby up
for adoption. Jenny Grove, a mother of two beautiful
children, had not been able to see how wrong it had
been for her to give up that first baby. It was a waste of
time even trying to reason with these people.

Suddenly angry with herself for having thought she
could make them understand, make anyone understand,
The Daughter raised her fist over head and slammed it
against the door. She wanted this to be over. She wanted
to strip Sister Julie naked, burn her clothes, and throw
her body into the pond where *The Birth Mother*'s soul lay
in the muddy murk.

But *The Daughter* would have to be smart. She would
have to be patient.

"What are you talking about?" Delilah shot out of the
chair in front of Snowden's desk. "You can't call off the
surveillance."

He looked at her across the desk, thinking how pretty
she was. Thinking what a hell of a cop she was. In the last
two weeks, she'd followed every possible lead on the
Julie Thomas case, no matter how tedious or unpromis-
ing. She'd been relentless in pouring over each victim's
life, trying to make connections between them.

Snowden missed Delilah. He tried to tell himself this
was all for the best, their no longer seeing each other.

He was her boss and it was wrong. And even if they could somehow make it right, he was already married to his work. He could never devote the time needed to make a relationship work.

But he was lonely.

In the last few weeks, he had come to realize that no matter how many hours he spent at the station, he still had to go home eventually. Home to an empty house. An empty bed. An empty life.

The remarkable thing was, it wasn't even the sex he missed the most. What he missed was her smile, her looking up at him the way she had once done with those big brown eyes of hers. He missed her laughter. Her tiny bare feet propped in his lap while they both read on the couch. He missed the anticipation of seeing her again, knowing he was the one person she wanted to be with, despite the issues that stood between them.

"I don't understand," she said, leaning over his desk, bringing her face closer to his.

He didn't have many men in the station who were bold enough to question him in that tone of voice, fewer willing to posture so aggressively. He had to make an effort not to smile. "Detective," he said sharply.

She stood up, but did not back away from his desk.

"Sister Julie has been missing fourteen days," Snowden told her, knowing his role had to be that of the chief of police right now. This couldn't be personal. "I can no longer in good conscience dole out taxpayers money to pay for overtime and double shifts."

"Chief, *The Daughter's* waiting on us. She's determined to dump her there. We have to keep investigating, keep putting the pressure on her. She'll crack, I know she will. She'll make her move and we'll be there to catch her."

"If this is our killer, she could easily dump the body in

any number of ponds, local or in another county. She could take a boat out twenty miles and drop the nun in the Atlantic."

"She *won't* do that," Delilah insisted. "I know she won't. That pond has some significance."

"There was nothing to link the pond to the two murders except that it was where the bodies were disposed of. Neither lived in the vicinity nor even fished there."

"There *is* a link. We just haven't found it yet. Maybe . . ." She looked away, then back at him, obviously grasping at straws. "Maybe it has something to do with Alice Crupp dying there last year. Maybe she's obsessed with Alice's death for some reason."

"The ME confirmed—"

"Damn it, Snowden!" She slapped her hand down hard on his desk. "I know what the ME confirmed. She fell in and drowned, but I'm telling you, this has something to do with Alice!"

Suddenly realizing that she had just shouted at her boss, Delilah lifted her hand gingerly from the smooth cherry surface of his desk and took a step back. She gazed downward. "I'm sorry," she said quietly when she had found her voice. "I apologize. That was completely unprofessional of me."

He could see her face reddening.

"Completely inappropriate," she murmured.

He gave her another moment to collect herself and then spoke quietly, but firmly. "I understand why you're upset. I also know that you understand these budget issues and you understand that by severely overspending now, we'll be putting other citizens of Stephen Kill at risk, further down the line." He let that sink in before he continued. "As it is, if I can't figure out where to cut costs this fall, I'll have to lay off at least one, possibly two officers and then we'll have fewer police patrolling our streets. Our response time will be slower because our resources will be more spread out."

"I know." She exhaled, hanging her head. "You're right, I know you're right. It's just that I hate to give up."

"We're not giving up. We're backing off and we're regrouping."

"Semantics. You think she's dead, don't you? Delilah said.

"If she took her, in all likelihood, yes."

Delilah's eyes grew moist and Snowden felt like such a heel. But he knew he was right. He knew he had to do what was best for the town, and best for his officers.

"I wanted to tell you personally before I made the changes in the shifts," he went on.

"Effective when?"

"Today. Evening shift. We'll continue to patrol the pond as often as we can, but we'll no longer assign units to that strict task and you do not have my permission to run some kind of stakeout yourself. In fact, I forbid it."

Delilah glanced at the clock on his wall. "It's already after five. I have to go. Callie will be waiting for me." She turned away.

"Delilah . . ."

She halted in the doorway, her hand on the knob, but didn't turn to face him. "Sir?"

"No matter what happens here, you've done a fine job."

"Thanks," she said. "I'll tell that to the girls at Maria's Place."

"Glad our new Friday schedule is working for you. Tell me how your week was." Trubant sat back on the couch and propped his ankle on his knee. He slowly opened his portfolio and plucked a fancy pen from his shirt pocket. He did everything he could to try to pretend he was relaxed, the adult in charge, but Callie suspected otherwise.

Yesterday, while working at the library, Izzy had told her that he was acting even stranger than usual. He kept changing when he was coming for group and individual sessions, messing up the new "daily schedule," and Sister Agatha was getting pretty pissed. She hummed a lot around him. And yesterday, he had received two mysterious calls on his cell during their hour group therapy session. Both times, he looked at the number on the display and then excused himself, stepping out onto the deck so the girls couldn't hear what he was saying. Izzy thought he was cheating on his wife.

Callie watched him carefully from across the coffee table. She'd never liked the jack-off from *Day One*. Of course he was cheating on his wife. But she wondered if maybe he wasn't something worse than a jerk and an unfaithful husband.

What if he was a serial killer?

Izzy had said that was the craziest thing she had ever heard, but then they'd talked about it and Izzy had said that maybe it wasn't as farfetched as it sounded. He knew Sister Julie and the other lady from Maria's. Maybe he knew the college kid, too. Callie didn't know why he would kidnap and kill them, but maybe he did it because he was nuts. Wasn't that why Freddie Krueger and Son of Sam and the BTK Strangler all killed people, because they were crazy?

Callie definitely thought she and Izzy were on to something. She and Aunt Delilah had been talking about how police investigated this kind of crime and they talked about what it meant to think outside the box, especially when they didn't have much to go on. Callie was trying to think outside the box. Maybe help Aunt Delilah out. Maybe if she could help her find Sister Julie, find the killer, her aunt wouldn't be so stressed out and maybe she'd see what a good idea it was for Callie to stay for the school year.

The closer it got to school starting, the more certain Callie was that she didn't want to go home to her mother and that jerk of a stepfather. She liked it in Stephen Kill. She liked living with Aunt Delilah and she wanted to stay.

"Callie?" Trubant said, cocking his head like some kind of stupid parrot or something. "Not feeling like talking today?"

She didn't answer.

"You seem down."

She narrowed her gaze, wondering how uncomfortable she could make him. "Sister Julie's been gone more than two weeks and she's not coming back." She continued to look right at him. "We all know she's not coming back."

"And how do you feel about that?" he intoned in a placating voice.

"How the hell do you think I feel?"

Callie didn't curse much anymore, but she did it for the shock factor. To see if maybe she could rile him.

It didn't work.

"I sense fear, but anger, too. Are you angry that Sister Julie is missing? Do you somehow feel as if she's let you down?"

Callie reached for her limeade lip balm in the front pocket of the new jean skirt she'd bought with her very own money. "Let me down?" she said, talking to him like he was an idiot. "It's not like she sent an invitation to the killer and said 'Hey, would you like to kidnap me, hold me prisoner, let me die of thirst, and then could you throw me naked into a pond.'" She shook her head. "Are those diplomas on your wall real or did you buy them off the Internet?"

The expression on his face didn't change, but he uncrossed his legs.

Callie had definitely pushed a button there.

"A lot of hostility today. Have you and your aunt and your mother decided whether you'll be staying in Stephen Kill or returning to Georgia? Is that what's bothering you?"

"Nothing's been decided." She popped the lid back on her lip balm tube, wondering how far she could push him. She didn't want him calling Aunt Delilah, but if she and the girls were right, and she was sure they were, she doubted he'd be on the phone ratting Callie out. Somebody important like him in a little town like this probably didn't want to share with the cops that he was banging women other than his wife.

"I'll tell you what I'm upset about, Dr. Trubant." She leaned forward in her chair. "I'm upset that I have to come here every week and talk to you."

"Callie, you and I, you and your aunt, I know, have discussed the benefits of counseling. You seem so much happier these last weeks. You're making such good choices. Surely, you can't argue—"

"I don't have a problem with the counseling," she interrupted. "I have a problem with you."

"You don't like me?"

"I don't like the fact that when you're supposed to be counseling teenagers, you're on the phone with your girlfriend."

Something in his face changed.

Callie smiled to herself. She believed she'd just hit button number two.

Trubant shifted on the couch. "Callie, what would make you say such a thing?"

"You think I'm stupid?" she asked. "You think we're all stupid? Or just blind?"

"That will be quite enough, young lady."

He stood up suddenly and Callie shrank back. *Oh, crap,* she thought. *What if he is the killer? That was stupid. I piss him off and I might be the next one in the pond.*

But he didn't come toward her. He closed his portfolio and set it on the table. "I think we need to take a break, Callie. Continue this next week, if you're still here." He didn't sound angry, but she knew he was.

She jumped out of the chair, going around the back of it.

"Go ahead and go back into the waiting room and wait for your aunt there."

"You going to tell her what I said?"

"I think we'll have to talk more about that next session."

Needing no further invitation, Callie made for the door. She couldn't wait until she got to the library to talk to Izzy.

Paul stood there until Callie closed the door behind her and then dropped down onto the couch, wiping his forehead with his palm. He felt a little winded. Dizzy.

The little brat knew something. He didn't know how. But she knew.

Would she tell her aunt? Knowing teenagers, it was unlikely. They rarely told on others if it was going to seriously incriminate themselves. Callie was just acting out a pattern she'd obviously already developed. She wouldn't say anything.

He lowered his head, sinking his face into his hands.

But this was it. This was absolutely his wake-up call. He had to get some help and he had to break it off with Kitten.

The question was, how was he going to do it?

Chapter 29

Sunday night, Delilah stood in her shower and let the hot water pour over her head as she fought her tears and the urge to grab the phone and call Snowden. Tell him about the baby. Tell him she wanted to run away with him, now, tonight. Take Callie and just go. She'd heard Costa Rica was nice.

A sob rose in her throat and she choked it back.

Sister Julie's body was found in Horsey Mill Pond at approximately one fifteen in the afternoon by a father and son fishing. She had not appeared to have been in the water any longer than the others.

Delilah had failed Sister Julie. She had failed the good folks of Stephen Kill.

Leaning against the shower stall with one hand, she drew the other across her belly and fought another sob.

How was she going to take care of this child? Who was she kidding to think she could raise a teenager and a baby? How had she ever thought for a moment she was a good cop? Could ever measure up to her brothers? *The Daughter,* whoever the hell she was, had bested her. Again.

Delilah was scared. So scared she could only take short, shallow breaths.

But she was angry, too.

Who was this woman? Why had she done these things and why had she singled out Delilah? Did Delilah know her? Was she from this town? This neighborhood?

What right did she have, to do this to Delilah? To those she loved? To Stephen Kill?

Resting both hands on the tiled wall, Delilah tipped back her head and opened her eyes, staring at the white ceiling. She inhaled deeply, exhaled, and took another slow breath, embracing her anger, using it to push aside the terror that gripped her.

She wasn't a quitter.

She couldn't go to Costa Rica. Not at least until she found this crazy woman and saw justice done. She owed it to the town she had sworn to protect. To herself. To Sister Julie and to the other victims and their families.

Taking one more breath, Delilah hit the faucet and the water shut off. She pushed out the shower door and grabbed a towel.

She has been telling herself all afternoon that she had no real leads. No suspects. But that wasn't entirely true. There were pieces to the puzzle here; the suspect's MO, the pond where the bodies were disposed of, the mysterious phone call to Sister Julie supposedly from Dr. Trubant's office, the tape on the street in front of the diner. And now, the latest morsel; possible trace evidence, at last. A smudge of black on Julie's scalp, just along the hairline. By some stroke of gruesome luck, or perhaps by divinity, the nun's body had gotten tangled in weeds on the shoreline, her forehead and a portion of her face kept above the murky water.

Delilah wrapped the towel around her wet body and

stepped out of the shower and in front of the sink to comb out her wet hair. These were all pieces to the puzzle, she told herself determinedly. And she was going to put them together.

Paul flipped on the lights in his office and went directly to the file cabinet, carrying with him the metal trash can from Muriel's work station. He'd resisted the temptation to call Kitten all weekend, reasoning it was better if she contacted him the way they always did. She was smart. If he had called her, she might have gotten suspicious. She might have showed on his doorstep, made a scene in a public place, or called Susan, all of which she had threatened to do in the past.

So, all weekend, he waited for her to call. By this morning, he had begun to worry that she wouldn't. That something was going on he didn't know about. Of course, logically, he knew it was harder for her to get away with Sister Julie gone. Her responsibilities had to be even greater.

Poor Sister Julie. Paul and Susan had been out on the sidewalk this afternoon watching the kids ride their bikes when a neighbor had come over to tell them about the discovery of the nun's body. Paul had been surprised when Kitten called his cell just before nine. Susan had been in the bathtub. He'd told her he had an emergency at Beebe hospital, an attempted suicide of one of his clients. He didn't usually utilize such drastic alibis, but this was the end. This was it. There would be no more lies to his wife. There would be no more excuses. Tomorrow he would call his psychiatrist and make an appointment.

Paul set the trash can down and retrieved the keys from inside the papier-mâché mask his daughter had

made that he displayed on one of his bookcases. Back at
the file cabinet, he opened the bottom drawer that
always remained locked and pulled out a file from the
rear. From his pocket, he removed a lighter, set the file
on top of the cabinet and opened it. On top was a sheet
of paper with a name he'd printed neatly and a photograph paper-clipped to it. Below the name, was a neat list
of details. Where. When. Anything out of the ordinary
they had done or she had said.

Even when he looked at her face, he barely remembered her.

Paul struck the red plastic lighter and a blue flame
flared. He held it to the corner of the page and watched
his handwriting disappear as the brown edges turned to
ash and drifted downward into the trash can. When it
became too hot to hold, he dropped it and watched
until the color Polaroid photo began to melt. Then he
picked up the next page in the file. It was a rearview
photo. She was wearing thong panties, looking over her
shoulder, grinning, a large vibrator in one hand. He lit
the corner with the lighter.

This would take a few minutes. He had to be careful
not to start too large or smoky a fire or the smoke alarm
would go off and he'd have an office full of volunteer
firefighters gawking at his very personal collection of
porn. Wouldn't they be surprised by some of the women
in the file? Women they knew. Loved. Wives. Daughters.
One was even a grandmother, though she hadn't yet
reached her fifty-fifth birthday when they'd carried on
their brief affair.

Letting the burning paper and photo fall into the
garbage can, Paul sighed. He wanted desperately to keep
one, maybe two photos, only his favorites, but he knew he
shouldn't. Couldn't. Dr. Ramirez had said that destroying

the mementos would be part of the recovery. Paul hadn't believed him at the time. He hadn't thought it necessary, but he knew now that it was. If he wanted to conquer his sexual addiction, keep his family and his practice, he had to give himself fully to the treatment. He had to want to truly end it. He had done it with his alcohol addiction. He could do it again.

As always, *The Daughter* did not park the vehicle behind Paul's office or on the street in front of it. She had lots of places to park in town. After dark, it was easy to cut across yards. Go down alleyways. Sometimes she looked in windows, peeked in garages. She liked to watch people living; families having dinner together, sharing popcorn in front of the TV, watching a movie together. Things she had never done as a child.

That was how she had found the perfect place to keep them. She had known where the house was since she had come to town, but it had only been this spring, after speaking to Cora Watkins, that she'd had the nerve to poke around in the dark. Explore.

Staying out of the path of light that spilled from the quaint street lamps, *The Daughter* took a shortcut through an open gate. The office was on a residential street, mostly homes, but also a doctor's office and the office Paul rented. Over her arm, she carried a black vinyl bag. Once inside the office, in the restroom, she'd change into the bustier, black miniskirt, stockings, and heels she carried. There was also a new addition to the costume, long black gloves that reached her elbows.

The Daughter had been pleased when Paul had seemed eager to meet her when she'd called. She'd been worried about him. Worried he was tiring of her. No longer appreciated her. Obviously, her concerns had been unfounded. He was just being careful, for her sake.

She passed through the side yard of a white bungalow that had room air conditioners hanging out the windows. The air conditioners hummed like big bees. It was hot and humid tonight. Perspiration gathered above her upper lip. But *The Daughter* felt good. With Sister Julie dealt with, she could relax. Focus on her relationships with Paul and Delilah.

Only half a block away now, *The Daughter* quickened her pace. She was going to be nearly half an hour early and she no longer had a key, but she would just wait in the rear parking lot where no one would see her. Maybe Paul would also be early, excited to see her.

Somewhere down the street, a little dog barked. There were voices. Teenagers. Life taking place around her. It made her feel good. Almost whole. She slipped through the gap in the old stockade fence that ran along the rear of the office property and was pleasantly surprised to see Paul's Audi.

He *was* eager to see her. Taking a quick look around, spotting no one, she hurried across the parking lot and slipped in the open back door, quiet as a mouse. She thought she might change right here in the hall and ambush him the way they did on that silly show on TLC where they gave poorly dressed people a new wardrobe. As she set down her bag, she wondered what the host and hostess would do to improve her wardrobe. Wouldn't they be shocked to look in her closet?

As *The Daughter* leaned over to remove her sensible shoes, she caught a whiff of something burning. She stood up, inhaling curiously. Brush outside? No. There was a burning ban on in the county. It had been a dry summer.

This smell, very faint, was coming from here in the office. Candles, maybe? No . . . not candles.

Puzzled, *The Daughter* quickly changed, foregoing the stockings because they were tricky to roll up and she usually sat on the toilet seat to put them on. Slipping her bare feet into the spiked heels, she pulled on the new satin gloves. Down the dark hall, she found that the door to Paul's office was closed.

She made a husky growl deep in her throat as she opened it.

Paul, standing in front of one of the black file cabinets, turned quickly toward her. "Kitten."

The smell was stronger in here.

She looked quizzically at him. "What are you doing?"

"Nothing. Cleaning up files." He didn't look directly at her. "Let's sit." He took her elbow, steering her toward the leather couch.

Something was wrong. *The Daughter* could smell it as strongly in the room as the tang of burning paper.

"What were you burning?" she asked.

"Client files." He offered a quick smile. "Copies that had to be destroyed. Shredder's not working. Silly of me, I know. I should just wait and replace the shredder."

He wasn't that good a liar. She wondered how he got away with it with his wife.

She pulled her arm from his grasp, looking back at the metal trash can in front of the file cabinets. "Paul, what are you up to?"

"Nothing." He grabbed her hand, stopping her. "I need to talk to you."

There was something in his voice that made her look up at him. This was bad. She could tell. She could hear it in his voice.

And she was afraid. She could feel the darkness closing

in on her. She had displeased Paul. *Been a bad girl.* He
didn't want her any more. No one wanted her.

Panic gripped her.

She shook her head, backing away, feeling exposed in
the tiny skirt and bustier that thrust her small breasts up
and almost over the black lace.

"Kitten, please. We really do have to talk. I think it's
time we re-evaluate our relationship."

"No." She shook her head, almost in a daze for a
moment. How could she have been so stupid? How had
she not seen this coming tonight?

"Just hear me out." He moved his hands downward as
if quieting a small child or a dog. "I'm not talking about
ending it. Just a time out. Time to—"

"There's someone else, isn't there?" Her fear was
giving way to anger. "Isn't there, Paul?" she asked
sharply. "I told you. There could be no one else. Not
when you were with me. I told you, this wouldn't be over
until I said it was over. You were the one who started it."
She pointed accusingly. "And now you have the nerve to
seek out someone else?"

"There's no one else, Kitten." He took a step toward
her. "No one else I would rather be with."

"You're a liar," she accused, backing up. "And you're
bad. You're a bad man." Her heel hit the metal trash can
and she looked down.

There were ashes in the bottom of the can. Ashes and
bits and pieces of paper and . . . a half-burned photograph. More photographs, singed, melted. Nude photographs just like the ones she knew he kept of her.

The Daughter thrust her hand into the can of ashes.

"Kitten!"

The contents were still warm. The half-burned photograph she lifted from the refuse was of a naked woman

she did not recognize. *The Daughter* lifted her lashes to look at Paul, her anger exploding in her chest. "Is she better than me?" she demanded. "Is that it?"

"No, no not at all. She's no one, Kitten. Nothing. Long in the past."

The photograph slipped from her fingers, her fury suddenly overwhelming. All-consuming. "She's better than me, so you're just going to cast me off, as if I was nothing!"

He flailed his arms, stuttering, stammering. He tried to make excuses. All *The Daughter* wanted to do was shut him up. Shut *The Father* up inside her head.

She grabbed the nearest object she could reach. A trophy off the file cabinet.

"Kitten, please—"

She swung upward with every ounce of rage bottled inside her. The corner of the heavy metal object hit him in the temple.

It made more of a crack than a thud and he fell where he stood, striking the file cabinet on the way down, just missing the trash can of ashes that would have made a mess on the beige carpet.

The Daughter stared at Paul for a moment, a little surprised. There was no need to check his pulse. He looked dead. She knew what dead looked like.

She set the trophy back on the file cabinet and took a step back. Now that the haze of her anger had subsided, she could see she'd made a mistake. A terrible, impulsive mistake.

But a mistake didn't have to be fatal for everyone.

Delilah walked into Dr. Paul Trubant's personal office and halted, taking in the scene. The place had been trashed; the table and chairs overturned, lamps broken, the cushions removed from the upholstered furniture. Every drawer in his desk was left open. The carpet was littered with books and papers.

On the floor, in front of open drawers in the file cabinets lay Paul's body.

"B and E gone bad," Officer Lopez observed from behind her. "He's already been declared. Once we're done with the photos, we'll let the EMTs take him."

Delilah slowly approached the body, trying to take the entire scene in as a whole, before she began to break it down and analyze it. "Who found him?"

"Secretary."

On her way in, Delilah had seen Muriel sitting in the back of an ambulance, sobbing.

"He usually come in to work ahead of her?" she asked.

"Back door looked to be kicked in. And um . . . he's been here a few hours, Detective. He's stiff."

She glanced at the officer. "Excuse me?"

"He's already stiffened up." Lopez gestured to Trubant prone on the floor, his head turned to one side. There was a very small spot of blood on the carpet near his head. Blunt force trauma.

A B & E homicide? Delilah thought with disbelief. How could this happen in Stephen Kill, where people still left their doors unlocked at night? The closest thing to robbery the police force had dealt with in the year since she'd been here was kids stealing Tootsie Rolls at the counter at the minimart.

She moved closer to the body, taking care to try to step only on carpet and not disturb any evidence that might be on the floor among the books and papers. A shattered papier-mâché mask, obviously made by a child, lay at her feet. "Anyone talk to his wife yet?"

"Thought you and the chief would want to do that," Lopez said taking a step back as someone entered the office from the rear door. "Chief."

Out of the corner of her eye, Delilah spotted Snowden. He came to stand beside her, beside the body.

"Place is pretty trashed," he said quietly, glancing around.

"I wonder what they were looking for. I doubt he ever had any cash. Appointments were paid for by insurance, check, or credit card, I would imagine," she thought aloud.

"The guys outside say he's been dead a few hours, maybe all night," Snowden lowered his voice. "His wife report him missing?"

"Not to my knowledge, but I haven't been at the station. I got the call at home, ran Callie out to Maria's so Monica or Sister Agatha could take her to work at the library when it opened." She pulled on blue latex gloves plucked from the rear pocket of her khakis.

"You could have called my mom," he said under his breath.

She ignored his personal remark. It was her new way of avoiding what she'd left unfinished between them. "He's already been declared. Once the body's been photographed, we'll get him out of here and up north for an autopsy." She squatted to get a closer look. "Although a blow to the head looks like a pretty good guess." She studied his handsome face for a moment, the eyes half closed. She stood up. "Wonder what was used."

"Probably that." Snowden lifted his chin, indicating an object on one of the file cabinets.

Delilah's gaze settled on a garish foot tall trophy with *World's Best Dad* engraved on it. On one corner of the heavy base was a dark, wet substance. Blood.

"Okay," she said, thinking aloud again. "The doctor comes to the office to do some late night paperwork, and someone breaks in, looking for money, whatever, gets scared when they see him. Maybe they get into a tussle and Trubant gets clobbered."

She hesitated. "But if he heard someone break in the back door from all the way in here, why didn't he call us?"

"Fell asleep on the couch?" Snowden offered. "Never heard him?"

"Could be." She glanced at Snowden again, then away. The tension was so tight between them that it seemed to crackle in the air. "You been in yet? I was hoping the lab report on the substance in Sister Julie's hair would be in this morning."

"I'll call in," he answered. "Check."

She nodded. He nodded.

Officers moved around behind them. The EMTs were waiting in the hallway with a stretcher. Delilah needed to go out to her car and get a large evidence bag. She needed to get the guys on duty organized and start going through the mess on the floor. The thing was, it looked like client files. She had no idea what the regulations were on these kinds of records. She knew they were private. Probably covered by HIPPA. She wasn't even sure the officers were legally permitted to collect them.

"I'm going to go to my car and get some evidence bags," Delilah told Snowden, feeling as if she needed to get away from him for a few minutes. "I'll take a quick survey of the room. Collect the trophy and then I guess we need to get over to the Trubant's house."

"Yeah, before she hears on the scanner. Everyone has a scanner these days. Even my mother."

"Your mother?" she remarked, unable to help herself.

"Well, her neighbors. But she sits around with them

on Saturday nights and listens, too." Snowden walked away from the body. "You see the back door?"

"Came in the front." She followed him. "Preliminary autopsy might be in for Sister Julie today, too."

"Might," he agreed, leading her out the rear door and down a hallway.

They walked through the splintered rear doorway together and Delilah turned around, standing back to scrutinize it. "Could have been kicked in," she observed. "Might get a shoe print."

"Or it could have been knocked in with that piece of fencing." Snowden pointed to a weathered board leaning against the rear of the building with some other junk; a cinderblock, a cracked flowerpot, an old fish tank. The lumber was about six feet long and the thickness of a two by four.

Delilah surveyed the parking lot. They were alone. Trubant's Audi was there and Snowden's cruiser. "I'll get Lopez to check out the car," she said.

"Delilah," Snowden said under his breath, brushing her arm with his fingertips. "I've been thinking. We need to talk."

She looked at him, genuinely surprised. "At a scene?"

He let his hand fall. "It wasn't what I had in mind, but I'm out of options, here. You won't let me come by. You won't talk to me on the phone . . ."

"Snowden," she exhaled, looking back at the busted-in door again, just so she wouldn't have to look at him. She *did* want to talk to him, but what was she going to say? What was *he* going to say? Nothing seemed right in Stephen Kill anymore. Nothing seemed possible. "I just don't know," she whispered, "if—"

She halted midsentence. "Snowden, check out the door again." She pointed. "At the door jamb."

He turned toward the building, then took a step closer. "Anyone touch the door?"

"I can check, but I doubt it." She joined him, reaching out to close the door half way, with a gloved hand. "You see what I'm seeing?" she murmured.

"It wasn't locked when they broke in," he observed. "Not the dead bolt, not the door knob."

She met his blue-eyed gaze. "So why would you break in a door that you could walk right through?"

Chapter 30

Delilah stood at the communal printer and waited for copies of Sister's Julie's preliminary autopsy to print. She'd read them when they'd been e-mailed earlier in the day. Nothing new there, nothing unexpected except that Julie died only a day before she was put into the water. *The Daughter* had kept the nun alive a full two weeks.

The idea made Delilah shudder.

Where could the killer be keeping the victims? It had to be local, didn't it?

Delilah was praying the lab report on the black substance found on the nun's scalp would give them an idea of where to look. Snowden had checked on it already, though, and it would be at least another two days before they got results.

The printer stopped, the green button flashed, and it began to print again. Copies of her notes on the Trubant case, which was getting more interesting by the hour.

It turned out that Susan Trubant had not been aware that her husband hadn't come home last night. He had had an emergency call to the hospital in Lewes and when she woke up this morning and he wasn't there, she had assumed he was still at the hospital. She'd been genuinely shocked when Delilah and Snowden showed up at her door at nine thirty this morning. Delilah seriously suspected there had been no breaking and entering at Trubant's office.

The fact that he had nothing of real value to steal, combined with the unlocked door, made her think whoever went there hadn't intended to kill him. There must have been an argument, then a struggle. Trubant had lost. There were a couple pinprick splatters of blood under the scattered papers; the room had been trashed after he was dead. The door had been broken in after the crime had been committed as part of a cover-up. The scene had been set up to look like a robbery gone bad.

Delilah removed the second set of copies from the printer and wove her way around desks and cubicles, back to her own. She glanced at the clock on the wall. It was after eight P.M. Sister Agatha had sent Monica to pick up Callie and Izzy after work and the teens had gone back to Maria's Place. When Delilah had talked to Sister Agatha on the phone, the nun had been uncharacteristically kind, offering any help she could give Delilah to free her up for the investigation. She had even suggested allowing Callie to spend the night, but Delilah was feeling selfish. She wanted Callie home with her tonight.

Delilah was just sliding into her desk chair when Snowden leaned over the cubicle wall. "You should go home," he said. "Get something to eat. Get some sleep."

"I'm going." She began to slip the copies into the appropriate folders.

He continued to stand there.

She didn't look up. "You want to hear what I'm thinking?" she said quietly.

He came around the corner of the cubicle. The office was quiet except for the background sounds of the dispatcher behind her safety glass.

"Let me guess." Snowden crossed his arms and leaned back against her desk, facing her. He was so close she could smell the starch in his uniform and the scent of his skin. "You think we should throw in the towel here, catch the next plane to Las Vegas, and get married in the Elvis chapel tonight?"

She looked at him as if he'd gone mad, but somewhere deep inside, she felt a little trill of surprise. Had he just used the word *married?* Kidding or not. It was interesting. Intriguing . . .

But Delilah didn't have time to even think about exploring such outrageous ideas. "I was thinking," she said, "that what if Trubant's homicide is somehow related to the other three."

He cocked his head. He was listening.

"Trubant, Sister Julie, and Jenny Grove all worked at Maria's Place. Trubant counseled Jenny and Rob. The phone call, made by a woman the night Sister Julie was kidnapped, was placed from his office." She hesitated. "You know, Callie was seeing Dr. Trubant for counseling and she dragged her feet every week. She said she didn't like him. She never came right out and said so, but she suggested that the gossip among the girls at Maria's was that he was a bit of a ladies' man."

"I've heard that before," Snowden said quietly. She could tell he was thinking. "But Sister Julie was a nun; I highly doubt he was having his way with her. And Rob?"

"Not even a hint that either Rob or Paul was homosexual." She pushed away from the desk, looking up at him, thinking. "No, it's more complicated than people sleeping around, but I just have the feeling this is the direction we ought to be looking."

"A little far-fetched."

"True. But, you know, Jenny Grove had an affair. Marital issues were what she saw Paul about. What if . . ." She hated to even make the accusation. And she knew she was grasping at straws. "What if she was having an affair with him and using the counseling as an excuse to be alone with him?"

"It all seems pretty unrelated, but, maybe it's not. Maybe tomorrow we need to work up some kind of chart. See how many connections we can make to the victims, Maria's Place, Trubant's counseling service." He pressed the heel of his hand to his forehead. "But I'll give you another little tidbit to throw in. I talked to Beebe Hospital. Took me all day to get through the red tape, but Trubant was never there the night he died. There were no suicide attempts made by teenagers, not only at Beebe, but any hospital in the area."

"So Trubant lied to his wife about where he was going. Think he was meeting some chick at his office?"

"Or an angry husband?" Snowden suggested.

Delilah closed the file on her desk. "We need to be careful we don't get ahead of her ourselves. We're basing this all on the assumption that Trubant messed around. I don't think we can use a bunch of teenage gossip to build a case on."

"No. So tomorrow we start investigating Dr. Trubant's personal life." Snowden stood up to go. "But not tonight. Now, you're going home."

"I'm going. I'm going." She lifted her hands in surrender.

"Good night, Detective," he said almost tenderly, walking away.

"Night, Chief."

Delilah was still sitting there like a dunce, all dreamy-eyed, a minute later when her cell phone rang. She picked it up off her desk and seeing that it was Callie's cell, she hit the receive button. She started shoving files into the box she intended to lug home. "Sorry, hon. I'm on my way."

"Now?" Callie whispered.

Delilah stopped what she was doing to concentrate on Callie. She could tell by the tone of the teen's voice, at once, that something was wrong. "What's going on, babe?"

"I need you to come right now. Only park in the back, and meet me on the deck."

"On the deck?"

"Please, Aunt Delilah. Just hurry."

The phone went dead.

Delilah grabbed her leather backpack out of the bottom drawer of her desk, dropped the lid on the file box and taking them both, hurried out of the station.

As Delilah pulled into the rear parking lot of Maria's, she saw Callie dart in front of the police cruiser. The teen was standing there when Delilah parked and opened her door.

"Amanda's running away. Hurry or Sister Agatha will see the interior lights of your car. If she knows you're here, she'll want to come out and talk to you."

Delilah climbed out of the car and Callie shut the door behind her. "What do you mean, Amanda's running away? Isn't she due any day?"

"We don't have much time. Sister Agatha thinks we're out here catching fireflies. She'll be calling everyone, in any moment." Callie waved Delilah in the direction of the potting shed.

Delilah followed Callie out of the light of the backyard and deck into the shadows where she had sat on the bench and talked to Snowden a couple of weeks ago.

"Amanda says Sister Agatha is going to make her give up her baby. She says she's going to run away and take care of the baby herself."

"She doesn't want to give her baby up for adoption?" Delilah whispered, following Callie.

"I don't think she knows what she wants. She's really upset about Sister Julie being dead and . . . and I think she's just scared, Aunt Delilah."

"I think we all are, Callie," Delilah agreed softly.

"Hey," Callie called into the dark. "Where are you guys?"

They walked around to the rear of the toolshed to find the silhouettes of several girls, all in various stages of pregnancy. In the dark, it was hard for Delilah to make out who was who. She hung back.

"Amanda," Callie said, joining the group. "My aunt's here."

"You shouldn't have brought her here," someone hissed.

"Callie—"

"No, it's okay." Callie took one of the girl's hands.

As Delilah moved closer, she could see that it was Amanda.

"You can't stop me," Amanda said. "If I don't get away tonight, I'll just go tomorrow night. You can't make me stay here. You can't handcuff me to my bed." She threw what appeared to be a backpack over her shoulder.

"No one's handcuffing anyone," Delilah said quietly,

entering the knot of girls. "Now what's going on, Amanda? How can I help you?"

"You can't. Only Sister Julie could help and now she's dead."

Delilah could tell that Amanda had been crying.

"See," Callie said quickly, "Amanda's been worried about giving up her baby because there was this little boy, somewhere in another state, who died because his adoptive parents put him in a closet and starved him to death. And Amanda wants to do what's best for her baby, she wants it to have a good home, but she doesn't want anyone to put her baby in a closet."

Delilah was quiet for a second, trying to take in and analyze everything Callie had just said. It was a pretty outrageous story, but Delilah knew from her own recent behavior that all bets were off when it came to the hormones involved with pregnancy. "All you girls back up and give Amanda a little room to breathe." It was so hot and humid that Delilah was sweating in her khakis and blouse. "Better yet, go sit on the deck and watch for Sister Agatha."

"I'm not going back in there," Amanda announced stubbornly. "I'm never going back in there."

Delilah grabbed Callie's arm. "Go on," she told her. "Take the girls and go. I'll stay with Amanda."

Reluctantly, the four girls slipped away into the dark.

"Okay," Delilah said. "Is there a place here to sit?" All she could think of was that she didn't need Amanda fainting from the heat right now.

The girl shook her head.

"Sure there is." Delilah glanced around, and spying a stack of large terracotta pots, she lifted one, turned it upside down, and pointed. "Sit." She grabbed another makeshift stool for herself. "And drop the bag. It looks like it weighs a ton."

Delilah waited for Amanda to obediently sit. The teen set her bag beside her, but on her far side as if she was afraid the cop might swipe it.

"Now, I want to hear this story from you. Why are you running away?"

Amanda hung her head and wiped at her eyes. "I don't want to stay here anymore."

"Because you've changed your mind about the adoption?"

Amanda nodded. Then shrugged.

Delilah was quiet for a minute. Sitting in the dark, looking at the small, slight girl with the big baby belly was hitting way too close to home tonight. When she looked at Amanda, she saw herself.

"So you have some concerns," Delilah prompted, taking care to sound objective and to keep her own emotions to herself.

Again, a nod. "Sister Julie said I didn't have to give up my baby, but she said it would go to a good home. She was going to make sure." Amanda sniffed.

"And now you're afraid your baby won't go to a good home?"

Shrug.

Delilah smiled sadly. "Ah, sugar, the church probably already has a family picked out for your baby. A perfect mom and a perfect dad. Parents old enough to have a good job and a house, and a bedroom all decorated, just waiting for this little baby inside you."

"I can't believe I'm going to give my baby away." The teen looked up, tears glistening on her cheeks. "What kind of person gives away their baby, Detective?"

Delilah looked away, her own eyes filling with tears.

She made herself look back at Amanda. "Someone like me," she whispered.

"You?" Amanda breathed.

Delilah nodded, giving herself a second to find her voice. "When I was sixteen I had a baby and I gave it up for adoption, because it was the best thing for my baby, for me, for my family. I graduated high school, I went to college."

"And . . . and your baby's okay?"

Delilah smiled sadly, reaching for the teen's hand. "My baby's okay, Amanda."

A sound on the far side of the potting shed made Delilah lift her head suddenly.

"What?" Amanda whispered.

Delilah brought her finger to her lips and waited.

She heard the croak of frogs. The twitter of insects. The distant, hushed voices of the girls on the deck, whispering.

But it felt as if someone was there.

"Callie?" Delilah called softly.

No answer.

Delilah waited another minute and then she turned her attention back to Amanda. "You're doing the right thing. By giving your baby to a family who really wants it, who probably can't have a baby, you're giving the greatest gift you can ever give anyone. The greatest gift you could give this baby."

Amanda sat quietly for a moment. "You think it's the right thing to do?"

"I do. And so did Sister Julie."

Amanda wiped at her eyes, again.

Delilah gave her a moment. "Listen, about what I told you about me. I have to ask you not to tell anyone. Not any of the other girls. Not Callie. It . . . it could hurt my job."

Amanda looked up. "Callie doesn't even know?"

Delilah shook her head.

"And you trust me not to tell?" the teen marveled.

"I trust you." Delilah rose off the pot and carried it back to where she found it. "Now, come on." She offered her hand to help Amanda up. "Let's get back up to the house before we both get in trouble."

By the time Delilah and Amanda reached the deck, Sister Agatha was standing at the French doors. "Inside, all of you," she instructed. "Monica should have your snack prepared and then it's off to bed with you."

Delilah slipped Amanda's backpack off the girl's shoulder and gave her a nudge toward the deck. "I'll leave it in the shed," she whispered. "You can get it tomorrow."

Amanda hurried into the light and up the steps of the deck.

"I'd better be going," Callie said cheerfully, giving a wave. "Thank you, Sister Agatha, for the ride today and for dinner."

"Where are you going? You have to wait inside for your aunt."

"She just got here. See." Callie pointed in the direction of the police cruiser parked next to the white passenger van.

"Oh, all right then," Sister Agatha said. "Good night. God bless you and keep you."

Callie hurried off across the paved parking lot and Delilah went back by the potting shed to hide Amanda's backpack. She met Callie at the car.

"Is Amanda okay?"

Delilah looked up to be sure the nun had gone into

the house and then got into the car. "She's fine," she said
as Callie slid in beside her. "She just needed some reassurance." She stole a quick glance at the teenager. She
was pretty sure that someone had been on the other side
of the potting shed listening in on the conversation. She
wondered if it had been Callie.

Callie fastened her seat belt. If she'd heard any of the
conversation, she was playing it cool.

Delilah started the engine, backed up, and headed
down the paved driveway. She'd told Amanda about her
own pregnancy on impulse. It had probably been a
stupid thing to do. No one in Stephen Kill knew anything about it. Worse, neither did Callie. The whole Swift
family had agreed from the beginning that that was the
way it had to be. Otherwise, some day, Callie would put
two and two together.

The Daughter sat down on the edge of her neatly made
bed, her eyes tightly shut, her fists balled at her sides.
The rage that had overcome her in Paul's office had returned. Increased, if that was possible. She thought she
might explode from it.

Never, in her entire life, had she ever felt so betrayed.

Her Delilah. Her sweet, beloved southern belle, up-
holder of the law, rescuer of abandoned pets, was an im-
poster. A liar. A hypocrite. The woman who had been
her hero, her most adored, had hidden from her, from
everyone, that she had committed the greatest crime,
the greatest sin against humanity one could commit.

And she was getting too close . . .

The Daughter breathed deeply, releasing her fists, flex-
ing her fingers. This anger wasn't good. She had learned
that Sunday night. It made her impulsive and impulsive-

ness was dangerous. She had to stay calm. Make plans carefully before executing them. That was the best way to stay unhurt. Unseen.

There had been multiple calls to Maria's Place today from the police station. With the death of Sister Julie, the entire town was a wealth of information. Everyone wanted to talk and phone lines had buzzed continually, a long stream of volunteers passing through the house today. Everyone wanted to express their sympathies. It was so easy to remain invisible, to listen.

The Daughter had learned things today within minutes of the police receiving the information. Trace evidence had been found on the nun's body, but the lab reports weren't back yet. Paul had been sleeping with women all over town. Before her. During.

The Daughter was glad he was dead. She wished she could kill him again.

She retrieved her scrapbook from the bedside table and opened the cover. Pages of clippings, some that went years back. Her life.

On the most recent page was a photo of Delilah, only last week, clipped from a weekly national news magazine. It looked like a photo newspapers kept on file. Maybe the one on her ID.

"You bitch," *The Daughter* whispered. "How could you do this to me? To us?"

She pinched the corner of the carefully pasted photograph and pulled on it, tearing it in half. "You want to throw away your child? Lock her away in the dark with the spider webs, wallowing in her own filth?" She balled the photograph in her sweaty hand. "Let's see how you like it."

* * *

The next morning, Delilah took Callie to breakfast at the diner before dropping her off at work. They briefly talked about Callie staying for the school year and after Callie begged, Delilah agreed they would call Rosemary that night. She didn't promise the teen anything. Mostly because she still didn't know what to do.

If Callie had overheard any of the conversation between Delilah and Amanda the night before, she gave no indication that morning. Delilah dropped Callie off at the library, went to the station and spent the day making charts of connections between the victims found in Horsey Mill Pond and Paul Trubant. She tried to think outside the box. She wrote down the names of any women who had had any connection with any of the victims, including Paul. Sister Agatha, Alice, Muriel, Susan, Monica. Any one of them could possibly be suspects, she reasoned.

Delilah waited all day to hear from the lab and when she called at five to five she learned that the sample had still not been evaluated entirely.

Delilah had left the station frustrated on multiple levels, both personal and professional. Snowden was right. They needed to talk. She wanted to talk. She was being completely irrational in not being willing to even talk to him about what happened with their relationship. She was being completely irrational in telling herself she wasn't in love with him.

And she had to make a decision about Callie. Today. Tonight. Obviously, Rosemary wanted Callie to stay. Callie wanted to stay. Delilah just didn't know if she was ready . . . no, she was ready. She was just afraid of failure.

And she had to start thinking about the baby.

But first, she had to solve these murders. She had to stop this murderer.

Delilah pulled up in front of the library at ten after

five, but Callie wasn't there. She waited another ten minutes and then went up to the glass doors. They were
locked.

Puzzled, trying not to be annoyed, she walked back to
the car and called Callie's cell from hers. She got Callie's
voice mail. Delilah leaned against her car, thinking. She
considered calling Izzy at Maria's, but last night Callie
had said the teen wasn't coming to work, that she
wanted to stay with the girls at the house and help make
plans for Sister Julie's funeral.

Where could Callie be? She'd never once not been
here after work, unless she had made previous arrangements to go to Maria's Place or somewhere in town with
other girls.

Delilah walked back up to the doors of the library and
knocked. Then pounded with her fist. After a minute or
two, Snowden's mother appeared at the inner door and
recognizing Delilah, unlocked the outside doors.

"Miss Calloway, good afternoon." Delilah smiled, nervous, though she had no reason to be. His mother had
never been anything but kind and friendly to her. "I was
looking for Callie."

She was petite with short-cropped hair, still attractive
for a woman her age. "She left right at five." She sounded
concerned, at once. "She came out to wait for you."

"I got here at ten after. She wasn't here." Delilah
glanced around as if she might have missed her standing
right there. All she could think of was that maybe Callie
had been eavesdropping last night and had heard Delilah's confession to Amanda. Maybe she'd taken off.

Delilah looked back to Snowden's mom. "She didn't
say anything about walking up to the diner? Maybe
coming to the station?"

"You think she's okay?"

"Oh, sure." Delilah waved, backing away from the doors. "Our wires probably got crossed. It would be an understatement to say I've been preoccupied." She gave a little laugh that was without humor. "Maybe she went to the video store or something."

"Well, all right." Tillie stood in the doorway, watching Delilah go back down the sidewalk. "I suppose I'll see her tomorrow. She's a good worker, you know."

"Thank you." Delilah waved, trying not to worry. Callie had to be in town. She had to be here somewhere.

Chapter 31

Delilah tried not to panic. She checked the diner, the video store, the drug store, and the station. No one had seen Callie. She called Izzy. Izzy hadn't talked to her all day. She called home multiple times, but all she got was her own voice on the answering machine.

After driving around for over an hour, Delilah broke down and called Rosemary, wondering if maybe Callie had called her. Delilah got the answering machine at home and voice mail on her sister's cell.

It was almost seven when Delilah finally decided to go home. Maybe Callie was just out walking. Maybe she had eavesdropped on the discussion the previous night, drawn conclusions, and was working them out in her head. Maybe she was just preparing to really give Delilah hell when she walked in the door.

Delilah found the house empty. She changed into shorts and a T-shirt and walked around, cleaning up, debating her next move. She picked up Callie's dirty shorts on the laundry room floor and tossed them in the washer. She carried a cup and a plate from the computer desk into the kitchen.

What if *The Daughter* had taken her?

Delilah had been holding off that thought for almost two hours. There had been no threats in the letters from *The Daughter*. Not made to Delilah or her family. But to her knowledge, the victims had not been contacted by the killer previously, either.

Should Delilah call the station?

She didn't want to overreact. This was a teenager, for heaven's sake, and prone to whims. Delilah didn't want to cause a ruckus at the station over a misbehaved teen when the guys were already overworked and on edge.

But how could she not call them? *What if, God forbid* . . .

Dropping the dirty dishes into the sink, she reached for the house phone. Her cell phone on the counter began to ring. She grabbed it up. To her relief, Callie's name was on the display.

"Callie, where are you?"

"Aunt Delilah?"

Her words were slightly slurred. It didn't sound like her.

"Callie?" Delilah repeated. "Callie, where are you? Have you been drinking?"

"I . . . I don . . . don't know. Caaan . . . can you come and g . . . get me?"

She was either drunk or high, or both. *No*, Delilah thought. *If she got caught again, she would go to juvie.*

But Delilah didn't holler. She didn't lose her temper. There would be time for that when she had Callie safely in the house. "Tell me where you are."

Callie didn't answer. Delilah thought she heard another voice. Maybe voices. Was she at a party? "Callie," she repeated firmly. "Callie, I'll come for you, but you have to tell me where you are."

"Roun . . . round back. Shhhhh," Callie murmured. "I'm . . . sorry, Aunt De . . . lilah."

"Tell me where you are."

"Where 'm I?" Callie said to someone else. Then she came back on the line and gave Delilah an address.

Delilah was surprised by the location. It was a quiet, older neighborhood. She wasn't sure which house, but it would be easy enough to find. The Bread Ladies lived on that street. So had Alice Crupp. "I'll be right there," Delilah said into the phone. "You wait for me, Callie. Do you hear me? Don't go anywhere."

The only response on the other end of the phone was dead air.

Delilah took her pickup rather than the police car. All the way across town she thought about what she was going to say to the teen when she got her home and sobered up.

Delilah was so disappointed. It had seemed as if Callie had come so far this summer.

But she'd also been through a lot. Delilah couldn't deny that. Her mother putting her on the plane, her staying with Delilah, who was in the middle of a murder investigation. Sister Julie being murdered, then the teen's counselor. If Callie had heard Delilah tell Amanda about her pregnancy, no one could blame the kid for going a little nuts. And a little nuts was maybe okay, but drugs and alcohol weren't. Delilah was going to have to make Callie understand that.

By the time Delilah reached the other side of town, the sky had prematurely darkened and it was beginning to rain. Perfect. It hadn't rained in weeks.

When she realized which house she was looking for,

she wasn't as surprised as perhaps she should have been. All looked quiet from out front. She drove around the back, turning the windshield wipers up a notch. She was so angry with Callie. So relieved she was okay. Delilah would find her another counselor. They'd get through this. Together.

She parked her truck in the alley, locked it, hanging the keys on the pocket of her jean shorts and walked through a rusty gate, left open. Thunder rumbled and lightning zigzagged across the sky. She was getting soaking wet, but she didn't run.

The cellar door was open.

It was a perfect place for a party on a rainy summer evening; she'd give the kids that.

Halfway across the yard, Delilah began to wonder why Callie wasn't waiting outside for her. Surely she didn't want her aunt, the cop, to see who she'd hooked up with. But the alley had been empty. No cars. No teenagers. She couldn't hear any music. Any voices.

Was Callie sick? Had she overdosed and her newfound *friends* left her behind? Or had they dumped her here? Had the party been elsewhere and some quick thinking, numb-brained kid had known the cellar door was unlocked?

"Callie?" Delilah called.

She halted at the doorway that led down the cinderblock steps, into the dark. She'd left her side arm locked in the truck and she briefly debated whether or not she should go back for it. But she wasn't Delilah the cop right now, she was just Delilah the frightened parent. She wasn't here to get anyone into trouble; she just wanted her kid back.

She took a step down, trying to peer into the dark. Rain drummed on the aluminum door hatch. She couldn't see anything. More thunder rumbled. Now thoroughly wet, she was chilled. "Callie?"

Delilah was three quarters of the way down the dark staircase before she heard Callie call out to her.

"Aunt Delilah?" the girl sobbed.

Whatever good sense and training Delilah had learned on the job flew out of her head. She wasn't thinking about the precautions she usually exercised in any unknown situation. All she was thinking about was the safety of her child. She bounded down the last steps, spotting Callie lying on a dirt floor leaning against wooden crates. "Callie, honey . . ."

It wasn't like the movies. There was no ominous music. No shadow looming over her. Delilah saw Callie react, realized someone was behind her, and started to turn. She felt an exploding pain in the back of her head. Heard Callie cry out. The hard-packed dirt floor came up under her. Then nothing.

"Goodness," Tillie said, waving both her hands as Snowden ducked through the curtain of water flowing over the gutters and through his mother's back door. "Take your shoes off."

"We need to get someone out here to repair these gutters, Ma." He eased off one tight, black leather shoe and then the other, stepping in his socks, into water on the floor. "They're supposed to drain the water away from the doors, not funnel it over them."

"You're soaked." She handed him a tea towel from the stack on her washer. "You should take your clothes off and let me toss them in the dryer."

"I'm not that wet, Ma." He accepted the towel,

though, and wiped his face. "I don't have anything to change into."

"You can sit in a towel while I dry your clothes."

He walked into the kitchen, forcing her to back up into it ahead of him. "Ma, I'm forty years old. I don't sit in my mother's kitchen wearing nothing but a towel. I'll dry. I'm fine."

"I made you dinner. Meat loaf and boiled potatoes and Brussels sprouts."

Snowden's stomach clenched at the thought. His mother made the worst meatloaf in the county, possibly the state, and he despised Brussels sprouts, especially the way she cooked them to a pulp. "I'm not hungry, Ma. I just came by on my way home from work to see how you were."

"You're not eating?" She drew up her petite frame indignantly. "But I made extra."

"Fine, I'll take it home with me." He crossed the kitchen. "I'll just have some juice. I need to get home. I have a mountain of paperwork."

She took the damp towel out his hand and leaned against the counter, watching him retrieve a glass and the orange juice from the refrigerator. "You're certainly testy tonight. Been testy for weeks. Is everything all right, son?"

"You mean other than the serial killer loose on our streets and the dead psychologist in the morgue?"

"I didn't raise you to get smart with your mother," she snipped.

He poured the watery orange juice into his glass. "Sorry, Ma. You're right. I just have a lot on my mind."

Still holding the towel, she crossed her arms over her chest. "You're not seeing that nice policewoman,

Callie's aunt, anymore. That's why you're so contrary with your mother."

He shot her a look.

She tossed the towel on the counter. "I'm just saying you haven't been yourself. A man needs a woman, Snowden. It's in his nature."

He returned the orange juice carton to the refrigerator door.

"Oh," she said. "Did she find her?"

He sipped his juice, standing where he was. "Did who find whom?"

"Detective Swift. Did she find Callie?"

He lowered his glass. "I wasn't aware she was missing."

"I don't know that she was *missing*. But Callie wasn't there at the library when her aunt came by to pick her up. The detective thought maybe she'd walked down to the diner."

"When was this?"

"After five, when the library closed, of course."

Snowden looked at his wrist watch. It was eight forty-five. He'd stayed at the station later than he intended. He'd called the lab and chewed someone out about the report they were still waiting on for the evidence found on the nun's body. They had promised he would have it tomorrow morning.

Callie missing? She couldn't be missing. Delilah would have called him immediately. Just the same, the whole idea made him uneasy. He hoped to God Delilah wasn't foolish enough to search for the kid on her own, if she had taken off.

He removed his cell from its holder on his belt and dialed Delilah's house. He got her answering machine and left a brief message simply telling her to call him as soon as she got home. Then he called her cell. Voice mail. He slipped his phone back onto his belt.

"I think I'm going to take off, Ma."

"You going to go see her? Because I think that's a good idea." She followed him back into the laundry room. "You know, no problem is insurmountable. We can't help who we fall in love with, Snowden."

He leaned against the dryer and pulled on a wet black sock. What was she talking about? Who had she been talking to? Had Delilah told Callie about him and her? Had she told her niece she was in love with him?

The idea scared him . . . and made him want to smile at the same time.

"You two should sit down and talk about this," Tillie went on, offering his other wet sock.

He snatched it out of her hand. They felt disgusting on his feet, but he certainly wasn't walking out of his mother's house in uniform, wearing dress shoes and no socks. "Call Jerry tomorrow, Ma. Ask him to come out and give you an estimate on repairing these gutters."

"He's expensive. He takes too long for a lunch break." She stood behind him as he untied his shoes and put them down on the rag rug to step into them. "You know, the last time he worked for me, putting those new shingles up, he drove all the way to Rehoboth to go to Arby's. Took him more than an hour."

His shoes tied, Snowden leaned over his mother and gave her a kiss, something he rarely did. "Talk to you tomorrow, Ma. Take your medicine."

She rested her hand on her cheek, watching him go through the door. "I always do," she called after him, her voice drowned out by the rain.

* * *

Snowden had never been a man who depended on hunches, or a *feeling*, as he had heard many cops call it. He liked evidence. Numbers. Eyewitnesses. But by the time he reached Delilah's dark town house, he was fighting a feeling. *A bad feeling.*

Her truck was gone, her cruiser parked prominently out front. Front and back doors were locked securely. He tried her cell phone twice more on his way back to the station. Her truck wasn't there, either. Sitting in the rain, in his own parking space in the rear, he called the desk sergeant, who also functioned as the shift commander at night. Detective Swift had clocked out at five oh four. She had not returned or called in.

Snowden sat in his car, rain pouring down, trying to decide what to do. The fact that he couldn't find his girl-friend—his ex-girlfriend—was no reason to put out an all-points bulletin. She could be a hundred places. She probably found Callie at the diner and they went to eat, maybe out to a movie. Cell phones had to be shut off in a movie theater.

It made perfect sense, he thought, the rain drumming on the roof of the car. School was getting ready to start. The niece would be returning home to Georgia. It was only natural they should do some things together.

That was sort of what Snowden had been waiting for, until Callie went home. He'd been trying to talk to Delilah for weeks, but he knew she was overwhelmed with the investigation and the teenager in her home. It made sense that they should wait until this all died down and then they could have some serious dialogue. He would tell her how he felt, she could shed some light on her own feelings, and they would discuss their options.

Snowden started the engine, flipped on the wipers, and pulled out of his parking spot. He'd go home and change out of his wet clothes, work on the pile of papers beside him on the car seat, and wait for Delilah to call.

"Aunt Delilah? Aunt Delilah?"

Delilah felt as if she were spinning. She was nauseous. Disoriented. She had been dreaming she was on a roller coaster in a dark amusement park where it was raining. Callie was with her. She didn't like the ride either. She was crying.

"Aunt Delilah, please wake up," Callie moaned.

Delilah's eyelids fluttered. Darkness. She was surrounded by it. *Was she blind?* she thought in sudden terror.

"Callie?" She felt the teen's thin arms around her. They were lying on the ground and Delilah was on her back, her head cradled by Callie's leg.

"Oh, God, oh, God, Aunt Delilah. I thought you were dead. I couldn't w . . . wake you up," Callie groaned. Her speech was still slightly slurred, but she sounded better than she had on the phone.

The phone call . . . Delilah remembered it. Remembered looking for Callie. Walking down the steps.

She blinked. Not blind. It was just dark. Very dark.

She tried to sit up, but the back of her head hurt so badly. She lifted her hand to it. Wet. Warm. Sticky. Callie was holding a ball of fabric against it.

"It was b . . . bleeding so hard. I didn't know . . . know what to do. Didn't have any . . . thing to stop it. Used my T-shirt," Callie sniffed.

Delilah closed her eyes for a moment, trying to clear her thoughts. Trying to separate what was actually happening from the past. From the crazy dream.

Reality was Callie here in the darkness with her. Her

bleeding skull and pounding headache. The hard, cool dirt floor under them. Her damp T-shirt. "What . . ." Delilah tried to think what she wanted to ask.

"I'm so sorry. She said you sent her to pick me up. It made perfect sense. Izzy wanted me to come over," Callie sobbed. "We were . . . were going to help write the eu . . . eulogy."

"Oh, sweetheart." Delilah fought her nausea as she tried to sit up and take Callie in her arms. "It's okay, baby." Her dizziness came in waves.

"No, no it isn't okay. Oh, God, I think I'm going to throw u . . . up again," Callie moaned.

She leaned over and wretched and Delilah managed to get to her knees and hold Callie's hair back for her.

"She . . . she brought me a Coke. It tasted so good. It was cold." Callie coughed, then vomited.

And drugged, Delilah guessed, her thoughts seeming to float aimlessly. *She drugged Callie to lure me in and I fell for it. So much for being a supercop.*

When Callie, who was wearing just her shorts and bra, had stopped wretching, Delilah wrapped her arms around her again She was a smart girl. As wet as the T-shirt felt, she may very well have saved Delilah's life.

"Shhhhh," Delilah soothed, clinging to Callie in the pitch dark. "It's okay. Don't cry. We're going to get out of this."

"But . . . but we're not. You know we're not. She's going to let us die. She's going to throw us in the pond."

"Who?" Delilah whispered, although she thought she already knew the answer. How could she have been so naïve? So easily taken in by stereotypes. "Tell me who picked you up at the library, Callie."

Chapter 32

Snowden waited patiently . . . as patiently as he could . . .
until twelve fifteen, before he punched Delilah's phone
numbers again. Nothing.

Then he got in the car and drove back to her house.
Her truck was still gone and he wished he had a key to
go in and look around, although the place looked undisturbed. He wished their relationship had progressed to
the point that they had exchanged house keys. Snowden
sat in front of her town house, in his car, for more than
twenty minutes, wondering what he should do. The
thunderstorms had passed and it was barely drizzling.
He sat in the dark, the windshield wipers off.

He didn't want to appear so concerned as to step outside the bounds of professional behavior, and he didn't
want to cause any suspicion about him and Delilah. But
this could mean the difference between Delilah living or
dying.

He called into the station on his cell phone, rather
than the radio that could heard by the two cars on duty
tonight, and whoever was listening in on the band who
shouldn't have been. He asked Johnson to have the two

cars on duty begin looking for Detective Swift's pickup and told the sergeant he'd join the patrol, but not to send word out over the radio, in case the murderer was listening.

Snowden drove up and down the dark streets of Stephen Kill. He started at the library and took routes he thought Delilah might have taken, depending on where she and her niece might have been going. He drove from her house downtown, from her house out to Maria's Place, and then he took the main country road out to Route One. He had Johnson call the local state police troop to be sure Delilah hadn't been involved in an accident near the beach, and then he began to drive around town randomly.

Snowden found Delilah's pickup at four fifteen about a quarter of a mile off the paved road, on the old mill road, close to where Rob Crane's vehicle had been discovered. He was sick to his stomach by the time he reached the driver's side door.

The keys were in the ignition, her backpack on the seat with her wallet inside, and the glove compartment, where he knew she kept her firearm, was open. Her Glock .40 caliber side arm, issued to all Stephen Kill officers the previous fall, was not there.

"Monica," Delilah said sharply. "Are you out there? Can you hear me? You have to let us out. You can't do this. You won't get away with it."

"Please, Aunt Delilah," Callie moaned, lying on her side in the tiny, dark room where they'd been imprisoned. "I'm telling you, she's not there. She made me get in here, she dragged you in, took your keys and your cell, and then she locked the door. I heard it. She's not coming back. Not until we're dead."

Delilah crawled the short distance between her and Callie. "Why did she do this? Did she say why?"

"I told you." Callie, by the minute, was beginning to sound more like the surly teenager Delilah had picked up at the airport two months ago. "She didn't say anything. She just picked me up. We were talking about the new books that came in to the library. About Amanda getting to meet her baby's new Mom and Dad, if Amanda's parents agreed to it." She curled into a tighter ball. "We drank our Cokes and we talked. She was being really nice." Callie's voice caught in her throat. "That bitch. She was being so nice. She was always so nice. Now we're going to die."

For once, Delilah let Callie's cursing slide. When she realized how ridiculous it was that she should even *think* about something like that at a time like this, she almost laughed out loud. Instead, she reached out to smooth Callie's hair. "Don't say that. We're going to get out of here. I'm going to get you out of here. I swear it."

"How? We screamed for hours. It's got to be morning by now. If someone was going to hear us, they would have. No one heard the others."

Delilah sat up, drawing her knees to her chin. She was thirsty already. She knew Callie had to be, too, but neither had mentioned it. Neither wanted to think about it.

What she was trying to figure out was where they were. She knew where, but what she couldn't figure out was what the room was where Monica had imprisoned them. It was obviously old. No windows, no door she could find, although she had felt with her fingertips the edges where the flush door met with the wall. She wondered if the room had been here since the house was built. But for what purpose?

"I'm sorry I got us into this," Callie whispered miserably. Her voice was hoarse from yelling. They both were hoarse. "If I hadn't gotten in the van with her—"

"Don't be silly, Callie. If you'd called me and asked me, I'd have given you permission to go to Maria's Place with her." *Because I never really suspected her,* Delilah thought miserably. She'd been on her most recent list of *possible* possibilities, but she hadn't seriously considered quiet, mild-mannered, hard-working Monica as a ruthless killer.

Of course she'd had contact with Jenny, with Sister Julie, with Paul. Delilah still didn't know how the first victim, Rob, fit in, but that was only because she didn't know how Monica had picked her victims. What did they all have in common? Was Delilah included, or had Monica simply decided the investigation was getting too close to her and it was time to eliminate the threat? She had, after all, been looking hard at Maria's Place. Monica might not have realized it was Sister Agatha who Delilah had seriously begun to suspect.

"I'm tired," Callie whispered.

Delilah scooted over to lean against the wall. "Come here," she said. "Use my lap for a pillow."

Callie crawled to her without hesitation, resting on Delilah's bare legs, using her own arms to help cushion her head.

Delilah stroked the teenager's hair, leaning her head back, wincing at the pain. "Go to sleep," she whispered. "You'll feel better when you wake up. The drug she put in your Coke should be out of your system soon. You'll feel more like yourself."

"I can't believe I fell for the drugs in the soda scam," Callie muttered, already half asleep. "Didn't you tell me just the other day about date rape drugs, about how I should never accept an open drink from someone?"

"Shhhh," Delilah soothed. "Go to sleep, Callie, and let me think."

By noon, with no sign of Delilah or Callie, Snowden was fighting hard to remain calm. There were no fingerprints in her vehicle and due to the heavy rainfall, no distinguishable footprints leading away from where it had been abandoned in the woods. By three, he felt as if he could have peeled himself off one of the white walls of his office. Everyone on the force had come in whether or not they were scheduled to work.

And the lab report was still not in. Snowden called again, leaving a message for a supervisor, and went to Delilah's cubicle. From along the wall, he retrieved the posterboard charts she had begun making the day before and carried them to the break room, where he could spread them out and get a better look at them.

If Callie had gone missing first, it was logical to Snowden that *The Daughter* had used the teenager to lure Delilah into a trap. *Why Delilah, though?* he wondered. She'd been on the case since the start. The logical explanation was that she was getting closer to the killer and somehow the killer knew it.

He studied the boxes where she had written her clues. There were circles with names inside them. Red circles for the victims. Blue for others. Lines drawn between the names with notes written on them. At first, it looked like a jumble of nothing. Words. Names. Timelines. But as he studied it, he began to see patterns. And everyone but Rob was connected to Maria's Place . . . including Callie and Delilah.

And there was a tiny asterisk next to Sister Agatha's name.

Sister Agatha? Could she be *The Daughter*?

Snowden decided it was time to take a drive out to Maria's and talk to the good nun himself.

Sister Agatha welcomed his unannounced visit coolly and businesslike. She offered him iced tea, which he declined, and then asked if they could speak somewhere privately. He suggested the back deck. She thought it too warm outside.

They settled on the small office she and Sister Julie and their administrative assistant shared.

"The girls are working on the obituary and eulogy, Monica," Sister Agatha said as they passed her in the hall. "Could you please monitor that? We don't need any hysterics. And check on Amanda. She was feeling poorly this morning." The nun looked up at Snowden. "Right this way, Chief Calloway."

Sister Agatha took a chair behind a desk. Snowden closed the door behind him. There were three desks, filing cabinets, the usual office equipment, a clock on the wall that could have been seen in any office in the United States, including his own. The only thing that made the office stand out was the plain wooden crucifix that hung on the wall between the two windows.

"I suppose you've heard by now that Detective Swift and her niece are missing."

"I had not heard, sir. Please, sit down." She indicated a chair to the side of one of the desks.

He pulled it up in front of hers and sat down, watching her carefully. "Have you heard from her?"

"From who?"

"Either of them?" he said sharply.

She sat back in her chair. "I'm sorry to hear they're missing. I have not heard from them. I can check with the girls, though. One of our girls, Izzy, has become good friends with Callie. She's a pleasant young lady."

The nun held herself stiffly, her words carefully chosen, formal sounding. He couldn't read her. Was she just an uptight, sour woman with a power complex, or was she a killer?

"Did you know Rob Crane, Sister Agatha?"

"I did not. I only came to Maria's Place last October, Chief Calloway. I believe he had already left Stephen Kill for his freshman fall semester. According to the newspapers."

He rested his ankle on his knee, watching her. She was quick. She had the right answers. He wondered if Delilah had begun backtracking, trying to determine where Sister Agatha had been when each of the victims had disappeared.

His cell phone rang. "Excuse me," he said.

"Certainly." She started to rise. "Would you like me to leave the room?"

"That won't be necessary." Snowden hit the *receive* button. It was the station.

"Johnson here, Chief."

"Yes?"

"I been watching the fax machine just like you said. The lab report came back."

Snowden glanced up at the nun across the desk from him. She was tapping on the keyboard on her desk. Opening her e-mail.

"What was it, Johnson?"

"Coal dust, sir."

It had been all *The Daughter* could do to stay until her day was officially over before leaving Maria's Place. Sister

Agatha had looked at her strangely when she had told her she was going home for the day. She rarely left at five. She rarely left before dinner. Because she had no life. Sister Agatha knew that. The girls all knew it. The little bitches. Little bitches who would give away their babies.

If she'd had the time, maybe she would have thrown them all in the pond, too. What had she been thinking all these weeks, reasoning that they had not yet actually committed the sin? That they were innocents, being led astray by the nuns? They were bad. They were bad.

Only now, *The Daughter* had to get out of town.

She drove straight to where she rented a tiny second floor apartment from an elderly couple who lived on the ground floor of the old house. She climbed the outside staircase, unlocked the door, and went inside. The apartment was plain. Ordinary. Just like Monica Dryden, who had been born Sandra Alice Crupp. *The Mother* and *The Father* had changed her name when the adoption had taken place.

The Daughter dragged an old suitcase out the closet. She would take care of the business in the cellar and then she would move to another state. Become invisible somewhere else. Continue her efforts.

She stuffed clothes into the bag without looking to see what they were. It didn't matter. She didn't have that many clothes and they all looked the same anyway. She got the shoe box from the closet where she kept her money. There was plenty in there because she always cashed her paychecks, never deposited them, and spent very little beyond rent and gas for her car.

She packed the little plastic drawstring bag of mementos. A quarter she'd found in the swimmer's pocket. A pack of mints from Jenny's purse. Sister Julie's crucifix. A photo of

Paul on a sailboat. She had burned their clothes. Not safe to keep them.

Next, *The Daughter* went to the nightstand and collected the scrapbook. She wondered if she should burn it, too, in the burn barrel in the backyard. The Andrews weren't supposed to have a burn barrel; they weren't legal inside the city limits. The fire chief had even stopped by one day a few months ago and warned they would be fined if they continued to use it. Monica had told them it was dangerous, at their age, to be burning trash. They thought the city charged senior citizens too much for curbside pick up.

The Daughter ran her hand over the cover of the scrapbook. So many memories. She flipped open a page to look at Delilah looking back at her. Tears filled her eyes. She hated her. Hated her! And yet . . .

She wiped at her face. She still loved her.

Of course, that wouldn't stop *The Daughter* from doing what had to be done.

She carried the scrapbook to the suitcase, set it on top, and went back to the nightstand. She pulled out Delilah's pistol. *The Daughter* didn't like guns, but she knew how to use one. *The Father* had collected guns.

Exhausted from screaming for help, then searching the entire room for a way out, Delilah had finally lay down with Callie and slept fitfully on and off all day. By the time she woke to feel Callie stirring, she sensed that it was dark out again. By now, someone had to be looking for them. She hadn't showed for work. Snowden would know that Callie had disappeared from the library. He would be looking for them.

"I'm thirsty," Callie whispered.

"Me, too."

"But you can go a long time without water, right?" She scooted up so that she was sitting beside Delilah. "Right? I mean, we have a few days."

"A week, at least. Maybe longer." Delilah patted her knee. "You cold? You want my shirt?"

"No," the teen whispered. "I'm fine. How's your head?"

"Fine." Delilah was surprised to hear herself laugh. "Well, maybe not fine. It hurts like heck, but you did the right thing using your shirt to stop the bleeding, Callie."

"Health class." She exhaled, leaning her head back. "I guess I was listening better than I thought I was. You think there are spiders in here?"

Delilah smiled. "Nah, what would a spider want—"

A sound beyond the wall tapped Delilah's attention and she went quiet. "You hear that?" she whispered. She waited.

"Hello? Is somebody there?" Delilah crawled on her hands and knees in the direction she thought was the door. She slapped her hands on the rough boards, feeling for the seams. "Monica! Monica, it's Delilah. I want to talk to you."

There was definitely a sound on the other side. Someone was there. Monica was there.

Callie scooted across the short distance between the walls to kneel beside Delilah. "You better let us out of here," Callie threatened. "You don't, Monica, I bet Sister Julie is going to want to talk to you when you die, and I bet she's not going to be happy with you."

"Shut up," came a voice from the other side of the door. "Shut up. Shut her up right this minute or I'll come in there and I'll shut her up," Monica threatened.

Delilah sensed they were only inches apart. That Monica was right there on the other side of the door.

"I have your gun, Delilah," Monica taunted. "I got it out of your truck, so I can do it, you know I can."

"Monica, how could you—"

"Callie, be quiet," Delilah whispered, grasping in the dark. She caught the teen by her shoulder.

"I want her to let us out of here," Callie cried angrily, striking out at the wall, hitting it hard with her fist.

"Shhh," Delilah soothed. "She's not mentally stable. We have to be careful what we say." She grasped her shoulders and eased her back. "Now you have to be quiet and let me talk to her. Let me convince her she needs to set us free."

Callie sat back on the hard-packed dirt. "I hate her," she whispered.

Delilah moved to the door again, pressing her hand against it. "Monica," she said softly. She waited. "Monica, do you want to talk? I know you and Sister Julie talked," she said, taking a wild guess. Everyone who knew Sister Julie found her to be a good confessor. Even Delilah had. "You miss her, don't you?"

"She had to die," Monica said in a small voice.

Delilah was trembling all over. She was dizzy. She was probably more dehydrated than Callie because of blood loss. With that and the pregnancy, she wasn't real sure how long she'd be able to think rationally.

She tried to dig into all her past psychological training. "It's all right, Monica. We can talk. I can't hurt you. I'm locked in here. You have the door locked."

"I locked the door," she repeated.

"That's right. You're in control."

"I'm in control. I'm in charge. I'm the boss of you."

"You sure are," Delilah encouraged, thinking what an odd phrase that was. So childish sounding. "You are the boss of me. You want to tell me why?"

* * *

At eight forty-five that evening Johnson walked into the chief's office. Snowden had been on the Internet for hours, first trying to find out where the closest coal mines were. There were none in Delaware, of course, and the killer had to been keeping her victims locally. Then he searched to see if anyone was still burning coal in the area; a factory maybe. Another dead-end. Next, he started looking for places coal had once been stored for factories, in the area. Trains had once run on coal. He wondered if maybe some local, abandoned train depot still had storage bins standing. Common coal was what the lab said Sister Julie had in her hair and it hadn't come from Maria's Place or the diner, so Snowden was sure it had come from wherever the killer had been holding her.

"Sister Agatha's on line two," the desk sergeant said. "I figured you'd want to talk to her."

Sister Agatha calling him?

He picked up the phone and hit the appropriate button. "Chief Calloway, here. What can I do for you, Sister Agatha?"

"Chief Calloway, I have to confess I've been praying over this for hours. Unsure . . ."

Snowden sat up in his chair, gripping the phone. "Sister, if you know anything about the whereabouts of Detective Swift or her niece, you're under legal obligation to tell me. Moral obligation."

"Yes, yes, I understand. This really isn't about Detective Swift per se, Chief Calloway. It's about . . . about an employee."

"Your employee?" His first thought was of Mattie

McConnell. He had been a suspect in the murders the previous year.

"Monica Dryden."

"What about her?"

"Well, I've been thinking. She was behaving oddly this afternoon, after you paid your visit and she left right at five. She never goes home that early, Chief."

"Okay." He wasn't sure where she was going with this, but at this point, anything anyone could tell him was more than he had right now.

"And she said something very odd the other day. Something that . . . frankly, worried me."

"And what was that?"

"I may have misunderstood her."

"Sister Agatha," Snowden said firmly.

"She said . . . she said that Mattie McConnell was her brother."

"Her brother? How so?"

"I don't know. When I questioned her, she insisted that wasn't what she had said, or meant, or something. *She* said she said she had a brother *like* Mattie, I suppose meaning mentally handicapped."

"But you don't think that's what she actually said?"

"People tell nuns a lot of things they would never tell others. We're under obligation to listen, Chief Snowden. Try not to judge. Never repeat what we hear."

The nun went on, but Snowden was barely listening now. If Monica was Mattie's brother, somehow, that meant that Alice could have been her mother. If they shared the same mother . . .

Delilah had sworn from the beginning that there was some connection to Alice Crupp's death and the others'. Could she have, somehow, been right?

"Sister Agatha," Snowden interrupted, not even knowing what she was saying now. "Thank you for calling me."

He hung up and dialed for operator assistance. Rachel Gibson answered the phone on the second ring. Snowden identified himself and got right to the point. "Did Alice Crupp have another child besides Mattie?" he asked.

"Snowden, what's the matter? Is Mattie in trouble?" Rachel questioned. "He's right here. He just went to bed."

"Rachel, please. I don't have time to explain myself. I know that Alice Crupp gave birth to Mattie out of state and Jack McConnell brought him back to Stephen Kill to raise him. But could there have been another baby? Could she have had another child later?"

"Not that I know of," Rachel said.

"You're sure?"

"I never heard anything—" She paused.

"What?"

"It was just a rumor," she said softly. "You know this town. People are always talking about other people. Making up lies, adding to them over the years."

"There were rumors she had a second child?" he pushed.

"Someone once told me it was twins. That Mattie had a sister."

"Twins?" he asked incredibly. He did the math. Mattie and Monica were likely the same age.

"They said she was healthy so she was put up for adoption. Mattie's father took him because . . . you know, his disability."

Snowden hung up as he leaped out of his chair and ran for the door.

* * *

Delilah didn't know how long it had taken her, but at last, Monica was beginning to talk. At first, she hadn't made much sense. She kept ranting about *The Mother* and *The Father*. From what she said, Delilah gathered that Monica had been abused as a child. She had been punished by being locked in a dark closet, threatened with guns and knives her father had collected. He had beaten her, burned her.

But none of it had really made sense. Delilah still couldn't figure why Monica was killing people. Sadly, many children were abused, and *they* didn't turn out to be serial killers. And there seemed to be no logical explanation as to why Monica had become fixated on her, except that Delilah was simply someone she had admired. It wasn't until Delilah heard her say something about *The Birth Mother* that any of it began to make sense.

"Monica, you were adopted, weren't you?"

She didn't answer.

"That's why you worked at Maria's Place. Because you wanted to help those girls."

"I didn't want to help them give away their children," she snapped. "No one should ever give away their children. They should pay. Pay for what they do to their children."

"She's crazy," Callie whispered.

"Shhhh," Delilah hushed Callie. "Monica," she then said, trying to get her captor to refocus. "You said they had to pay. You mean the birth mothers?"

"Sister Julie gave a baby up for adoption," Callie said quickly under her breath. "She told Amanda and Amanda told Izzy and Izzy told me."

Delilah looked in Callie's direction, then back at the wall. She was too scared to be shocked. "Monica, I know Sister Julie gave away a baby. Is that why you punished her?"

"She wasn't what you thought. She was a bad person. Bad," Monica said. "She was making those girls do a bad thing, too. I should go now. You . . . we all have to go. I have to take care of you, you know. Get rid of you."

"No, no, wait Monica." Delilah tried not to sound panicked. "I'm still trying to understand. You want me to understand, right? That's what you said in your letter. What about Jenny? Did she have a baby and give it up for adoption?"

"It was all in the files."

"What files?" Delilah was confused. Maria's Place hadn't existed when Jenny would have had her baby. "In the file at Maria's?"

"In *Paul's* files," she said as if Delilah was an idiot. "It was all in the files."

"How was she in his files?" Callie whispered. "There were locks on them."

"Did Paul counsel you, Monica? Is that how you saw his files?"

He wasn't *counseling* me, Delilah. He was *screwing* me."

Delilah couldn't see Callie's face in the dark, but she heard her sharp intake of air. "You were having a relationship with Dr. Trubant?"

"Told you he was a jerk," Callie whispered.

"Apparently, I wasn't the only one," Monica went on, sarcastically. "There were other women in town. So many. He took their pictures like he took mine."

"And you found out."

"I found out," Monica said. There was a sound at the door as if she was moving a latch. "Enough questions. We should get this over with."

"No, no wait." Delilah rose up on her knees again,

pressing her hands to the wall. "I still don't understand. Rob Crane couldn't have given birth."

"The girlfriend he knocked up in high school did. Then she and her parents moved away and put the baby up for adoption. Rob was in Paul's office boohooing about what a hard decision it had been," she sneered, "and then he was in the newspaper. Everyone thought he was such hero, but he was bad."

"Okay, so Rob, Jenny, and Sister Julie had to die for giving away their babies. Did Dr. Trubant put a child up for adoption?"

"I didn't mean to do that," Monica said. "He just made me angry. He hurt me."

Delilah ran her hand over her face, trying to think, knowing what she had to ask next. Wishing she didn't. "What about me, Monica?" she said quietly.

"You did it too. You lied to me! You lied to us all. You made us think you were good." She kicked the door.

"No, no," Delilah insisted. "You're mistaken."

"I'm not. I heard you. You admitted it to Amanda that night."

So it had not been Callie listening in. That was going to make this even harder. But Delilah knew she had to say it. She had to say anything she could to save Callie, to save herself so that she could save her unborn child. "No, Monica. I didn't tell Amanda the whole truth. I told her what she needed to hear, but it wasn't the truth."

"What are you talking about?" Callie asked, trepidation in her voice. "What's she talking about? What did you tell Amanda, Aunt Delilah?"

"Monica, listen to me." Delilah did not cry. She didn't give in to the fear . . . the shame of her past. "I did have a baby out of wedlock when I was sixteen, but I never put her up for adoption."

Hunter Morgan

"You did what?" Callie whispered.

"It's true, Monica," Delilah went on. "I never put her up for adoption. I only gave up custody . . . to my older sister. This is my baby here. I never gave her away. Callie is my baby."

Chapter 33

Snowden walked up the crumbling brick steps to the empty house that had once belonged to Alice Crupp and would soon be sold. The house was dark. Seemed empty. He pointed his flashlight beam at the window. He saw draped furniture through the half-drawn blinds, but no sign of anyone. He checked the door. Locked.

"Come on. Come on," he murmured under his breath. "Think, Snowden. Where is she?"

He had sent a patrol car over to Monica's apartment. They had already radioed in that her car wasn't there, and the couple she rented from hadn't seen her. He would radio Snowden after searching her apartment.

Snowden went back down the steps and along the side yard, into the back. No cars in the alley. The back door was locked as well. He drew the flashlight beam across the rear of the house. There was a cellar entrance covered by aluminum hatched doors, just like his mother's house, built around the same time. Closed.

He walked back along the side of the house, between Alice Crupp's and the Watkins sisters'. Their room air conditioners hummed. It was hot and humid and he was sweating in his uniform. "Where are you, Delilah?" he whispered.

The state police had offered their assistance. He would call headquarters in the morning and accept whatever help they had to offer. He couldn't let Delilah go. Not without telling her he loved her. Not when he had so many things to tell her.

He walked back out to the sidewalk and turned to study the dark house. Coal? Where would coal be stored? *Why* would coal be stored? No one had burned it in years.

He walked down the sidewalk toward The Bread Ladies' house. Cora and Clara Watkins were the last people he wanted to talk to tonight, but they had lived in the town their whole lives. Maybe they would know something.

He walked up the steps, onto their front porch. There were lights on in the house. He could hear a TV, the volume up high.

Cora came to the door, dressed in a chenille bathrobe similar to the one his mother wore.

"Chief Snowden, what a surprise. Clara," she called over her shoulder. "The chief of police is here."

"Miss Watkins, I need your help and I don't have time to explain myself."

"He needs our help, Clara. Come quick!"

He wanted to throttle her. "Please, Miss Watkins. I'm looking for a place coal might have once been stored, possibly on this street. Is there some kind of underground storage along the railroad tracks that I don't know about?"

"Let's see. No one has used coal in years, Chief Calloway."

"I know that." She had switched on the front-porch

light so he turned off his flashlight. "An abandoned shed maybe?"

She plucked at her chubby chin. Clara stood behind her.

"We burned coal when we were children, Cora," Clara said. "Remember Daddy shoveling coal into those big buckets and carrying them into the kitchen?"

Snowden's heart beat a little faster. "You mean he shoveled it here at the house? Where did your father store it?"

"Let me show you, 'round back." Cora started onto the porch. "In the cellar."

Could Monica possibly have broken into the Watkins' cellar and be using it to imprison her victims? It was a wild shot, but anything was possible. "No, no." He held up his hand. "I'll go. Is it unlocked?"

"Lock's been broken for years. Nothing of value down there. There's a little room, built floor to ceiling. The big truck would pour the coal down a chute, through a little window, and fill the room up to the top. There were two doors, a little one in the big one," the middle-aged woman explained excitedly. "You used the little door when the coal was first delivered and later the big door."

"Go inside, please," Snowden said. "Lock the doors and wait for me to come back." He took the porch steps two at time. Running along the side of the house, he tucked his flashlight into his belt, unhooked the strap that secured his Glock, and used his radio to call for backup at the Watkins sisters' address. He then hit the mute on the radio so it wouldn't come on, taking anyone by surprise.

In the backyard, Snowden approached the aluminum doors that led down into the Watkins sisters' cellar.

* * *

"What are you talking about?" Callie demanded, staring into the darkness at her aunt, even though she couldn't see her. "You're kidding, right?" She lowered her voice to a hoarse whisper. "You're just saying these things to make her let us go."

Aunt Delilah didn't say anything and Callie got really scared. Something inside told her Aunt Delilah wasn't lying. "How could you?" she accused.

"Callie, please, not now."

"You lied to me? My mother . . . my *aunt* who I thought was my *mother* lied to me my whole life?" Callie sputtered.

"Please, Monica. You have to believe me," Aunt Delilah said. "You can check state records, honestly, you can. My sister Rosemary and her husband took Callie home from the hospital after I gave birth to her. It was all done legally in the courts."

"So that worthless, deadbeat bastard my mother used to be married to wasn't my father?" Callie asked, dazed. It was probably the best thing she'd heard all day.

"Callie, please," her Aunt Delilah moaned. "Let's get out of here and then we can talk. Then I'll tell you anything you want to know."

Callie's eyes welled up with tears, but she didn't cry. Maybe she was too scared or too dehydrated. Or maybe at this moment, it didn't sound too bad to have Aunt Delilah for a mother. Especially if that crazy bitch on the other side of the wall was getting ready to shoot them.

"I can't talk any more," Monica said. "I have to finish this."

A bolt squeaked on the other side.

"Get back," Aunt Delilah ordered Callie. "As far back

in the corner as you can get, and when I tell you to run, you run. You understand me?"

Another bolt on the door squeaked. Slid.

Callie couldn't believe she sounded so calm. Her Aunt Delilah . . . *her mother* . . . was one tough chick. Callie heard the door begin to groan open and faint light from outside the room came through the crack in the door.

Snowden opened one side of the aluminum doors and it made a hideous screeching sound at the hinges. There was no way he was going to sneak up on anyone.

He knew he should wait for back up. But Delilah was down there.

He flipped on his flashlight, drew his weapon, and charged down the steps.

Delilah didn't have time to think. Only time to react. She didn't know if Monica planned to shoot them here and leave their bodies or take them elsewhere to kill them, but she knew either way, their chances were close to nil.

In the back of her head, to this point, she had still been thinking Snowden would show up and save the day. But they'd had the same training. She was as good a shot as he was. As good an investigator. Maybe better. Delilah couldn't depend on Snowden to save her. She had to save herself. And her children—both of them.

Waving Callie into the corner furthest from the line of fire, Delilah rushed at the door, hands stretched outward, shoving it open just as Monica slid the last bolt back.

Monica screamed as the heavy door hit her.

Callie screamed.

Delilah didn't hear the gun go off so much as she saw the flash of light and smelled the acrid powder as it discharged.

Snowden was standing in the middle of the Watkins' sisters cluttered cellar, staring at a tiny cell-like room that had once held coal when he heard the gun go off. He turned and raced up the crumbing steps, realizing now where Delilah was. She wasn't in the Watkins' cellar. She was in Alice Crupp's cellar.

At the same time that the Glock went off, Delilah heard Monica go down, knocked over by the door. Delilah burst through the opening. It was dark in the main room of the cellar, but nowhere near as inky black as the little room had been. Light from outside street lamps and security lamps effused from the tiny windows into the larger chamber. Delilah spotted Monica on the ground, struggling to get to her feet, to get a good grip on the weapon again.

"Run, Callie! Run for help!" Delilah cried.

Callie streaked past them as Delilah threw herself onto Monica. Monica kicked her, flailing for the pistol. They rolled, wrestling first one on top, then the other. Monica was a couple of inches taller than Delilah. Heavier.

Delilah felt the barrel of the pistol press into her side even as both her fists connected solid one-two punches. Monica hit her in the lip with the butt of the gun. Then her ear. Delilah grasped a handful of blouse at Monica's breasts and pulled as hard as she could. Fabric tore. Delilah cocked back her head and struck the woman in the face with her own forehead.

Monica howled like an injured animal.

Delilah couldn't get a good hold on the gun.

She heard Callie's feet pounding up the stairs. The kid was screaming like a wild woman.

Attagirl, Delilah thought. *Wake up the neighbors. Get them out on the street. Get them all down here.*

At least Callie would be safe.

The fingertips of Delilah's left hand touched the cold barrel of her firearm and she threw the weight of her body full force against Monica's. They knocked something over that clattered as it fell. Stretching, groaning, panting, Delilah's hands found the barrel, at last, and she wrenched the pistol out of her attacker's hands.

An instant later, Delilah was on her feet, shaking from head to toe, holding the gun on Monica, who lay prostrate in front of her.

"Go ahead," Monica said, suddenly quiet. Still. She looked up at Delilah. "Shoot me." Emotion filled her voice as she choked back tears. "Please, for the love of God, shoot me."

Delilah seriously considered it.

There was no one in the cellar now but the two of them. No one to witness what happened. There were obvious signs of struggle. No one would think twice if decorated Detective Delilah Swift walked out of the cellar alone, leaving this hideous killer dead on the dirt floor.

But Delilah would know.

"Don't move," Delilah threatened, her voice amazingly strong.

"Don't move," Snowden called from the bottom of the staircase.

Delilah didn't have to look up. She knew it was him. She didn't know where he'd come from or how he'd found her. She only knew that he was here.

"Chief," she said in her best cop's voice. She felt the blood from her head wound running down the back of her neck. Her lip was busted and her earlobe hurt. She still held the gun steady on Monica. "You think you could take over, here?"

And for the second time in little more than twenty-four hours, Delilah went down.

She woke later, knowing she was in a hospital before she even opened her eyes. She heard the sounds; the squeak of nurses' rubber clogs on the clean floor, the beep of IV pumps, the hushed voices. And she knew Snowden was beside her because she could smell the faint, masculine scent of his skin. She could feel his presence.

Her eyelids fluttered. "Callie," she murmured.

"Right here," he said.

Delilah heard a chair scrape and felt someone bump up against the bed. Callie's warm hand clasped hers.

"You okay?" Delilah asked. She opened her eyes just long enough to see the teenager, to be sure she was real and then they closed again.

"I'm okay."

"She okay?" she whispered to Snowden.

"She's fine." He leaned over the bed. "I made her submit to a full exam in the ER. I told her you'd have my hide when you woke up, if she didn't. They hydrated her with an IV."

"It really hurt. I still have the needle in, in case they have to give me some more tomorrow." Callie told her. "Oh, and they gave me these cool scrubs to wear. I look like I work here."

Delilah smiled. She felt woozy. Almost a little drunk.

"Monica?" she whispered.

"On her way north to Baylor's Women's Correctional, as we speak."

"She was abused, Snowden. Terribly abused. She thought it was because she was adopted."

"I already told him the whole story," Callie said matter-of-factly.

"She makes a pretty good witness. I took her statement myself. Excellent recall of details."

Delilah smiled sleepily, still holding onto Callie's hand. "We need to talk, girlfriend."

"I know," Callie answered softly. "But not tonight. I'm just glad you're okay. You had a whole bunch of stitches and the doctor said you have a little crack on your skull. He says none of your brains squirted out, though."

"You're going to be okay," Snowden whispered, leaner closer.

Delilah suddenly thought about the baby and she opened her eyes, trying to focus.

He held her gaze. "Callie, would you mind giving us a minute?"

"Oh, man," Callie groaned. "Is this where they start playing that stupid, sappy music at the end of the movie?" She leaned over and gave Delilah a quick kiss on the cheek. "I'll be out in the waiting room. They left the TV on for me." She let go of Delilah's hand and was gone.

Delilah waited until she heard Callie's footsteps in the hall outside. "The baby?" she whispered.

"Fine. They did an ultrasound. I have the Polaroid for you."

Tears ran down her temples.

"I'm not going to ask you if the baby's mine," he said, taking her hand, smoothing her hair on her forehead. "I'm just going to ask you when you'll marry me."

A lump rose in her throat. "Marry you? You can't marry me; you'll lose your job."

"So I'll find another," he whispered.

"Snowden, you can't do that. You've wanted to be Chief of Police of Stephen Kill your whole life."

"Okay, so how do *you* feel about a career change? Callie tells me you've been researching graduate studies in psychology for weeks."

"She's a nosy kid." Delilah fought another wave of tears.

"Delilah, look at me." Snowden leaned close, over her.

She opened her eyes, looking up into blue.

"I love you," he said. "I'll go where you want to go. I'll be what you want me to be."

"I want you to be this." She brushed her fingertips across his badge.

He caught her hand and kissed it. "Go to sleep, Detective Swift, and we'll talk tomorrow."

She drew his hand next to her cheek and snuggled against it, her eyes drifting shut. "Sure, Chief."

She heard him sit back in his chair and she felt herself drifting. Suddenly, she opened her eyes again. "Snowden?"

"I'm right here."

"I do."

"You do, what, hon?"

"I love you, Snowden. I've loved you since the day you hired me and warned me I might not be up to the job."

As her eyes closed again, she saw him grin.

"I know, Delilah."

Nail-Biting Romantic Suspense
from Your Favorite Authors